D0499680

LOUPS-GAROUS

NATSUHIKO KYOGOKU

LOUPS-GAROUS

NATSUHIKO KYOGOKU

TRANSLATED BY ANNE ISHII

SAN FRANCISCO

LOUPS-GAROUS by KYOGOKU Natsuhiko
Copyright © 2001 KYOGOKU Natsuhiko
All rights reserved.
Originally published in Japan by TOKUMA SHOTEN PUBLISHING CO., LTD., Tokyo.
English translation rights arranged with OSAWA OFFICE, Japan through THE SAKAI AGENCY.

English translation © 2010 VIZ Media, LLC
Cover Design by Frances O. Liddell

No portion of this book may be reproduced or transmitted in any form or by any means without
written permission from the copyright holders.

HAIKASORU
Published by
VIZ Media, LLC
295 Bay Street
San Francisco, CA 94133

www.haikasoru.com

Kyogoku, Natsuhiko, 1963-
  [Loups-garous. English]
  Loups-garous / Natsuhiko Kyogoku ; translated by Anne Ishii.
      p. cm.
"Originally published in Japan by Tokuma Shoten Publishing."
ISBN 978-1-4215-3233-2
I. Ishii, Anne. II. Title.
PL872.5.Y64L6813 2010
895.6'36--dc22

                                                                              2010001684

The rights of the author of the work in this publication to be so identified have been asserted in
accordance with the Copyright, Designs and Patents Acts 1988. A CIP catalogue record for this book
is available from the British Library.

Printed in the U.S.A.
First printing, May 2010

CHAPTER 001

THERE ONCE WAS a beast called the *wolf.*

If you saw a picture of one, you'd as soon assume it was some kind of dog.

At least that was what Hazuki Makino thought as she looked at Ayumi Kono's back, though why she was thinking about it in the first place was a mystery. It had nothing to do with anything. One minute she was just thinking how uncomfortable her school uniform was—the fabric too thick, making it hard to move around. Then, wolves.

Ayumi's short black hair was very *garçon manqué*; running long from her hairline to the collar of an off-white shirt, her crisp white nape.

Hazuki had first seen her at the area center's summer session, but later Ayumi became a common sight.

"Aren't you ever gonna grow your hair out?" she'd called out, and then, "Hey, I'm talking to you," before Ayumi finally turned around.

Her eyes, tinted green, pierced through long eyelashes like a young doe.

"Smells feral."

Ayumi ignored the question and kept her arms around her knees as she turned away from Hazuki.

"Feral?"

"Yeah. It's gross," Ayumi said into her knees, tucking her head into the crook of her crossed arms. Hazuki, still seated, inched closer.

"What's that mean? I don't think I've ever smelled an…animal before."

"Me neither, dude." Ayumi guffawed. *Then how do you know you're smelling it?* Hazuki asked. Ayumi thrust out her right arm.

It was white. It was thin. It was smooth like alabaster. Hazuki wasn't sure but it looked like the arm of a girl. Not a beast.

Hazuki lowered her nose to Ayumi's arm.

"It doesn't smell like anything. Just your shower gel, maybe."

"Yeah?"

Ayumi put her arm back around her knees. She was looking far off into the distance. Hazuki scooted farther up so she was sitting diagonally right behind Ayumi. She had clean-cut features and a dignified profile—*God, what a lame way to describe it.*

"What do you mean by *feral*?"

"I'm not sure. It's just the thought that came to me."

Ayumi lowered her eyes. Hazuki looked to where Ayumi's gaze had just been fixed—a cityscape of no distinction that promised no futures. Buildings stood like CGI creations.

Utterly. Boring.

No movement. *What was she looking at?* Probably just staring off into the distance. Nothing, technically. Just the distance between them and the view itself. You couldn't measure distance in a computer monitor.

After a long silence she saw it—the air, the wind, or something.

Hazuki and Ayumi always came here after their communication session ended. They'd sit at this spot and stare at the view in silence. They were supposed to go straight home after classes, but who ever did? If you were already used to going out on your own you weren't going to stop now, and if you weren't, this weekly class was the perfect opportunity to do so. Since the kids were forced to go out once a week anyway, it made sense to take advantage of the situation. The counselors stayed out after sessions too. It being a weekly encounter group on communication, it could be argued that one would actually be remiss not to learn how to interact with society; to go into town.

Still. It wasn't as if there were much else to do besides wander.

The town was vacant. What real boutiques existed only sold luxury and collector's items. These things weren't inherently interesting to the girls and were totally unaffordable for children. They didn't appreciate being under constant surveillance at the restaurants and coffee shops, and it cost money just to sit there anyway. Some of the kids went to the "amusement areas," but it essentially amounted to camping before a bigger monitor screening the same "entertainment" you could get at home. Besides, half the time there were more adults than children. Not very fun. Mostly, the kids went to the park and pretended to play sports; they sat around and made idle conversation with each other. A useless endeavor that benefited no one. One would have to wait till nightfall to do anything more out of the ordinary, so there was no sense in using your weekly trip to summer school as an excuse to commit mischief, even something as innocent as detouring on your way home.

The communication sessions could get pretty long, depending on your district. Hazuki's was full of children sans legal guardians or who had other qualifying "special circumstances." This meant the classes were easy and ended early. Of course, they said it was because public safety in the area was so well maintained. It was to continue keeping order, discipline. This was why group had always been able to end at 3:00 PM on the dot.

They had so much free time they couldn't stand it.

However, Hazuki was just as bored sitting around making idle conversation. There was no story. It wasn't as if they were staring into their monitors, so it seemed ridiculous to be talking about schoolwork. If she wanted the news she could get that at home. There was absolutely no reason why children had to face each other to talk.

On the other hand, one could reason, they'd gone out of their way to come to school anyway, so it would be pointless not to take advantage of the opportunity to make the detour. If it was going to be pointless, it should really be pointless, was another way of looking at it.

And that was how the two girls got to coming here—looking out into the city, their arms wrapped around their knees.

Ayumi used to come out here alone in the beginning. Hazuki happened to see her one day on her way back from school and found it curious. Ayumi had just transferred to the area four years ago. They were assigned to the same room, so she knew at least her name. Before that, it was as if she didn't exist. Hazuki was terribly curious about this new girl and started researching Ayumi's profile. They were the same age because they were in the same group—she knew that much. But the students in each group had different learning-level assignments. Theirs were identical.

The next week they were in group together, Hazuki tried to sit close to Ayumi. Not to make conversation or anything. Just to be near her. They'd stayed that close after warming up to each other.

It wasn't as if Hazuki was trying to be like Ayumi or become best friends with her. It being a group setting, this was the perfect place for Hazuki to behave totally pointlessly. And that was the reason itself for her actions. Since Ayumi never complained, Hazuki never left.

Ayumi put her nose to her arm once again, then opened her right hand wide. Staring into the empty space inside her palm, she suddenly clenched her fingers into a hard fist.

"What kind of smell?"

"I dunno. Maybe human."

"You just said it was an animal smell."

"Fine. I meant *living being*."

"Then that's your own smell."

"Yeah, but…"

Ayumi was a beautiful young woman. Her hair was very short and her style plain, but, Hazuki thought, she was still more feminine than her own self, long-haired and accessory-laden. *Why can't I pull off short hair?* But as she started to mouth the next words out loud, Ayumi abruptly stood up and turned around. Hazuki turned her head.

Leaning against the handrail of the staircase was Mio Tsuzuki.

"You're going to get in trouble," Mio said. "They told us to hurry home today."

"What about you?" Ayumi responded. Mio grinned and leapt over the handrail to Ayumi's side.

"I'm bored."

Her eyes were feline, her face compact.

Mio Tsuzuki was in the same class as Hazuki and Ayumi. But while they were the same age, she was far higher in level placement. It would be more accurate to say there was no other objective correlation between them than to claim one smarter than the other two. According to public records, Mio had completed her compulsory groups at the age of nine and finished her secondary groups in an astonishing two years. In following with the line of college curricula she'd completed, she was ten years ahead of her age group. Her learning speed was the best bar none. *She's what we used to call a genius*, adults would say.

Still. A fourteen-year-old was always a fourteen-year-old.

And in that respect, they were all the same.

"There's nothing to do," Mio said.

"Why don't you go study?"

"I'm tired of it." Mio sounded as uninterested as she claimed to be with life, and turned her back.

"Does that mean you've learned it all?"

Hazuki compared Mio's back to Ayumi's face.

She thought it unusual.

Mio was hard to like at first. Hazuki had transferred to this neighborhood ten years ago, but until today she had not once had a normal conversation with Mio. They knew nothing about her personal life, and Mio didn't seem to have anything in common with them anyway. There was clearly nothing to ask about, so naturally, there was nothing to talk about.

But it wasn't just Mio Tsuzuki. Hazuki and Ayumi were hardly in a position to have mundane social interactions, so they knew next to nothing about any of their classmates. In terms of the personal information you could gather on someone, excluding the public data everyone was legally obliged to provide for public consumption, there was no way of knowing if the arbitrary information people gave about themselves was true or not. Of course everyone agreed on this point. Besides all of which, the groupmates only saw each other for a few hours a week—conversations wouldn't last much more than five minutes if they happened at all. Hazuki always thought it strange that people could sit in front of a monitor for five hours without a problem.

As for the weekly group format, more and more kids were having difficulty with normative human interaction, or would be soon. The groups were utterly useless. People already able to communicate effectively with others didn't need this group, and the kids who couldn't communicate would never learn anyway.

Mio Tsuzuki would never learn. At least that was what Hazuki thought.

On the one hand, Ayumi went totally unnoticed. She, like Mio, had no outstanding characteristics worth digging up from public records. If you didn't know any better, you'd think Ayumi was the superior learner. The fact that these two were having a normal conversation was hard for Hazuki to swallow.

Mio dropped her purse on the ground and squatted down. Her eyes were huge. Her glare was piercing. Hazuki wasn't used to being looked at. She felt like a monitor herself when people looked at her. It wouldn't matter the query you input, she would not be able to respond. Mio kept staring at Hazuki and said, "You from the ranch, was it?"

"The ranch, yeah."

"Your dad's the politician, right?"

"Step-dad."

"You're adopted?"

"I see my dad maybe once a month."

"That's nothing. I see mine less than once a year."

"Hmph."

The conversation was going nowhere.

"Why aren't you staying after group today?"

Ayumi's voice came from above her. "Yeah, aren't you teaching our proctors physics or something?"

"She's teaching the proctors?"

Hazuki looked at Mio's eyes for confirmation. Mio smiled. That she couldn't deny it probably meant it was true. It was entirely possible. It didn't occur to Hazuki, but if Ayumi had this information, it was probably common knowledge.

Mio looked up at Ayumi and said, "It's not the proctors I'm teaching. It's the counselor, Ms. Fuwa. And it's not physics, it's statistics."

Ayumi kept staring at Mio. She didn't respond. Mio continued.

"She told me to go home. The proctors told us all to hurry home."

"They always do."

"Today's different. They said it's dangerous."

"Dangerous?"

"They're saying someone might get murdered tonight."

"Murdered? You mean that..."

Yes. People were being murdered. The body count was at four so far. They were all fourteen to fifteen-year-old girls. It didn't matter where you were logged on, the public news bulletins announced the murders every hour, and it was all anyone would talk about on the TV tabloids. Even online, anonymous tips and news items ran alongside each other in a barrage. Hazuki hadn't been reading any of it, but she'd heard they'd started a bunch of conferences. Still...

"It's not news, you know."

Every year there was some serial killer on the loose. One who somehow evaded capture. Just last summer, six people had been killed, and the culprit was never arrested. There were probably several killers living in plain sight, leading normal lives. Nothing to get all freaked out about now. The only reason anyone was talking about it now was because the victims were all minors.

"It's all happening nearby," Mio spoke up.

"You mean in neighboring areas," Hazuki said. In other words, it was always someone else.

The murders had all taken place in adjacent areas. No one had been killed in Hazuki's neighborhood. Public safety was the one thing the town had going for it.

"*It's not* just *nearby*," Mio said importantly, clasping her hands behind her and looking up at the sky.

"It could happen to us, you know. The neighborhood associations and our local police are all freaking out."

"Why—someone die?"

Hazuki tried to think. Had anyone been missing in group today? She hadn't gotten the impression anything was amiss at the session. But it could just be that Hazuki hadn't been paying attention.

Wait. There was something...

"Someone was absent today."

What was her name?

"Yabe."

"It was Yabe!"

And just as quickly as the name came to her did she think she knew her well. But Hazuki hardly knew the names of half her groupmates. Ayumi, still standing, said, "It wasn't her."

"She's not dead."

"She's not dead?"

What a weird conversation, Hazuki thought.

"It was someone else who died," Mio said.

"They found the body this morning."

Ayumi shot a look at Mio. The sun shone in her eyes, making Mio's face impossible to see.

"Under the Central North-South Line overpass. Right at our district borderline."

"But I haven't…"

Seen anything. Heard anything.

"There's nothing in the news yet. The local police, prefectural police, and sheriff are all investigating it now."

"Investigating?"

"Look. The local government and the head office on the case will differ on whether it's part of the serial killings or if it's just a singular incident. If the events have spread out across areas and prefectures, the case becomes a wider concern. The methods change, the system changes—historically it's how the country's been run. Of course, the initial investigation is always a failure, so there are tons of holes in the case later."

Mio spoke like an adult.

"How do you know all this?"

"I nosed around. Infiltrated."

"Hacking into computers again? You're going to get caught one of these days."

"I'm never getting caught." Mio was still looking up at the sky as she dismissed Hazuki. Perhaps Hazuki had Mio all wrong. Something about her was off. Hazuki looked back up at Ayumi but couldn't see her face.

"The victim supposedly had the same eyes and mouth as the others. Face and throat were slit."

Still looking up. Kill the victim and then slash her with a sharp knife—that was the serial killer's pattern. One person, one move.

"Thing is…"

"They say the victim's a boy." Mio slid down and kept looking up. Hazuki turned her head up too. The sky looked weird unframed, so she immediately looked away.

"A boy…and from our neighborhood?"

"Yeah. We probably met him during that coed session last week, right? Not that I care or anything. I didn't look at his data profile, so I don't even remember his name. But he's from around here."

"That may be…but still."

Hazuki looked at Ayumi again. It was too bright to see.

"And…" Ayumi started.

"What are you doing here?"

"Like I said. I'm bored. They say *go straight home*, but that's where I'm most likely to get killed because then I'd be alone. And all these victims have been attacked on their way home from school, so if they tell us to go straight home, I'm saying, at least escort us back. Right?" Mio was still lying on her side looking up at the sky without expression.

She really had a way with words.

"They aren't escorting anyone, eh? Not even important geniuses like you."

"They're having a conference."

"Conference?"

"When you talk to a group of people face-to-face. Adults like to meet in person and talk to each other. Such a waste of time."

Mio went on importantly about how *meeting each other in person and talking face-to-face isn't going to catch the killer*, then sat up straight. Dried grass was stuck all over her backside and hair. She started clapping it off her shoulders, then shook her bob haircut furiously. The grass stuck to everything it touched and wouldn't fall.

"This is stupid."

"Everyone's freaking out though."

"No one is freaking out. It's always like this."

"They don't usually clamp down like this though."

Mio stuck an index finger into her collar and wrung the neckline as if to open up a little space. "Sounds like you know what you're talking about, Kono."

"I don't." Ayumi looked down.

"You really like pestering people, don't you, Tsuzuki."

"It's *fun*." Mio laughed.

"What is?"

"I can't stop wondering."

She never knew how people would react…probably.

Ayumi stared blankly at Mio's feet and said without thinking,

"You mean you don't know what stupid people think?"

Mio's eyes widened.

"If we think at all. I bet it's hard figuring us out. Or is that what we're learning in this communications group?"

"You're such a model participant," Ayumi threw in.

"Whaaat?" Mio's voice went up several octaves.

"That's a pretty boring comeback."

"Unfortunately, I'm no comedian," Ayumi said, looking back at Hazuki. "Am I?"

Their gazes moved on as Hazuki lowered her head, unresponsive. The weeds snapped at her calves.

"What I'm saying is…it's not cool for you to be investigating us."

Investigating. Mio furrowed her face.

"I'm doing no such thing."

"You were just staring at us, weren't you?"

"I can't talk to you unless I see you."

"You can't even look at me."

It was true. Ayumi had never actually looked at Mio.

In fact.

Ayumi had never faced anyone. Not even Hazuki.

She suddenly came back at Mio and gawped.

"What?"

Mio shifted her sight line past Ayumi's temple.

"See. You can't even maintain eye contact. You don't want to be looked at either." Mio made a bored expression.

"Jerk."

"Yep."

"That's why I choose to be alone," Ayumi said as she sat back down and looked at the stick building far away. The gesture was like a curtain call declaring an end to the conversation.

It was true.

Ayumi was vetoing.

Mio raised both her eyebrows at Ayumi's still back and let out a sigh.

"Oh well." She stood up.

She'd apparently had the same thought as Hazuki.

"That was fun, guys."

Was it? Ayumi glimpsed Hazuki, who continued to avoid eye contact. Mio shimmied over the railing and walked away. She was so different in person. Nothing like what the public data said, nothing like in the encounter group.

Ayumi, without so much as looking after Mio, repeated to the far-away that she had been staring at,

"I hate being watched."

"Tsuzuki said it herself just now. There's no point in talking face-to-face."

"Yeah, but…"

Maybe I'm bothering her too, Hazuki said to herself in a small voice. She certainly didn't like being watched either. And yet, she couldn't stop staring at Ayumi.

Couldn't stop.

It was involuntary.

"Am I a bother?"

Her voice rose. She spoke doubtfully.

"You're not bothering me," Ayumi answered. "You weren't saying anything, Makino."

"Oh…really?"

I wasn't trying to be quiet. She'd said a few words here and there. Nothing useful, nothing important. Otherwise the two were just staring into the distance in the same direction. Except that…

Ayumi was always in Hazuki's line of vision because of the way they sat. Hazuki created the landscape Ayumi had to be a part of.

So.

So Ayumi had no idea Hazuki had been staring at her.

Or did she? Impossible.

They'd not yet made eye contact, despite their having sat there side by side. Ayumi couldn't have seen Hazuki watching her. There was no way Ayumi would know what Hazuki's eyes said.

It was a comforting discomfiture.

I guess it's only normal.

Hazuki reassured herself in an internal voice only she could hear, then stood up.

"I'm going home."

"All right."

"You're not coming?"

"Huh?" Ayumi was distracted.

Now that she thought of it, Hazuki had never called back to Ayumi like that before. If she didn't want to leave what was it to her? Think of all the times they'd parted ways without saying anything at all.

"I mean, it being dangerous and all," Hazuki explained, though why she felt she had to justify her comment, she did not know.

"With the murderer…"

"I'll be all right."

Ayumi spun around and looked Hazuki straight in the eye.

Her eyes.

"I'm fine. The field's…" Ayumi said.

"Dangerous, you think?"

"What do you mean?"

Without answering her question, Ayumi said she smelled water.

"Huh?"

"Look up."

Ayumi's mind was preoccupied upward, then the instinct hit Hazuki. She looked skyward as one cold, piercing drop of water crashed into her temple.

"Rain."

She hadn't brought an umbrella, and it didn't look like Ayumi was going to budge. Hazuki held back despite herself. Ayumi interrupted Hazuki as she prepared to tell her she should get out of the rain.

"I'll be fine."

Hazuki didn't understand what would be fine about it.

She turned around and started to head up the incline when she felt something against her foot. She prodded it with her toe and discovered under the grass a half-buried hard drive.

She picked it up and arched up to face Ayumi. It was definitely not hers.

"Is this…?"

Yours, Kono? Knowing full well it wasn't.

Hazuki returned to Ayumi with the disc.

"I have no use for a drive with that much memory."

It *was* quite large. If the number on the drive were any indication, Hazuki could put all the data she'd ever collected in there and still have plenty of room for more. The thought of that much memory made the object between her fingers heavier. It was uncanny. The drive shouldn't weigh any more because it could hold more information.

Ayumi said, "Only someone like Tsuzuki would need that much disc space."

"So it's Tsuzuki's."

Could be. Mio had put down, no, dropped, her bag right around here.

"What do we do with it?"

"She'll probably come back to get it, right?"

"I doubt she knows it's here though."

There was a lock on the drive, making it impossible for there not to be any content.

"If it's important, she's going to come looking for it. Just leave it where you found it."

"But…"

Hazuki looked skyward.

The cold water droplets continued to pound her forehead. A giant frameless monitor screened two layers of dark gray sky mapping out a texture without cadence.

It was raining.

But it certainly didn't smell like water.

CHAPTER 002

SHE WAS STARING at the edge of her desk because looking at the leathery old face of the supervisor made her sick.

She might not see him but could still hear him.

In other words.

Even from this vantage she could hear the *huh*s and *hah*s of his breath. When she thought of how they shared the air they breathed, how it filtered through his animal-like male body, through his filthy nasal cavity and viscous mouth hanging agape, it was enough to make her nauseated.

I hate conferences.

It was just a way to communicate the news, but they had to make it a pointless meeting.

It was not constructive. Nothing that came of these meetings had anything to do with the deliberation items. Discussions in person didn't augment or add any information, nor did they refine what was already known. It was just a collection of advertised opinions, everyone's comportment, body odor, grating voice, extraneous data collected for intellectuals. Of no use. At this rate there would be no real discussion or deliberation.

It was maddening.

You know what you really need to effectively research communications is just your damned self, thought Shizue Fuwa.

This was the only place she'd make eye contact.

There were faces to look at all around her. And…

Shizue hated the walls, the ceiling too. Actually, she hated the entire room.

It was wide and had a high ceiling. It was supposed to evoke a sense of space but instead made her feel trapped somehow. In other words it was *pretending* to be spacious.

Compared to this, the screen on her terminal was infinitely more spacious.

And suddenly all the inorganic designs felt like a total lie. It was an outright lie. Unabashed gussying up, at the end of the day.

The truth lay only in ideas.

Yet people created the facsimile of a truth and pretended it was the real thing all the time. They told themselves that bumps were straight lines. If they were so able to convince themselves of the lie, why bother saying it was straight?

Room 3, Section A, Area Community Center.

She didn't know how many centers there were across the country, but each region had a community center and each community center was built according to a uniform standard. The materials, the design, everything.

A public platform had no need for embellishments—or so the thinking went. Austere, hygienic—that was the ethos of the design. But putting up the facade of austerity was costlier than putting up a cheap design. They talked about hygiene but weren't really doing anything to disinfect the air—the spores were still there. What was more, you could see the dust. It was so bad you couldn't really go anywhere without moistened wipes or a cloth.

Shizue wasn't saying there should be embellishments and decorations everywhere. She just wondered why no one else saw how trying that hard to be austere just made it all the more obnoxious. It wasn't like you could walk into a space that really looked like a monitor.

It was because they made rooms like this that organic humans did dirty deeds together.

I hate it. They'd just had their *monthly* meeting…last week.

Today's was a unique summons.

The Ministry of Culture, which brought together the National Welfare and Development System and the Committee on Adolescent Welfare and Development—comprised of center personnel from each locality—was meeting under the auspices of an emergency session of the 122nd Area Branch.

Shizue had been brought in from central.

They called her a counselor, but it wasn't like she was an accredited therapist. She had a license but mostly advised minors in their plans for the future and assured they were in good mental health.

She had no idea what it meant to deal with a serial killer, but they were saying at least one of the victims attended the 122nd.

The conference seats were filled with police associates and local cops, as well as local governance that didn't usually show up to these things. It wasn't any ordinary conference.

This was obviously a big deal.

Being in the same room as these people for any amount of time depressed Shizue. On top of which, the facilitator of the emergency meeting —the very man she was judging—was the dumbest one of them all.

Shizue's melancholy was pitched at an all-time high. His whole introduction was pointless and over-long.

"There's been a rash of bizarre crimes," he waxed impassioned.

What's bizarre *mean anyway?*

It was an obsolete term.

Bizarre. Derived from words signifying anger, wrath, and fascination with both.

Bizarre, eh?

Bizarre was a word that was popular a hundred years ago in detective novels, its time long since passed into history.

Making such distinctions between normal and abnormal was in and of itself passé.

Shizue thought the real crime was this attempt to apply the distinction to an unquantifiable territory and to the psychology of its inhabitants, its society.

Unusual simply meant outside of the norm.

It could also mean reality was less than ideal. Be it in excess or in its lack, significant idiosyncrasies were impossible.

In other words, before one could begin to use a word like *bizarre* one would have to define *normal*, and that required envisioning an ideal. This conference was not doing any such thing.

There was no such thing as a normal psychology or a normal society.

Things changed. Things were complex and had aberrations. Things couldn't be easily territorialized. Besides it being impossible to draw lines, how was one ever to measure deviations, if they'd deviated successfully?

Ideals required ignoring the defects and deficiencies of a reality and replacing them with theoretically and carefully composed goals of superiority. Ideals were just ideologies. In which case, something was wrong with you if you tried to fix an ideal in this day and age.

Also…

It was stupid to be calling this a *rash* of incidents.

Who knew why they deemed this a bizarre crime. It wasn't like "bizarre crimes" had never taken place before.

Even if in each era there were some vague trend of events noticed or unnoticed, the events were probably the result of several other events that occurred over the past several hundred years. Shizue was convinced that even if one tried to give numerical value to the events that led to the aberration and averaged a rate, there would be instances of too many or too few to come to a conclusion.

People had been the victims of mass murder from a long time ago, every single day. Of course you wanted to stop it, or if not stop, control... This savage country used to slit the throats of murderers. It was also a country that under the guise of war rendered tens of thousands of lives useless. The only difference now was that children were being uniquely targeted, the method of killing was atrocious, and they couldn't figure out how it happened. It was certainly disturbing but there was no right or wrong with a killer. In any murder case, a murderer was a murderer. Which stood to reason that there was no reason to get all up in arms now. You want normal?

This is normal.

This concept of the abnormal was no longer valid.

And if you took the things that were abnormal or bizarre, you would eventually see they had no meaning.

"The situation is imminent. We need a more concrete plan."

Shizue was through staring at the corner of her desk, so she looked to the right and saw the face of a fellow member of the welfare department. He looked obsequiously at the terminal, nodding stupidly along to everything the supervisor said.

Did he feel anything? Or was it coded behavior, involuntary gesturing, meant for precisely this kind of situation.

How insensitive.

Really...

He must not have felt anything. What did you expect from such insensitivity toward language?

These people—a generation from the end of a millennium—were all obtuse when it came to language.

You had to define your terms before starting any argument. Words were ambiguous; limiting the breadth of your words assured no confusion in argument. Terrible things happened when you didn't respect this very basic premise, even when it came to something as simple as collecting data. It was impossible not to be prudent if you couldn't see the face of the person you were talking to.

It was hard dealing with people coming into a still-developing culture. They lacked skill and numbers, and because they had such low comprehension levels they were too eager to believe everything and too easily convinced to take sides. That was why they had to be personally confronted with information in order to get the information. Whatever it took...

Whatever...

Shizue's larger generation, born in the twenty-first century, was raised to be personally offended by words whose use lacked consideration. *Whatever.* That was a pretty thickheaded thing to say. It riled her up despite herself.

Still.

Shizue held her breath. Then slowly let it out to calm the ire in her belly.

The people who raised the insensitive generation that bruised Shizue now were probably even more insensitive. She tried to re-examine the bureaucrat's face with a more historical appreciation of his stupidity.

It made her feel better.

He kept blathering.

"—the body was discovered in this locality, and what's more it's a resident of the area, but besides the fact that the victim is a minor, and the possibility of this being one in a string of serial killings notwithstanding, we can't treat this case as anything less than alarming."

That went without saying.

Shizue looked at the clock on her monitor.

They'd wasted 1,050 seconds just confirming the obvious.

In other words.

The murder discovered this morning wasn't deemed part of the greater killing spree because this latest victim was male. The others had all been female.

Based on this information it was decided the prefectural police would take over the investigation. The special investigations unit leader had the chief of Area 122 reporting to him, but otherwise the area chief reported to the prefectural police.

That was all. They could have gotten all this information in writing and saved themselves a lot of time.

Still.

The problem was what had happened before this.

It just so happened this murder had taken place outside of their jurisdiction. What did they think they'd accomplish now? It was beyond conference meetings to determine protocols for emergency notifications.

Plus, all these incidents had taken place in adjacent neighborhoods.

It wasn't as if there were some physical shield protecting the boundaries between those neighborhoods. Any distinction between inhabited areas was purely theoretical, nothing real. The ground kept going. The fire across the street could have started in your next-door neighbor's house. Of course it was going to spread. There was nothing you could do if people weren't worried about the fire in area 408 just because it wasn't *their* quarter. *They weren't worth saving*, thought Shizue.

"As people who work with adolescents…"

It had always been a dire circumstance.

"As far as we're concerned…"

The area chief of police, who sat next to the center's supervisor, spoke with a long face. Despite his severe face, the chief hardly moved his lips when speaking, making his speech come across as ambiguous at best and difficult to hear.

"So…we're in the throes of smoking out our suspect, but as you can see in the documents we have provided for you, the murder took place outside the residential quarter, and we believe that it took place late at night once again, on top of which we think getting any verbal statements from witnesses of this random killing will be difficult."

What about it, then?

What did he think was going to happen by presenting this to a group of youth counselors?

"At the moment…"

Shizue had a horrible feeling about this.

"As of now, as area patrols, we are compiling a list of deviants who live in this residential quarter."

"Wait a second."

She'd gone and opened her mouth. She knew it was going to end badly but couldn't stop herself.

"How are you determining that this is a deviant? I'd like a clear definition of what makes this person deviant. Otherwise it's just discrimination."

Perhaps because she'd just thrown the conversation off course, the area chief went silent, furrowed his brow, and said "discrimination" under his breath.

"Of course it's not discrimination. A deviant is a deviant. It's someone who can't be normal."

"I am just asking as a matter of setting a standard. Are the police using a medical standard or else a sociological standard when using this term?"

It was useless.

"What for?"

The area chief looked perplexed and shifted his gaze to his right at another participant. That participant then shot a look at Shizue.

"C'mon, Fuwa."

He sounded retarded.

"Stop saying things that make no sense. It runs our discussion off course. It's a waste of our time."

This whole conference was a waste of time.

"What's not making any sense, Counselor Takazawa? I should like to repeat, as a counselor, that these baseless accusations are discriminatory. I should like you not to use these terms if you're not prepared to define them."

"Discriminatory..."

The police chief looked like he didn't know what it meant and this time shot a glance at the counselor on his left.

Was he a superior? The skinny man gave the police chief a cold look, then faced Shizue.

"I am Ishida, from Division R of the prefectural police, head of the violent crimes investigation unit," he said. "This is, as you say, a term we don't want to have misunderstood. Let me try to explain. The deviant Officer Yokota is talking about will have committed crimes that are wholly removed from typical crimes prosecutable or non-prosecutable by the police, or else has attempted these crimes or is a person suspected of having participated in such crimes."

"What does 'wholly removed from typical crimes' mean?"

"This is a very crude way of saying it, but sexually based crimes including stalking, for example. If I go any further than that it will seem discriminatory, as you say."

"In other words—"

"You are correct. Distinguishing 'normal' from 'abnormal' is a very delicate issue. For example, there is nothing we can do about a person's behavior if their proclivities remain personal, with no effect on others. Even if he stepped outside those bounds, even if we are able to prove that he is a poor influence on society, if we can't arrest or prosecute him, we can't legally call him a criminal. However, if we're to solve this crime swiftly, or prevent it from happening again, we must know what kind of person we're looking for. We've aggregated all the information we need, and the prefectural police has a database of sorts."

"That's—"

Before Shizue had a chance to respond, Ishida sharply interjected.

"Could you say this is infringing on privacy? Sure. However it is not as if we were taking any extreme liberties into anyone's information."

"Does that mean you're simply collecting public information on citizens into a database?"

"Public or private, we're taking information deemed important to the general public, as well as secondhand information parlayed by others. We're not invading any personal information sources."

"Of course not."

"Right. This is information the average person could gather without a police badge. However it's the mass of information. It's on a scale the average person would never be able to collect. That having been said, for the police to collect this information in a calculated fashion...could raise issues."

"I'm sure."

"That's why we can't speak in simple terms."

"That's why you have these vague definitions of elusive notions?"

"That's right. It's like you said. There are too many different kinds of people in the world. If you look at our barometer, there are a good number of dangerous types out there. But no matter how dangerous they are, if they haven't committed any crimes, they won't spill out of the 'lawful citizen' category. And so I think our officer here dares to use the term 'deviant.' I'd like your affirmation on this terminology."

This was all too convenient.

"So essentially, the authorities will draw the line on what is to be considered normal," Shizue said.

"We're determining which personages demonstrate a potential danger from the stance that we are to protect society at large. We are calling them deviants for the convenience of this conference."

"That's enough," Shizue said quietly.

"Pervert or deviant, who cares. You're stalling the conversation."

"It's important."

"You're just a troublemaker now, aren't you, Miss?"

The area chief had made a reckless comment. Must have been in his fifties. Definitely born before the turn of the century. Shizue scowled at him. Ishida reprimanded him.

"Officer Yokota. That's a clear instance of sexual harassment. We don't approve of comments made on the basis of difference in age or sex."

The area chief looked totally dissatisfied and stared at Shizue. Shizue looked away. She didn't want to look at him.

"But as the counselor points out, there seems to be some unsatisfactory terms in the local police's explanations, which the prefectural police will hopefully clarify," Ishida said, as if to correct the situation. At least his delivery was acceptable.

"As I've just proffered, my prefectural police team, through the area patrol, will investigate the current situation and use the database to survey those who have the potential to commit violent crimes in the neighborhood."

They were talking in circles.

"We're working on a very minute survey process. And in that regard, we're requesting the participation of the residents in the area in question. We will formally request their cooperation."

Ishida turned toward the superior assemblyman.

"Of course," he said.

"But, if I may be frank, the reality right now is that the police force is facing a difficult investigation. Truth be told we have a huge gap in our database."

"Gap?"

"There is a remarkable lack of information on minors." Ishida looked out at the group, one by one. His gaze finally landed on Shizue.

"We don't have any data on the minors save what's already been made public."

"You mean the data *we* have collected?"

"Correct. All we have right now is the public data collected by your local community center—the local register of residents aggregated by each local youth welfare department and local government," the representative said.

"There must be a lot of heinous youth crimes unmentioned in that data, eh?"

What an irresponsible thing to say. A lapse in judgment. The head chief of the area youth protective services gave a sideways glare at the representative.

"May I have a word, Assemblyman? Crime among minors has decreased drastically since its peak in 2002. It has not risen at all."

It was something she'd say.

Actually, no she wouldn't. It would imply counseling was totally useless.

"Whether the rate has decreased or not does not matter. Obviously since I was elected assemblyman, the laws have been repeatedly revised."

Ishida replied that anyone who'd committed a crime would be charged and prosecuted, even minors.

"As you know, this will involve a criminal penalty. If it's covered by existing laws, there is no distinction in criminality. Other than that it takes longer in court, there is no difference between criminal cases involving adults and minors. Just that in the case of minors, we have no legal access to personal information about them other than what's been made publicly accessible. It's the entire police organization's judgment that accordingly, there is no need to gather that information."

A man sitting next to Ishida who looked like a police officer said, *You mean there's no budget for that.*

"All this data aggregation is difficult as it is."

Hearing this wasn't going to get anything started. The bug in Shizue's gut started to act up again.

"I get that the police have no budget, but what about it? Maybe I'm not understanding what you're saying, but this meeting itself is a waste of our time and hence your budget."

Ishida spoke without change in expression or intonation.

"Let me be totally forthright. I want the information you all have on people over the age of ten to be handed over to the police."

"That's not right."

Shizue looked at the counselor sitting next to her.

He wouldn't move.

Is he shocked, or does he not think anything of it?

"What is the meaning of this?"

"Just as you heard. These minors—who until now were bundled up and referred to as 'children'—in the residential quarter number approximately 3,200. We are respectfully asking you to provide nonpublic information about them."

That's not right.

"We can't do that," Shizue said. "As a rule, we do not make public the personal information collected on the children in each community center. Even if they are over the age of ten, if they are under supervision, you need their consent to peruse their file. It doesn't matter that you're the police."

"These are rules by default," the police chief said. "I'd like you to think about the situation. It's a serial murderer."

"People are killed all over the country every day. This isn't even the first time someone's been killed in this quarter. I've never heard such an illegal request."

"It's not illegal. This is a necessary measure we take as a matter of mitigating extralegal circumstances."

"You're twisting the words."

"Hey, hey, Fuwa," the head assemblyman said, stroking his hair back in an awkward gesture. He scratched his head, but his hair flopped back into place. It was depressing. *Memory-hair transplants were truly one of the most regrettable innovations of the age*, Shizue thought. *If you're going to grow hair like that, at least don't try to make it move.* He probably wasn't held enough as a child.

"You're overreacting, but we understand that. That's precisely why we've organized this conference, so if you could just bear with us."

"You're saying you're suspecting children now?"

They think they're gonna get the last word here?

The assemblyman dropped the end his sentence and just flapped his mouth.

"You believe that there is a killer among these children at the center, do you?"

"It's a possibility."

"They're under suspicion then."

"Enough, Fuwa. C'mon—"

"They are," Ishida said matter-of-factly.

"The victims are minors and have to be within shooting range. Of course we haven't narrowed it down that far yet, but we need more information to do just that."

Relationships.

There was no age limit on friendships. If they were communicating via monitors, there was no saying what age or sex their associates were. It had nothing to do with anything. If anyone were having frequent in-person exchanges there'd be no need for communication sessions.

I know what you want to say, Ishida said as if reading the look on Shizue's face.

"We're not just assuming that because they're minors their friends are all the same age. The police are well aware of the reality. We've studied the monitor histories of these victims, and we're in the process of filtering their public records. The victims all seemed to be fans of cel-based animation and seemed to be corresponding frequently with other fans. Of course, the age, sex, and nationality of their friends is all scattered. If anything, the average enthusiast shows to be older. However..."

Ishida looked briefly at his own monitor.

"In murder cases like this, it's almost always the case that the victim and the culprit will have had physical interaction. You already know this. It was not poison or explosives used in these killings. Because the victims sustained physical damage, we know for a fact the killer was in personal contact."

He did not have to explain all this again. She understood.

Ishida looked around.

"Since we're talking about kids who aren't just passing information around, since we know there was real physical interaction involved, the investigation is terribly limited. In any case, children these days don't interact with people. Their only interactions are through communication labs. Learning levels and counseling notwithstanding, classrooms are divided strictly by age, after all."

"You're right," Ishida agreed.

He didn't want to answer.

"None of the victims had siblings. Other than their counselors, these kids had no physical interaction with anyone but groupmates and children in other groups they might have seen at their local centers."

"That's not necessarily true. It's difficult to be certain as the police don't yet have all the information on these kids, but the kids do have *some* interaction with society."

"Right. So we'd like for you to share that data with us," Ishida said directly at Shizue.

They probably thought that if Shizue relented now they could end this conversation. By settling one argument when confronted with two, the police side of the room was able to circumvent the original issue of the appropriateness of police requests for extreme lawful diligence.

Shizue was a scapegoat.

Who are my allies?

"As you've just mentioned, each of you has personal data on each of these children. It should be your job to collect the data and supervise the lives of these children."

"You say 'supervise the lives of these children' like it's nothing. No matter how you look at it, supervision comes down to information. We aren't directly supervising the children."

"Don't you think that's the same difference?"

"No, it isn't. If a problem arises, resolving the issue will always end up being the individual's responsibility. We will counsel them, and the children will respond according to their own whims, but our hypothesis is that our advice is absolutely not legally enforceable. It's fundamentally different from back when school institutions strictly enforced a down-the-middle sociability on these kids, like they were animals or something. Those minors who seemed like social weaklings—we protect their basic human rights, and in order to maintain a position of aiding in the exercise of the right to full development, we expunged the word 'education' from our vocabulary, remember?"

Shizue thought to herself that this wasn't her normal spiel. This was something the area bureau chief of the juvenile counselors cooperative should be saying.

The chief in question was scowling and simply sat there trying to see where this was going. He wasn't upset. He was resigned. It probably didn't matter to him what happened either way.

"And so…" Shizue continued. She had no choice but to. "And so the information I have on the children is all provided to me by them. We are forbidden from acting as a third party without any notice to the child in question. Doing that would be a violation of the relationship of trust between the center and the child, and it cannot be done."

"Relationship of trust…" The area chief wrinkled his nose. "Well, I'm just a patrol officer, and I don't understand these more complicated things, but speaking on my own behalf, with or without this counseling you're talking about, the world isn't a better place at the end of the day. Crimes committed by minors have certainly shown a tendency to decrease, and I don't know about the numbers, but the actual reality of the situation hasn't changed. When you say we can't use the word 'education'…"

The police officer looked around for reactions from other people of his generation.

"When we were growing up there was still school, but everyone complained that we were just being trained. I mean, as you pointed out, no one really trusted the schools, but what we have now is not so different, I don't think. If anything I think it's gotten worse. There's no discipline. That's probably not good."

"Could you not make this personal? Subjective interpretations are unacceptable to further such discussion."

The police officer went "Oh" and cowered at the neck. He was no good.

"The point is, I'm against it."

"You're a counselor. You were just brought out here from central, weren't you?"

"Of course I don't have the power to make any decisions. I'd like to hear what the regional head and area chief have to say about it."

The two in question both voiced strange sounds.

"In any case we have no precedent. We have to come to a consensus with the whole national organization of youth counselors."

"There's no need for that," Ishida pronounced.

"No need?"

"Yes. Actually we've already broadcast news of this to all reporting areas outside the one in question, pursuant to the requirement."

The local center's director muttered in an uncertain tone that he *hadn't been told anything about this.*

"There was no established route of communication for this kind of broadcast announcement."

"Of course, the very fact that we had information of this nature was in itself not to be made public, so..."

"Are you covering something up?" Shizue asked.

"Covering up? We are simply not publicizing it is all."

"You're covering up precisely because you know this will be recognized as uncouth behavior."

"That is not true."

Ishida spoke up affirmatively again.

"This situation calls for immediate action. However, the reality is that there is no prior legal protocol for this kind of response. That's why we requested cooperation and reached out to the adolescent welfare department through the respective prefectural offices—to see if we couldn't find the most legal way to do this, in a best-case scenario. As it is, we are unable to compel compliance. But we were able to obtain the consent required. Rest assured they thoroughly studied the request. However, as has been mentioned more than once, this is an incredibly delicate situation, without so much as being illegal. Which is why we're issuing a formal gag order so as not to create any confusion with the public."

"You're saying the welfare department answered positively to your request to keep this sharing of data a secret?"

"The gag order was issued by the police, but if anyone's going to benefit from it in the event of such a data share, it's the adolescent welfare department that provides the data."

He'd been holding this information back as a courtesy, or at least that was what it sounded like.

Shizue stared at the bureau chief.

His mouth was a perfectly upturned V.

"You're saying there is a precedent then."

"Yes, that's right."

"That's how we convinced central."

The bureau chief and Shizue stood up.

"Either way it's a very unique illegal precedent. It's clear this isn't just the piecing together of established facts. It's an abuse of power backed by destructive legalese."

"Whether it's an abuse of power or not, it falls in line with legislative privilege."

"Our job is not to make laws, of course, so there's nothing we can do about this."

Shizue looked at the edge of her desk.

It was useless. There was no arguing this.

It was a foregone conclusion.

This wasn't going to be documented.

And that was exactly why they'd gone out of their way to assemble this emergency meeting. Everyone was now implicated.

Shizue stopped breathing.

She couldn't stand the smell.

CHAPTER 003

HOW DO I *describe this smell?* Hazuki couldn't stop asking herself.

RGB. CMYK. Describing colors was easy. Hazuki didn't know the words herself, but there were apparently any number of ways to describe various timeless color palettes. There existed even a plentiful lexicon for shape and texture. Brightness and temperature could be quantified. Sounds had wavelengths, and there were even ways to describe timbre. Sound itself was a way to describe aural input. There were even mimetic words to describe touch.

Sight, touch, sound could all be described.

When it came to taste and fragrance however, things got really miserable.

Even taste though could be described with any combination of sweet, spicy, bitter, and sour. There weren't such categories for smell. If you took apart the components of a smell you could probably quantify aspects, but smell could not be understood in numbers. There was unfortunately no figurative translation of this hypothetical math.

That was why there was no more concrete way to describe a smell than to announce what it was you were smelling.

But if you said something smelled like roses, a person who'd never smelled a rose would not know what it was you meant. You could say it was intoxicating or stimulating, but those things meant nothing. You could also say something smelled sweet or sour, but those were expressions associated with flavor; well, except for something that smelled fishy, but that described a situation, not necessarily a smell.

Something either smelled good or it smelled bad.

Smells were generally categorized as pleasant or unpleasant.

Particular distinctions or unique characteristics could not be precisely described. This smell was not necessarily good or bad. It was unlike any other smell. The smell of the city. The smell of outside. The smell of air.

So this was the smell of water.

Water from a faucet didn't smell like this.

In any case it wasn't a smell you found indoors.

"I'm wet," Ayumi said. "Is this material really water repellent?"

Hazuki didn't know either. "A small clear droplet of water crystallizes like dew."

When she said that, Ayumi told Hazuki that real dew was whiter. Hazuki didn't know what real dew was. Was it like when the cable broke down and data got noisy, creating a white haze?

The air was clear but the town was dark.

The buildings were old. There was not even a uniform architecture.

If it looked sooty out it was because the building materials were blackened. Verticals were all a little crooked. Cables connecting the tops of utility poles to individual doors drooped, only adding to the effect of incoherence. This region hadn't been retrofitted with underground cables. Meaning that the town must have built at least twenty years ago.

It was Section C.

More commonly known as an extinct red-light district.

Of the two great residential zones in the region, one of them was Section C. As the name implied, it hadn't always been a living quarter, but if asked, Hazuki could not say what it was. She had the impression from the phrase "red-light district" and the age of the buildings that the area must have been a low-level living quarter, but she'd been told over and over that there was nothing different about the people who lived here.

That much was obvious. Where someone came from or what they did was no reason to judge them. It wasn't possible. It was so obvious it didn't bear repeating, and careful instruction on that matter made such discrimination actually seem less natural.

However, Hazuki'd just learned that there was a time in the past when geographic discrimination and physical discrimination had sparked conflict. Everything had a troubled history. She thought that to bring excessive attention to it would actually have the opposite of the intended effect.

If you keep saying we're all equal, people will start to think we aren't.

In reality, there happened to be a disproportionately large number of Section C residents who were economically depressed. Section C also happened to be located next to the most ethnically diverse residential section—Section B.

There may be no difference between us but there is disparity.

You could tell just by looking at the color coding of the *navigator*. Public institutions with green areas were all green, commercial regions were blue, and the industrial areas were gray. General residential sections—save for the one under development, Section A—were mostly marked white. And yet Section B was yellow and Section C was magenta. Where B and C overlapped was red. It wasn't to denote how dangerous it was. It was ostensibly just color-coordination, but red was officially designated a color of danger, and thus the association was impossible to avoid. Even a child could discern the significance of a map simply color-coded in red, with a little thought. So...

They couldn't conceive of discrimination against people who lived in that region, but Hazuki couldn't say with any confidence that if the preconceived notion of the area being dangerous wasn't germinating deep in the minds of these children.

But if they'd not kept insisting we were equal I'd never think about it, thought Hazuki.

People who lived in the same region didn't have intimate relations to begin with. Most communications took place on monitors through cables, so there was no way of knowing where they lived or what thy looked like; their gender, age, or even ethnicity.

The information broadcast through the wires was the only reality. Most of reality was a lie.

There was no difference between truth and falsehood.

There was no point in knowing it.

Proof of this lay in the fact that Hazuki had no idea of the names or provenance of most of the people she'd physically met in communication groups.

Under that circumstance, Hazuki thought it would be difficult for these same people to start any kind of antagonism.

Maybe these were just the ramblings of a child.

Hazuki took another look at the view. She couldn't get her eyes used to it. She couldn't get used to either the front or back. If the cityscape were in a monitor, it wouldn't matter how dissimilar the elements were on screen, she'd just turn her head and be in her room again.

She couldn't get stable. The width of the road, height of the buildings, and layout of the city were all curiously inconsistent, her sense of scale totally inverted. She couldn't place herself in it. She felt as though she might just float off into space.

She looked around and ended her gaze upon Ayumi.

Ayumi was looking at her portable monitor.

"It should be around here. Tsuzuki must—" Ayumi bent her neck before finishing the words, tilting her face away from Hazuki. *She must live in Section C.* Ayumi swallowed the rest of the sentence.

Hazuki, uncharacteristically, was also thinking about this. Mio Tsuzuki and Section C didn't go well together. But the address they got from their search clearly indicated that she lived in the area.

Yet for her to think such a thing must mean that despite herself Hazuki had some prejudice against Section C. Because all she knew about Mio Tsuzuki was that she was at an unusually high study level, she assumed that Tsuzuki couldn't be from Section C, and therefore assumed this was some kind of coincidence. Considering she wasn't conscientiously disdaining the assumption, there was no mistaking Hazuki had some kind of prejudice.

"Oh." Ayumi made a small sound.

Hazuki expanded her gaze out toward where Ayumi was looking.

Just beyond an unusually narrow road.

Another even narrower road sandwiched between walls made of cheap building material.

"Yabe."

A groupmate.

She had trouble putting a face to the name. In regular clothes, it'd be even harder. She concentrated her eyes. She started to recall what she'd looked like. Skin nearly translucent, wearing pink contacts that were popular a while ago. It looked good on her, so it didn't strike Hazuki as outdated.

She didn't know much else. But that she remembered that much must mean Yabe was a girl from her class. No matter how tenuous the relationship, she could at least distinguish between people she'd only seen on monitors and those she'd physically met. And if she'd met them in person it couldn't have been anywhere outside of the communication group.

Speaking of which...

Yabe, Yuko Yabe...she hadn't been in class today.

I wonder what she's doing.

Yuko Yabe looked up, exhausted, and stood under the eaves. She didn't appear to be wearing any rain gear and had on only a light layer of clothing. She must have been soaked.

"She's wet."

Waterproof materials are made precisely for this kind of thing, Ayumi thought, just as she stepped into a flooded road. "Let's leave quickly," Ayumi said without turning around.

I'm glad I didn't say anything pointless, Hazuki thought.

Still, was Ayumi not concerned about that girl?

Wouldn't you normally be concerned?

It wasn't really any of their business. Thus revising her opinion, Hazuki stepped out under the rain and into the unsettling city. That was when it happened.

Ayumi had turned away from Yabe's face. Probably on purpose, so she didn't have to look at her.

No matter the situation, of course she didn't like being looked at. Hazuki did not look at her either, so she wasn't sure why she thought it. But for some reason she did. It seemed Ayumi had the same thought occur to her, and they both stopped moving.

Wait. The sound just came through the shushing of the rainfall.

Ayumi wasn't sure whether she'd stopped or heard the call first.

As she turned on her heel the pink-lensed Yuko Yabe was approaching them.

"Wait," Yuko repeated.

She was talking to Ayumi, because Hazuki had already stopped and turned around.

"Is everything okay?" Yuko asked. Ayumi didn't turn around. "Hey," Yuko probed, and Ayumi said, "I'm fine." Hazuki didn't know what was going on.

Yuko tentatively stared at Ayumi's back, which showed no sign of turning about, and eventually put Hazuki back in her field of vision.

"Did something…happen?"

She asked as if her thoughts were deep somewhere.

Hazuki probed further instead of answering. "What do you mean, did something happen?"

"Well you're…acting strange."

"You don't know then?"

She apparently didn't know about the murder that had taken place in the area.

News had gotten out about an hour ago.

Hazuki had confirmed it on their way here. If Yuko had been at home she should have known. This kind of emergency data would be displayed on any active monitor, no matter your profession.

When Hazuki asked if she really didn't know, Yuko said it was because her monitor was broken.

"Broken?"

Was there some kind of trouble? Even so, she should have been at home. Was she saying the main terminal was broken too?

"Murder. In this area."

"Murder?"

Yuko raised her eyebrows.

"Random killing under the North-South Line bridge."

"So."

"So?"

"So that person, after that thing…"

"This time it was a boy," Ayumi said and turned her body.

"Here."

Ayumi showed her own monitor to Yuko.

Portable monitors have small displays, which made it hard for Hazuki to see, but she was sure Ayumi was showing information on the victim.

"Ryu Kawabata. Age sixteen. Son of an average insurance and hygiene clerk."

Ayumi brought the monitor closer to Yuko after speaking. The pink contact lenses reflected the screen.

"This is the victim."

Yuko stared at the monitor until the mist on her temple collected enough moisture to trickle down. Then, tensing her forehead, she glanced at Hazuki.

"What are you doing with this?"

That's what I'd like to know, Hazuki thought.

But…

She couldn't help but think Ayumi and Yuko were sharing some kind of information, just from having listened to the way Yuko spoke earlier.

He wasn't dead. Ayumi must have known why Yuko was absent from class today.

Still…

If that were the case, the way Ayumi saw Yuko looking at and then ignoring her, and then acting like she couldn't get away from her fast enough, was all unsettling.

As if Yuko noticed Hazuki was unusually deep in thought. What. What was it?

"That can't be."

"Don't worry, we didn't come here to check on you," Ayumi said.

"We're looking for Mio Tsuzuki's house."

"Why?"

"Because it's raining."

The raindrops grew heavier, lengthening. They fell harder.

"Her house is over there, by where the car is parked."

"Car?"

"Yeah, one of those gas-consuming things that moved people around a long time ago."

On the road at the edge of Section B was an old-fashioned personal car, one not to be ridden. Did it still run?

"Her entrance is on the second floor. The ground floor is a store. Only people from China in there."

"What do you mean store? Is it a Real Shop?" Ayumi said that it wasn't.

"It's a deli that resisted the trend of distributing legal drugs like alcohol and tobacco. Even though they're legal, people didn't look favorably upon them, so it was impossible to get vendor licenses in the commercial zones."

"Alcohol...drug-related then."

Ayumi chuckled for some reason and said, "That probably wasn't all."

"It used to be that kind of place," Yuko said. "...since it used to be a red-light district and all."

Hazuki didn't quite understand.

As Ayumi dithered, she had already started heading toward the buildings.

Yuko was still getting wet from the rain.

Hazuki selected and without inputting any more words, followed Ayumi.

She felt Yuko's pink lenses on her back all the way down to the corner of the block. Something was making an unrecognizable cracking sound. She turned and looked over her shoulder to find Yuko still standing there. In the distance behind her, the concrete wall was ablating, slowly falling apart.

The city was decaying.

No, buildings from the twentieth century weren't made with proper materials.

The design was passé. The windows didn't match, and on top of it all, strange ornaments with ancient messages decorated the walls.

She'd heard that those were called "advertisements."

Are advertisements like notifications? she wondered.

Exposing so little data to the outside, and in that dirty way, making it stand out, exactly what kind of notifying purpose was it serving?

Hazuki could not fathom. She could not fathom the way people in the past thought.

The middle of the poster was blackened. There were several women in outdated fashions sitting on chairs.

"You shouldn't peek in."

Ayumi circled the building as she spoke and stood by a glass door that looked like an entrance.

She said, "This place looks old-fashioned. I wonder if we can go in," and poked the keyboard she found at the entrance.

"We can't use our ID cards."

"There's no card reader. We can't even connect our monitors? What about vocal recognition readers?"

"I'm pretty sure they had PINs back then. Otherwise we have to actually get permission from someone on the other side of the door."

Ayumi said what an ordeal that would be and stood in front of the door.

The door creaked open.

"It's open. There's no lock."

The building lobby was lined with well-worn cheap imitation marble. The old elevator had long been out of service, and beyond a sliding door left open were scattered plastic utensils and empty glass bottles. Some of the walls had long since collapsed and exposed all the cables, some of which had been yanked out and connected to what looked like a golden box on the floor. There was yet another thick cable coming out of the box as if crawling on the floor and along the wall. Ayumi looked at it nonchalantly. Then glanced at Hazuki. "Let's go?"

"Isn't it kind of amazing?"

"Maybe."

To come all the way here just to go back? It wasn't like the rain was going to let up anytime soon. Their uniforms wouldn't get wet, but their hair was already soaked. Hazuki pulled the disc out of her bag.

"Here," Ayumi said as she followed the cable on the floor with her eyes.

"But...Tsuzuki has severed communications on her monitor." *Which is why we came here*, Hazuki thought.

In other words.

She doesn't want to see us.

"Isn't that what you were thinking?" Ayumi said. She hadn't said anything but probably read the look on her face. Even though they wouldn't look at one another's faces or anything.

"We'd be a bigger nuisance if we just left."

"Do you want to access the terminal at home?"

"Not really."

"It looks unused. It should be fine," Ayumi said as she approached the cable.

The cable wound up the stairs.

Her footsteps made thumping sounds. There was an endless buzzing. It must have been either an old lamp or an electric fan.

Or was the cable running something?

"She said it was the second floor, right?"

Three along the hall, one around the corner, four doors altogether. Ayumi looked at the floor. The cable extended not just from the bottom of the stairs but out from the top of them too. Two outlets were conjoined at one point, then the cable ran down the middle of the hall and through the doorway around the corner. The wall on one side of the hall was slightly peeling, with a hole dug through where the cable ran.

"It's so primitive," Ayumi said smartly as she went straight to the door at the corner. There was no sign on it or anything. There was no way of knowing which room was Tsuzuki's. The address they found online indicated only the neighborhood and building number. Hazuki hadn't even considered that the building might be some old tenement housing complex.

"Wait."

She couldn't possibly just know where to go. Ayumi definitely knew a lot of things Hazuki didn't, but this building had been pretty hard to find. Ayumi pointed a finger.

"We can't get in."

The doorknobs had been plucked off all three doors in the hallway.

Ayumi stopped dead in front of the door around the corner. It was a nondescript door. It had a doorknob at least. There was no residential name plaque on it, nor a visitor scan sensor. Ayumi peered into the hole through which the cable ran.

Probably, this was where the old-fashioned interphone used to be back in the day. You'd see houses like this in old moving pictures. Complicated machines that combined mics, cameras, and speakers so that residents could communicate with people outside.

"Can you see anything?"

Ayumi answered, "Nothing."

They briefly stopped moving.

Ayumi has probably never visited another person's home. She's not used to it.

The buzzing continued.

Suddenly, Ayumi grabbed the doorknob.

The door opened easily. The volume of the noise increased.

"It opens," Ayumi said as she opened the door and took one step in. Hazuki stuck her head in.

Hazuki was at a loss for words. The interior of the room was beyond her imagination.

Black. That was the impression she got. It was neither a wall nor a ceiling, but thick black cables winding everywhere. There were chips and parts and exposed machine insides, various displays, and other metal objects Hazuki had never seen before scattered all over the room. Black cables twisted around everything and connected each and every object together.

It's the insides of a monitor, Hazuki thought matter-of-factly.

When she was small, seven or eight years ago, an engineer came to repair the main terminal at her home, and she was able to sneak a look at the disassembled machine.

Happy things, shameful things, proud things, problematic things, and, of course, messages from other people, notifications and warnings, all of it appeared on monitors. She had wanted to look at the insides of that monitor, beyond the window on which information appeared.

Inside was just black.

It was a flavorless dry enclosed space built out of a variety of cables, chips, and materials. Be it lines or boards that broadcast onto a contained box, it was the entirety of the world, and suddenly the young Hazuki had realized that must mean the whole world was an illusion.

Realizing this did not surprise her, nor did it make her feel sadness or joy.

She thought she might have experienced some tightness in her chest.

There was something fake about the world. But she soon forgot about it. Afterward, what with walking around holding the portable version of this world in her hands, knowing this rarified realness, Hazuki assimilated with the fake reality and forgot about the insides of the box.

This room was…

This looked just like that inner room.

zzzzz

That was the sound of that intangible electricity and data that circulated through black lines.

This was the other side of the world.

"There are no cable guards or anything around here. We could get electrocuted."

In the midst of all these cables and boxes stood Mio.

"It won't kill you or anything."

Mio did not look at all surprised.

In fact it was Hazuki who was shaking.

Ayumi told her to get her monitor connected already.

"Thanks to you I'm all wet."

"It's such a pain. The outdoors I mean," Mio said, and placed some kind of tool on the counter by her hip. "More importantly, what's going on? People have never come inside here before."

Ayumi turned her face toward Hazuki and prompted her with a raised brow. Hazuki held up the disc they had brought with them.

"This..."

"Oh."

Mio had a bored expression on her face.

"I didn't even notice."

"We thought it might be important."

"It's not that it's important. I mean, it serves no purpose."

"Really?"

"It's just for fun."

Hazuki stepped forward, careful not to step on any of the cables, and handed the disc to Mio.

"So you didn't need it back?"

"No...Well, if I'd lost it I would have had to redo some calculations, though we're talking about a few minutes to do the math, and it's re-entering data that's the most bother."

Hazuki had no idea what she was talking about.

Ayumi looked over the room expressionlessly.

It looked like the three doors in the hall, though separate, all opened onto an adjoining room.

"This is an amazing place you live in. Administrative counselors must not come here much."

"Administrative counselors?"

"Youth protective services people. You know...people who come in to take care of kids who are in less than ideal living environments."

"Ah. Well my parents live above this floor, and there's nothing going on there. Except that they're never home. I don't think they've ever laid a hand on me, and I'm pretty sure I didn't experience any serious parental deprivation. But well, my place is okay. Fuwa came here once, but she was disgusted and went home."

"Because you're a genius."

Right.

"So this is only your room."

"At first it was only this room, but everyone left, so I've taken over the floor. Breaking down the walls was pretty hard."

"You broke down the walls? Yourself?"

"*I totally broke them all!*" Mio said, laughing. "I didn't have a place to sleep anymore. Thinking about it now, it would have been better to leave the entrance by the stairs. I started to pile things against the wall down there, and then soon it was no use."

"No use…What was no use?"

"What do you mean what? The machine."

"I know about the machine, but…"

"My main monitor."

"This whole room is a main monitor?"

"Yeah. But you know, thinking about it, a monitor implies that you are looking at something. That's weird, right? Why do we call it a monitor when it's a number-crunching unit with the capability to send and receive information? Don't you think that's amazing?"

When she put it that way it seemed right. But Hazuki didn't think it was "amazing."

"They say in the past a machine that received on-air information was different from online monitors."

"Hmph," Ayumi interjected, unimpressed.

"But reception devices were totally normal back then. They even had sound-recording equipment. But it would only record sound. How pathetic, right? Of course it only received information; the devices couldn't transmit or manipulate data. Wired communications were also audio-only."

"Only sound?"

That was inefficient.

It was like being blind.

"Actually it was just sound-based reciprocal communications offline too. Something called a *telephone*. I don't know what language that is.

As for images, especially moving ones, they were exclusively received communications. And the diffusion rates of these exclusively reception machines were unusually high, so the styles persisted and evolved into the terminals we use for news in the home to this day. And the device that displayed this visual information was called a monitor. That's why we call it that, apparently."

"You're quite the know-it-all," Ayumi said. Mio ignored her and continued.

"But here I thought it was called a monitor because through them individuals could observe the world. Like, *Let's really observe it then!* So I reconstructed it."

"Still, look how ugly this is."

"I'm a genius, so I don't have a sense of aesthetics. It's got great performance. It has approximately twelve thousand times the data-mining power of an average household monitor. It has memory capacity at, I'd guess, around eight thousand times the average. Of course I've only used a hundredth of it. But for that matter, it can connect to any kind of data origin in a split second. It runs fast and can do heavy lifting."

"Meaningless. We're just kids."

"Like I said, it's just a hobby."

"Like your disc."

"This is *The Monster*."

"Monster?"

"I saw something about it in a moving picture, a fiction. This giant turtle-like thing has fire come out of its mouth."

"What are you talking about?" Ayumi furrowed her face.

"An old moving picture! Like what they show in optical science class."

"A fire-breathing turtle?"

"Yeah, it's amazing." Mio then pointed toward the back of the room, that is to say, the room next door.

In the next room was a piece of equipment they'd never seen before.

"I couldn't wrap my head around a turtle doing something humans couldn't. That's a plasma generator, designed to emit plasma streams, but I failed."

"It's a weapon!"

"It's a crime," Ayumi said.

"It's a *failed* weapon. I have to think of another way. It won't be like in those entertainment motion pictures from decades ago. So I thought up a different method. And this guy has all the data on that plasma-spewing machine. The Monster."

"That's dangerous."

"Just because I make it doesn't mean I can use it. There's no use for it. Things are different now. Nothing changes when you destroy things, but there is still the impulse for destruction.

"It's an instinct," Mio said in the midst of humming electric waves.

Ayumi bared her hatred.

CHAPTER 004

WITH HER HEAD tilted all the way back and the muscles taut, her windpipe collapsed a little and started to choke her.

I can't keep doing this.

Shizue had supposedly fallen into a depressive fit that doctors said was the result of eye fatigue.

This was clearly a retaliatory move on their part.

Of all people, they'd named Shizue—the spearhead of the opposition against this information mining of the authorities—head director of the new martial law on gathering information.

This was nothing but their way of getting even.

That councilman with the *memory hair* no doubt maneuvered this with the center's bureau chief. Probably getting back at her for being embarrassed in front of the area chief.

It wasn't like Shizue was trying to embarrass the filthy bastard. She might have thought slanderous and libelous thoughts, but it wasn't as if she'd voiced them. It was, to be sure, Shizue's fault the conference didn't go smoothly, but it was hard to imagine it didn't bother the man responsible specifically for making the conference run at all.

Those guys would prefer a seamless conference to actual results.

How pathetic.

The Information Act was unlawful. Even if it weren't, it was at least problematic. Each and every thing about it needed to be obstructed.

But now Shizue was complicit.

If the truth came out and the crime in this were recognized, Shizue was in no position to criticize the program or shut it down.

In any case, Shizue herself was doing the actual work on this now, so no one would hear her excuses.

She couldn't say she didn't want to do it after the fact, and no one would listen if she said she was forced to accept the position. It would just sound like a bunch of excuses. That was totally unlike Shizue.

Of course she'd thought of saying something before, but now that she'd started the work, it would be difficult to back out.

Shizue frantically pounded the keys.

It's no use.

"It's no use." The officer brought in from the prefectural police spoke out in a nerveless voice.

Kunugi, she thought his name was. A boring forty-something-year-old man. As far as police officers went, he was probably not very important, Shizue decided.

She didn't determine that based only on outward appearances.

It was because he'd demonstrated such a lazy attitude that he'd reluctantly and needlessly been brought around to this job. That much he had in common with Shizue, but this man didn't seem to then ask himself why he was here at all. So, burrowed in this room since noon doing futile work was the consequence of his being incompetent, whereas Shizue was here as a result of having offended the system.

"It's such a waste. I don't know why we have to do this," the officer continued, peeking at Shizue's fingertips. "Isn't there…I don't know, something else we can do?"

"Are you saying you're less than satisfied with the results of my work?" Shizue looked straight at the officer. Not that she wanted to look at him.

Kunugi looked like he didn't know what to do with his obstinate body, all clenched up on his seat. He had no presence. His saving grace was the fact that he didn't seem gross.

"What would you do yourself? Anyone can do this in the time it takes to make copies."

"That's not what I meant," Kunugi said. "How do I put this…I'm just wondering about the way we're obtaining the information. I'm not really in a position to be saying this, and it's probably nothing, but isn't this medium obsolete?"

"We can't transmit this information online."

"The program doesn't support it?"

"No. Of course it *can* be done. It's just been specially encrypted. Even perusal of this data requires a secret PIN, so as it stands transmission connections are tenuous and copying the data would be impossible."

"But aren't you copying it now?"

"Yes, I am. That's why it's a question of what's going to take longer—renewing the whole system and exposing all the data, or adjusting all the information and copying it to traffic media."

Putting their hands in the system would probably guarantee a better quality of work. But there was a problem. If they altered the mainframe, all of the information stored in there would, for a moment, be exposed. Information about children under ten wasn't given to the police, and beyond that, there was no small amount of top secret information the details of which couldn't be publicized collected on the mainframe. In addition, once the system had been altered, it took as long to return it to its original state. Shizue was no expert, but she knew enough to know that a serious mix-up during that brief moment of exposure wouldn't be unheard of.

Data leaks from everywhere. That much was determined in the 2030s. Copyright and trademarks, privacy…None of it was protected by ethics or morals. If you wanted to protect something, never save it as electronic data.

Ultimately, people depended on things.

There were supposedly old people who had homes packed full of paperwork from the past, but was that how it was all going to end?

People needed concrete objects.

"The police just decided it would cause too many problems, so they want to put everything on discs," Shizue said, as it was too complicated to explain the rest.

"I don't know about that," Kunugi replied, unimpressed. "That seems…oh I don't know. I'm not good with words. I'm sorry."

"It doesn't bother me," Shizue replied.

The truth didn't bother her.

Things like words were good when communicating something. The issue was that the words actually had to say something. Shizue's problem was that there were so many idiots who didn't. Saying something politely didn't make it all right either. Things like vocal tone were displayed on-screen through things like typeface, but that had nothing to do with meaning.

Kunugi had no doubt heard things about Shizue from either that guy Ishida or the area policemen near Yokota.

I bet they told him I'm a frigid bitch.

"As you can tell, I'm an awkward cop, plus, I was at the police academy before the turn of the century, so I'm from the old century in every way. So you see, with young people like yourself…There I go again. That's harassing language isn't it. Well, unlike those of you who were born this century, I'm totally inept with current technology."

"I'm no specialist either."

"I'm sure. But still, when I was young, old men my age didn't even know what a computer was. I was often asked what they were for. But I didn't know how to answer. All I could say was that it could be used for anything. But if it can do everything, then you need it to be efficient before you can understand it. It was simple. When I became a cop, the Internet and the something something revolution still caused a commotion."

"Was that wrong?"

"Wrong?"

"Computers were viewed strangely for too long," Shizue said. "Clearly the excessive illusions about computer technology wrought confusion at one point, and society thereafter attempted to adapt midcourse, and these thoughts overflow in this generation of people who can't let go of their outmoded ideas."

"Our generation," Kunugi said.

Shizue pointed at the edge of the keyboard with her index finger. "You think too hard about this everyday technology. You still believe computers can do everything. These are all programmed machines. They can only do a set number of things."

"I'm sure that's right, but is that all?"

"Of course. It goes without saying scissors are good for cutting paper, but you can't use scissors to suture paper. Similarly, the best accounting software can't make music. Computers are nothing more than calculators. It's a system built to do the math necessary to accomplish a task. If humans were able to do several calculations at once there'd be no need for computers. No matter how grand the calculation, nothing but cutlery can cut paper."

Kunugi's lips creased at the corners. *Hmm*, he muttered.

"What I mean is, those old men from when you were young were already right on about the purposes of computers." Shizue spoke as calmly as she could, then returned her gaze to the screen. It was more settling.

The download status bar gave no sign of movement. Only 10 percent of the work was finished. This would take at least another half hour. More specifically, it would be another 1,820 seconds.

Shizue just had to sit there and silently wait.

It was that kind of work.

And Kunugi's job was to watch Shizue sit there and silently wait. Otherwise there was no point in him being here. Cooperation was a pretext. There was no need for two people to do this very basic work.

She could think of only one reason this boring old man who had no data-mining knowledge or technology was sitting next to her. To make sure Shizue didn't tamper with or eliminate any data. She was sure of it.

Out of her peripheral vision Shizue could see packaging that had been folded over several times sitting on top of the disc. Kunugi must have been really bored. If he was really just watching over her, then he was certainly bored. Shizue herself was bored, and she was actually doing the work.

"Maybe it is just an illusion," Kunugi said. "This hard drive is meant for copying this, right? I was just thinking, isn't this taking too long? If we've only gotten this far, there must be some other way, right?"

"Isn't it always like this?" Shizue looked back at her screen.

"I feel like it used to be faster."

"Used to be…You mean circa FDs and MOs?"

"Yeah. You don't see that anymore. We still had them when I was in school. Recording methods have changed since then I guess."

Kunugi resumed fiddling with the packaging between his fingers.

"Recoding methods in and of themselves haven't changed much from the past, but compression technology has advanced leaps and bounds. Obviously, there was less information to have to move in older media. Of course it transferred faster."

"Hmm, so the disc format is considered old now?" Kunugi asked.

"Changes in format take a long time. The diffusion of hard drives is not complete, so for now, discs are still being used."

"So we have no choice then," Kunugi threw out, and the police officer shrank as he watched Shizue continue to work.

"Well, I'm just sitting here, so I guess it's fine."

"I'm just thinking this must be annoying for you," Kunugi added.

"Me?"

"Weren't you unhappy about this assignment? You look annoyed."

"Please don't judge me by appearances," Shizue said coolly. "I'm always like this."

If he saw through her it was because she *was* annoyed.

The cop furrowed his brow. "I'm sorry if I'm wrong. I can't know what's going on inside, so all I have is the outward appearance. I asked precisely because I didn't know. Sorry."

How awfully polite. Made things hard.

"Well, honestly I was just trying to lead in to asking if you wanted some tea or something. I can't get used to all this."

After assuring herself that the download status bar was in fact moving,

Shizue turned her gaze toward the nondescript man. As soon as they made eye contact, Kunugi broke his gaze from Shizue and went into a tizzy.

"Oh, no, I mean, I'll get it. What do you want?" he said.

"I'm fine. This is my workplace. You just wanted tea, then?"

"Is there any *Japanese* tea?"

"Flavonoid drinks are popular right now," Shizue said as she stood from her seat. She didn't usually pour tea for anyone besides herself. And she'd also never taken the same drink as someone else. That was because she didn't feel like drinking something someone else made. It wasn't as though Shizue was worried about being poisoned or anything, but she felt that one could never be too sure.

As she poured tea into a disinfected rental cup for visitors, she sensed the haze lifting.

The way he's behaving…is he…

Kunugi must have been what they called a gopher, responsible for getting tea, at his workplace. For some reason, the term *gopher* was used derisively in organizations. Shizue didn't know why. What it was about bringing tea that merited discrimination she would never know.

When Shizue returned with the tea she found Kunugi sitting in her chair and making a confused face at the monitor.

Not that staring at it improved the quality of the work or anything.

"Oh, sorry."

The cop scrambled up. *Maybe he's easier to get along with than I thought*, Shizue thought.

However, Shizue detected what looked like a fingerprint on the armrest of her chair. "It's fine," she snapped, as she wiped down the armrest with a disinfectant wipe. The chair she'd picked out because it was easy to clean was made of synthetic leather, but that made keratin stand out all the more. If it were lined in fabric she wouldn't have noticed.

"Germophobe, eh?"

"That's normal. Lately anyone who isn't is called a germophile."

"That's what I am then," Kunugi said. He sipped his tea.

"It says there's another twenty minutes left."

"Looks like it."

He must be around my father's age, Shizue got to thinking.

"You want to have *a real conversation* while we wait?"

Shizue looked Kunugi in the face and said half aggravated, "Aren't you supposed to supervise me?" Just when she'd started to warm up to him he had to go and do something like this. She had to admit she'd been played with a little.

"You know…" Kunugi shrank again. "I know that talking about private matters in public is considered offensive, but I want to say something knowing as much. I'm single. When I say 'real conversation' it's not a joke. What would you do if I really did it? If it's a joke, it's a joke, and it's sexual harassment. And yeah, I'm definitely here to supervise you, but that's because it's been a while, and people like me don't often get the chance to be this close to women your age. And if I might add, the prefectural police don't think you're going to do anything dishonest here."

"Is that right?" Shizue said. "I'm sure you're well aware, but I was strongly opposed to having the private data on minors be handed over to the police. And now I'm the sole person responsible for copying that data. It's so obvious. For example, you don't think it's completely possible that information that could raise suspicion with the police can be tampered with?"

"Of course not."

"How can you be so sure?"

"I am positive."

"Why?"

"I have proof."

"Proof? There's no way."

"No, I do. If they truly thought you were capable of committing such a crime, they wouldn't have stuck a useless old man like me with you." Then Kunugi laughed. "My head stopped evolving around twenty years ago. You could be performing some operation through those keys, but I don't have the knowledge to discern that. If I asked what you were doing and you told me a lie, I'd have no way of knowing. I would not be able to stop you. I'm a useless middle-aged man. I'm sure the longer I sit here the more unpleasant it'll become for you."

"Unpleasant…"

Was that what it looked like?

She couldn't deny it.

"You looked really unhappy," the cop said. "Of course, once again, that's based simply on what I see. Well, that's the only reason I could come up with for being transferred here, which in other words just means I'm here to bother you. The fact that they want to bother you at all must mean someone doesn't quite have positive feelings about you, but they definitely don't suspect you."

"Is that so?"

"It's like that," Kunugi tied up. He made a weird face and sipped more tea.

"Mmm, this tea is good," he said, very deliberately.

It tastes the same everywhere.

It was just something that came out of a dispenser.

Because so many people sued for cases of dysosmia and hypergeusia, food products of late had enhanced flavors and smells. It was all a little acidic for Shizue's taste.

After a brief silence, Kunugi asked, "You were really that opposed to this?"

"What do you mean 'that opposed'?"

"Well, you just said you thought the police doubted you because you were so opposed to their plan. Is that a way of saying you're tired of doubting your own pupils?"

"No, it…isn't."

Shizue immediately regretted having answered such an off-kilter question so earnestly.

"I'm just a counselor."

She went on. "There are no longer such things as educators. Proctors help with specialized subjects, and supervisors are responsible for teaching basic social mores and rules. There are staff for running communication courses, but I'm sure that will be phased out soon."

"So you're telling me there are no more educators."

"I'm saying the word 'education' no longer connotes teaching and fostering. It has negative connotations of discipline and organization. Looking at past data it seems the word had a broader meaning before, but even so, by the end of the twentieth century it was no longer clear *what* was being taught, regardless of the methodologies used."

"I wasn't taught how to live either," Kunugi said. "I certainly didn't like my teachers. I don't know about before my time, though."

"With no one learning anything, using the word 'student' was silly too. 'Teacher' is a weird word too. I don't think 'teacher' originally signified the primacy of older age, but that's the meaning it took on. There's nothing guaranteeing an older person is inherently superior."

"I guess that's a form of age discrimination."

Well, yes.

"For about ten years, all kinds of contradictions erupted, and these arcane educational pedagogical systems collapsed. Concurrently, the term 'education' was banned. Today, minors are all children—they are only recognized as such by the different rights and responsibilities they bear."

"I don't really understand. Well, I'm the one always lectured on profession-based human rights issues, but clearly things are different from the past. When I was young, there were laws protecting young people, but…" Kunugi paused. "What am I trying to say here? W-*well*…" The policeman stammered.

"You're *confusing* the issue," Shizue said. "I know what you are trying to say. I'm no youth rights revivalist. There is no clear delineation between children and adults, so it's no one's right to make them up. Whether you have knowledge or experience or superior physical function isn't determined by age or gender, so to create arbitrarily separate groups based purely on age is problematic. I realize this will seem like a gross exaggeration, but to say a minor can't have a criminal record is in principle the same as denying a woman's right to vote. You're having to protect and shelter both, but beyond just protecting basic human rights lies responsibility."

"So what don't you like about all this?" Kunugi asked. "I mean, what is so important to oppose now, to the extent that you hate the police?"

"Why are you asking such questions of me?"

"Hmm…"

Kunugi put his empty cup down on the desk and brought his right hand to his chin.

"If I had to identify the problem…In brief, there are no guidelines as to how we are to use this data we're accumulating."

Obviously.

That was because it was illegal.

"How to use it then?" he said.

"Using this data will produce terrible results. I think it's a popular delusion fostered by people born in the twentieth century."

The policeman smiled weakly and pointed at his face. "You mean me."

Unable to confirm or deny, Shizue went on. "The data itself has no meaning. The data is nothing more than organized numbers and signs. No data has any meaning at all. If we find meaning in data it's because the people using the data are determined to find meaning. The same information can be interpreted differently by different people. Various meanings can hence be derived from the same information. The question is which meaning will we adhere to, and then what shall we do with that information. Ultimately, the result is influenced by the people using it."

"You say it would be used badly."

"I'm sure at the very least the police wouldn't do anything bad with it."

Shizue was just being sarcastic, but Kunugi said with a completely straight face, "Of course."

"Today's police force spends most of its time looking for criminal usage of data. Two-thirds of the entire police force is dedicated to protecting information exchange. As I've already made clear, I'm just a lug in this department, but this data we're looking at—isn't it just records on children? I can't imagine how it could be misused."

"I can't imagine anything but it being misused."

"You're suggesting the police would misuse it?"

"This isn't just information about children's lives. In this drive is contained information necessary for the *mental care* of minors. Information about their performance in classrooms, obviously home environment, likes, dislikes, hobbies, changes in habits, physical characteristics, exhaustive medical records, dream records…everything has been databased. That's why there's so much to be downloaded."

Kunugi looked beyond Shizue at the screen. She continued, "The police are going to try to suss out a suspect from this information."

"No, they're trying to create a profile of a hypothetical perpetrator…or that's what they're saying."

"That's even worse."

Kunugi turned his eyes from the monitor to Shizue. "Worse?"

"Yes. Let's say, for example, there's a question of psychic trauma. There are instances in which such psychic trauma can be a hindrance to a healthy social life. But to say it is the root of criminal behavior, to use it to explain criminal actions, is complete nonsense."

"Hmmm, trauma was definitely a popular term in the past."

"It still is. Obviously, reductionist explanations of patterns of human behavior have limitations. They're close to superstition. So to say that if you suffered some kind of abuse as a child you will inflict abuse as an adult is—"

"That doesn't happen?" Kunugi asked.

"Of course it does. There are cases of it, but there are also cases where it doesn't happen. Childhood abuse is of course of great concern to everyone, but there is no set pattern that leads to actual abuse. Sometimes an endearment results in abuse, other times, it's just a communicated exchange that creates abusive stimuli."

"Isn't that taking it a bit far?"

"No. Past interference is a problem, but the quality of the problem is different. There are those types of people who are perplexed by attempts at normative communication. Reaching out to these children will feel to them exactly like physical pain. Remember five or six years ago the phrase 'give it your all' was banned?"

"I was reprimanded for using the phrase myself, actually," Kunugi said. "I wasn't deliberately saying anything mean or anything."

"That's what communication is. It's lopsided. Reciprocal comprehension is a delusion. Communication is the ability to overcome this one-sided way of thought by embracing the possibility of misunderstanding each other in any situation. These days, fewer people know how to misconceive things. That's all."

Kunugi held his chin again.

"In any case, contrary to expectation, this analysis of the information hasn't produced any one result. Pre-modern disciplines oriented toward understanding human behavior, such as psychology, have totally collapsed. In that sense, religion is a much more useful tool. Surveys, statistics—they're all useless. We've realized too late that humans cannot be understood. That's why there are still people who sustain primitive beliefs in the effects of trauma on character or personality."

"Like the police."

"I'm sure. That's the impression I got from the way your superior sounded off at the conference. This data is supposed to be used by the police to ascertain extreme characters—to pick up dangerous persons. The police are the ones determining what makes someone unusual, so I'm assuming they'll look at home environments, proclivities, medical records..."

Shizue wondered how dangerous any of these things were, or why they would have gone unnoticed.

Legislating this data mining is well within our vision, Ishida had made clear. Wasn't he just saying they'd be applying this ridiculous criteria to organize and analyze every citizen?

Race, provenance, profession, class, gender—because these distinctions had lost importance, the police decided to discriminate by educational environments and habits.

Shizue got a little emotional as she explained this, and as expected, Kunugi just said that sounded like an exaggeration.

"This investigation has been a really hard ride."

"It always is. But arrest rates have gone down, right? Plus, I hear that there's a program in development that will sequester people who are genetically prone to act against society."

"I've heard the same."

"This data becomes material for programs like that. Society didn't come before humanity. Deviants definitely need to be arrested in order to support the framework, but is it right to preemptively weed out what might be deviant behavior? Isn't that a kind of eugenics?"

"I understand what you're saying." The policeman straightened himself. "Truth be told, I'm not comfortable with it either. But I'm not as knowledgeable about this as you, so I don't know what exactly is wrong about it. That's why I'm asking so many questions."

Then, "Hey!" Kunugi pointed over Shizue's shoulder.

She turned around exactly as the download completed. The drive made a short sound to signify that the job was finished and popped out a disc.

Shizue put the disc in a hard case and put a protective cover on it. They'd been working since morning and only gotten a third of the way through. Shizue brought out another disc to continue working, but Kunugi stopped her.

"This is good for today."

"We've got a lot of work left. If we have until five o'clock I can probably manage another two or three discs."

"It's not that. I have to deliver this disc to police headquarters by five. In that ugly government-issued solar car you see out there, driving from here to there will take exactly thirty-eight minutes. Add to that all the paperwork, and I have to leave here in twenty minutes. That's not enough time to do another disc."

It'd take at least thirty minutes.

"The proviso states a police officer has to witness the work, so when I leave this place, the work you do alone will be invalid. We are all bureaucrats, if nothing else." Kunugi spoke matter-of-factly as he took the disc from Shizue and put an organizational number on it. Then after taking a deep breath, he counted the disc along with the others and wrote the number down on another card, then put it all in a box. Then he stowed the box in his bag.

"Maybe it's just an illusion, but I have a feeling this will all be pointless."

Kunugi put on an old-fashioned jacket not seen much anymore.

Shizue sterilized her fingertips.

In other words...

I have to work this way for another two days.

"Pointless or not, the regulations have created a real obstacle, haven't they."

She couldn't have anyone substitute as a counselor, and one never knew if a problem might arise. She wasn't even able to perform routine mail checks. Two more days of this would certainly be a problem.

"You don't prefer the regulations?" Kunugi, now standing, asked.

"I can't do it like this. We're in charge of a hundred people. Our division is short-staffed, and I myself have seven or eight people in each age group, totaling ninety kids I'm responsible for. Normally we each get thirty. Any more than that and we lose focus."

What use is it complaining to this guy?

Shizue opened her mail on the monitor. As if waiting for the right moment, Kunugi stood again.

What?

Shizue's eyes froze.

There were no messages.

No messages from concerned children. She converted to the room monitor and summoned a roster of the children.

Kunugi decided that maybe he shouldn't be looking. He turned toward the wall and asked if there was a problem.

"It's not a problem, per se." Shizue checked that she was connected. Her message to Yuko Yabe...

FAILED DELIVERY.

She double-checked the address and connectivity.

The connection wasn't recognized.

Is the monitor broken?

Shizue felt a shiver up her spine.

A broken monitor wasn't unheard of. But it was something she should have noticed when she sent the message yesterday. No, she could just try a voice message or at least check the connection on her home terminal. Shizue had been preoccupied with this data mining last night.

"There was a child who didn't come to yesterday's communication group. There was no notice of it, so when the proctor notified me I sent the student a message, but..."

"There's no reply?"

"Well, that's not uncommon, but it's not that there's no return message.

There's no...monitor."

"No monitor?"

"I have to go," Shizue said. And she left.

CHAPTER 005

AS HAZUKI DISCONNECTED, some rote on-air news appeared on-screen.

At the bottom right of her screen floated a file called VIOLENT CRIMINALS OF THE TWENTIETH CENTURY.

The on-air menu flooded the screen with text, so she knew the basic gist even with her speakers on mute.

A middle-aged man with old-fashioned dyed hair was rapidly moving his mouth. Words appeared in a text box below his face in conjunction with the movement of his mouth.

NO WEAPONS / THEATRICAL / CALLED A PSYCHO-KILLER / MINORS / "EDUCATIONAL" / IN THE HOME...

AROUND THIS TIME THE STALKER / FAMOUS / BIZARRE MURDERER...

The words ran so quickly she couldn't read them all.

Not that she wanted to.

To begin with, Hazuki wasn't sure what *bizarre* meant. She just thought it must mean something bad.

Well, not simply bad, but immoral. That was the impression she had. She didn't know why, but probably because of the way the word looked. Even if the meaning wasn't apparent, the appearance of that series of characters could signify so much. She might be totally wrong, but there was still the unspoken meaning that was implied.

She tried viewing the word in English. Still, she recognized words by spelling, which vexed her. At wit's end, she switched to Arabic.

Then, suddenly she didn't understand anything. The middle-aged man with brown hair or anyone from any country. She didn't know what they were saying.

They showed picture after picture of young girls.

They were explained with words she'd never seen before.

These must be victims. Judging from the age of these girls they couldn't be perpetrators. Their clothing looked unfamiliar to her, meaning they could have been of foreign nationality. Yet their faces looked recognizable, meaning they must have been Japanese.

These were children from a really long time ago.

If I were murdered, I wonder if I'd appear foreign to people looking at me in the future.

More familiar scenes on her monitor.

Though surrounded by incomprehensible words, the images were clearly taken from the area where Hazuki grew up.

However, it was only for a split second that the images were familiar. The footage soon took on a morbid cast. These were probably images from the murder investigation of the local killings—under the North-South Line overpass—Mio had been talking about, which was more accurately said to be taking place under the Central North-South Line directly adjacent to her neighborhood.

Hazuki could point out on a map where this was but had never seen it herself. This broadcast was the first time she'd seen it.

They went back to showing headshots.

These must be of the latest victim.

It was a boy. Hazuki tried to remember his name but couldn't for some reason. No, it was because she hadn't ever known it.

This was a foreigner too.

It was because of the Arabic writing on the screen.

In any case this was a language from a world Hazuki had nothing to do with, she reasoned.

She looked at her monitor.

Four fifty-one PM and twenty seconds.

It had been at least five hours since she connected to the area center cable. She'd long surpassed the suggested amount of time for connectivity. Or rather, Hazuki's group had been instructed not to spend more than two hours at a time on work.

Hazuki put her monitor on sleep mode and got up from her chair.

Dinner should be ready now.

She left her room and went down the hall.

In the dining area was, as expected, a neatly laid-out meal.

She was four when they pulled her out ten years ago. Hazuki had been eating this same kind of meal every day in this room ever since. Her foster dad was a busy man who only came home about once a month. She no longer had a caretaker, so she was frequently alone.

She wasn't hungry.

She drew water from the faucet and drank one glass. She felt full.

Whether Hazuki decided to eat or not, every morning the dining table would be set for breakfast. The home helper sent over by the security center was very conscientious, correct, taciturn.

She thought of throwing away the food. She knew it would be a waste, but if she left it, there would be an ordeal later. If you left a meal out twice without touching it, the security center automatically notified a counselor.

Then they'd start sending you all these messages, and pay visits, notify your caretaker, and generally create a bother.

She wasn't without a caretaker, but what would they make of this kind of behavior? They might bring her to a medical caretaker. If you were under sixteen and determined to have an eating disorder, they would abruptly cart you out to a rehabilitation center.

This diagnosis was apparently made through a medical interview conducted via another monitor. If you answered the questions poorly, it wouldn't matter if you were healthy—they would declare you ill. Conversely, you could be suffering from a grave illness but answer the questions correctly, and the monitor would not diagnose you.

Unlike other illnesses, psychological ones like eating disorders were problematic. *Still, what child would answer these questions honestly,* Hazuki thought.

She kept looking at the food.

I'll keep it for now. She might want to eat it later. It wouldn't matter when she ate it as far as anyone was concerned. It would just be cold.

But just as she'd resolved this—

A *thunk.* Was the helper still around? Usually she tried not to be seen. She considered it a matter of custom. Hazuki would only see the caretaker on days she cleaned the house.

Today?

Not cleaning day.

She expected no visitors. It couldn't have been her foster father. He never did anything alone. Whenever he came home he'd have an entourage trailing him. And then there were all the people who'd come the day before to prepare everything for their return.

She heard the clicking of the doorknob moving.

Hazuki looked at the kitchen monitor. If there were someone at the door the monitor there would automatically turn on. All she saw displayed on it was the time. Hazuki pulled the emergency receiver from her main monitor and gripped it tight, then turned on the monitor.

The monitor beeped, and the front door clicked open.

Hazuki reflexively moved to push the dial button, but her fingertip stopped at the button, paralyzed. What came on her monitor was so unexpected it arrested her stiff.

"What a huge house," came the voice through her monitor speakers.

On her monitor screen was Mio Tsuzuki.

"What's…going on?"

Hazuki was confused, but after hesitating a moment, she advanced to the foyer with her emergency receiver. She couldn't feel at ease. Wasn't sure what exactly was going on.

Mio was standing in the foyer.

"I failed at breaking in."

"Hey!"

She was about to ask what the hell was going on, but her voice didn't let her. But Mio probably didn't know she was disoriented. Hazuki remained quiet and stared down Mio's small animal-like eyes.

"I meant to sneak in unnoticed. But then there was the distance between the gate and the door, and even after opening the door I wasn't in, and when I thought I'd gotten into the room it turned out to be the foyer."

"How did you…get in?"

She left it at that for now. Mio pulled out her card.

"This opens almost everything."

"Is it a forgery?"

"It's all-purpose. When you say forgery you mean like a counterfeit. This isn't a fake. It can work in any place, so it's all-purpose. It opens locks and passes most clearances. Now if it could just bypass sensors."

"You can bypass sensors?"

Sure you could.

"But here, even if I get past the door I have this big surveillance AI to deal with."

Mio pointed at the machine hanging from the ceiling.

"That's recording, isn't it?"

"Probably. That would be normal."

"Maybe I should erase it then. Ugh, what a drag." Mio craned her neck.

"Erase…What are you talking about?"

"Look. If there's video of me visiting, the counselors find out. That we became friends or whatever. Or that we could be. Don't you think that's annoying?"

"Annoying…I guess."

"Besides, I passed the sensor at your gate and then in your foyer. If the house determines that was a system error they'll send a repairman. If not, they send an area patrolman. My face shows up on it, they arrest me."

"Arrest you," Hazuki said, looking to the side. "Aren't you doing this in order to get arrested? I have nothing to do with it." It was all she could think. A genius like Mio had no use for Hazuki. Even if she did want to talk, a simple connection to her monitor would suffice, and if for some reason she couldn't do that and decided to come all the way up to Hazuki's house, a proper announced visit would do the trick.

If she'd known it was Mio to begin with...

...she would have let her in.

Hazuki was vaguely presuming these feelings.

It wasn't like she hated Mio or anything.

She didn't mind talking to her, seeing her or being seen by her...It wouldn't bother her the way it usually might.

Still, she was tired of it. She got tired of it. She didn't want to talk anymore.

"Go home."

Hazuki didn't want her face looked at. She raised her emergency receiver.

"Wait. You're being weird," Mio said.

"You're the one being weird! Didn't you see my *vacancy* light turned off? So..."

So by running their personal ID card through the reader the visitor would be properly identified on a screen inside the door.

If the words *Mio Tsuzuki* had appeared on her monitor to begin with, if her ID number appeared, then Hazuki could have graciously let her in.

If.

"You didn't need to use some fake card. You have your personal ID, don't you?"

"Yeah I got one. But this is payback. Payback. I don't know about you..." Mio pulled her hair back. "You guys just came into my place yesterday. You came in unannounced."

"Huh?"

Hazuki stole a glance. Mio sneered.

"We're even."

"You came here for revenge?"

Is that why you secretly invaded my house? You wanted me to know how annoying it is, that's why you did this? Still...

Hazuki dropped her emergency receiver and faced Mio. Mio was wearing unornamented pants made of industrial-strength textile—she was dressed like a maintenance person.

Yesterday at her house, Hazuki hadn't thought Mio looked at all bothered. She hadn't seen any indication of annoyance. She didn't even remember any negative impressions from her on their way out. But that was all Hazuki's personal viewpoint, and maybe the sudden intrusion had been a horrible nuisance after all. Actually, it probably had been. If Mio's break-in today bothered her this much, Hazuki's visit yesterday must have upset Mio even more.

"Are you upset?"

"It's not that." Mio scrunched up her face. "Here."

She jutted out her arm. Something small hung from her fingertip.

Hazuki looked closer. It was shiny.

"Is that a piercing?"

"Is that what it's called? I don't really know, but you're supposed to put it on your body, apparently."

It was a pink gemstone.

Judging from the size she decided it was for the ears or cheek.

"What about this?"

"What about it. This isn't yours?"

"Mine?"

Hazuki hated piercings; seeing them made her want to tear them out.

"It's not yours then?" Mio placed the object in her hand and stared.

"I brought this back to you since you'd come out to bring me my hard drive."

"This is your payback?"

"Sure. I'm just returning the favor. Right?"

"That's not called *payback*, Mio."

Hazuki suddenly became self-conscious and looked Mio dead in the face.

"Tsuzuki, are you really a genius?"

"Bona fide. I'm sorry. But, well, this must be Kono's then."

"Ayumi?"

Had Ayumi been wearing a piercing?

She couldn't remember. Hazuki had only seen her from behind, and then diagonally, so if Ayumi had been wearing it in her left ear Hazuki wouldn't have noticed it. Hazuki wondered allowed if Ayumi would ever wear something like this.

"Yeah, I figured you'd be the one to wear a dangly little thing like this. No offense."

"None taken."

It was true. Hazuki tended to buck the trends. Ayumi was more...

"She's really simple, you know?"

Right. Ayumi didn't do anything excessive.

"I don't think it's hers," Hazuki answered.

It wouldn't suit her. Of course that was just a personal opinion, and even if that personal opinion coincided with the general consensus, whether such a thing suited Ayumi or not would be up to the person in question. It didn't preclude Ayumi's wearing a dangly piercing.

"This guy's neo-ceramic, so it's really sturdy," Mio said.

"It doesn't matter."

"I guess it doesn't, but you two are the only ones who came over, and no matter what anyone says it's definitely not mine. If it's not yours it's hers."

Mio closed her hand on the stone.

"More importantly, can I use your main terminal for a second? I need to erase the security tape in less than fifteen minutes or it'll report me."

"Can you erase it?"

She sounded like she could.

"You don't have any more surveillance cameras?"

"There's one in each room, but they don't act unless something happens."

"Wow, one in each room?" Mio took off her shoes, said she was coming in, and went to the monitor. Before Hazuki could stop her, Mio was down the hall, walking toward the dining area.

"Gotta hand it to the prefectural housing people. This place is solid. It feels lived in, like an old house."

"They built it to feel that way."

Hazuki followed her.

Mio opened the dining room doors.

"There's no sensor here, right? Wow."

Mio approached the dining table.

"That looks good!"

"Yeah?"

"That's a home-cooked meal."

"Not really."

"I mean like, as a style of menu," Mio said. "Just like there's French food. No matter who made this, I'd call it home-cooked. Probably."

"Probably."

"I don't have a family either. So where's your terminal? Oh, this will work." Mio sat in front of the kitchen monitor and started tapping at the keys. Her fingers moved effortlessly.

"How's it going?"

"Nothing really. I just have to switch the times. I came into the foyer at 4:57 PM and twenty seconds. It's 5:10 now. Not a lot of time here."

"You're going to...switch the times?"

"I'm going to cut it out, then splice in the same time frame from yesterday. No one came yesterday, right? The time in here is made up anyway. It'll be like nothing happened."

Was that all?

"Can you believe we depend on this meaningless math? I can't believe this world. Would you notice if all your clocks were wrong?"

"I wouldn't if they were only off by a little bit."

"What's a little bit? One second? One minute? You wouldn't notice if it were twelve hours, would you?"

It was true she lost track of time when sitting in front of a monitor.

"I suppose, but I'd know as soon as I compared my portable monitor against them."

"What if that was off too?"

"It can't be."

"I'm just saying *if* it were. Actually all these clocks are regulated now, so normally, an isolated clock won't get derailed. If one clock went off, all the clocks in the world would be off. If all the clocks went off by a whole day, I bet a lot of people wouldn't notice. No, even half a day. If we were off by a half day, people wouldn't question their clocks, they'd just wonder why it was so dark at noon."

Mio laughed at her own joke, then continued. "So I can cut and paste this moment and no one will notice. And...there. We're set. I am no longer here."

"But you are."

"I'm not here," Mio said, and turned in her chair to face Hazuki. "You can see me, but according to the data in your house you have no visitors, so historically speaking, I am not here. It's magic."

"Magic?"

"People in the past were carefree, so they thought up stupid things like time travel and teleportation, but, like, they really believed in it. But people from even earlier eras thought realistically, so they called those stupid things—like time travel and teleportation—magic."

"Magic is more realistic?"

"Of course. Magic is not real. A real attempt at magic would be unrealistic. If it were magic, it would be easy. The time for easy living, for thinking you can do anything you wanted, is over. We're finally back to the old times we were living in originally."

"I don't know what you're saying."

"The time for the real has been left running. Order—the unidirectional flow of time—must be preserved."

"What do you mean, preserved?"

"Meaning you can't go against the stream or do something over again. If I explained it quantitatively you wouldn't understand. According to the laws of physics, moving around in a closed linear timeline is impossible." Mio rolled her eyes once and looked at Hazuki. "People from the past had all kinds of convenient theories, like *superstrings* or *wormholes*, but it was all a bunch of false logic that existed only on paper. It was useless. Those of us in the space-time continuum cannot alter the continuum itself. But a continuum will do anything without these silly theories. If it's going to be limited to being on paper anyway, it doesn't need these exhaustive theories behind it. You can just say or write that you have flown through space or traveled through time. That's how people used to do it a long time ago. In other words, magic. The slightly less old humanity tried to actualize that magic and built planes and let electricity fly, but when all's said and done it was just awkward. Fundamentally speaking, you can't interfere with the system. There's no such thing as all-knowing magic. That's why they thought of this."

"Thought of what?"

"Today's world. To make everything numerical, digital."

"Numerical?"

"This is numerical," Mio pointed at the monitor.

"This is all signs. The images, the words, they're all composed of numbers. We look at these compositions to understand the world. In which case, it's a free-for-all of magic. Since it's just numbers, I could be 150 years old, or a man. Erasing just over ten minutes was a piece of cake.

"No one would *not* do it," Mio threw out, then faced the dining table. "Still, magic can't help an empty stomach. Aren't you going to eat that, Makino?"

"You can eat it," Hazuki said.

Why had she said that? Hazuki twisted her neck. Mio hadn't asked to eat it. She'd just asked if Hazuki wasn't eating it. Normally one would have answered that she was going to eat it later or that she wasn't going to eat it at all. If they'd been chatting through their monitors this wouldn't have happened.

In a daze, Mio went to the table.

"I eat Chinese food from downstairs every day, so..." Mio started, and as she spoke she reached out for the ratatouille.

Hazuki was amazed at how much of a conversation could be understood with so much left out of it.

"Downstairs?"

Anyway. Hazuki sat down across from Mio.

She didn't like being agitated by something like this.

"You saw when you came. The foreigners. Half of them are Chinese. I don't know what ingredients or seasonings they use. I don't know what they use or how, but it tastes good."

Mio marveled at the delicacy of it all as she spoke. She ate the raw vegetables, the warm vegetables, and the main course. Hazuki watched her mouth move in a daze.

"Are you vegetarian?"

"No, but there's always a protein in those meals. I don't know what it is, but...they don't have any good produce there. What's this?"

Mio pushed the broccoli in the casserole around and uncovered something else.

"Looks like some kind of clam."

"Clam? You mean like seafood?"

"Well, yeah. Tsuzuki, you've never seen it before?"

"I don't know. I've seen turtles, but I have no interest in nature." Mio pierced the bit of food with her fork and inspected it up close. She wondered aloud how it was cultivated, then popped the whole thing into her mouth.

"It's pretty good. Even though I don't know what it is."

"You're weird."

"You think so? I think that's pretty normal," Mio said and placed her fork back down on the table. It looked like she'd just played with the food.

It wasn't like she'd simply tasted the food, nor was it like she savored the whole meal. Plus she said it was *delicious* like someone much older might have.

"Food is important."

"Well, sure."

"I think our ancestors must have been really weak," Mio said conversationally.

"Weak?"

"Sure. They were the ones being eaten. I'm sure of it. That's why they took such pains to get out of the food chain. We've all collectively stopped killing animals, right? No one in this country eats animal meat anymore."

"You mean it's wrong to kill."

"But we used to kill. We'd kill animals and then eat them."

"You can make food without killing it."

"Of course you can."

"You can even make vegetables," Hazuki said. "People have been making vegetables since a long time ago."

"Make. You mean grow them. Grass is a living thing too. It's different from being made. *Making* things from scratch is only a recent thing."

Oh…

"But since we started replacing everything from grass to beasts, humans have extracted themselves from the food chain. It took us millions of years, but we've done it. We've been able to improvise edible food out of nonliving things. Not so long ago, synthetic food was talked about like it was a bad thing, but it's no different from what we use to make food now. People lacked the proper technology in the past, making the first synthetic foods toxic, but that was stupidity on their part. Still…"

"Still?"

"If you don't eat or aren't eaten, you are not an animal."

"Animal…"

"Beast. Even in the sanctuaries, beasts eat beasts. They survive this way. Humans are the only ones that don't do this."

Is that a bad thing?

"There are animals that have gone extinct because of humans' killing them."

"You're talking about tigers and stuff, right? But humans stopped killing whales, and now they're rampant. They eat every living thing in the ocean."

"Whales don't eat every single thing."

"Don't they eat clams?" Mio said. Despite being a genius, Mio seemed to be lacking much knowledge of animal biology. Hazuki liked animals for some reason. She'd hardly seen any in her life, but she liked looking at old pictures and had even filed some of them.

Like wolves.

One night ago, she'd been researching a file on extinct animals and came across one that from the picture looked like a dog. Like a dog she'd seen as a very small child.

A dog...

Where was that?

She couldn't remember.

"Animals. That's derived from *anima*, which means life, breath. To be animated." Mio wiped her mouth with the thick fabric of the sleeve of her maintenance uniform. "We aren't very animated, are we? I think we're trying to stop moving altogether."

The chair squeaked as Mio got up and went back to the monitor.

"We sit here for hours on end. And yet we continue to live. Anything else would die."

The sound of keys being punched.

"What are you doing?"

"I'm about to copy the next ten minutes of yesterday into today. I have to go now. If I'm found walking around too late in the evening the police will give me trouble. They have more guys on the street now with this killer and everything."

"Tsuzuki, you going somewhere else now?"

"Somewhere else? I'm gonna go return this stone, of course. I'm going to Kono's house."

Ayumi's house...

"This time it'll be a real payback. All right, it's as though I was never here."

Never here. So this was all a lie.

"It was all a dream?"

Mio turned back and laughed.

CHAPTER 006

SHIZUE SMELLED SYNTHETIC resin. She smelled a cheap synthetic leather sheet.

No, wait, that wasn't all. She smelled something medicinal. It was mixed with a volatile astringent.

People who were bothered by potent smells once liked this kind of smell, but at the end of the day, this wasn't pleasant to the human olfactory sense. To be frank it was a noxious odor.

Research on pleasant smells was thriving, and a perfume boom was spreading through the younger generation. Some of Shizue's kids had taken up a hobby of perfuming but unfortunately had never experienced a delicate fragrance. If they knew a fragrant odor it was smelled in passing.

It was no wonder, with odor-deficient people suddenly increasing in number.

Shizue opened a window.

It wasn't as though it smelled better outside. The air wasn't invigorating by any means, but the mere presence of the breeze made her feel better. The atmosphere and landscape ran without end throughout the residential quarter like an ancient scroll of parchment.

"Is it stuffy?" Kunugi asked. "I might be a, uh, *germophile*, but the person usually riding this car is a clean freak of a woman. She's always sterilizing everything. I figured you'd be okay in here."

"She probably has anosmia."

"Oh yeah?" Kunugi sniffed the air a couple times.

"More importantly, are we all right? It's already almost five."

"We're fine. I told them if they waited around it was pointless. We couldn't get our finished work in during business hours. I made the call directly to the prefectural police headquarters through the center's terminal and not my portable one, so they won't suspect anything. I'm ostensibly on my way home. That said, I'm going to stop by headquarters on my way to your office tomorrow. Though that means you can't start working till I get there."

"That's fine."

"More importantly... is that girl who didn't show up to the group one of your kids without a guardian?" Kunugi asked.

"No. However, her parents have been gone for three days."

"Gone?"

"They're traveling."

"Well, isn't that nice?"

"It's not private. It's a public matter."

"*Ohh*," Kunugi let out in neither a sigh nor a word. "They're one of these couples that are both employed by the same people, eh?"

"Yes. It's one of those awful 'partnership' systems. Supervising and protecting children under sixteen is obviously mandated of guardians, but this partnership system exempts those guardians who have applied for paired status. It's a matter of work productivity, apparently. When the child is thirteen they're allowed to be left home alone. Minors between the ages of fourteen and sixteen have the right to be under guardianship, but that right can't be enforced."

"Wherever there is a law there is a loophole."

"Our system is riddled with loopholes," Shizue said. "It ends up being the center's responsibility to protect children during those years. However, there aren't enough people designated to do that there. Counselors end up having to be extra careful. But even when careful, we can't watch over one child the whole time. We can't actually take over their guardianship either. The center forbids us from infringing on their individual freedom. We can only initiate communication with them via monitor. Fortunately, most kids these days aren't without a portable monitor, so we've not had any problems communicating, but—"

"Have you contacted her parents?" Kunugi asked.

"I approached them immediately. They're *en route* right now but are supposed to be back home tonight."

"I know they're working, but do parents not contact their kid themselves?"

"I guess they must not. There's nothing to talk about."

"I don't have a family, so I wouldn't know. Come to think of it, I come from what would be described as a broken home."

"That's a play on words. Family is a concept and not a thing, after all, so it can't be broken."

"I guess not."

"No. It just means the concept has changed meaning in your case, Mr. Kunugi. The concept of home or blood relations were defined differently in your youth, and back then as now, a family was a living arrangement in which you cohabited with blood relatives or else assigned relatives, so it's not that the 'family' was broken. The model family is structured according to each era, obviously, and right now this is just what happens to be your definition of a home. That it differs from the past does not mean it is broken. What do you think?"

I actually think that's stupid, Shizue wanted to add.

They were from different times.

"You just called me by my name for the first time," Kunugi said out of nowhere.

Shizue turned her head, regretting she didn't go with the more appropriate "officer." Kunugi looked ahead and smiled.

"Well, maybe. But when I was young, these bureaucrats would come and talk down to my family, talk down to me, and it made me feel out of place. Stupid phrases like 'self-discovery' and 'broken homes' were probably all coined during that time."

"It's a given that in every age there will be stupid words."

"Well, probably. But I thought I didn't understand them because I was young at the time, and you'd think I'd know now that I'm old, but I don't.

"It's not like I gave up or gave in," Kunugi said as he switched something in the navigator. "It just means that before I felt out of place with the gap between me and the older generation, and now it's a gap between me and your younger generation."

"Humans are protective. It'd be difficult for them to change internally. Younger generations will always be viewed as being dumber, more frivolous, and useless. But of course it's that dumber more frivolous person who creates the next generation."

"You are one well-argued woman," Kunugi said. As Shizue turned her face, the middle-aged man let his line of vision shift over to the passenger seat ever so briefly.

"I'm allowed to say something like that since we're just talking privately, right?"

"Technically, but…"

"Yeah, so, for me…I'm just wondering if parents don't worry, that's all."

"That's something we're responsible for at the center."

"I see."

That was a rote answer, no doubt. It felt empty. This middle-aged man probably detected that Shizue did not speak from her heart, and responded accordingly.

Who would trust the center or the counselors anyway?

"So... she's supposed to live somewhere around here."

"Okay."

Shizue looked at her monitor. Her current location was marked.

The solar car slowed down to a stop. Kunugi ran his personal ID card through the side of the navigator.

"This is a police vehicle and all, so anything I do with it after hours is on my personal record."

"Then should I file an applica—"

"Hurry up and go," Kunugi said upon pulling up his own monitor.

Shizue pushed open her door and stepped into the dark city.

Normally, no one from the center would go directly to a child's home. In extreme situations there might be a shut-in that required counseling, or a special circumstance that required a counselor to examine the home to determine whether the home environment was a safe one. Otherwise, visits were once-annual affairs.

Shizue had only been to Yuko Yabe's home once.

She was not a child with problems.

Still...

Shizue didn't remember any of this.

The assigned living quarters were identical from the outside throughout the country. Remembering it would have been impossible.

Inside the house...

She remembered the inside of Yabe's house being a shambles.

It was full of deformée character toys from the twentieth century.

No, that was...

That was something she remembered from the database.

Most of the personal data on the kids she had was in her head. She'd memorized their habits and proclivities. This information on them, the preconceptions about the kids, formed imaginary memories in Shizue's mind. These detailed pieces of information could take on a life of their own. And on the whole they'd not be far off and would occasionally jibe with reality.

This was the worst kind of profiling, and she hated it.

You couldn't measure or understand a human being that way, Shizue believed.

She'd always believed this when it came to her work. Subjectively profiling people was a kind of personality analysis, no different from the mantic arts.

That was the right thing.

Subjectively speaking such an analysis was necessary in any given situation. Curbing that analysis at the level of reference was the appropriate thing to do.

That went without saying, Shizue thought.

Still, even today there remained those adherents to profiling. Idiots who believed it was the only way to distinguish people. All of it...

They believed it because sometimes they ended up being right.

This was obviously not because the profiling technique was so advanced.

No matter how minute the survey or how exacting the analogy, that analogy was never the reality. And if the analogy kept hitting the bull's-eye, it was not because of advanced technology.

If the assumption were true, it was because people were able to visualize the prototype having parsed him or her self. It was because so many people grew up in this environment. It should be assumed there were simply more people who were able to self-regulate according to the stereotypes they might match.

Shizue sighed and chased out the image of Yuko Yabe's room from her head.

She confirmed the apartment number on her monitor and refreshed her connection just in case. The main monitor announced a vacancy, and the portable monitor was not being recognized. It was possible to deny it a connection, but monitors almost always recognized one another. Maybe Yabe's was broken. Maybe it was broken into.

Shizue turned around and saw Kunugi's back leaning against the driver-side door of the car. The thinly armored vehicle most definitely did not suit this man.

Yabe's home was supposed to be in the third building from the corner.

The vacancy indicator said it was unoccupied.

If anyone were in the room that sign would not be lit. Either the sensors were broken or no one was home.

Shizue swiped her card through the reader and left her visiting information.

Her ID number displayed along with the time: 5:20 PM.

She inputted the reason for her visit and connected the monitor to the card reader. She then downloaded information and discovered that no one had been in there since 8:12 PM two nights before.

No one's been here since then?

It'd been forty-five hours since. Meaning Yuko Yabe had now spent two nights outside of her own home. According to her file there were no other residences Yuko would have been able to stay at. Meaning...

It was possible she was caught up in something.

Shizue looked back at Kunugi.

He stood there staring at nothing, as if thinking he had nothing left to do, having brought Shizue out here.

He couldn't have had ulterior motives. He was probably just sticking around in case something was wrong here.

A model policeman.

She thought of calling to him but stopped. Her unease kept roiling inside her, but she didn't want to acknowledge it.

She looked at the door again.

Yuko couldn't be inside...

"What's going on?" Kunugi's voice sailed over her head. "Not home after all?"

Shizue didn't answer. His voice came closer.

"When were they last here?"

"Two nights ago."

Kunugi was right behind Shizue.

"That's odd."

"Can't you get us in?"

"I could, but...even if I held up my badge and let us in it'd be no use," Kunugi answered. Now he stood by Shizue's side. "The police are only allowed to take out a lock in case of emergencies, and Class D emergencies at that."

"This is an emergency."

"Anything over a Class B must be handled by at least a captain. This is barely a Class A. You just report this to the local precinct and that's it. If it says no one's in there, no one's in there. It wouldn't say that unless absolutely no one was in there. If there is really someone inside, it just means the sensor is broken."

"It might be. It doesn't even recognize my monitor."

"Well, that's the kid's personal monitor, right? The house's main terminal should still be on."

That was true.

"Besides, if we barge in I have to file the report." Kunugi turned his rugged face to Shizue and made a weird expression with his eyebrows. "Well...a suspicion is a suspicion. I suppose I can do a vacancy sensor check."

Kunugi pulled his police ID monitor from a holster. Shizue hurriedly pulled the cable from her own monitor from the card reader.

"The visitor's record is normally locked, you know. We can find out who visited without being let in. Sometimes it's visitors you don't want. That's just a Class A offense. Something even area patrol can handle."

Something beeped.

"Huh?" Kunugi's face clouded over.

"Something wrong?"

"No, well…" He said it seemed there'd been two visitors here during Yabe's absence. Both of them were minors. "Does this girl have a lot of friends?"

Not really. Generally speaking Yuko's friends were friends via monitor. She wasn't known to have any special friends that would come visit her personally.

"I'll take that as a no," Kunugi said. "Not even once in a while? They're kids, after all."

If it were just one friend that would be something, but two visits from friends in such a short period of time? Kunugi kept typing into his monitor, but he started to make a funny face.

"You aren't allowed to tell me the identity of those visitors, are you?"

"Not normally. But…"

Kunugi typed some more, then let out a small "whoa" and lifted his face.

"I've found a precedent."

"What do you mean precedent?"

"I was searching cases in which protected information accumulated by police can be made public. If there is a precedent, a written explanation will suffice…"

Kunugi showed Shizue his monitor display as he made up this excuse. "I'm showing you. They're both kids who go to your center though…"

There were countless children in her jurisdiction. Unless she worked with them, a mere name and ID number would be futile.

But…

"This is…"

She knew these kids.

"Do you know them?" Kunugi asked.

"This second one, Hinako Sakura, is one of my kids. She's in the same communication session as Yuko."

"Are they friends?"

They had no interactions.

At least Shizue didn't know of any.

"Sakura is a child of special tastes and has little interaction with any of the other children."

By special tastes, she meant…an interest in the occult.

Hinako Sakura had a strong inclination for mysticism. A good 10 percent of any child population would demonstrate that kind of interest, but when it came to Sakura, it could only be said that she easily surpassed her peers in fervor. She'd been seriously studying divination techniques of the Middle Ages and had, moreover, begun practicing them.

People like Shizue couldn't think that a good hobby, but it wasn't causing any problems, so it wasn't a target of counseling.

Regardless, whatever the subject, there were those who would continue to further their knowledge in a specialized or academic way; coercive counseling at the juvenile stages was discouraged.

Shizue agreed.

It was no different with kids who were difficult to handle.

How about this one?

Yuji Nakamura.

She didn't know him. The name looked familiar to her, but she'd seen the register of names and the kids before, so it wouldn't be unheard of to remember the names of other counselors' kids.

"He's…" Kunugi cleared the display. "He's apparently a person of interest."

"You mean in the killings?"

"Yeah," Kunugi said and put his monitor back in the holster. "My monitor signals when someone related to the investigation is mentioned. Apparently, this minor, no, child, was with the last victim, Ryu Kawabata, the day he was murdered."

"Apparently?"

"He denies it, but…"

Kunugi stopped talking and took two steps toward the car, then continued to talk, practically to himself.

"He visited last night. So he came to this house right after being interrogated."

"Does that mean Yuko Yabe is implicated in this case?"

"It means she could be. I will need to report this." Kunugi turned around. "This will be extra work for you too. When I send this information, I will have to explain why we got this information from a private residence. In order to explain how this is a Class A situation, I need your statement."

"I don't mind that, but…" Shizue's gaze wandered.

This was unexpected.

"Hmm?"

On the other side of the street sandwiched between the buildings moved a black *thing*.

"What's wrong?" Kunugi asked.

"Over here, just now."

The person Shizue'd been looking at hid in the corner where she shifted her gaze.

Kunugi seemed to swallow the scene in one moment, jutted his chin, then returned the look and bolted down the road. Shizue followed.

That was…

Shizue tripped once on the road. It was like she'd forgotten how to run. Running was a decent enough activity certainly not beyond her abilities, but she had never run on asphalt in her life. Even though it was true that it had health benefits.

At just this side of the median she stopped and looked around her.

It was like this everywhere, but at dusk, the neighborhood was particularly inactive. In an age when over half the people worked from home, and home delivery of food and sundry goods had become mainstream, there was no more need to be wandering around the city. The sun started to sink and the streetlights went on.

It was practically real.

Even with a sense of dimension, merely seeing how sandy the sky looked made it feel less than fresh.

"Hey, come over here," Kunugi said.

When Shizue looked up in the direction from which his voice had come, she saw the rough man holding the delicate arm of a girl in a mourning dress.

"Let go, let go." The girl twisted and tried to pull herself from his grip.

"Stop squirming. I'm just—"

"I have nothing to do with it. Please let me go."

"You don't—I just asked your name."

She was wearing old-fashioned black clothing. Heels that looked like they came from a *real shop*.

"Is this…the girl?"

As soon as Kunugi let go of her arm, Hinako bounced off to the light pole.

Perhaps because of the way her black clothing absorbed the light, or because the light outside had no warmth, Hinako's face took on a pale blue cast. Like it would break if you touched it.

Hinako jerked her face away.

She was refusing him.

"Miss Sakura—"

"I had nothing to do with it."

Shizue reached her hand out to the girl's emaciated shoulders but stopped just short of touching her.

She was known to inflict incredible violence at a mere touch.

"Hinako, didn't you have something you wanted to do at Yuko's house?"

Shizue couldn't mention she knew the girl had come for Yuko Yabe. With her face still turned away, Hinako nodded her head several times. Then she turned her head up slowly and shot Shizue a hard look.

"I didn't think I had to report that to a counselor."

"You're right, but—"

"You do have to report to the police." Kunugi jutted his police badge in front of her face.

"Police…" Hinako twisted her neck and assumed a difficult-to-read expression, then looked at Kunugi.

"I've been saying that this whole time."

"Police…but you're not in uniform."

"The area patrol wears uniforms. They're citizen police. I'm with the prefectural police. I'm a regional officer."

Hinako looked alternately at Shizue and Kunugi several times as if to compare their faces. The jet-black bangs cut dead straight across her forehead fluttered. There was something doll-like about her.

"Ms. Yabe got it after all…"

"*Mizz*?" Kunugi had started in a falsetto but continued in a deeper voice. "What do you mean, 'after all'?"

"Well, *has* something happened to Ms. Yabe?" Hinako paused. "I knew it." Hinako grabbed at Kunugi's sleeve. Kunugi, stunned for a moment, looked at Hinako.

"What makes you think that?"

He tried not to sound too aggressive. Just enough. He wasn't used to having direct conversations.

"Because…"

"What do you know?"

"I don't know anything," she said without any energy, and turned her head so far her neck could've snapped.

She wouldn't break.

Kunugi hadn't thought to depend on Shizue for this.

"You said you had nothing to do with this, but that doesn't seem to be the case now either, does it?" Shizue asked.

"I don't have anything to do with it."

"Then why are you saying things that would get us anxious about what's happened to Yuko Yabe?"

"Because..."

Hinako finally looked toward Shizue.

She had dark circles under her eyes. That was one of the reasons her face looked so sallow, Shizue realized.

Hinako looked up at Shizue with her black-rimmed eyes.

It was a pleading look...

In their counseling sessions Hinako would make this expression before revealing anything. It wasn't that she thought she needed approval to say things of importance, but she needed a firm reason. Instead of nodding, Shizue returned her gaze. It wasn't how a counselor should behave. Sure enough, Hinako, looking defeated, broke the gaze.

"I predicted it."

"Predicted?"

"A less than good outcome."

"Less than good outcome?"

Kunugi made as if to let Hinako loose and turned toward Shizue, implying, *so this is what you meant.* It was hard to explain. Shizue moved a step forward.

"Sakura, why were you looking into Yuko Yabe?"

Shizue couldn't understand the relationship between them.

Even in their communication sessions they sat far from each other.

"You girls..."

"We were called out during last month's medical checkups."

If that were true Shizue hadn't known about it.

Of course as the number of chronic illnesses and handicaps increased among younger people, so did routine exams. The center where Shizue was employed had started requiring these exams three years ago. With a relatively large number of people in their center the ordeal would end up taking over two days, so it wasn't like the counselors would be able to see every one of their charges during that time.

"Does Yabe know you know about these things?"

"She looked into it," Hinako answered in a small voice.

Now that she thought of it, it was in Hinako's public profile that one of her hobbies and subjects of research was the occult. For information exchange.

"Actually she'd asked me to read her fortune. She might have been joking."

She probably was. She couldn't say it to Hinako's face, but there were probably not many children who believed in that kind of thing these days.

She couldn't know Yuko Yabe's intentions, but she couldn't have been serious. Shizue kept looking at Hinako's pale, almost translucent, skin.

"I read her fortune," Hinako said. "And I saw a dark star. But I was scared to tell her. But then she didn't show up to class yesterday. I got worried. When I went on my monitor she wasn't connected. So..."

Kunugi stiffened.

Hinako's lips quivered.

That was when Shizue noticed Hinako was wearing gray lipstick.

CHAPTER | **007**

IT SOMEHOW FELT moist outside.

She must have been imagining it.

Yesterday's rain had dried up. It'd been sunny all day today.

Though Hazuki hadn't once confirmed the weather outside herself.

The wind struck her cheek. Her hair was pregnant with the gust and billowed up. Hazuki held her chest. Her palpitations sped up. She'd just run for the first time in a while.

This road never ended.

It kept going and she couldn't see ahead.

It made her uneasy. The city was a large box. It didn't suit Hazuki's scale. It was like looking at a low-resolution image on a large-screen monitor. It felt hollow and the edges were blurred. How was it that with such low density, reality could draw up the images so clearly?

She could see a black shadow straight down the road.

"What are you doing?" asked the shadow.

"If you're coming along let's go together."

"Together?"

She hadn't planned on going together.

Why had she flown out like that? She wasn't sure herself. Maybe she'd wanted a last word with Mio for jimmying her way into her house and then leaving as abruptly.

No...

That couldn't be.

"You're so *weird*," the shadow said. "If you didn't want to come along then what are you doing?"

"What am I doing?"

"I mean, are you just going to follow me?"

"Yeah."

Just then a street lamp went on.

It illuminated Mio's face.

"It's late."

"Yeah, and dangerous," added Mio.

"If you're not coming you should just go back now. Even if there isn't a murderer out there, you'll be stopped by the police walking around wearing that."

Hazuki wasn't in regular clothes.

Still, Mio had no right to talk.

"What about your clothes?"

Hazuki ran up to Mio. "I'd run away," Mio said. "I'd just up and run. I don't know what 'up and run' means, but I'd do it."

"I would too."

"Impossible. You ran thirty meters and are already out of breath."

"Out of breath?"

"You're panting, right?" Mio said, a little snide. "When you pant, they call that being 'out of breath.' Your shoulders go up and down. You can't run at all, Makino. You're weird."

Was she?

In indoor athletics at least, Hazuki was of above-average physical strength. Even in her medical exam, she ranked an A-minus.

"That's not what I'm talking about," Mio said. "You're funny. Let's go to Kono's place."

"Funny?"

Hazuki didn't know what was so funny.

She didn't understand why Mio insisted she come with her. Should they have been going to Ayumi's house in the first place?

"Can we walk there?"

She had a feeling it was far away for some reason.

"Of course we can. I'm pretty sure she's really close." Mio got up on a stone ledge by the sidewalk and looked up the address on her monitor. "She's in Section A, right?"

"I think so. She's not in *my* neighborhood, that's for sure…Oh, here we go."

Mio went into a side alley. "This is an unusually old neighborhood. It could get dicey up ahead."

Up ahead. There was so much depth to the city. It was gross. Different from the maps.

Or so Hazuki thought.

Mio went into the alley. If Hazuki fell behind she'd lose sight of her. She brought out her monitor and opened the navigator. Confirmed her location. Until Hazuki determined her placement in the world with an axis of coordinates she wouldn't feel grounded.

Should they be uncomfortable walking forward into an unknown?

She'd have a bird's-eye view of the city with a map. She'd know what lay ahead five meters to the east, know who occupied the building behind the wall. But right now she couldn't see anything. In which case…

"Hurry up already. We're not in official residential quarters anymore, so it's easier to get lost."

"There's a nonofficial living quarter in Section A?"

"Idiot. Sixty percent of Section A is nondesignated. Cities were originally built ad hoc. Short of demolishing everything and building anew, no area can be perfectly designed."

I didn't realize it wasn't all built at once. Of course it wasn't. I just hadn't really thought about it, Hazuki said to herself.

This world had been the same since Hazuki was born. At the very least, the world she'd seen and heard hadn't changed. The world of the past she'd learned about was certainly cut from a different cloth, but it was wholly removed from the present. The remnants of that past were certainly still felt in parts of Section C, for example, but for Hazuki at least that was all another world.

The earth kept going.

They couldn't have been walking more than twenty minutes, but the sky was already completely different.

Perhaps because of the time.

She never went outside at this hour. Of course everything looked different when the light changed.

Even so, this view of her block was beyond her wildest imagination.

"The city implies the time."

"It's not something you can just reset," Mio said. She grabbed a pole on the sidewalk as if to hop off it. "Look at this. It's not a cable pole. It's just a plain column. A useless pole. Made of concrete, no less. They don't even have these in the red-light district. Doesn't make a lot of sense to leave just one. It truly is just ornamental. It has no use!" Mio cackled. "It's a Section A under heaven. Of course the cables are laid underground."

"What do you mean 'under heaven'?"

"What do I— Don't be stupid. That's what this is called. This neighborhood. Haven't you ever been here?"

"I've never had to."

It was difficult to walk here.

Hazuki concentrated on the tips of her feet. The road was hard. She didn't want to look up. The sky was in the midst of turning to night, and she didn't want to see the exaggeration in scale. She heard Mio's voice. *The area patrol is making its rounds*...the voice seemed to say.

"They're making rounds. Let's not run into them. Oh, over here."

Mio slipped into a side street as if to hide herself. As she turned on her heel a red signal bled in the distance.

"What are you doing?"

Caught zoning out, Hazuki was pulled into the alley by her sleeve.

It was a hilly road.

It was a public road that had only been half completed.

"This used to be a burial ground."

"Burial ground?"

"Where you bury dead bodies."

"Really?" Hazuki asked. "Probably," answered Mio.

There were very few street lamps. The houses lining the street looked like black clumps.

The shadows stretched toward their distant destination.

"Isn't there a forest up ahead?"

"We're not by a nature preservation area, so it's probably just a natural outgrowth. Our area's ecological standard is met with the green area cocooning the community center, so if we see forest, it's just land that's been left alone. It's really started to become decrepit, hasn't it? People used to love growing trees and stuff, so it wouldn't be so weird to do it again."

"Still."

It looked like a forest.

"Hey, there it is, Makino."

Mio pointed at the very forest.

There stood a new-looking house against the backdrop of the black forest. Mio ran up to the gate. The white cheeks on her small face lit up green, reflecting the monitor's display.

"This is it," Mio said. "Kiyomi and Ayumi Kono. I didn't realize Ayumi lived here with her sister. I heard her sister's out of the country right now."

When did she hear that? Hazuki remembered hearing something about it too.

Hazuki advanced up to where Mio was.

The gate display said no one was in the house.

"They're out."

But Mio made no sign of moving. Kept staring at the building.

"You plan on going in anyway?"

She was going to use her new modified card.

"It's a crime to go into a house when no one's in."

"It's a crime even if someone *is* in. But I don't think I'll need this." Still expressionless, Mio jutted her jaw forward, apparently distracted by something she saw on top of the building. Hazuki also lifted her gaze.

It was a standard three-story building.

But...

"What's that?"

There was definitely some kind of square object on the roof. It had been obscured by the blackness of the forest at first. The dimensions were illuminated from within, meaning there was light inside.

"It's moving."

"Moving?"

Mio fumbled through her clothing and eventually came out with a clunky-looking object Hazuki had never seen before.

"What is that?"

"You can see things more clearly with this," Mio said as she brought the binoculars to her face. "So that's what that is," Mio whispered, and walked past the gate forward to the building.

"What is it?"

"Well..."

"Well what? Besides, you still can't just barge onto property like this. The cops will show up."

"This isn't like your house, Hazuki. There aren't surveillance cameras everywhere. Until I'm inside the building I'm not actually on anyone's property. It's no different from being on a public road. If they can do it, we can do it."

"I don't understand what you mean."

"Listen..." Mio said, exasperated, and went along the side of the house between the fence and the building to get to the back.

"Kono is here."

"It said she wasn't."

"She is. Watch."

The knocking sound of beating metal.

It was hard to walk. Nonstandard width. The ground was made of a material not conducive to walking. Hazuki finally made it through the gap to the back of the house, where Mio struck a pillar with the palm of her hand and looked up.

"Look. It's a spiral staircase. They must have attached it after the place was built."

"Why? Why would they put something like this on the back of their house...?"

It was hard to see in the dark, but this was the sort of metal staircase one hardly ever saw anymore.

"Obviously it's to get to the top," Mio said, and turned around.

"Top?"

"You really *are* stupid. To get to the room on top of the roof."

"That was a room?"

That was...

They added a room to the roof? But by the time Hazuki had realized this Mio was long gone, up the stairs and twirling upward toward the sky.

Hazuki started up the hard metal stairs.

The more energy she put in her legs the higher she got. Repeat. Her view kept rotating. It wasn't her spinning, but the world. Hazuki eventually found herself at an incredible height.

Mio's back. And beyond it...

A white nape she was too familiar with.

And very short hair.

Ayumi was leaning against something and looking at the night sky.

"Illegal entry," Ayumi said without moving.

"Illegal building structure," Mio answered back.

"You're clever. We *are* outside."

"What's it for?"

Ayumi turned at the neck only. From behind Mio, Hazuki could see Ayumi's pale face.

"Makino." Ayumi confirmed Hazuki's presence with the short utterance.

Though she couldn't tell from Ayumi's voice, Hazuki thought they must have surprised her.

Ayumi let her eyes wander and stepped outside.

It was pretty wide.

A third of it was the square room with a small window. Light shone from inside it.

"What...is this?"

"A dove house."

"Doves," Mio repeated, and thrust her head through the door left open. "Where are they?"

"I don't know their schedule."

"Hmph."

Mio withdrew her head and said sarcastically,

"I didn't realize doves slept in beds."

"That's mine." Ayumi stood up. Mio closed the door.

"You here all the time, Kono?"

"Yeah."

"It must get quiet. You turn on the vacant sign and turn off your main monitor. But what do you do about homework? You couldn't possibly do it out here."

"I go downstairs for that. About once a week."

"You go home once a week, eh? That's pretty savage."

"You can't eat up here either."

"Hmph. So you cook too?"

"What do you want?"

"Wait a minute." Mio walked up to Ayumi and stopped at the handrail.

Hazuki and Ayumi were forced to face each other.

A round red orb glimmered behind Ayumi's shoulder.

The moon.

The moon truly hung in space.

Ayumi stood with her back against the moon.

Hazuki lowered her eyes and said just inside her mouth, "Sorry."

She probably didn't hear that. No, she definitely didn't hear that. Ayumi didn't respond.

But...

She hated this. No doubt about it she hated this. Ayumi hated facing people like this, being seen. Talking like this was a total nuisance. Hazuki regretted ever coming here. Palpitations vibrated in her throat.

"What can you see from here?" Mio asked in a loud voice. She grabbed the handrail and leaned over it, looking out in the direction Ayumi had been facing. She listlessly stretched her neck.

"The sky."

"The *sky*?" Mio spun around and leaned her hip against the rail. "I don't see anything."

"That's because there's nothing there."

"Then you're not looking at anything."

"I'm looking at nothing, then."

"Philosophical, aren't we?"

Hmph, Mio let out idiotically and brought out her binoculars, then turned back around.

"That's…the elevated freight road. What they used to call the high-way."

"It's the North-South Line," Ayumi said nonchalantly.

"It's bright," Mio said, and she lowered her binoculars. "It's the lamps on the side of the road. These make everything look a lot brighter."

"You can't see without those things?"

"Human eyes aren't that good. If you can see it, that means *you're* the unusual one, Kono."

Mio shrugged, bored, and approached Ayumi, holding the piercing between her fingertips and bringing it up near Ayumi's cheek.

She wasn't sure what it was reflecting—Hazuki thought maybe the moonlight—but for a moment, the pink stone glittered.

"This."

Ayumi moved only the pupils of her large eyes over to where the object reflected light.

"What about this?" she said.

"This was left at my house."

"And?"

"Isn't it yours?"

Mio leaned in toward Ayumi.

"It isn't?"

Ayumi suddenly dropped her shoulders as if they'd lost all strength and crossed her arms. She compared facial expressions on Hazuki and Mio.

"You came all the way here for that?"

"Was that wrong?"

"It's weird."

"It's fun," Mio said as she walked around Ayumi.

"Fun?"

"Yeah. Isn't it, Makino?"

Fun…

What does fun feel like? Hazuki wondered.

But before she could answer her question, Ayumi plucked the piercing from Mio.

"This thing." Ayumi stared into it.

"I wouldn't be caught dead wearing that," Mio said.

"Then we'll just have to put it on you after you've died," Ayumi said.

Mio narrowed her eyes.

"I'll let you because you're special. But if it's not yours or Makino's, whose is it?"

"This is Yabe's."

"Yabe?"

Yuko Yabe...soaked by the rain, pale skin. Pink pupils.

It matches her pink contacts, Hazuki thought.

"You mean *that* Yabe?"

"You know any other Yuko Yabes?"

"No...but why would Yabe's piercing be in *my* house? I don't even know what she looks like. I've never connected with her online and her house is nowhere near mine."

Her house was far from hers?

Nowhere near?

If Mio said so...

But that day...Yuko Yabe had been in Section C, where Mio lived. Moreover, that girl with the drenched pink hair was the one who told Ayumi and Hazuki exactly which building Mio lived in. What was that all about? Was that some kind of mistake?

Could have been a mistake, Hazuki thought.

Just because they'd seen and heard her didn't make it a reality.

"It's my fault," Ayumi said unexpectedly.

"Your fault?"

"I had a physical exchange with Yuko Yabe a couple nights ago."

"*Real contact?* You met?"

"Liar," Hazuki blurted out.

"Liar?" Ayumi made a puzzled look.

Ayumi didn't meet with people.

Ayumi hated being looked at directly.

Ayumi would never directly exchange words with someone.

Ayumi had never even made eye contact with Hazuki.

But.

Yesterday.

Yuko Yabe and Ayumi...

They did something together. Some kind of shared information Hazuki wasn't in on. That was what this was.

If that were the case.

Maybe...

Hazuki looked back, and Ayumi, still facing the other direction, said, "We had an encounter."

"An encounter."

"Yeah. I'm sure her piercing must have fallen in my bag or something. And I took that bag to our communication session, then on the way home I found myself breaking into your house. It must have fallen then. That's the most logical explanation. I was bumping into a lot of that crazy wiring in your room."

Ayumi adjusted her seat away—a wooden chair—and sat back down on the edge of it.

Mio rounded in front of her again and leaned in.

"When you say you met, you mean you deliberately interacted with her?"

"Yeah."

"Why would her piercing get stuck on your bag from merely meeting? You saying her ear brushed against your bag when you met? Is she like some kind of pet?"

"Yes, already. God you're annoying." Ayumi moved away again. "Yabe was clinging to me."

"Clinging?"

"Yeah, she clung on to me, and like you said, she rubbed her head against my bag. That's probably when the piercing fell off."

Ayumi looked up slightly.

"Actually, her piercing might have been taken off by then already."

"Huh?"

Ayumi looked down at herself and turned her face to the right.

"Either way, it's because she'd used my body as her medium that it got to your room."

"Where?"

"Where did you two meet?" Mio asked. Ayumi simply pointed forward. She was pointing at nothing in the dark.

It was the direction in which Mio had been staring before.

"Huh? At night? What was going on?"

"None of your business. Just walked."

"I don't mean you. I don't care what weird shit you were up to. I mean Yabe."

"I don't know," Ayumi said indifferently. "She was being chased by someone. She was running away."

"She was being chased?"

Mio's eyes widened. She looked over to Hazuki.

"This isn't some kind of movie. People don't get chased," Mio said.

Hazuki couldn't answer.

She didn't understand what was going on.

"Yabe was attacked?" Mio asked. "By whom?"

"How the hell should I know?"

"And...you tried to save her?"

"No, I didn't. I just ran into her. The girl in the Chinese clothes saved her."

"The girl in the Chinese clothes...You don't mean the girl with the cats!"

Mio stood up.

Ayumi didn't.

Hazuki...looked up at the heavenly orb above her.

CHAPTER 008

AS CHIEF LIEUTENANT Ishida neurotically wiped his screen, a horizontal crease formed on his cheek.

Ishida was a man of delicate health.

Ishida's blatant repugnance gave a worse impression than the worst indifference to filth she'd encountered. Shizue thought that with a little perspective, anyone would see it that way. The Ishida she witnessed at the conference left her with a good impression, but you could contrast him with the rest to no end. You'd be comparing him to idiots, no less.

It turned out...

He too was no good.

Shizue shot a venomous look at Ishida and then scattered her poison-filled glare all around the sterile room—a room almost identical to the center.

Everywhere, everything was constructed homogeneously in the deceptive guise of cleanliness, right angles in the guise of order, when really it was a crooked building. A man who'd put himself in this lie and coated the lie with a faux obsession with cleanliness was a truly despicable man.

Shizue dwelled on the mighty rage she felt and then swallowed it down.

She felt like the lining in her head was being rubbed raw.

In this situation she felt closer to being a masochist than just an aggrieved observer.

All her vilification came right back at her.

Give me a break.

"Why do we need a survey conference?" Kunugi said from the side.

"We don't need one for now," Ishida answered.

"Should I run this information to the investigators then?"

"That's not for you to worry about. The work has all been meted out. Whether the information is to be publicized or not is entirely the determination of the bureau chief, and that's me. You're just one investigator."

"In that case, should I forward just the information on the missing child?"

"That is also not in your jurisdiction," Ishida said. "I can only tell you the responsibility belongs to someone else. Right now in another room this missing child's guardians are being brought up to speed, and if they file a search request on their charge, then we will send the information to the person who will take necessary measures. You, you should consider your one concern to execute the one job we gave you."

Yuko Yabe's guardians had returned home last night. It followed that the responsibility to guard her went back from the center to the guardians. In other words the guardians' disposition became the highest priority.

In that case, a counselor's opinions had no more use than secondary corroboration. In Shizue's estimation, neither the police nor the local authorities would move on this.

In the end...

"Was there any point to this?" Shizue asked rhetorically, looking at the display behind Ishida's back. She said it in a way that made it explicit she was being sarcastic. But whether this bureaucrat actually sensed the sarcasm was hardly discernible.

Just in case, he coldly replied that it wasn't pointless and touched his display with a fingertip.

The data on the screen disappeared and was replaced by a huge police logo.

"As a consequence of your accident, we got a great deal of very interesting information for the investigative unit, so I want to thank you for that, but..."

Ishida fiddled with the display again.

"But I stress that it was a consequence."

Shizue commenced a pre-emptive strike.

"Are you suggesting that because I didn't turn up very interesting facts regarding a person of great interest in the murder investigation that my assessment as a counselor was flawed? That my actions were a deviation from the work responsibility of a community center counselor?"

"That is not what I am suggesting," Ishida said without so much as a change in expression. "In fact your assessment and actions were entirely appropriate given the circumstance. As the head counselor for a student with an unexcused absence from the communication session and whose personal monitor was no longer transmitting a signal, of course it is your responsibility to survey the residence at once. There was nothing inappropriate about that. No—"

Ishida cut himself short and pointlessly tapped at the tablet screen and said, "If anything your response came too late."

"Late? That's not possible. I responded as soon as I could."

Ishida shook his head.

"You were late. You know that better than anyone. You know full well you took a police escort in order to pretend that you were hurrying to the scene."

Ishida glared at Kunugi.

Kunugi pretended not to notice.

"If a child's guardian is exempt from supervision, the responsibility for care of the child in question becomes the community center's. If the child misses labs without a note, you are supposed to confirm the circumstances at the moment you learn of this absence," Ishida said.

"You're right. However, this is customarily..."

Shizue stopped herself short in the midst of her apology. Whether it was customary or not, even if the statute Ishida alluded to was unrealistic, the fact of the matter was that the center's response was exempt from the statutes.

"I'm sure you're busy with all kinds of business matters, but you must have known as soon as your mail didn't send that her terminal was offline. You should have, at the very least, known at that point something was wrong. You were almost an entire day late responding to the situation, so if anyone's going to notice it's you."

He was right.

She should have noticed.

But the reason she didn't notice sooner was that damned conference.

The pointless conference and their insincere work was what threw off the timing of her correct actions and astute judgment.

"That's all I mean when I say this was a consequence," Ishida continued. "If you had acted sooner, the connection between Yuji Nakamura and this uh...what was her name...Yuko Yabe would have been known sooner. No?"

Sure, if they hadn't had that conference, Shizue would have known about Yuko Yabe's aberrance much sooner.

If they hadn't had the conference she could have left right after work for the Yabe residence that night, before 6 PM.

This Nakamura child had supposedly headed to the Yabe home after being released from interrogation after 8 PM. Shizue couldn't know, but she thought she might have been there before him.

Moreover...

"Also, as far as this case is concerned, the fact that a police officer just happened to be there is interesting. If you had gone on your own you wouldn't have known about the visitor log. That just seems to be too nice of a coincidence."

Ishida glared at Kunugi again. Kunugi shot back a look of disagreement.

"Coincidence? I moved on my own accord."

"Kunugi. Neither I as your superior nor the police organization has the authority to restrict your actions on your private time."

Ishida crooked his face and compared looks on Kunugi and Shizue.

Kunugi let out a short breath.

"I've turned in a report." He looked quickly at Shizue with narrowed eyes.

Whatever was being suggested, *any* activity with this man outside of their civic duties did not appeal to her. If Ishida thought for a second that Kunugi had any imprudent thoughts or that Shizue went along with them, that would have been a serious misinterpretation; an outrageous one.

She got goose bumps. Kunugi looked like he'd had enough.

"In any case, I had no ulterior motives. I didn't mean to do anything outside of the police code either, but it's still your judgment as police chief."

Ishida was unable to respond.

"More importantly, Ishida. What about this kid Nakamura?"

"After our interrogation, he was released from our custody but didn't return home. He's still missing."

"That's—"

"Yes, we were negligent," Ishida said as if to pre-empt Shizue.

"You are acknowledging as much?"

"Of course. It's clear as day we bungled. Of course I can only say this now. We let a potential suspect up and run away. Still—"

"Let him run away? That's not what I'd call it. It's more like making a criminal," Shizue interrupted. "He's not a criminal, he's a subject of interest."

"That's precisely why we were unable to keep him. Unfortunately, we weren't able to restrain him. He has categorically denied having anything to do with this case. He says he wasn't with the victim. But the probability he was giving false testimony is remarkably high."

"Do you think you should be saying this? In front of a civilian like me?"

"I am not saying he is a suspect. All I *can* say is that his testimony, our investigators' information, and the testimony of numerous eyewitnesses are inconsistent."

"So you're treating him as a suspect."

"That is obviously a distinct possibility."

"That's just sophistry. If that's a distinct possibility, it's also distinctly not a possibility. The word 'possible' is entirely meaningless except to contextualize the impossible."

"Ms. Fuwa!" Kunugi put out his hand as if to calm her. "All this information has been made public. I'm sure you don't need me to tell you, but I'd recommend you refrain from making these provocative accusations." Kunugi suddenly slid into formal speech after having yelled at her.

Ishida snickered. "Well, I understand your uncertainty. However, now that we've declared this much to a civilian like you, it remains to be seen whether this is reliable information."

"I don't think the information is unreliable."

"Really. It's just…all it indicates is that the victim and our witness were doing something together during the alleged time of the crime. We unfortunately do not know what the witness had to do with the event itself. In other words, as regards the specific murder investigation, we police don't have any hard evidence that refutes the witness's testimony."

"We can't arrest him," Ishida said.

"Of course not," Shizue responded. "Arresting him now would be unacceptable. But the fact remains he's a significant witness, and the fact that you lost track of him after interrogation is a bit careless, no?"

"Hey," Kunugi said.

"You're right. That's why I'm acknowledging this frankly as a mistake on the part of the police," Ishida said. "I was easy on him because he was a minor."

Easy?

Ishida's diction touched a nerve in Shizue. She took a deep breath.

It was odorless.

"That's inexcusable."

What was?

The police chief blinked but otherwise seemed unphased.

"There's a problem with your statement, chief. In that context, it's clear why the police held the child as a potential suspect."

"Is that so?"

"Even if you didn't mean to, it's an illegal admission. Even if it were a misunderstanding. I'm an employee of the youth protection and development center. I speak from my position as such, but in this situation, it was your responsibility as a public employee to guard him."

"Guard...him?"

"Yes. This child...If, as the police have determined, this Yuji Naka-mura gave false information, it could be because he personally witnessed the criminal act. The fact that he was with the victim of this violent crime at the time of the incident does not make him the criminal."

"Right, that makes him an eyewitness. So?"

"That's all the more reason to protect him."

Shizue looked for some exculpation in Ishida's expression.

"Witnessing the violent murder of an acquaintance is a highly pecu-liar experience, one that has the potential to cause what you police like to call Post-Traumatic Stress Disorder. He should have been immediately seen to."

"I see. However, we received no such suggestion from his primary counselor. We weren't hiding anything. In fact we sent over all this infor-mation to your department."

"Who's his caseworker?"

"Someone named Shima."

"Shima..."

She was a lazy woman.

She wouldn't have done a very detailed inquiry.

"I understand. If the counselor didn't see the need for supervision then that is that. However, Police Chief, how could you have simply released him?"

"What do you mean?"

"You could look at it this way. This child, Yuji Nakamura, could be considered simultaneously a potential suspect and also the second victim in this case, right?"

"What?" Ishida narrowed his eyes and lowered his eyelids. It wasn't a look of anger but rather confusion. "Victim? Are you saying the mur-derer had his sights on him next?"

"It's absolutely possible. I'm not a criminologist, nor have I done any investigating, so this is all pure conjecture, but..." Shizue looked at the ceiling. Whenever she spoke a small red light next to the mic would turn on. She was being recorded.

The police chief stroked his hair as if to disguise his confusion. "Please go on."

"For example, couldn't we assume Nakamura was as much a target as the first victim? Even if the account of his actions rings false, it might not be to hide criminal behavior. Doesn't that happen?"

"Yes, but—"

"If all the other murder victims were girls from another neighborhood, all this information changes, but this time the victim, Ryu Kawabata, was the same age and sex as Yuji Nakamura. Furthermore they are known to have had *real contact*. They clearly had commonalities."

"I can see that," Kunugi said.

"In which case, the killer's motive against Ryu Kawabata becomes problematic," Kunugi said.

"It doesn't matter the motive," Shizue countered. "Investigating motives is like improving your odds gambling. It's still a gamble. It serves no purpose. Profiling is the same. It's nothing more than astrology."

"There are scientific foundations for profiling."

"No there aren't," Shizue retorted coolly.

Kunugi strained at the neck.

"I don't mean to state the obvious, but going forward I'd like for you to choose methods that exclude such suspicious fallacies."

"Fallacies…"

"Superstition. In this case too we're only looking at the facts. The victim and the person we know to have been with him shared commonalities. The murderer for some reason killed only one of the two similar boys. This is a fact. Right?"

Ishida nodded.

"It's meaningless to think about psychological aberrations when determining what led the murderer to make this choice. The interpretation may be accurate, but it also takes away absolute certainty. You hinge on one of those uncertain elements and leave yourself with very few alternatives. First, that Nakamura was in fact not there."

"The likelihood of that is very low."

"Just low. Not impossible. One more thing. Whether he was there or not, he was not killed. The police understand that much, right?"

"Making Yuji Nakamura the obvious killer."

"That's not the police's position, Kunugi," Ishida said.

"It's not my position either. I'll repeat myself, but this is just one of the possibilities," Shizue said.

"Right. Just one of the many possibilities. That Yuji Nakamura was not killed because he is the culprit. It's an alternative theory based purely on the evidence. However, these aren't the only answers. He might have been hiding somewhere; he could have been attacked but rescued somehow. Or…the killer might have targeted just Kawabata and not even noticed Nakamura. Technically speaking, a possibility is any potential, non-contradictory, occurrence. It's an alternative. In that sense there are endless possibilities. His being a suspect is just one. But…"

Shizue looked up at the mic in the ceiling again.

"If Nakamura is the criminal, the circumstances under which you've marked him offer very little certainty, and if another crime occurs, that certitude goes up."

"That's true."

"But. Conversely, if Nakamura is considered a victim, the present culprit remains at large, and the crime becomes more serious. That's why it's so important the police protect him. The police department's duty is not just to mine data and catch criminals, now is it?"

Ishida's expression tightened.

Kunugi sought meaning in that face. "Chief, this might not be for me to say, but I think she's right. Because—"

"No, I agree," Ishida interrupted Kunugi. "Since I received your notice last night, I've assigned many more investigators to the search for Yuji Nakamura. But, Ms. Fuwa…" Ishida faced Shizue, his posture now open and candid. "Your opinions have been very fruitful. This is embarrassing for me, but we hadn't considered that because the victim, Kawabata, and Nakamura had so much in common that the latter could have been another victim. Whether witness or culprit, Nakamura is likely one or the other. Frankly, we still can't determine what relationship these two had."

"Shima had nothing?"

"Counselor Shima had nothing positive to add."

"Was she uncooperative?"

That's just how she is.

"She cooperated, but all she knew was that the two had shared interests in twentieth century cel animation, and that the two of them had shared files on the subject. We didn't need to hear that from a counselor of course, as it was all in their terminals."

"What other information do you have?"

"I can't divulge that information without guardian consent."

"I see."

That was probably good.

Still…

"Shima had nothing to add, then?"

Of course she didn't.

Ishida nodded.

"That's why we needed to go ahead and mine the data on these children. Do you understand now?"

"These are two different…"

Issues. No. Were they the same problem? Shizue was confused.

"The data on Nakamura on the disc you brought us—"

"There isn't any."

They'd only transferred a third of the database.

"Nakamura's file and Yuko Yabe's file are probably not on this disc. We went in alphabetical order. If yesterday's pace is any guide, we won't be finished with this for another couple of days. Not to mention, when we have to stop for *discussions* such as this, it delays us—"

"Two days…"

Ishida looked at the screen. "If we could hurry this up…Wouldn't it be prudent to have the director of the center brought in on this and add staff to get things moving? This work can be done in parallel processing, so a supplemental staff would be productive. And for what it's worth, the police can send staff with better background in systems management and operations than our Kunugi here."

Kunugi furrowed his brow without a word.

"What an astute suggestion…"

Ishida looked up slightly and said in a louder voice, "Subject. As regards Ms. Shizue Fuwa's discoveries. Requesting increase in staff representatives for swift reprisal of systemwide adolescent data-mining activities. Attention, community center director. Sent from chief investigator on Case 388765. Also requesting R investigating officer, name Ishida, be moved to duties on V investigation. Requesting expert staff on systems management and operations. Location, Area Community Center. Request number, Case file 388765. Over."

The words appeared on the monitor in front of Ishida. He took notice and tapped his ten-key ID, then hit ENTER with his index finger.

"It's done. I should hear back immediately."

Some things could get done so quickly here.

Yuko Yabe's investigation hadn't been taken up yet, probably.

Her parents were apparently being briefed in another room.

At the other end of the terminals, two systems engineers heard of their daughter's absence and panicked. Back when Shizue had accessed the residence, the possibility of Yabe's absence being the result of a crime seemed low, but for law-abiding public servants the disappearance of a daughter was already a big event.

The circumstances had changed drastically since they'd returned. They didn't know what the police were going to call it, but it had to be called something, and it was impossible to think it wasn't connected to the larger crime. Though not definitive, this was part of a murder case. When a connection was made from a child's disappearance to a murder investigation, of course the parents would lose their minds.

Still…

What were they talking about in there? It didn't seem they were responsive to questions about Yuko.

Yuko Yabe's guardians didn't know a lot about her. It wasn't a matter of deprivation or failing to meet their responsibilities as guardians. They had quite simply not known this girl at all.

The rights of a child…

One could assert that child rights were about protecting their privacy. In other words, acknowledging a child's rights was about a guardian recognizing that every child had boundaries you could not cross. That was why so many parents knew nothing about their children. *That's probably the correct way, the normal way*, Shizue thought. It was nothing new. Shizue's own parents knew nothing about her. The difference was that parents of the past thought they ought to know everything about their children and pretended to know as much. Everyone used to believe that was the core of parental responsibility.

That meaningless delusion was dead today.

Shizue was about to inquire how the Yabe investigation was going but stopped herself short because there was nothing she could do about it.

Besides…

Counselors had ever so slightly more information on children than their parents, but it didn't mean they knew the children any better.

Shizue didn't know anything about Yuko Yabe. She saved information on her and organized it for work only.

One could only know oneself.

No…

Shizue looked at the police department monitor.

This knows everything about everyone.

Humanity had gone from recording history to being recorded by history. No one would remember private citizens, but all of history would be reduced to numbers and signs stored in a place with no address that no one would know about.

Life would be entirely virtual.

Ishida looked at his own monitor.

"I've got a response, finally. From the director. Five staff representatives will join you tomorrow at eleven to resume work. I'll be sending two members well versed in systems operation from my end as well. Your center has sent orders to your monitor, Ms. Fuwa."

"Excuse me..."

She pulled out her portable monitor and switched it on. As soon as she opened it, her display was filled with emergency instructions. There were commissions purporting to relieve Shizue of her duties as head of youth data copying. When she pressed ACCEPT she then received a notice from the prefectural police that it had been decided that a team of highly skilled administrators would be formed. They would wait for a status report to be submitted immediately.

This must be from memory-hair man.

Shizue wordlessly sent the work log she'd prepared the night before.

That should be enough.

"Looks like you won't have to do this crap anymore," Ishida said in a manner not befitting him.

Shizue could obviously not know his intentions in saying such a thing, but she thought he was being sarcastic. "Thanks to you. Now I can go back to doing my regular work."

"I hear counseling is quite a busy job. You can leave now."

Now she got it. The formal interview was over. Their conversation was no longer being recorded. That was why his tone had changed.

Ishida stood up. Then turning around as if he'd forgotten something, he stopped his gaze on Kunugi.

"Kunugi."

"Yes," Kunugi responded childishly.

"I need to get you another job. I can't just send you back to headquarters. You've already been given one warning. You agreed to an easy job and this is what happens? It's as if none of those lessons had any calculable results."

"I'm no good at studying," Kunugi replied.

"That's not good."

"Does this mean disciplinary action? Even with our staff shortage?"

"Staff means people who serve a purpose, Kunugi. If you were able to produce a report on Yuji Nakamura or Yuko Yabe I wouldn't have to cut you from this, but until I get further instructions, maybe you should just request some personal time off."

Kunugi nodded once and said he'd *do as you suggest, sir*.

The police logo on his monitor disappeared.

CHAPTER 009

IT WAS HER first time seeing a real live cat.

Hazuki didn't think it was as cute as it was supposed to be, though it was spry and she couldn't see it very well.

It was rare to see feral cats, even in the city. Almost every household used to own a cat or a dog in the past, but for some reason there weren't any more now. You needed a permit to have a pet animal now. Each household required a confirmation of a specific living environment for the particular species in question, and until the permit was issued, owning a pet animal was not allowed.

Therefore the only people who would keep a domesticated animal for fun were those with means.

Still…

Hazuki felt it would be vaguely disgusting to have some animal just moving about at will in your house.

Hazuki had an interest in living things. There was a nature preservation area where animals still lived that she'd always wanted to see. They looked so cute on her monitor—be it in still or moving pictures. But maybe they weren't like that in real life.

"There are dogs too," Mio said.

"Dogs?"

"Yes. A species called 'stray dog.'"

"That's not a species, I don't think."

"I'm not sure either. I'm weak in the nature department. I have no interest in animals. All I know about are turtles and alligators, maybe. And dinosaurs."

Hazuki was a little shocked.

This genius truly knew nothing about anything in which she had no interest.

The young genius, completely clueless about the animal kingdom, sat on some scrap wood and shook her head from side to side.

"I wonder if this is another kind of preservation area too."

"Preservation area?"

"Yeah. When you leave the tacky old stuff as is and preserve it," Mio said, adding, "The old red-light district is unsanitary. It doesn't clear environmental sanitation standards at all. I think what they want to do is make it more government housing, but the residents won't consent. Though I hear the residents actually want to demolish the area anyway. It's sort of a residential thing. There are all these people without money and a lot of unsavory types. A lot of foreigners, a lot of people without ID cards. So of course there are going to be some cats and dogs."

Another cat darted to the side of a warped building along the windowsill.

Mio widened her eyes at the cat and said, "*You know?* Look, they have everything out here. All kinds of animals I don't know anything about."

"What about wolves?"

Why had she said that?

Hazuki doubted herself just as the word came out of her mouth.

"Wolves?" Mio said in a high-pitched voice and made a bewildered face.

The wind blew.

They were in an empty area of Section C.

"Wolves are extinct," Ayumi said, her voice vibrant.

She was wearing a suit fitted tightly to her body and an industrial-strength vest, a khaki waist bag, large racing shoes. Leaning on a steel frame.

Ayumi was standing.

"Tsuzuki, what kind of person calls out strangers to a place like this?"

"What kind of person actually shows up?" Mio jumped up, excited, and sprang from the scaffold.

"We also got one idiot just watching."

Mio nodded at Hazuki.

Ayumi looked down at Hazuki's feet.

Ayumi said nothing but stared down Mio.

"Yesterday is yesterday. You barged into someone's house. Now, less than a day later you call people out in the morning. You're an anachronism. Not even adults do stupid shit like this."

"C'mon, it's not that bad," Mio said, looking up at a stick building in the haze. "Aren't you bored?"

"I'm not like you, Tsuzuki."

"Then why'd you come?"

Mio turned around and stood directly in front of Ayumi, arresting her line of sight.

"You came because you wanted to, no? Am I wrong?"

"I came because I was called."

"Hmph."

Mio crossed her arms.

"Why're you playing it off? If you didn't like being called out, you could have just ignored me. I'm just a minor. I have no authority over anyone. Even if I were a cop, I have no power other than to ask you to come voluntarily. Whether you came or not was up to you entirely. If I were you and I was put off by something someone said, I'd definitely ignore it.

"Definitely," she repeated.

"And?"

"And?! You come and then blame other people for making you come? That's not fair. Look, even Makino's enjoying herself. Aren't you, Makino?"

Hazuki had gotten excited when she was called. Her blood coursed faster. Her vision blurred; it felt like she was going blind all of a sudden. Her field of vision contracted.

Two days ago Hazuki had been the ringleader.

You could say it was her actions that had led to this situation.

Mio finding a strange object in her room and determining that it was evidence left by intruders, then thinking to bring it directly to the culprits, had all been triggered by Hazuki's aberrant actions.

Ayumi turned her eyes away from everything and said, "Tsuzuki. You're like an extinct species yourself."

Mio was left speechless for a moment, then said under her breath, *Take it easy.*

"So what did you want with me?"

"Why didn't you ask in the first place?" Mio said, scrunching up her face. "I went to Yabe's after that."

"You went out there? You're *really* bored. You're like the demon of surprise house visits."

"I had no choice. There weren't cops, and I didn't want to go to three houses in one day either. Only perverts do that. But she doesn't have a terminal."

"She went offline?"

"Not offline. Like, she didn't have a monitor. It probably broke. Short of smashing the machine itself, a terminal is supposed to be able to connect, even when the power is out. But her terminal wouldn't connect at all. That's why I went over. I had no choice. But she wasn't there. It was vacant."

"You went at that hour?"

"She hasn't been back. Since three nights ago."

"Since the night of the attack?"

"Yeah. Isn't that suspect? I got to her place after nine. The only people who go out at that hour are criminals and weirdos."

"People like you and me," Ayumi joked. Mio ignored her.

"Well, if I'm to believe your story, Yabe was violated by someone, and there's a murderer out loose in the city. I figured she might have run off to somewhere safe. But then..."

The two girls both turned their heads toward Hazuki.

"W-what?"

"What do you mean, what? You said yourself you saw Yabe near my house."

"I did, but..." Hazuki gave Ayumi a petrified look. "She was really there," Ayumi said.

"She's the one who told us where you live."

"That's the first weird thing. I don't think she's ever been to the old red-light district."

"I don't know."

"I do. I was raised here. It's a horrible neighborhood."

Mio looked around at her surroundings. Hazuki also broadened her scope. The alien nature of the scene flew right at her eyes.

"Weird, right?" Mio said. Hazuki didn't know if it was weird. Perhaps because Hazuki was quiet, Ayumi said, "This isn't exactly a suitable place for a minor if they think they're in physical danger, is it?" She sounded unperturbed.

"Right, of course," Mio said, incredulous.

"Section C, of all places. Wouldn't you normally go to the center? What kind of kid who's been violently attacked one night runs and hides in an ancient red-light district full of murderers the next? Also, if the center knew her monitor was broken, they would do something about it. They'd come in thirty seconds to give her a replacement."

"Maybe. So?"

"The adults don't know anything."

Don't they?

It wasn't just the adults. Kids wouldn't know anything about other people either. No one wanted to know and no one wanted to be known.

So no one knew anything about anyone else. They weren't bothered by not knowing. They weren't bothered by not being known. Moreover…

They actually hated being known.

"I wanted to know what happened," Mio said. "So I tried to get some data from her monitor."

"That's a crime."

"Right. Private information piracy. Illegal residential entry, sensitive protective data falsification—all misdemeanors really. I'm a misdemeanor girl. But you've got an illegal building and unpermitted animals. Doves."

Doves. Last night, they hadn't come back.

Hazuki had wanted to see those birds dance back to Ayumi's rooftop.

"Those were wild doves that just took up residence on my roof."

"That's still a violation, no doubt. Well, I don't care either way. Anyway, when I checked her data it was just as I'd expected. Fuwa had been there at 5:20 PM. If a counselor came checking on a vacant house, it means the center itself didn't apprehend Yuko Yabe. Fuwa probably came over in a hurry after realizing something was wrong two days after the fact, but that means the center has no idea whether Yabe was attacked or not."

"What about her guardians?"

"They were gone too. They'd been gone for three days when I checked. What's more, there were two kids who came to visit—Yuji Nakamura and Hinako Sakura."

"Sakura? You mean that funeral girl?"

"Funeral? Ha ha ha. Come to think of it she's always wearing that funeral outfit under her center uniform." Mio laughed, satisfied.

Hazuki wasn't sure whom they were talking about. Should she tell them as much? It sounded like they were talking about someone who was in their group.

"Weird, right?" Mio stopped giggling and made a serious face. She looked at Hazuki and repeated, "Weird, right?"

"Do people usually see that many visitors?"

"Probably."

Ayumi nodded at Mio.

"Stop joking," Mio answered.

"Look, would someone of a different gender and a different group come visit? This isn't twentieth century nymphomania. You think Yabe is having relations with boys now?"

"Who's this Nakamura?"

"He was in the same class as that kid who was killed, Ryu Kawabata. Nothing alarming in his public data profile. Average sixteen-year-old. He collects old paper magazines, apparently. And also…"

Mio took off the night-vision goggles that were hanging around her neck.

"Two nights ago, you said you ran into Yabe after she'd been attacked, right?"

"Right."

"What if the person who attacked her was this Nakamura kid?"

Mio said horrible things so easily.

"Huh?"

Ayumi looked bothered. Then immediately, "I don't know."

"You saw it, right?"

"I saw it but I didn't see who," Ayumi responded. "I don't know who this Nakamura is."

"But if you saw him you'd recognize him, right?" Mio asked.

"No, I wouldn't," Ayumi responded curtly. "It was already a free-for-all by the time I saw it."

"Free-for-all…Oh, you mean between the attacker and the girl in the Chinese clothes who was defending Yabe."

"Yeah. She's the one that probably saved Yabe. That's how she was able to run away, and into me. But like I said yesterday, I didn't want to get mixed up with them, so I took Yabe to the other side of the street and sat her down in the shadows, then kept walking past the brouhaha."

"Unbelievable," Mio said, disgusted. "You couldn't panic a little? Anyway, the point is that you didn't see a whole lot. But you remember the girl in the Chinese clothes."

"Only because the fabric was weird. It looked old."

"Old fabric—is that something you'd know at just a glance from so far away?"

"Like, not a man-made synthetic fiber like our clothes. Old."

"One of those anti-man-made fibers people, eh?"

"Older. It looked like it was made of animal skin. It looked like something my sister bought abroad."

"I see. Then I was right."

Mio chuckled to herself, crossed her arms, and then headed toward the building where the cat had gone.

"What do you mean, you were right? What are you saying I should have done? If that's it I'm going home."

"Wait. I want you to confirm something."

"What?"

"We're almost there. You can see a woman." Mio pointed at an old-fashioned low-rise building. "I want you to look at her face. I think that's the woman with the Chinese clothes. As they used to say, we're gonna have you ID the suspect."

"Hey!"

Ayumi looked at Mio's profile, then turned her back to Hazuki.

"This isn't some samurai movie. You could have sent me a picture of her. I could have confirmed this in two seconds."

"If I could do that of course I would have," Mio retorted.

"Why couldn't you? My monitor's not the one that's broken."

"There's no image of her."

"Then take one."

"I can't."

"Why not?"

"She won't let me," Mio said. "And I haven't been able to sneak a picture. There are no pictures of her."

"That's impossible. We have to get pictures taken twice a year. The public data department requires us to take a picture of our face and our whole body, front, back, right, left. If this is indeed the girl I saw, she was right around our age."

"That's true. She said she's fifteen."

"Then?"

"She...doesn't have a family register," Mio said, facing the building.

"She doesn't?"

"There are all kinds of people in this city. There are a lot of foreigners."

"I know that. But a family register and nationality are unrelated. We learned that regardless of our nationality, everyone living in the country gets equal rights and duties. They all get ID cards."

"Well, yeah," Mio said. "If you do all the paperwork. I don't know if you don't."

"What do you mean by paperwork?"

"Paperwork. It's not the case anymore, but back in the day there were a lot of undocumented and illegal residents. Until the laws loosened up for them, a lot of them had to hide. If they were found they'd be prosecuted or deported."

"Not anymore," Ayumi said.

"Right. There are even those who missed their chance to leave. How'd you like to be hiding so long you have grandkids who are still hiding? Data analysis today isn't slipshod like it used to be, and everything from A to Z is recorded. You can't just blend in, so you have no choice but to live in hiding. Those guys are the ghosts of the past. They couldn't go back to places that have been officialized. That's why they come to live in these ruined parts of the city—to blend in."

"That sounds shady."

"Yeah, totally shady," Mio affirmed. "My parents run a business they can't be very proud of. They're not doing anything illegal, but nothing they'd allow in Section A. That's why I was raised in this dirty old red-light district. Actually, most of the people out here are legit in that sense. But there are a bunch of shady types mixed in."

Mio looked around at the rubble.

"When I was a little kid, before I knew anything, I played with everyone because there wasn't any discrimination yet. There wasn't segregation. But one day I realized. I noticed that there were a bunch of kids who didn't need to go to communication sessions. That's when I realized they were different. These kids who'd been my friends until then were suddenly *people from the past.*"

"People from the past?"

"I don't really understand," Ayumi said.

Hazuki thought she understood. Mio was probably referring to the same kind of kids that had been on her monitor the other day. The ones that looked like they came from another country.

In which case, she knew very well the look.

Just like scenery from the past looked like it could just be from another country, Hazuki thought this neighborhood looked like a foreign country. This was probably because of the distance from normal daily life. But to Mio who lived here, this *was* her daily life. As long as you lived in it, you had no distance from it. In which case, you had only the distance from time.

That was why they were people from the past.

Still…

It was harder for her to understand this bit about having been friends with them until a certain point.

"Her name's Rey Mao."

Mio brushed her hair.

"I don't know if that's her real name. She acts like a cat. Her old

Chinese clothes are for *gongfu*. She's strong."

Ayumi turned on her heel and looked where Mio was looking.

"If this is the girl I saw...then what?"

"Look." Mio leaned in. "If Rey Mao is the one who saved Yabe, she's probably still protecting her now."

"Protecting?"

"She might have brought her here. Because it's not dangerous."

"You think Yabe's still in danger?"

"Possibly. For example, what if Yabe's a substitute for Kawabata?"

"Substitute..."

Ayumi looked grave. Hazuki got nervous for some reason.

"That can't be. The victim was a boy."

"But she was attacked the same day that kid was killed, and isn't the location nearby too?"

"Yeah, it is." Ayumi said coolly. However, thinking about it, she was in serious danger there herself.

"But if that's the case, the police or the center would have been notified, normally."

"What if the monitor was broken right then? Plus, Rey Mao doesn't have a monitor or ID card. If the police came, she'd be the first one in trouble."

"Yabe's a normal person. She would have gone straight home. She has a main terminal there."

"What if she was attacked on her way home? Rey Mao's existence in and of itself is illegal, so even if she did save Yabe, she couldn't have seen Yabe to her designated housing. It wouldn't be out of the question that Yabe didn't make it home from outside the city in one piece."

"So you think Yabe asked Rey Mao to take her with her?"

"Because her parents weren't going to be home anyway. At the time the murder hadn't occurred yet, and neither the area patrol nor the prefectural police would have responded quickly. If Yabe was really attacked, she wouldn't want to be alone for even a minute." Then, "Isn't that right, Makino?" Mio turned to say to Hazuki. "It's hard to press that emergency receiver button when it comes down to it, isn't it?"

Whatever the reason, Hazuki had in fact not pressed that emergency call button. On top of which, she learned that what was supposed to be a foolproof security system turned out to be full of holes.

"Plus, Nakamura actually went to Yabe's house the next day. This is consistent with my theory that Nakamura was targeting Yabe. Since it didn't seem he was going to be apprehended a full day after the first attack he probably thought he could do it to her again."

"I see..." Ayumi was seeing Mio's point for some reason. "In other words, you just want me to confirm whether that woman I saw was this Mao character or not. And if she was, you think it's likely Yabe is still in this area. And you *really* want to get that piercing back to her, don't you."

"We've gone past the point of no return, or something like that. You know the expression," Mio said. "It just doesn't feel right if we leave it here. Right, Makino?"

"Huh?"

Was it really?

Hazuki had lost her bearings. Mio might have been right, but Hazuki felt like she could also just forget about this and not care. This had nothing to do with her. It was someone else's business.

Besides, she didn't think it likely someone would make such an aggressive effort and change things for the better. There was no reason to get involved.

Even if they were to return the piercing to Yuko Yabe, probably nothing would happen. She might be happy, but were she in Yabe's shoes Hazuki would not feel any different. First of all, she wouldn't necessarily want to have returned something she'd accidentally left behind in someone else's house while snooping around. In fact she might even be displeased that people would investigate her like this. No...

Definitely.

She'd definitely be displeased. Hazuki was sure of it. The fact that people who had nothing to do with Yuko Yabe were talking about Yuko Yabe in a place that had nothing to do with Yuko Yabe was plenty horrible already. If right now, somewhere far away, some group of people were speculating wildly about her, Hazuki'd be so pissed she'd want to die. Merely thinking about it made her nauseated.

"I don't necessarily..."

"Just ask her straight up."

Ayumi spoke before Hazuki could finish her drawn-out sentence.

"Tsuzuki, you're acquainted with her, right? Since childhood? So just talk to her directly. That would be the quickest way. Why bring us into this?"

"I can't ask her," Mio said.

The wind stroked the construction beams and blew through.

It smelled like something from childhood.

"I can't get her to listen to me. I haven't heard from her since the summer we were eight. Even though she lives right by me. Plus she doesn't have a monitor. And she's always moving. You can't catch her," Mio said. "Looking at her is the easiest thing to do. She always comes out around now and collects food from over there to feed the cats. Section C's rapidly developing, so it's become harder for cats to survive. These days the sanitation department and the environmentalists are out here a lot, and if the cats are caught they get taken to an animal sanctuary, but cats that grow up around here can't survive in wild places like that. I don't know for sure, but they apparently can't take meals, and they're defenseless against their natural enemies, so only 3 percent of the animals brought to the sanctuary from the city survive. That's why—"

"That's normal," Ayumi said indifferently, and turned her gaze toward the low-rise building.

"That just seems unnatural, 'animal sanctuary.' I hate it."

Then Ayumi poised herself.

Ayumi looked up at the sky and spoke.

"In the end, everyone who dies, dies. Those who live, live. Leave it be...That's nature. But we arrogantly claim to be protectors. We aren't protecting the environment or nature. Whether you like it or not, it's the earth that's protecting us. Protecting animals is no different from those twentieth century idiots keeping animals in their homes with stupid euphemisms like 'pets' and 'companion animals.'"

Who was she facing?

Who was Ayumi talking to?

Hazuki was suddenly worried.

"Living things live to live. If you give them food of course they'll get attached to you. There's a huge difference between making a pet out of an animal and respecting an animal. To have a pet is just to bribe animals with food so you can project your own selfish feelings onto them. Capturing animals and protecting them is the same as feeding animals in the wild. It's a narcissist's contradiction. I think."

A long shadow slipped up onto the roof of the building.

Straight long hair. Protective leather spats. Red embroidered Chinese clothing. There were cats milling all around her; they began to meow.

The sound of the cats disgusted Hazuki.

CHAPTER 010

IT SMELLED OF her mother.

For some reason the image of her mother's left shoulder came to Shizue's mind. Her eyes narrowed. In her contracted view sat one Hinako Sakura, wearing ghostly makeup.

"What...is this smell?" Shizue asked. Hinako eventually said *incense*, indifferently.

Hinako then squirreled up and looked up at Shizue.

It was a look beseeching approval of her response.

This occult-obsessed young girl probably thought it would be useless to tell Shizue the kind of incense and therefore chose the most uncomplicated answer.

If Shizue had to ask what the smell was, then the particulars of why Hinako bought the particular incense would be lost on her. However, one could say Hinako's choice of incense was very well informed. Shizue didn't know varieties of incense. She wouldn't know any complicated incense names. Besides, she wouldn't know to ask. Hinako's choice was perfectly appropriate indeed.

This smells like my mother.

Shizue probably had it all wrong. It was just a thought.

Shizue had gone to what was called a funeral for the first time in her life four years ago. There, she'd smelled incense for what was probably the first time in her life as well.

She couldn't be sure of the exact smell, if it was powdered or stick incense, but it was certainly the smell of the air she breathed on the occasion of her mother's funeral, and it was an air she had not breathed since.

Therefore.

No. I must be mistaken.

That couldn't be. Shizue chased worthless anguish out of her head. She tried to focus on what she could see instead of smell.

Hinako's room was monochrome, as was Hinako herself.

There were no elaborate designs.

There were piles of discs around her desk, books lined up systematically. None of them had been published recently. They were of the scant remaining old volumes that hadn't ever been digitized. It didn't seem appropriate for a fourteen-year-old. They were probably very expensive.

"I didn't realize you liked incense."

"It's calming. I don't tolerate perfumes and volatile man-made fragrances well. Do you hate it?"

"I don't hate incense. It's as you say—calming," Shizue said, and Hinako made a strange face.

"Strange."

It wasn't a response, but Hinako's gaze shifted to Shizue's bag. Shizue caught on. People probably associated her directly with the disinfectant wipes she carried around with her everywhere.

"I don't like filth or anything, but I actually can't stand the smell of antiseptics. I'd sooner smell smoke."

Hinako looked like she sort of understood but not really.

"I said this in the beginning, but..." Shizue tried to rein in the conversation from this tangent. "This isn't an official visit, so if you refuse to talk to me I will go. Please don't hesitate to tell me now. I did go ahead and ask your parents for permission to speak with you today."

Forcing an interrogation of a minor could be considered violence in certain cases.

That was why you always had to speak with a guardian whenever you were interviewing them, to gain consent from the subject. If anything happened as a result of a direct conversation with the subject, regardless of their consent, the meeting became inadmissible as evidence.

Still, as a counselor, Shizue was in a position to insist upon an interview, and in this case, legal enforcement would creep up out of nowhere if guardians refused, no matter how unofficial the interview request.

Hinako's parents seemed perplexed, and though they'd approved the interview, it was impossible to know what Hinako was thinking.

"What do you want?" Hinako asked.

"Huh?"

Shizue was caught off guard.

"Please go home. I don't want to talk."

Shizue had been prepared for that response somewhere in her mind. No, she'd even been anticipating it.

"Is there a problem? Was there some trouble with the paperwork?"

"Yes, there is. There *is* a problem. Even if this is a personal visit, I don't like that it's being recorded."

"I wanted to consult with you privately about something," Shizue said.

"Consult...me."

"Well, yes. I have a question for you."

"That's weird."

Hinako sagged the celluloid-like skin between her eyebrows, fogging her features. "A counselor, learning from a child..."

"Yes."

Shizue slackened her shoulders.

This was obviously a way of gaining the respect and trust of her counterpart, but it was also a means for Shizue to get over her confusion. Shizue had a lot of reservations about coming to this interview.

"Is it strange?"

"Isn't it? Usually it's the other way around."

"Really? I don't think so. You learn about topics you don't know much about by questioning people who do. I want to ask something of someone who knows a lot about it—that's not particularly strange."

"I'm...a minor," Hinako said.

She was still looking at Shizue's bag.

"Age has nothing to do with this. People who've lived longer don't necessarily know more. I get lectured once a week on statistics by one of my kids."

"But I don't have anything I can teach you."

"What about the mantic arts?"

She had to start somewhere.

It was still a difficult subject to ask about.

"How do the mantic arts work?"

Her motives had to be so blatant.

Sure enough, Hinako dropped her shoulder, disappointed.

"Are you suggesting that my hobbies and tastes are ill-advised? In that case as in the past, counseling—"

"Look, that's not what I'm here for. What I'm asking is...are your mantic arts always right?"

What kind of question was that?

Shizue was once again disgusted with herself.

"Right?" Hinako's brow furrowed.

"Yes. No offense, but there are not many people who believe in mantic arts in this day and age. I mean, all kinds of people did before my time. Mantic arts were extremely popular. There were even on-air broadcasts. Astrologists on, every day."

"That's not mantic arts."

Hinako darted a sharp glare at Shizue.

Shizue jumped. Hinako had never spoke out like that before. Not once...

"What do you mean it's not mantic arts?"

"It's different."

Hinako adjusted her seat. "Information obtained in such stupid ways...to make predictions. They cannot be trusted. Am I right?"

"Yes. There was a lawsuit about twenty years ago. The court ruled that dissemination of baseless future projections with any pretense of truth couched in a lack of specifics was a menace."

The media had exercised some self-restraint toward mantic arts since then. Actually, it probably started as self-restraint, but it was difficult to call it restraint now. People just stopped seeking it. They stopped trusting things they couldn't explain. That was all.

Moreover, what went on *underground* was totally beyond Shizue's knowledge.

"You're referring to the court case over astrology broadcasts from twenty-two years ago," Hinako said.

With her cutting in so matter-of-factly, it seemed Hinako was much more familiar with this case than Shizue.

"It's as you state, Ms. Fuwa, that the media had been broadcasting baseless conjecture of the future on a daily basis. If you look at it from today's ethical standards, the media at the time were without consideration or integrity. Those plaintiffs from the lawsuit were people who'd suffered economic and physical consequences of believing in these predictions, and also those who'd exhibited symptoms of neuroses or dependence on it. The defendants claimed it was only for recreational use and whether or not one believed in it should be left up to the viewer, but that was not any kind of excuse. It's irresponsible. If it's information, it's worth believing. It is positively criminal to be proclaiming this information as fact. It all happened before I was born, but I still resent that this happened."

"Really?" Shizue was more impressed by how she spoke than by what she said and for a moment was unable to respond.

I didn't realize she was so open-minded.

Shizue was a little surprised.

"Eventually the media and the governing department that oversaw the media's actions lost the case and paid an unheard-of settlement. The verdict was appropriate, but it resulted in a major misconstruction."

"Misconstruction?"

"Yes. Today, people have the mantic arts confused with baseless predictions of the future. Such foolish predictions are simple, but the phrase is in everyone's mouth. Of course those things will be disdained, but as a result, the mantic arts also have been disdained."

She seemed remorseful.

Shizue got that impression clearly from the way Hinako spoke about it.

She didn't know what could be the basis of that remorse. This itself was a baseless thought.

"The mantic arts are not the same as predicting the future."

"You're right. Then it's more like a presentiment?"

"That's even worse," Hinako said. "A presentiment simply means there is a 'pre'-existing 'sentiment.' That kind of thoughtless use of words is what damages society."

That's...

Shizue had only just thought the same exact thing a few days ago. Shizue examined Hinako's face a second time. The view transfixed Shizue's eyes.

"You're the one who taught me how destructive thoughtless speech can be, Ms. Fuwa. I have been deeply affected by that wisdom since I received it three years ago. I believe culture is the same as the human heart."

"Ahh." Shizue remembered something about this conversation now.

However...

Shizue was somewhat astonished to hear her opinions coming from other mouths. To be affected by it and realize that no matter how careful she was, she would be a careless adult too.

"I'm sorry."

She meant it.

"But this is precisely what I wanted to ask you about. I'm not making fun or disdaining it. I really don't know anything. The mantic arts are—"

"The word *uranai*."

Hinako interrupted Shizue.

"The word is composed of *boku*, divination, and *kuchi*, or speech."

It was only after Hinako continued to explain the meaning of divination that Shizue realized it was the Chinese character she was referring to.

"*Boku* is like '-mancy,' and refers to divination. Are you familiar with osteomancy—the idea that glimpses of the future can appear in the bones of long-dead animals?"

"Well, no."

"The theory is that one can interpret fortunes in fissures that have formed in a heated tortoise shell or other sort of bone matter. However, we know now that a shell cannot crack solely through exposure to the sun, and so some other physical event must have contributed to the fissure. In any case, the character for *boku* is a shape that appeared on tortoise shells that were used in these divinations. The character for 'mouth' was added for ideological reasons."

"Please don't be mad when I say this," Shizue became stern. "I think I now understand the etymology of the word *uranai*. But you know, isn't it still a form of divination? I'm only saying this because I don't know, but if the symbols of divination are created by heat or wear or whatever other kind of physical effect, can't the results be swayed?"

"I suppose you're right," Hinako said plainly.

"In which case, they appear to be coincidences, or else they are artificially handled, but either way, it's a mystery."

"In this situation you can't really claim artificial manipulation. Making something appear to be a coincidence still implies a mystery."

"What do you mean?"

"A divination implies that god has kept a secret. It implies we do not know why something has become the way it is. But the cause of the symbols of divination in and of themselves are not unknown."

"Coincidence is divine, in other words."

"Strictly speaking you can't define a coincidence. Every phenomenon is only ever the result of one exact cause. Like you said, it is possible to fabricate the fissures in a shell, but there are so many processes required. Then by some interwoven process of application and nature, the complex process leads to unique grooves in the shell. There are an infinite set of minute and subtle circumstances that lead to the finished object of divination. To grasp every single one of the circumstances involved in the meta-phenomena that creates the symbols is not humanly possible. If it were we'd just do the math. And if that were the case we would in fact actually be predicting the future. Am I wrong?"

"No, you're not. I guess that would be a calculation of the future."

"Yet even in this modern age of machines, we still cannot quantify these circumstances."

"You're right," Shizue said.

"Even the central mainframe that runs this country can't predict the way a tortoise shell will crack. At best it is an estimation. And likely to be off."

Even hundreds of years of forecasting the weather hadn't yielded any amount of certitude.

"So people now call the unpredictable mere coincidence. However, it is not amazing that a tortoise shell can be broken with heat and penetration."

"You're right. It's just physics."

"Divination can't escape coincidence. It is merely the understanding that coincidence is the will of god. It doesn't affirm that something abnormal will happen, and it's not especially unscientific."

"It's a question of speech."

"It's a question of interpretation."

Shizue thought for a moment.

"This will of god you speak of. What is the god that—"

"Naturally, god's existence was disproven many centuries ago, and what remains of synthesis religions have been disproven as well. There is no god."

"Then?"

"To presume the existence of a god is itself a contradiction because it assumes the need to have to prove it. In the last century, people were obsessed with pinpointing the way they ought to be thinking and feeling, but that was problematic too. They thought that questioning one's existence was the nature of existence. Obviously, 'to exist' doesn't exist."

Shizue raised a hand. "Wait. I get it. I didn't want to have a spiritual debate with you though. Besides I'm not very good at talking about these kinds of things."

She'd had enough of logic long ago. She remembered philosophy feeling like a cul-de-sac. But. A long time ago even children would espouse the limits of reductionism, and people today were still reductive in the explanation of *things*, but at the end of the day every *thing* was measured by deduction speculation. Shizue was the same.

It was because it was simple. Humans couldn't swallow the world whole. That was why they couldn't let themselves go without relying on something. While smart people waxed philosophical, what was once an unquantifiable world had slowly transformed completely into pure numbers.

With enough contemplation, the world Shizue lived in now could be completely digitized. She didn't know the specifics—binary codes, chakras, yin-yang, numerology—but she was in the habit of understanding the world through numbers.

Of course it was a delusion.

Numbers could be a concept and not always a reality.

Between one and two was an infinite number of numbers. But people ignored what lay between one and two for simplicity's sake.

A world expressed only in numbers was completely flat, without depth. Shizue lived by projecting depth onto this shallow world.

That was why it was difficult to talk about things between one and two.

"This...divination..."

"I understand," Hinako said curtly.

"Understand..."

"May I? On top of this disc?" Hinako lifted a thin finger and pointed at the monitor disc next to Shizue. "My writing utensils have fallen over there."

"This?"

It was a laser pen.

"Yes. Do you think the fact that it has just fallen is a good or bad thing?"

"Good or...I don't know."

"It's not that you don't know. It is neither."

"Well in that case, if we're being really serious, it's probably a bad thing. It will take physical effort to pick it up. Unless you just decide to ignore it, it's a minus," Shizue said.

"But say for example you discover something hidden under the desk when you go to pick up the pen. How about now?"

"Well in that case it's a good thing."

"Right," Hinako said. "However, there's no causal connection between finding something under your desk and dropping a pen."

"Well, no, you're right there. It's impossible. It's a coincidence...oh."

She was saying something about how you can't escape coincidence.

"Then drawing a causal connection between events which are unrelated is—"

"It's a little different," Hinako said. "By stating the possibility of a conclusive causal relationship through divination, you can correctly assume there is no relationship between the two events. Things always inevitably happen. It's not good or bad. Moralizing is a value judgment. Only humans make value judgments."

Of course they do. Only humans could have two opposing interpretations of the same phenomenon.

"It's an extreme example, but, say someone dies. Socially, it's considered a negative occurrence. However, say something big happens as a result of this person's passing, and all of society greatly benefits from it. You could say that it was actually a good thing."

"And you're saying that's—"

"That is fundamental."

Hinako looked up through her sharply cut bangs at Shizue. "Divinations do not predict what will happen. No one can know what will happen in the future. Divinations determine how what *is* happening and what *will* happen should be interpreted."

"Interpreted—"

"Remember that's what I said in the beginning," Hinako said. "The character *boku* means determining a fortune. It is not a prediction or a look into the future. It takes what is going on now and prepares you for what may happen next. A divination is the utterance of this suggestion. As it stands, nothing is positive or negative, so we don't have any determinations on how to interpret events. People are confused by this, which is precisely why once they've surpassed understanding the physical they make a positive or negative determination and label events as such. That is the nature of divination."

"I see…"

Shizue finally understood. At the least it was a more manageable explanation than anything at the communications center. Hinako had always seemed frightened during interviews. Unless she was talking about something she was very familiar with, she never had such cogent arguments.

It all amounted to the fact that nothing was learned from counseling.

No matter how much data they collected, it was just an accumulation. Meaningless. If you didn't know how to read the information, it was pointless. Merely organizing numbers couldn't even let you know a person's face.

"Prayer is the same," Hinako continued. "Sincere prayer to a god is not unreliable. But today there are more people who don't rely on it. Prayer is thought of as unreliable."

"Well—"

"But that's because people pray with a vehemence for some divine intervention to magically alter the course of nature. Consequently they are asking for a ready blessing, an answer to their prayers. That is the problem."

Probably.

"I feel very differently about these answers to prayers," Hinako said.

"Blessings are just positive phenomena, and in simpler terms they're just luck or fortune. Many people believe prayer is requesting good luck from a god. In that case prayer certainly is evil. But they are mistaken. Luck and fortune are rewards for particular actions. Prayer, in actuality, is to announce what actions you are about to undertake before God and to ask to be able to accomplish your goals."

"Like a declaration of resolve?"

"Yes, but before God, which is more powerful than proclaiming to man."

"God…"

It was inevitable they'd talk about God.

Shizue didn't want to start dwelling on this. That was probably why she'd never gotten much further than this point in the conversation.

Shizue tried in life never to dwell on this subject.

However.

There was one thing she was sure of. This Hinako Sakura was no victim of delusion. Shizue had probably wanted to perform this interview to make certain of that. In that sense she could say this was a fruitful interview.

"So I wanted to ask…" Shizue said with some force. Hinako immediately returned to being a shy girl.

Hinako lowered her gaze, shrugged, and said, "Sorry."

"Why are you apologizing?"

"I talked too much."

"That's not true. I think I really understand now. I'd like to hear more about it later."

She was half serious. Hinako demonstrated an indecipherable, impatient attitude.

"Oh…did you not want to have a conversation about this with me, perhaps?"

She probably didn't want any of this on record.

Hinako nodded weakly.

"I understand. Well, if I ever want to hear more I'll just come over."

Hinako certainly wouldn't want to hear that from Shizue. It would be unnatural for a counselor and her charge to meet and speak privately.

Shizue's voice dropped off, and she nervously looked down. Who was the charge here?

"I wanted to ask about Yuko Yabe," Shizue managed, if clumsily.

She was apprehensive.

"Was Yuko asking you these kinds of questions as well?"

"Umm…"

She didn't like how long Hinako paused. Once this door was shut she knew it would be difficult to swing open.

Hinako stole a quick glance at Shizue's eyes as if beseeching permission to speak.

Shizue nodded.

This was how she knew Hinako normally behaved.

"That girl just wanted me to read her a divination."

"Like tell her fortune?"

"Yes. It seemed she was frightened of medical exams."

"You mean the physical checkups we did recently at the center?"

That day, Hinako had run into Yuko Yabe.

"That girl's illness would probably go undetected in a simple medical exam."

"Illness?"

Shizue didn't know of any medical conditions that deserved special mention, and she'd just looked at Yabe's file not a day ago.

The results of her physical were good.

In fact her condition was excellent. Yabe was in the top tier of health. Level A, and even in that level she was in the top 10 percent.

"Was Yuko somehow convinced that she was sick?"

"She didn't appear to know beforehand," Hinako answered. "But she did say someone had indicated it to her."

"Indicated?"

"Yes. If it really were this illness, her life was in grave danger."

"Her life? She has a life-threatening illness?"

"But it was something that went undetected in the medical exam, so…"

"That's not possible," Shizue said.

Those physicals were quite meticulous.

Today's physicals bore no comparison to the ones Shizue underwent as a child. Today's physicals included a cancer screening and a full-body scan.

They were scrupulous but apparently still had discrepancies.

In the first place, the Food Agency and the Science Council and other central administrative departments lurked in the background to encourage extra diligence in these already minute exams performed on every child in every community center in the care of the National Youth Welfare Department.

What started it all was a sharp rise in deteriorated liver function in minors. A new division was formed to look into the cause in the preparation of elements of synthetic food products five years earlier. These exams were the result of those first tests.

There was no medical link established between the food and liver problems, but since there was no ubiquitous distribution of synthetic food products in the past, the central administration decided to be cautious.

"Is there such a disease that can't be detected by those exams?"

"I don't think there is," Hinako said. "That girl was…If there were a sign of misfortune following her, she thought it might be this illness."

"So were the results of your divination not good?"

"Terrible," Hinako answered in a soft voice.

"According to what you were saying earlier, Hinako, does that mean you determined that whatever her situation is now or is about to become would, uh, be bad?"

"It means not that she should stop being optimistic, but that she must be prepared for anything."

"I suppose I wouldn't understand the basis of that statement."

"You aren't supposed to, in principle. *Occult* actually means 'to hide.' Still…"

"Yes?"

"Her results were so unusual," Hinako said apologetically.

"Unusual how?"

"She would encounter a wolf."

"A wolf? You mean like the animal?"

"Yes. An animal that's been extinct since the last century."

"I know that much, but you said she was going to encounter one?"

What did that mean?

As if detecting Shizue's hesitation, Hinako said, "It's probably an omen. Like, a warning to avoid a situation."

"Avoid a situation?"

"That's the fortune I determined for her. As I said earlier, this is not a cut-and-dried prediction that she would encounter an extinct animal. Whatever does or doesn't happen to her…is simply avoidable. That's what the fortune meant."

"Avoidable…"

"Yes. I wanted to tell her as soon as possible, but simultaneously I was hesitant."

No doubt telling someone bad news would be difficult.

"But Yuko begged me not to send her the results virtually."

"Really. Was there a reason the results couldn't be sent in a message?"

"Otherwise I had no choice but to tell her at the communication session. But…"

Yuko Yabe did not come to lab that day.

Did that mean she had in fact encountered a wolf?

Shizue was confused.

CHAPTER 011

HAZUKI FORGOT WHERE she was for a moment.

The old-fashioned low-rise building. An old-fashioned human figure standing on the roof of it. It was all unreal. Hazuki thought it would actually look more real on her monitor. It would look less deceptive trapped in the frame of her screen with Arabic letters running along the bottom.

There was the sound of some atonal animal voice.

Meow. Meow. Meow.

"Meow cats!" Mio yelled. Mio's line of vision went straight to the person on the roof.

The girl in the red embroidery looked down, sans expression.

Mio looked intently at Ayumi's face. Ayumi didn't move. From where Hazuki stood she could not see what Ayumi was looking at. Hazuki kept her focus on Ayumi and walked up. Mio moved between them and, facing the cat-girl on the roof, took a wide stance and said out loud, "Meow. We have to talk."

Mio stepped forward a few steps and then looked back at Ayumi. Ayumi was still. Mio was likely not visible in the scene reflected in Ayumi's eyes. That gaze was fixed directly on the girl on the roof.

Mio yelled out for Mao to come down. But she wouldn't. Her long straight hair billowed across her face. She didn't even bother to pull it away from her eyes.

Mio kicked the ground once. "*Look over here!*" she yelled. She was angry.

Mio was…

Mio wanted this girl to look at her?

Yes.

No matter how loudly Mio spoke, Rey Mao made no indication of listening. She just continued to stare Ayumi down. Hazuki discerned that Mio wanted everyone to look at her.

"Hey!" Mio stepped forward. Rey Mao still refused to look at her.

It was just her dry voice, carried by the wind, that reached as far as Hazuki.

"Sorry, I'm busy."

"Busy?"

"Yeah, busy," Rey Mao repeated.

"Stop acting like you're important. You know full well kids aren't *busy*."

"Kids, huh? I'm not a kid. I don't have any kid friends."

"What?" Mio clasped her hands behind her head and made as if to flip backward.

"What the hell are you talking about? You're my age. We used to play when we were little. Have you forgotten? You can't be more than fourteen or fifteen. You are a kid. A kid!"

"Out here, a kid is someone who can't gather their own food."

It wasn't a conversation Rey Mao was entertaining so much as it was a sermon she was giving.

Since she wasn't even looking at the person she was talking to—Mio.

"Food? You're talking about economic independence. Well then, you ought to know we're not allowed to work, so we can't make money. That makes you a minor."

"And?" Rey Mao lowered her chin and dropped a laser-focused glare onto Mio.

"What do you mean *and*?" Mio winced.

It doesn't matter how badly Mio wanted to be looked at, she still cannot handle the effect, Hazuki thought to herself.

"There aren't any delineations like 'kids' or 'minors' out here. I don't know, but it sounds like something your people came up with. I have nothing to do with it. That stuff doesn't translate out here."

This girl…she had no nationality. She had no ID card or monitor.

As though she'd had enough, Rey Mao turned her back to the girls.

The small, mewing animals followed close at her feet.

"No offense, but I don't hang out with children."

"Really."

Just then…

Suddenly.

Ayumi spoke.

"Really arrogant. Tsuzuki, your friend's really arrogant."

Ayumi's words ripped through the delicate embroidery at the center of Rey Mao's back. The cats on the roof reacted instinctively to the voice and stopped dead in their tracks.

Hazuki took a deep breath. Her heart was racing.

Ayumi hadn't spoken very loudly, but the words were clear. In the midst of this fake-looking situation, her voice was unusually real.

Rey Mao stood there silent.

With her eyes still piercing her back, Ayumi continued.

"I don't know the difference between children and adults, but you know, I don't really care."

Rey Mao's back quivered at the sound of Ayumi's voice.

"Besides," Ayumi continued. "Sure the animal that can forage for its own food is on its own, but you're not going to tell me you're not human *animals* now, are you?"

Rey Mao threw in without turning her back, "I don't want to hear your pompous theories. Humans are still animals."

"Sure. Humans are animals. But they are not wild animals."

"What?"

"What you're talking about is the logic of wild animals."

"What do you mean 'wild'?"

Rey looked over her shoulder again at Ayumi.

Ayumi's look repelled the cats.

"An animal that lives simply to survive is a wild animal. Stop pretending you don't live in the same sheltered neighborhood we're in."

"Sheltered, you say? This neighborhood?"

"Sure. You are sheltered in this neighborhood. You are by no means totally on your own. And I can prove it. You can't step one foot out of here, can you?"

Rey Mao turned around without any change in her expression.

"You're an undocumented resident, right? It's nothing to beat yourself up about, but I wouldn't brag about it either. It doesn't make a difference to anyone. But you can't live anywhere besides this Section C, correct?"

"Are you making something of it?"

"I'm right, aren't I? This shit environment is the only one you can get your food in. One step out of here and your kind is powerless."

Ayumi quietly menaced Rey Mao.

"You're right that we live off the graces of guardians. We couldn't feed ourselves on our own."

"I bet you can't."

"We have it brought to us, as they say."

"Have it brought? You mean you are fed by someone else."

"That's not necessarily true. Without obtaining the food ourselves, we have the food obtained for us. We're not just a bunch of idiots with mouths open waiting for food to be poured in. Baby chicks have an insight on life that's only theirs."

"Insight?"

"Insight. There are no more guarantees that a parent bird is going to bring food. It's not that kind of world anymore. You can't just laze there waiting for something to come to you."

"Let me guess...and there isn't enough love or nurture. Spare me the sob story."

"Oh no. Animals don't care for their children out of love."

Ayumi rebounded off Rey Mao's interjection.

"It's instinct. Because animals don't experience things like love," Ayumi asserted.

"I don't know the specifics, but living beings are all programmed to behave the way they do. Rather, that's the essence of life. Children aren't raised because they are cute. They are raised to protect the seeds of the future. Love is a convenient word humans devised to differentiate themselves from animals."

Hazuki's eyes widened.

What is she saying?

Ayumi appeared to her like someone from another planet.

Hazuki had never seriously thought about the meaning of the word *love*. The existence of love wasn't something she debated.

But.

Ayumi stared into the eyes of Rey as she slowly continued her story. She was outside Hazuki's permissible scope.

"And what about it?" Rey Mao's voice.

"And so humans are the same. If humans can't care for children today, it's not the fault of bad homes or bad people. It's arrested development. It's an illness. They say approximately 30 percent of the world's population suffers from it. It has nothing to do with economic circumstances or living environments. Of course the situation is worse for poor people because their circumstances give them no other recourse. We've caught a stray blow from the thoughtless idiots of the twentieth century. As a result, we kids of the twenty-first century can't just go to sleep without a care. Because once you're born, you have to live."

"Then go get your own food."

"We're not allowed to," Ayumi responded. "Tsuzuki said it herself. We have to use our heads and survive in this cage of a boring society. Those who can't, die. You don't have to be in a fatal environment to die of malaise.

"Of course we have to live by this rule," Ayumi continued. "We're risking our lives by accepting food in our cage. There's no point in telling kids like you playing pretend 'great outdoors' in the completely sheltered preservation areas that you're outside the cage because you're not."

"Playing *pretend* great outdoors?"

"Isn't that all it is? If it's not, let me ask you this. Why do you feed cats? You think you're protecting the weak?" Ayumi said, louder now.

"I-it's none of your business what I do."

"It isn't. But don't get all cocky about it. Aren't you always feeding the cats? You've decided for yourself that they are weak and have enforced your protection of them, for yourself. That doesn't give you the right to lord it over us. Real animals of the wild live only to survive because to do anything other than what was required would lead to death. They're not in a position to be starting charities."

"Charities—" Rey Mao began.

"Sure. Those cats are in a unique position—they have you to feed them. If you sent those cats out to the wildlife preserve now they'd die. You would too."

Rey Mao looked as if the weight in her back had let out. She dropped what was in her hand. Several little animals gathered at the point where it landed.

"Do you remember me?" Ayumi looked up.

"It's you."

"I knew it. This is the girl who saved Yabe, right? Hey, Kono…"

Mio looked over at Ayumi. Ayumi didn't answer Mio, but lowered her face.

"You're not supposed to have seen my face."

"No."

"I know." Rey Mao adjusted her stance.

"It's you."

"Who do you think you are?"

"You want to go? I'll come down."

"I don't want to fight you. If you plan on fighting, I'm just going to leave while you come down."

"Why? You could win."

Win?

Ayumi would win?

Hazuki didn't understand what that could mean.

"I wouldn't," Ayumi responded. "Children raised in cages don't know how to fight."

"Oh really. You didn't even flinch that day. I was—"

"You were engaging in fisticuffs. You couldn't have seen my face. Right?"

"I didn't need to see your face to know it was you."

"Impressive."

Ayumi wasn't cowering.

"You recognize my smell. In that case you're definitely an animal. You passed out after that."

"I did."

Mio stepped in front of Ayumi. "The hell? Aren't you the one who saved Yuko Yabe, Rey Mao? Am I wrong? Kono, didn't you say she went at the attacker? What do you mean she passed out? What happened? What…"

"She was indeed the one who saved Yabe. You're right that she's strong. But no matter how strong you are, anyone punched that hard would lose consciousness."

"Punched?"

"This one round-housed the guy. At the same time there was another guy trying to swipe at her with a metal pole. That's when I came along. And Yabe went running and bumped into me. I took her to the other side of the street and sat her down. That's it."

"If that's it, then…"

"I didn't see what happened afterward. I just assumed she'd passed out."

"What do you mean you didn't see, Kono? You just left?" Mio asked.

"It was none of my business," Ayumi said.

"You are one cold bitch," Mio said and walked back a step. "You should have at least called someone. You got a monitor on you after all."

"Even if I'd called the cops, by the time they arrived the showdown would have been over. I couldn't help, and I wasn't going to stop the violence by dragging the police into it. And if I did, there'd be retaliation against me later."

"Okay, fine. But at least call for someone's help if you can't do it yourself."

"Who? There was no one there. If I screamed for help they would notice me. If they noticed me they'd kill me."

"I wonder," said Rey Mao. "I just don't think you'd be taken down so easily."

"I told you already. I don't know how to fight. I've never thrown or received a punch in my life. I don't know how to make allowances for fighting moves like you do."

"Kono. This isn't about knowing how to fight. Geez."

Mio raised her arms wide. "Y-you don't *plan* combat! Jesus. I don't know about fighting, but in that situation you just go at it with your all. I've seen it before, but this one will move like a beast." Mio pointed at Rey Mao and looked back and forth between her and Ayumi. They'd both certainly witnessed fighting at least once. Hazuki couldn't fathom it.

"I don't know about giving it one's all, but you certainly have to plan your actions."

"I didn't plan any of that," Rey Mao yelled.

"That's not possible. That *gongfu* you busted out is a thoughtfully exquisite fighting style. That's what it looked like, at least. You probably aren't allowed to kill anyone with it right? Yet if you struck anyone hard enough with your skills, they'd die," Ayumi said.

"If they died it wouldn't be a fight, would it? It's because people just grapple that it's called 'fighting.' People who are fighting aren't trying to kill each other. It's a savage form of human communication. Fighting isn't something that can be settled in one moment. Animals won't do anything that pointless. Eat or be eaten. Their fight for life ends in one move. Fewer losses the better. A fight only occurs when your attacker is weak and you can counterattack. When humans fight it's like a monkey fight for position."

"I don't give a damn about animals," Mio yelled.

"Monkeys, shmonkeys, I don't know anything about it. Makino might, but—"

"I…" Hazuki was just confused.

Ayumi peered at Hazuki from the side, then quickly returned her gaze to Rey Mao.

"When monkeys fight they have rules. Humans do too. You can't fight unless you know the rules, and you can't fight anyone who doesn't understand them. You fought with someone who didn't know the rules. That's why you lost." Rey Mao swept away her long straight hair.

"I see…"

"I get it," said the girl standing on the roof.

Hazuki didn't know anything. Not one thing.

"It's as you said. I take back what I said earlier."

"That would be wise."

Ayumi turned to one side. That familiar profile was once again in

Hazuki's line of vision.

"Since we're being wise, I wanted to ask. Do you care for anything besides cats?"

"What do you mean?"

"It looks like you're fond of caring for the weak. Besides these cats at your feet, say that night for example, did you rescue a little pink kitten? If you did in fact take in that poor little kitty, Tsuzuki here would like to have access to her."

Ayumi placed a hand on Mio's shoulder. "This Tsuzuki is one strange cat, so to speak. She's really put us all out, you know."

"What do you want with her?" Rey Mao asked.

Mio narrowed her gaze.

"You *do* have her."

"What if I did?"

"Damn. This bitch is slow or something," Mio shook off Ayumi's hand and stepped forward again, turning her face up high.

"I have to talk to her, so just let me see her!"

"She's being hunted."

"So? You saying I'm one of the hunters? Is that what you're saying?"

Rey Mao didn't say anything.

"Say something, bitch! You saying I can't be trusted? I just want to return her piercing."

"Calm down." Rey Mao spoke firmly, then finally looked Mio in the eyes. "Her opinion matters too, so I won't say anything to disparage you. And I won't brag about gathering food. But you guys and I still live in different worlds. Mio, you've long become a member of that other world."

"There's no *this world, that world*," Mio said, annoyed. "I don't live in this world because I like it. Neither do you. It's unrelated. You've been raised here the same way that little cat has."

"It's still different." Rey Mao turned her face away.

"What did you say?" Mio raised both arms and made as if to run at Rey Mao.

Ayumi grabbed her, and Mio screamed, her face twisted, "Fine! Then answer this, *bitch*! Yuko Yabe is also from a different world than yours. Why are you hiding her?"

"I'm not hiding her. She's here of her own will."

"Her own will?"

"She followed me here. Sure, she was scared. The man who attacked her was a pathological killer with no sense of logic. She told me he'd probably killed many people already."

"And so? You saying you're protecting her? Stop fronting. You think you're some kind of superhero do-gooder? Leaving her in this dump is more dangerous than anything else."

"I know that, but she can't move right now. She has a fever."

"That's why you extended your hand out to her?" Ayumi said, still restraining Mio.

"Ridiculous!" Mio shouted.

"You'd prefer I just kick her out? I told her to go home, but she won't. She said she doesn't have any guardians and that something was destroyed. It didn't make sense. You guys really can't function without that machinery, can you?"

Her monitor.

Right.

Hazuki thought about it.

They were monitors.

Society, the world…she wasn't sure what to call it, but say there was a large strict system in the middle, and they were all connected to it. That gave them security. They protected that safety. The monitor was proof of that safety. An existence based on accepting things that were predetermined to be harmonious, or ought to have been, was in one sense totally irresponsible, but generally considered a good way to live. The things you needed to survive were all prepared somewhere, and as long as the monitor had access to them it would distribute them to you.

The monitor was a tool to receive the entire world and a sort of passport. If you lost it…

It would be unimaginably horrific.

"We don't have things like that here," Rey Mao said. "There's nothing you can do. That's why I left her alone for a while. It's raining."

"I see. That's why you told her where Tsuzuki lives," Ayumi said, as Mio opened her eyes wide and turned her head backward.

"Me?"

Rey Mao turned to her side and whispered something. "You're the one who told her where I live?"

"Only because I didn't know anyone else with a normal house. But she didn't go. Maybe you two don't…get along?"

"We're fine. I've never talked to her. Right?"

Mio looked for assent from Hazuki.

What would Hazuki do?

She'd probably look for Mio too.

Probably.

Probably wouldn't go.

"Is that so?" Rey Mao said. "In any case she can't move. That's all."

"If she stays out in this rain she'll catch cold. At least take her to a doctor," Ayumi said.

"You probably can't," Mio let out.

"You guys are an inconvenience."

"Any way you look at this it's up to you. But until her fever goes down she really has to keep sleeping. I came here to tell you that. As long as she's here she lives by our rules."

There would be no medical intervention, to say nothing of police intervention.

"Not because she didn't have a monitor. People like me aren't allowed to have access to public institutions. In spite of doctors it's still dangerous. As far as I'm concerned, you are dangerous too," Rey Mao continued.

Maybe. Hazuki, Ayumi, Mio...they all had monitors. They were all connected.

"It's nothing fatal. If you want to see her, do it when she leaves here."

"How long do you think that'll be?" Ayumi spoke in Mio's place.

"Two, three days. Though I couldn't say that with any confidence."

"Why not?"

"I'm sure you already know. Someone has died."

"And?"

"You'll be arrested."

"That's got nothing to do with it. I didn't kill anyone."

"*That* has nothing to do with it. According to Tsuzuki, the person who last met with the boy who died visited Yuko's house a couple nights ago. Her disappearance has long been noted, so it's just a matter of time. Whether you're associated with this or not, you will be tied to the murder. And that means the area patrols or prefectural police will be here in no time."

"Wha—?" Mio raised her voice.

"Am I right?"

Mio hadn't thought that far ahead. She looked all the way around her and said, "They're coming."

"They are. They'll go through this area with a fine-tooth comb. If Yabe is being protected here you guys are the ones in trouble. You'll get arrested. It won't matter if you're not the culprit. It won't matter if you can fight. But if you're arrested, everyone like you in this area will be interrogated. For the police, it's a golden opportunity."

"I see…"

Rey Mao crossed her arms and looked up.

The cats at her feet were suddenly gone.

"You should return Yabe," Mio said. "In a worst-case scenario this whole town will be razed. The old red-light district will be trashed. These guys are pathologically clean, so they'll clean up all the trash. They'll use any excuse."

"But you see, the girl can't move right now. Are you suggesting she walk home on crutches? Just leave. I'm plenty satisfied with this area the way it is."

Rey Mao went silent. She looked lost in thought.

"I don't think you could call that a good move," Ayumi said as if to intercept the thought. "Right now, there are probably police all over Yabe's home. They would be extremely harsh. If you brought her home right now, it's like you'd be asking them to arrest you. Of course, if you were arrested there, it might not be a direct nuisance on the people who live here. But as soon as they found out about your situation it wouldn't make a difference.

"In other words, you're saying this: if I'm arrested and I tell the cops everything, it'll be a problem for everyone, including you. *I'm sorry*," Ayumi said and shrugged.

"It's already a major nuisance. I'll pretend I don't know. There's no evidence anyway."

"I'll tell. Yuko will tell too."

"I'll tell them it's mistaken identity," Rey Mao said.

"What?"

A gust picked up the air around them.

The slack in Hazuki's clothing became pregnant with the wind, then as quickly settled down. The cloth kept flapping in the wind.

The scene was practically unreal but for the sensation on the skin, and Hazuki was stuck confused between the two. There was no sign anywhere of anything the others said being a lie or the truth.

Rey Mao's hair was flying. Mio's worker's clothing was rustling. Ayumi had no excess fabric to rustle in the wind.

"Shut up!" Mio screamed. "It's decided. We're going to my house."

"Tsuzuki's house is in Section C too. If we can hide out there, when

Yabe eventually goes back home and explains the circumstances it'll have the same result. Unless the case gets solved in the interim."

Ayumi remained totally silent.

"You're right. If the killer is caught first then we have nothing to worry about." Mio's voice was elided by the sound of the wind.

Mio stood on some scaffolding and repeated herself out loud.

"That's right. If the killer is caught first, then…"

No one responded.

Everyone was sure the killer would never be caught. That was what Hazuki thought, and of course Mio knew that much. This case would never be solved. There was too little evidence, and it would take time to find him. The investigation would last years. They couldn't keep Yuko Yabe locked up that whole time.

"What do you suggest we do, then?" Mio said to Ayumi.

"This won't work, that won't work. Nothing will work!"

"Yes, but, Tsuzuki. All you wanted to do was give her back her piercing. Just give it to Rey Mao to give to her and we're done."

"You think that's all there is to this now?" Mio said and put her head in her hands.

"It'd be better if we could move her to Section A."

"There's nowhere in Section A to hide something this problematic. Unlike Section C, it's strictly controlled. It's visually monitored. You bring that into the cage and all foreign substances will immediately be flushed."

Ayumi was right. It wasn't possible. If they were just going to hide, Section C would be the best place.

"That's not true. A strictly controlled society still has holes. A world made of numbers is easy to co-opt. There's magic to be performed everywhere. Isn't that right, Makino?"

Mio looked at Hazuki and grinned.

Magic.

Mio had in fact used a sort of magic.

Mio had broken into Hazuki's residence and eaten her food, and Hazuki was even there to see it all take place, but it was no longer a fact, because no one would know about it. There was no record of it. It was as if it had never happened. It was made to not have ever happened.

Even now Hazuki couldn't help questioning her own memory.

"What's monitored isn't the truth, but information." Mio sat on the scaffolding and rested her elbows on her lap, resting her head on her hand. "Information can be rewritten. People who depend on a world made of numbers can't fathom deceptive numbers. Just like long ago when people believed their silly little brains saw ghosts, today's adult will think up ghosts because a mistake in numbers is unforgivable. So long as it's consistent no one will raise any doubts. Basically if it's not a bothersome type of human, it's all right. For example..."

Hazuki felt enveloped by Mio's large eyes.

"We can't go to Hazuki's. There's no one in her house, but there's AI everywhere."

Mio stared at Ayumi's back.

She's got a great little hiding place.

CHAPTER 012

THE PHANTOM OF her mother dissipated as soon as Shizue stepped outside.

But that feeling, the nostalgia, heartbreak, the extreme version of a small feeling—the sickly sentimental bathos clung to her. It was a feeling she'd never felt toward her actual mother, which made her all the more uneasy.

She was probably just turned around. Or else that smoky scent of incense had intoxicated her.

She drew in a deep breath of air outside. It was odorless but textured. *What am I doing?*

Spores in the air traveled through her nostrils to the depths of her body, invading it. It was an awful image. It was wholly unclean. She had a mountain of work to get through, but Shizue was not doing anything one could call constructive. The reason for her indifference toward paperwork would not come to her. She decided for herself that she was mildly depressed.

It couldn't be anything else.

Her actions were useless.

The request to investigate Yuko Yabe had already been accepted. Furthermore, the police had started investigating, probably. Yuji Nakamura's physical protection, same thing. There was no need for Shizue to go out now. She just couldn't fight the urge.

You could say.

That didn't mean she would find anything out from meeting with Hinako Sakura, nor did it clarify matters for Shizue. It wasn't as though Hinako had anything to do with the disappearance of Yuko, and this wasn't necessarily a murder case. Hinako hadn't even had *real contact* with Yuko. She'd just gone to Yuko's residence to check on her after Yuko was absent from lab, making it no different from what Shizue herself had done the next day. In actuality, the police had not come to Hinako. They'd apparently determined from reading Kunugi's report that the visit was unrelated.

But.

That was beyond consent to begin with. Actually, Shizue was confused by the mere fact of having met Hinako. It wasn't so much that it had been spurred by a desire to make something happen—the "fieldwork" was just the reflection of Shizue's inner consciousness telling her she didn't want to get involved with any run-of-the-mill office work. She'd been looking for a means to justify escape from reality by doing something out of the ordinary.

Shizue was disgusted.

There was such a thing as being disgusted with such self-analysis, but it was more likely the influence of having lost the excuse to escape from reality.

There was an insect flying.

Shizue watched the bug's path. Few things in the city actually moved. Beyond it.

A solar car.

"Kunugi."

Standing next to the solar car looking bored was Officer Kunugi. He waved a limp arm once and mouthed, without uttering, the word *yo*.

"What are you doing here…at the Sakura residence?"

"It's not like that," Kunugi said, rolling his eyes. "I need to talk to you."

"Me?"

"Yes, well, the outside line indicated this address. It's the fortune-teller girl's address, isn't it?"

"What's the problem? Is this about Yabe?"

"It's not like *that*." Kunugi waved his hand again. "It's a private matter. Don't take it the wrong way. It's not like *that* either."

"What do you mean by *that*?"

It was going to be too complicated to try to arrange an official meeting. Kunugi's already nervous face became tenser still, and he sighed.

Aghh.

"Our generation…we still have complexes about gender relations. Even if it's private, it's still sexual harassment. I'm sorry. I just assumed if you came here it was because Yuko Yabe is still the subject of an investigation at the center as well. Is that correct?"

"Why are you asking?"

"It's just, the police can't find out what the center is up to, and I'm not asking as a public matter. You aren't under any obligation to answer."

"You're talking in circles."

Was he just being careful?

"Other people of your generation are a lot less serious than you.

That's why you're so thoroughly hated." Kunugi let out a weak laugh.

They hate me when I use my senses, so maybe that's pointless.

"So what did you want with me?" Shizue said, cold. She felt more like herself. "I clearly just met with Hinako Sakura, but it was a private matter and unrelated to the center's activities. They're treating Yuko Yabe's disappearance as a possible murder, so the investigation has been turned over to the police."

"Is that so?"

"Of course, we've been instructed to cooperate in every way possible with the police investigation. That's why we've sent them all the information we have on the kids, but we haven't done any surveys on them individually, or their active social lives."

"You're talking in circles yourself," Kunugi said. "You were concerned and came out here, then. Was it useful?"

"That I definitely don't have to answer. It was a private meeting."

"I guess. I've been left completely out," Kunugi said, apathetic.

"From the investigation?"

"Worse. From the department. I've been asked to take a sabbatical."

"Sabbatical...Are you being blamed for our incident?"

In which case Shizue wasn't exempt from responsibility, though it'd be difficult for her to assume any if asked. When she asked if she was under suspicion Kunugi said *It isn't like that* again.

"Technically yes, but it's just words. I'd been eyed from the root. I'm a nuisance to them. I'm always somehow at odds with what the rest of the team is doing."

"In that case..."

Why was he here? If it wasn't to talk about his concerns, was he just here to complain?

"I'm just not satisfied with the explanation." Kunugi sounded hopeless.

"Of what?"

"With the turn of events. Things just aren't fitting, and at this rate it'll all go bad. But I seem to be the only one thinking that way. But it's because it's gone unresolved we have a serial killer on our hands."

"The police lose credibility."

"I don't care about that," Kunugi said and turned around. "What's credibility anyway? We weren't trustworthy to begin with. Kids and families might trust you inherently, but the police, we're just a bunch of functionaries. People hate us; they don't depend on us. Besides, the only people we have *real contact* with are suspects and the associates of known criminals. We don't even need to be human."

Shizue was at a loss for a response.

What was trust? In today's age trust had to be quantified. It would be measured with immutable numbers through a monitor, but it still had to be measured.

"Well then, what are you going to do?"

"I can't do anything. I told you. I'm not satisfied with the way things have gone."

Not satisfied.

That was one way of putting it.

It was how Shizue felt right now too. Mildly depressed. Not entirely satisfied.

"Wait. You're not suggesting investigating this matter privately, are you, Mr. Kunugi?"

"I can't. Off duty I'm a strictly monitored civilian. I have no authority."

"But are your moral standards making it hard for you to remain quiet? Or are you just curious about what's happening?"

Kunugi turned around again and lowered his brows. "I might be old school, but I'm not so old I borrow moldy concepts like 'moral standards.' Besides, I'm not curious about people dying. I might not have any authority, but I'm not totally useless. So I just need to, you know, *get it.* Just the stuff that's not sitting right with me. It might just be for my own edification. And that's why I had to talk to you."

"That's why you're following me?"

"If I use my monitor to arrange a meet it leaves a record. I had to run into you without an appointment."

"You're really a pain, aren't you?" Shizue said.

"Am I?"

"If I refused to see you and reported you to the police you'd be discharged. Those who are assigned authority by law can be prosecuted for forcing a personal meet without permission. It may be a soft offense, but I'm sure even off duty you'd be dismissed."

"Report me then."

Kunugi gave Shizue his monitor.

"I can report you anytime."

Shizue pulled out her own monitor.

"I would rather make an appointment than report you. Thanks to your little organization of cops, I have been suffering a tremendous amount of stress and am mildly depressed. I was going to buy myself some high-end cuisine to alleviate this stress."

Kunugi laughed weakly. "All I know are the police cafeterias. Three meals a day there. I had started to think about where I would eat off duty, but I didn't get very far."

Kunugi withdrew his own monitor and started typing into it. Searching for a restaurant?

"I'll decide after I've eaten whether I'm going to report you or not," Shizue said.

She'd never had any intention of reporting him.

Shizue'd inferred from his past reactions that if she told him he was bothering her he'd run away with his tail between his legs, and that would be a lot less work for her. But she didn't tell him he was bothering her.

She wasn't sure herself why not.

Maybe because this was her excuse to get out of reality.

That was probably it.

To be frank she didn't really want to have dinner with this man. She just thought it would be better than being seen on the road talking to him. He was driving a different solar car from last time. The model was the same but not the smell. It was apparently a rental and not for public use. It was a privately rented car meant for public welfare. Another datum demonstrating that public authority types liked to use these government-issued machines for personal use.

Kunugi made reservations at a Japanese restaurant at the top of an antique real shop.

Japanese cuisine contained many dishes difficult to re-create with synthetic ingredients. Produce notwithstanding, animal proteins all had to be synthetically produced, and so a cooking method replicating "rawness" was near impossible.

That was why it was so expensive.

They were in a private room.

She could tell it was a nice restaurant because the cameras mounted on the walls weren't visible. As a police measure, every real shop was equipped to record all actions by patrons. Especially in eating and drinking establishments, where people spent long periods of time, the area patrol would install surveillance units to record a facial image of everyone who came in. To respect their privacy their conversation wouldn't be actively listened to, but the recorded images and voice data would be saved for a period of time, and if any patrons were later involved in a crime the recording would be released by the police to the courts.

In low-ranking restaurants the mics and cameras were exposed. You knew your conversation wasn't being monitored in real time, but people were opposed to being recorded, and when you thought about the image of you eating being broadcast somewhere else, no amount of familiarity would reassure you.

A high-ranking restaurant recorded the same data.

"That must be it." Kunugi pointed at the light fixture on the wall with his eyes. That was where the camera was.

"All right, I'm screwed. I'm going to have to eat something I've never had before. Could you order for me?"

Kunugi looked at the menu on the monitor and had it downloaded into his own. It was set up so that once you ordered, the cost of the meal would be withdrawn from the account of the monitor's owner.

"Please don't go overboard. If you don't have enough funds to cover the food you've ordered, the difference gets deducted from me, since I'm eating with you."

"It wasn't like *this* in the past," Kunugi said as he punched keys. "When I was young, it was all credit cards. But it got to be too much data to analyze, right? There was a time lag between the charge and the payment, which meant there was always a debt at some point. It used to be you bought confidence. These days you can't confide in anyone. But seriously—what is this sashimi made of?"

"Sashimi is sashimi," Shizue said, but Kunugi said, "It's *different*. It used to be you cut up something that was once alive and then ate it. I think when I first joined the force we celebrated by eating the flesh of a real dead animal. That's the last thing I clearly remember. All right, I'll have the sashimi."

Kunugi tapped randomly on the keyboard and smiled, proud of himself.

It was endearing. It had been a long time since Shizue felt endeared.

As soon as he'd inputted his order Kunugi's posture collapsed.

"Do you think synthetic food really doesn't have any effect on the human body?" he asked.

"A public authority like you shouldn't be saying things like that."

"Nah, the fact that the government approved it doesn't necessarily make it safe. It's tied in directly with the biofood industry."

"Wouldn't it be exposed by the media, then?"

"Impossible," Kunugi said with a frown. "I'm an incompetent local functionary. They're not letting me investigate missing people, much less murder cases. The biofood industry has rooted into everything from the Department of Food and Welfare and even central administration. With its growth in the past five years it has the whole world in its hands. They're saying synthetic food products are what's keeping this country's economy afloat. No challenging that."

"Then…you shouldn't mix up your social standing. You're being recorded."

Kunugi huffed through his nose at Shizue's criticism. "When I was young, the biofood industry was a venture business. It started taking off about twenty years ago. What was that all about? Suddenly everyone wanted it, and it became really popular. The best minds in business transferred to that industry."

"There can't be a single exact cause for that."

"I dunno. I think the country gave them free rein."

"That was because cloning technology had finally gotten a foothold."

The moral standard for clone technology had also been established around that time, Shizue remembered. Shizue couldn't be sure what exactly the moral code was on biocultures. Maybe they'd been groping for a different, more ethical methodology at the time.

Kunugi tilted his head. "That's an alternative."

"Alternative…"

"What I mean is, as far as I can remember, acceptance of cloning only became widespread after the boom went down in flames. Cloning used to be harshly criticized. What's more, everyone was suddenly all for the databasing of everyone's DNA."

"Ahh." Shizue had heard of that much too.

"There was also the brazen idea of using the DNA data registration system in professional discrimination."

"Registration system…"

"Of course it was a national operation. I believe they got halfway through it. They knew it would be a definitive way to distinguish work classes. And much better than assigning numbers. Also really useful in criminal investigations. Though they're adopting this at the police station. It's more effective as evidence than fingerprints. If they have a prior record, DNA can find them. In other words it's used in place of family registries and ID cards."

"If I recall, weren't Human Protective Services vehemently opposed to that?"

"Yeah. But it's like you said earlier, it's probably correct to assume they couldn't analyze the data. I mean a private company could figure it out so easily."

"You mean there were technical obstacles," Shizue said.

"There were no problems biotechnologically. The issue was dealing with the information. It's not like how we have these things now."

Kunugi tapped at the monitor in his hand a couple times.

"There is an immense amount of information encoded in genes. Plus every individual is different, right? There just wasn't a way to even properly organize the system to analyze DNA. Half the police budget alone has been spent on systematizing our information on ex-convicts. The DNA project was going to cover every single person in the country! Besides, can you imagine the shitstorm we'd be facing if there were an information leak? Think of how opposed you were to the idea of distributing private information on children. If you think about it—no, you don't even have to think. The fact is, misuse of DNA information would lead to infinitely worse consequences. Half-assed data analysis could snowball into a national problem. That's why the plan was dismantled midcourse. And at that point, the government got itself in debt with the industry."

"Debt?"

"Yeah, they'd apparently spent an outrageous sum setting this up, but for nothing, right? The industry launched its own project of epic proportions specifically for that system, but since it was never adopted, their work was all for naught. Billions in investments were totally sunk. The citizens couldn't be asked to shoulder the entire cost, naturally. They had no need to. The government had to fill the hole they'd created."

Cloning was the solution.

Or so they say, Kunugi left implied.

"Medically speaking the deployment wasn't so lacking. Tissue culture technology was far more advanced in other countries. That alone made it difficult for the government to pay out its debt. That's why I'm convinced the laws encouraging the complete switch-over from animal to man-made animal protein five years ago are rooted in the failure of the government's system. It passed under the auspices of animal protection or environmentalism, but the venture capitalists are the ones who grew fat from the plan."

It was true that this country was a step ahead in man-made food stuffs technology.

What Kunugi said was entirely plausible.

Still...

Regardless of the backstory, the fact remained that the country was poised to adopt legislation banning the killing of animals for their flesh. There were more than a few voices of concern regarding the effects that synthesized food had on humans. Concerns were still expressed today, but even without them, humans had long ago lost the skills needed for self-sufficiency. *Generally speaking, this was the most appropriate outcome for all*, Shizue thought.

As they pondered these things, the synthetic sushi arrived.

It definitely looked high class. Aside from a few vegetables everything was synthetic, but the cuisine was real. The ingredients were still prepared and presented in a particular way.

Though of course Shizue couldn't know how exact a replica it was.

The complete conversion to synthetic ingredients took place five years ago, but organic ingredients were unavailable long before then, and synthetic products had been popular for a while.

Kunugi popped a piece of sashimi into his mouth and then made a strange face.

"Is it anything like that sashimi you said you were fed when you first joined the police force?"

Kunugi swallowed the sashimi and muttered, *Yeah*...

"I don't know."

"The monitor tells me it's got the exact same chemical makeup, and it's been put together exactly the same way, and that the coloring and texture should be identical. I just can't judge without having a real sense of the original."

"It must be the same," Kunugi said, bored. "But I'm not completely satisfied. Why is it so difficult to describe the sense of taste or smell? I just don't know how to describe how this is different."

Completely unsatisfied.

"More importantly..."

Shizue pulled chopsticks out of a sterilized paper sleeve.

"Did you have something you wanted to discuss with me?"

"Right," Kunugi said and adjusted himself.

"Pardon the bulletin."

"Well, let's be frank. This is just going to make my food taste bad, so say it quickly. Put it this way. I'm..."

Busy, Shizue said only to herself.

"Actually." Kunugi sat up. "You think I'm too informal in the way I talk, don't you?"

"I don't think that."

But since he'd mentioned it, yes, he spoke too casually. Still.

She hadn't noticed.

"Thank God. I only know how to talk this one way, you know? So yeah, I'll be frank. I guess I have, you know…serious doubts about this serial killing investigation."

It must have been difficult for him to explain.

"This time there've been four people killed in the vicinity. Actually, one of the murders took place farther away from the others, but they still think it's one perpetrator. There have been five victims. They've all been female. The oldest was sixteen, the youngest thirteen. The sixteen-year-old had just had a birthday, and the thirteen-year-old would have been fourteen in another month. Suffice it to say they were all around fourteen or fifteen."

Kunugi traced numbers on his plate with the tip of his chopsticks.

"The oldest one had been held back a year in communication sessions because of an illness. In other words all of the victims were in a section for fourteen-year-olds."

Shizue had followed most accounts of the crimes following the media coverage, but this last detail was news to her.

"So right now that's the only common denominator. But this Ryu Kawabata kid was a different gender and in a different session. Because he didn't share this common denominator, he was excluded from the case. All of this is public information."

"Not a confidential investigative matter."

"No. Or what I mean is that the information the police have been able to gather on this case is no different from what the average person already knows. By the way, do you remember the serial killings from four years ago on the west side?"

These kinds of serial killings occurred every year. Shizue felt like she remembered something about the case four years ago, but she didn't really know. She told Kunugi as much. As a matter of fact, the serial killings last year and the year before that were also so similar. It was hard to differentiate them.

"Last year six people were killed," Kunugi said. "Two men and four women, and they were all between the ages of nineteen and twenty-six. But you see, they all had one thing in common. They were all employed by the same conglomerate. What's more they were all employed at around the same time."

"Scion Enterprises, right?" She'd forgotten about it but she'd heard this enough times to go practically insane at the time.

"*That's right*," Kunugi said. "The killer still hasn't been caught. The investigation is ongoing, but no one's sure it'll ever be solved. There are no witnesses to date. The rest of this is off the record."

"You're still being recorded here."

"As long as I don't get violent or kill you or anything no one will listen to these tapes. They can't. And the recordings are erased after a year. But get this, last year we had our sights on a real criminal suspect. We were 80 percent sure, but we weren't even able to arrest him in the end."

"Why not?"

"He had an alibi. Of the six incidents, he couldn't possibly have been at the scene of two of the killings."

"Well then."

"It's no use. It doesn't matter if you were 80 percent sure. You could have been 90 percent certain and it still wouldn't matter. There is no gray area in these matters. You need to be 100 percent to be black. Anything less than that is white."

Kunugi responded that they were 100 percent on four of the cases.

"But there were problems with two of the incidents, right?"

"What I'm saying is that because the six killings were determined to be part of one serial killing spree, the percentage of certainty went down. There was no need to aggregate the certainty like that. If we had just considered them separate cases, it would have been settled. This suspect was responsible for four of the six killings. There's no doubt about that, as far as I can tell."

"But that wasn't the final determination."

"*Exactly*," Kunugi said, and tossed a mound of white rice into his mouth. "It had to be a serial killer, they decided."

"I seem to recall this was a really drawn-out investigation, and if the investigation unit concluded as such there must be a reason. Either way, it wasn't like one person made the decision."

"Maybe. According to witness testimony and the circumstances of the scene, there were no accomplices. Just the one killer. If it really were a serial killing spree, an alibi would be hard to come by."

His tone implied more.

"You're suggesting that the events last year weren't related? In which case, if the two killings for which your suspect had an alibi were unrelated, are you suggesting the last two cases might have been copycat killings?"

"That's where I run into problems."

"Problems?"

"It'd be simple if of the string of six killings the last two were different, and I wouldn't be here talking about any of this. Unfortunately, this prime suspect's alibis were for the third and fifth murders."

"Third and fifth?"

"Yes. At the time the third killing took place, details from the previous two incidents hadn't been released yet, nor had we determined that it was a serial killing. In other words a copycat wouldn't make any sense."

"Wouldn't make sense..."

"Not at that point. But that notwithstanding, the second and third victims happened to share a lot in common. On top of which the guy we had pinned for the other four incidents had a serious communications handicap, making it impossible to ever come across the third victim. It's improbable that our suspect had an accomplice."

"Then he probably isn't your criminal. There's no logical consistency. Isn't it a simple conclusion?"

"That's what I thought too until I read the reports. But you see, the third and fifth incidents were truly different. From the other four. On paper they all had a lot in common. It looked like it had to have been one person committing all the murders. But..."

Kunugi set down his chopsticks and scratched his forehead with his middle finger.

"Hear me out on this one before you think I'm crazy."

"I already do."

"Right. That's fine then. So outside of the third and fifth killings, the other four incidents all took place on *butsumetsu*."

"Butsumetsu..."

"You don't know? In the ancient Asian calendar there was a repeating cycle of auspicious days. Like a 'lucky week' every month. That's the butsumetsu. If you look in any old almanac you'll see it in there. It's based on the day of the Buddha's death."

"I know what it is. I just remember it being meaningless."

"It is indeed. Just from what I've read, there's no basis for the worries of dyed-in-the-wool believers. Up until about ten years ago you'd see these butsumetsu dates still listed in calendars. People would plan things around them. Stupid things, like signing contracts and delivering shipments. They were planning dates by baseless barometers. You can't call that a reasonable circumstance."

"The baselessness of it is what allows you to make a value judgment, right?"

"What's *that* supposed to mean?" Kunugi responded, furrowing his brow.

Shizue said, "They're divinations."

"I suppose they are. No one believes this crap anymore though, which is precisely why no one noticed it."

"*You* noticed. But then you said it's only four of the six murders that took place on butsumetsu dates. Maybe it's just a coincidence."

A coincidence.

There are no such things as coincidences. Is calling it a coincidence an excuse? Hinako Sakura would know a lot more about this… Shizue found herself preoccupied.

"You're probably right," Kunugi said in the interstice in which Shizue was at a loss for words. "But that's exactly why I think it's so questionable. It screws with the story. But you know what else? Our guy actually screwed up. One of his victims was left alive."

"Screwed up?"

"He didn't get it done. He was arrested six days after the last killing. He escaped while in holding, and when we caught him he had a murder weapon on him. And this is the thing. The sixth killing was supposed to look like an accident. The timing doesn't match, but the four other killings, plus the one failed attempt, all took place on butsumetsu dates."

"The butsumetsu."

It was still unfamiliar to her ears.

Shizue started to empty her plates.

She wasn't savoring the food so much as consuming it.

Because she was always thinking about something else.

"As I recall, there are six kinds of butsumetsu, right? Like, the *daian* day and *yubiki* day, etcetera. I don't know any others, but…"

"You're right. There's also *akaguchi* and *senbu*. I mean, we still have a seven-day week named according to some weird mythology, don't we? I think it's the same thing. Just that with the six-day system each day meant something like 'get stuff done,' or 'don't do anything.' You're not supposed to do anything bad on the butsumetsu."

In that case…

"There are many cases of crimes committed, repeatedly, on these dates. I'm sure it's a case-by-case thing, whatever sets off these periods, but if, say, there's a repeating six-day period of crimes, wouldn't you forcibly have to commit the next crime on the same day later? Regardless of the butsumetsu? But it doesn't work that way," Kunugi said.

"The six-day cycle occasionally has to adjust over a day. It's not always necessarily a six-day cycle. Plus this guy was a fanatic. For calendars. Actually not so much a fanatic as an obsessed collector. He collected calendars from the late nineteenth to mid-twentieth century. The police just considered him a classic art collector, but I didn't. He must have been looking at those calendars because he was curious to see how events of the past coincided with these auspicious dates. Comparing the events to their calendar years. Predictions in hindsight."

"Compare?"

"Comparisons. Calendars are made before the dates come to pass, right? And old calendars went so far as to tell you which days were good and which were bad. He must have been studying up on whether bad things did indeed take place on those bad days and good things on good days. It got worse and worse."

Bad things had to happen on bad days.

"You're saying the butsumetsu killings are a self-fulfilling prophecy?"

That's ridiculous.

"Isn't it?" Kunugi said. "But... I think it's the truth. In the end, people's motives for killing each other are really trite, no? When it happens it's always a big deal, of course. In the long history of humanity, an incalculable number of people have been killed, but how many of these murders seem justified when you hear the motive? Money, revenge... nothing's really worth taking human lives."

She couldn't but nod.

He was absolutely right.

Murder sans motive had become a popular cliché sometime toward the end of the twentieth century. But it wasn't as though motives for murder became more tenuous with time. Motives for murder had been lame since the beginning of time.

The value of human life was over-exaggerated in past arguments.

When you think of it that *way*, Kunugi started, and glared at the fish-shaped food product on his plate suspiciously, even though it had no bones.

"When you think of it that way, this guy would not commit any crimes on days that didn't fall on the butsumetsu. It's the daian," Kunugi said.

"But the MO is otherwise identical, right?"

"The shapes and kinds of weapons used, the way the bodies were disposed of, and of course, the victims' commonalities—these are all definitely related. However, if you look at the details there were things that didn't correspond."

"You're talking about just the anomalies in the two cases you think were committed by a different culprit?"

"That's right. You can distinguish the two cases from the other four with points of difference. Actually…"

Kunugi bit into the head of his boneless fish-shaped food. Then.

"Something's missing," he said.

"Missing?"

"Yeah, missing. With the third and fifth murders. There was an internal organ missing from each of them."

"What?"

"Last year the case was brutal. The murderer took apart the insides of his victims, and the remains were well…very damaged. Scattered everywhere.

"We probably shouldn't be talking about this over food," Kunugi continued. "But…I've told you the worst of it, so I'm going to keep going. You see, there wasn't a whole body's worth of parts in the remains we collected from the scene. The liver was never found."

"In just those two cases?"

"Yeah, *just* those two. But that any of them at all were missing livers…Anyway, we decided that a wild animal must have eaten it, but what's a wild animal, right?"

"There are cats and dogs in Section C."

"The bodies were found in Section B. There are no cats or dogs there."

"What does it mean?"

"I don't know." Kunugi played with his chopsticks. "I have no idea. All I know is that these six murders can't have been part of the same streak. There had to be, at the very least, two different sets of murders. That's my opinion. It's an opinion that got me reprimanded, but well, for what it's worth."

Reprimanded. Ishida had been saying something about that.

"I was reprimanded," Kunugi said shamefully. "I was trying to be constructive, but I got the veto from on high. I was speaking out of line, disobeying the normal protocol for investigation, reading data outside of the case's jurisdiction. I suppose I deserved to be scolded. I lucked out though. The old lieutenant didn't want to touch any sort of controversy because he was up for a promotion. They just reprimanded me. In the end no one heard my theory."

Kunugi pushed aside his flatware and leaned his face over the table.

"This time it's in our jurisdiction."

"Kunugi, you aren't—"

"Am I wrong?"

"No, it's not that. All we've said tonight is that these are not one string of murders. Last year's cases are different. Still…"

Kunugi clasped his hands up behind his head and waited for Shizue to finish her thought.

"Including the discovery of Ryu Kawabata in the area directly adjacent to ours, there have now been six murders. As you said, the Kawabata case isn't considered part of the serial killing. The reason being he's the only male victim so far. Conversely, the other five are being treated as part of the same serial killing spree. But you're asking whether that's appropriate?

"In other words, the murders believed to be related aren't, and the one murder believed to be unrelated is."

"I can't say anything about the Kawabata case." Kunugi touched his monitor and turned up the AC. "But as it stands, the reality is that this one case stands out. What concerns me though is what these victims have in common. Is it truly just that they are all girls of approximately the same age who live near each other? Isn't that too easy? There's got to be another way to look at this. Once we figure that out, I think we'll be able to fit the Kawabata case into this too."

Kunugi was looking for some key concept to neatly explain all the murders. Something like last year's butsumetsu theory.

There was probably a foreign idiom software for this. Certainly if you sussed out the rules a structure would appear. And if you had the structure, you had the translation and the definition.

But.

Shizue wondered if it could go that well. Unlike the imaginary space created by numbers, this guy, and reality, was full of impurities and discord.

Nothing could be predicted.

Nothing was going as planned.

Reality was something unusually scrambled and gross. It was an indefinite space without straight lines, a filthy world in which pure things could not exist. Even if you looked for something that happened to be beautiful, it was pointless.

Shizue started to realize that the idea that the world operated under one pretense was delusional.

"Do you have any clues?" Shizue asked, as Kunugi turned his head to the side.

"I was about to ask you the same thing."

"I'm not Ryu Kawabata's counselor."

"I know that. But your associates haven't been very cooperative, and besides, I don't know any of them. If I tried contacting them in private, I'd be reported in a heartbeat. Also…"

"Also what?"

"I think I have a key to the missing Yuko Yabe."

"Key…"

"You said it before, but she might be the next victim. Wasn't she into *deformée characters*?"

"What are deformée characters?"

"When I was a kid they were called comics," Kunugi said in an unusually serious tone. "Before that they were called manga. In other words it's non-real animation."

Yuko Yabe wasn't that into animation, as far as Shizue recalled. All she did remember was that Yabe's room was filled with toy figures. When she told Kunugi all this he answered, "She was a collector, then."

"I don't think she was a collector necessarily."

"But you gotta admit that these days you'd have to be collecting in order to find much of this stuff."

"I remember them being things her guardians gave her. I don't know if it was her father or mother, but I have it written down that one of them gave her these toys in her childhood, and that she kept them safe with her. Probably…"

Probably…

Her memory was hopelessly foggy. Diffuse. But Shizue did have some memory of hearing all this. If she looked at her counseling files, she'd know immediately. There were records of all conversations with the children. Even if compressed, the record would be totally accurate. Memories were all converted to digits. That way they would never deteriorate.

It could even be duplicated.

"You should check with the data we just handed over to the police," Shizue said, but as soon as she did she went silent for a long moment.

"But...you can't."

"That's why I offered you dinner. All right, so Kawabata it is."

"By the way, Kawabata's optical, uh..."

"*Animation*," Kunugi said.

"Its origin is the word *animism*, apparently. Because it's similarly an image that shouldn't move that does, as if possessed by its own spirit. I can't remember exactly. Everything on our monitors is an image, and most of them move."

"It might move but I didn't say anything about *fucking spirits*," the off-duty cop swore.

"Actually, the first victim was an aspiring character designer, and there's record of her having exhibited at the D.C. Biennial to a lot of acclaim. And the second victim was connected to that character—what was it? It's supposed to be the most popular anime character right now."

Kunugi uttered a proper noun that rang an bell, but it wasn't quite right.

She knew it was slightly off, but Shizue couldn't definitively correct him either. It didn't matter. It had nothing to do with this case.

"She was a regular on the fan site. The fourth victim was also a huge fan and even dressed up like the character. Made her own costumes and everything. The third victim was the one who got wrapped up in defor-mée characters. The other two had nothing to do with it.

"Ryu Kawabata is different too. In his case, he was into works from several decades ago. If I recall, he was into what I think was called *cel* animation. He did collect that. We're talking about artifacts from over thirty years ago. Yuko Yabe also. Her collectibles were not from the present. Other than those two, we're talking about three out of five like-lihood. What do you think about that?"

Hmm. Kunugi let out a low sound.

"I know. I'm saying this knowing all that full well, but well...it's as if wholly unrelated to the character, the other two victims are..."

"Like I said, they were missing internal organs," Kunugi said, his dark expression drawn.

CHAPTER 013

LIVE DOVES WERE really creepy.

The way they cooed, their stink, their texture, everything. But mostly their brilliant beady eyes. You couldn't guess what they saw. Those eyes rejected Hazuki. No, Hazuki's whole world.

"Groooossss."

Mio turned away after having stared at the doves cautiously.

"Animals are so disgusting. You like these things, Makino?"

Hazuki couldn't respond.

The window had been left open for the doves to come in and out, and the whole room had been fitted out for them. Hazuki could count six doves in all.

About a third of the room was dedicated to the doves.

Ayumi had said it was a bird*house*, but it was more like a dove*room*. In the space that remained were a table and three chairs, and against the wall was a very simple bed.

Yuko Yabe was sleeping on that bed.

Standing at the doorway was Rey Mao.

They were in an illegal building structure on the roof of Ayumi's residence.

This was Mio's idea of a refuge for Yuko.

There was no denying that even though they were in Section A there were no sensors or surveillance units here in the doveroom. There wasn't even an occupancy indicator.

It appeared to be a good hiding spot.

Except.

If you thought about it, this was also terribly inconsiderate.

In the midst of a serial murder investigation when there was probably an interrogation request out to anyone with any information, they'd hidden the one person, a sick girl no less, who had any information, and they did so without any semblance of a plan. Even a child would know this was totally dangerous.

But.

Hazuki ignored all of that.

They'd taken turns carrying Yuko on their backs beyond Section C borders.

The human body was squirmy, lukewarm, and heavy. The way they sweat, breathed, and smelled was intolerable.

Hazuki didn't know why she had to get her hands dirty with this. For that matter she didn't know why they had to move her to a different location or hide her in the first place.

Still, Hazuki was overcome with a feeling of obligation that couldn't be reasonably explained.

It was because Ayumi hadn't refused.

She thought. For some reason, Ayumi hadn't objected whatsoever to Mio's reckless plan to cart Yuko out to her place.

Just that…

Ayumi'd said she didn't want to have to touch Yuko.

That was why Hazuki had gone along like it was the most natural thing on earth.

Yeah, that was what it was.

After the matter had been decided, Hazuki had stopped by her home with Mio. If they'd parted ways there it would have been over.

But Hazuki had left again. With Mio's magic they'd tricked the occupancy sign to read positive. As far as anyone was concerned, Hazuki was in her bedroom right now.

After going to such illegal lengths she was forced to help move a squishy body.

But the transfer itself had gone smoothly.

Barring the business district, there was little human activity at night in the city. There was no fear of being seen by anyone if they took the route away from the weather observation point. They still ran the risk of being stopped by policemen on area patrol, but there was no time to consider another route.

Fortunately Hazuki and her associates were able to finish their task without any run-ins. Ayumi's home was in a different direction than Yuko's and also far away from the scene of the murders. Whether the way was clear simply because the police weren't patroling areas not of interest to the case or if fate had simply worked in their favor, Hazuki couldn't tell.

The task was complete in approximately seventy-three minutes, and Yuko Yabe was put to bed in Ayumi's doveroom.

Hazuki looked at the birds alongside Mio. In real life, little animals were not cute.

As she watched their bellies convulse, Hazuki gradually came to the realization that her current situation was quite unusual.

She peered at Rey Mao. The unregistered girl looked somewhat like a police officer standing in front of the entrance like that. Maybe she was guarding the room, but she was just standing there quietly. Hazuki just remembered that Rey Mao hadn't uttered a single word through the whole transport.

Rey Mao suddenly jumped.

The doors flew open.

Ayumi was standing just beyond them.

Rey Mao widened her eyes in surprise for a moment, then looked concerned.

Ayumi walked into the room without so much as looking at Rey Mao and put the box in her hands down on the table.

In the box was junk food and bottles of water.

"Just what we needed," Mio said with a laugh.

"Rations? They're disgusting! More importantly, you think she can take medicine now?"

Ayumi brought out a pill case from the box.

"All I have are these calming supplements."

"That's no good!" Mio interrupted.

"Getting drugs nowadays is really hard. If I try sneaking this stuff out I'll be instantly under suspicion."

"I'll say I took it."

"If they check you more than twice the medical center will access your file."

"I'll make something up," Ayumi said and moved to the adjacent room. "The sooner she's out of here the better." Ayumi waved her hand at Yuko.

"Even if she gets better she can't leave here," Mio said.

"We're not keeping her till she recovers. We're keeping her till the case is solved."

"Out of the question."

"I'm sorry." A frail voice. Yuko lifted her face.

"I'm sorry I'm…"

Causing so much trouble, she seemed to say.

"Just take your medicine. Then go back to sleep," Ayumi said. She moved to lift Yuko up. Hazuki tried to read Yuko's face, but Mio was blocking her view.

"Hey, Kono. You can say what you want, but you know that aspirin won't do anything, right? People were so worried about side effects it's been stripped of all its potency."

"I know," Ayumi said without intonation.

"If you know, then don't bother giving us placebos!" Mio whipped her head and scrunched her nose, grabbed a package of junk food from the table, and went to the bedside.

"The medicine will take effect better if you eat even just this little bit first. Here. This should get you back on track."

What would being back on track mean? Hazuki had no idea.

Mio said, "I'll have a bite myself," and pulled a chair up to the table, facing Rey Mao, who was still at the door. She told her *you should sit down too*. Rey Mao didn't respond and simply glared at her.

"Why are you fronting? You know you're hungry. I don't care if you think you're savage or an animal or whatever, but everybody needs to eat or they'd die. Isn't that right, Makino?"

Mio pushed some food at Hazuki.

"Even the grossest synthfood tastes good when you're hungry. Just sit down, Catwoman. Or are you still worried about what Ayumi here said?"

Rey Mao turned her body about-face so that her back was to Mio.

"Whatever."

Mio put the dummy meat in her mouth, brought some over to the wire fencing, and plopped down.

"You're *not* cute, you know. These doves are cuter than you. Ugh. This is meat? It tastes like meat. Ayumi, what do doves eat, anyway? Do they eat meat?"

From the room next door they heard a voice say *I don't know.*

"You don't know? C'mon, they eat meat, right?" Mio started tearing strips off the meat and asked Hazuki.

"I don't think so..."

Before Hazuki finished answering, Rey Mao said, "Doves don't eat meat."

"They don't? I guess meat-eating birds would be brutal. Like they'd resort to eating each other. They really don't though, huh?"

Rey Mao said *they don't eat meat* at almost the same time Ayumi yelled at them to shut up.

"What's wrong with you two?" Mio kept nibbling on her food and sulked. Ayumi stared her down cold.

"Don't interfere."

"You feed them, right?"

"No."

"But aren't they hungry?"

"I don't know." Ayumi was seated right in front of Hazuki.

"These birds just moved in on their own. I don't know what they eat or what they do. If I leave them alone they take over the whole room. That's why I put up the fence. So that they wouldn't take over any more space."

"Then why don't you shoo them out? Or put screens on your windows."

"This many doves doesn't bother me. You, here—that bothers me."

Mio scrunched her nose again. *Tch.*

"I'm worse than a bird, huh?"

"At least birds can take a hint. If I mark my territory the birds won't cross the line. Dividing land and selling it is a human endeavor. Birds don't care where you put them. And I don't need this space to live or anything. I have no reason to kick them out."

"You cohabit, then."

"The only thing is, if I let them come over here then I can't eat here."

"You're more pragmatic than I thought," Mio said, bored, drinking water from the pack. "I don't know about the birds, but this is still your territory right, Ayumi? They invaded *your* place. Accommodating them is the same as keeping them as pets. Why don't you just eat them?"

"Doves..."

"You can *eat* them?" Hazuki blurted out.

"Can't you? They used to. Right?"

Mio looked at Rey Mao. Before Rey Mao could answer, Ayumi said *yes you can* very matter-of-factly to Hazuki.

"Have you eaten one before...Ayumi?"

Why. Why did Hazuki feel fragile all of a sudden? Asking her such stupid things.

Ayumi faced the fence and bared the nape of her neck.

"I've never eaten one, no."

"Of course you wouldn't."

"I don't know how to prepare them."

"You prepare them?"

Hazuki's eyes shifted to the strange object that moved around by the wire fence. Its form was organic but its movement was machinelike. It was made of a shiny material, but it was hard to imagine what it felt like to the touch.

It definitely couldn't make itself understood. That was why it was so frightening.

This small animal had nothing in common with them.

"*Dove preparation*, huh?" Mio let out. "Sounds like a lot of work. I don't think I could eat something like that."

"Not just doves. I couldn't eat anything that was once alive."

"But people used to. And it looked like this." Mio took a bite out of her synthetic meat. Hazuki's hand hovered over her own container of meat.

"Dove cuisine is not normal in this country."

"So they eat it mostly...abroad?"

"I guess they must have to kill it and take it apart," Mio said. She waved at the birds on the other side of the fence.

"I read somewhere that doves used to be a symbol of peace."

"This one's pretty combative if you ask me," Ayumi said in response to Hazuki.

"He looks like war," Mio said with a laugh.

"They would totally eat each other."

"No they wouldn't," Rey Mao said coldly. "They only eat cereals. Only humans eat everything."

"But humans eat nothing. You know, I remember reading something once. That even animals that only eat grass will resort to eating meat if left hungry long enough. Pigeons look so fierce, I bet if they were left unfed long enough they'd start eating each other."

"Animals don't commit cannibalism."

"I don't know about that," Mio said almost regretfully. Then she looked through the fence again. "I wonder if living things taste good."

"You want to try, Tsuzuki?" Ayumi said.

"Aren't you curious?" Mio said.

Mio turned her head to Hazuki. "Don't you love animals?"

"I mean, I like them, but—"

"If you like them don't you want to eat them?"

"Eating them means..."

Killing them.

"Right."

Ayumi grabbed a food pack and said, "You can't eat them unless you kill them."

"Ayumi..."

"Makino would never kill an animal." Ayumi handed the pack to Rey Mao, who remained standing. Rey Mao accepted it without a word. *Why is that?* Mio asked.

"Because it's cruel? Because it's gross?"

"Because she's human," Ayumi said.

"That's a pretty obvious answer even for you, Kono. Didn't we already decide humans are also animals this afternoon? I think humans aren't animals anymore. Animals actually eat other animals, but humans have become totally emancipated from having to kill to eat."

"Emancipated?"

"Yes. We're no longer qualified to be called animals."

Speaking of which...

Mio had been saying humans had abandoned the animal kingdom. That timidity had, over a long period of time, forced humans out of the food chain.

"Humans are still animals."

"I don't know about that."

"I told you before. Animals live only to live. So if they're full they don't eat. They don't do anything in excess. Here..."

Ayumi opened a package of junk food.

"This does not run or hide and has plenty of protein, so why would a human go out of their way to prepare a dove? That's all. The absorption of excess nutrients only hinders the sustenance of life."

Mio said, "I still don't know about that," and started chewing on her second piece of dummy meat.

"I mean, going back to cannibalism, if you were starving and about to die, wouldn't you kill one of these doves, Ayumi?"

"I suppose I would," Ayumi said. "It'd be easier than eating you, that's certain."

"I'm edible too now?"

"If the situation were so bad that I would consider eating doves, it goes without saying I'd have to consider you as well. For that matter Hazuki would have to consider eating doves too."

"And killing them?"

"Yes, *killing them.* You have to kill it to eat it."

"I...I could never eat a dove or kill one for that matter," Hazuki said.

Why not.

Was it because as Mio had said, "it's cruel," or because "it's gross"?

She thought it was something else altogether.

Mio was definitely right, but it was more than that.

It was because it would be sad.

Yeah, that seemed the closest description of why she felt she couldn't do that. It would be sad.

"Animals," Hazuki said without power. She didn't command the gravitas that Ayumi and Mio did. "Animals don't think about how sad it is for other animals they kill, do they?"

"No, they don't," Ayumi responded without a pause. "Animals don't think of anything, actually."

"They don't?"

"I wonder what it feels like not to think of anything at all," Mio said as she looked over at Hazuki's face.

"But you know, I read somewhere that animals do have a consciousness. It said it's not like animals don't have emotions. I mean, I don't know about lesser life-forms," Ayumi said.

"Having a consciousness or emotions is different from thinking."

"Different?"

"In order to think, you need to be able to establish time. If you have no sense of time, you can use logic but you can't think. Animals don't know how to gauge time. Mammals only live for the moment."

"Oh yeah? But mammals have memories. They learn."

"They learn, they memorize, sure. But whether it's something that happens in a moment or over ten years, one event is still only ever one event for an animal. There's no depth. It won't matter if you can connect events—if they don't have any depth they won't be empathetic to a situation. So they are forever only in the now. That's what my sister told me," Ayumi said.

Mio stared at the ceiling, food still in her mouth, and eventually said, "I see."

"So you're saying they have the memory necessary for pattern recognition but they have no concept of the passage of time and therefore cannot connect pattern to pattern from separate experiential events? Now I get it. That's amazing," Mio said.

Did she really understand?

Because Hazuki didn't.

Why couldn't she just be "forever only in the now"?

Why couldn't that idea be learned?

Hazuki did not understand this at all.

Sad things were sad.

That's why humans stopped killing animals, Hazuki thought.

Hazuki didn't know anything about transcending the ecosystem or protecting the earth's natural environment the way Mio did, and she hadn't really thought about it in close personal terms, but everyone knew it was bad to kill animals and eat them. That was why humans had stopped eating animals.

Because it was sad.

"You think it's sad because you *don't think* of that thing as a dove," Ayumi said.

"That's not true. That's…"

A dove. It was nowhere as cute as it was on a monitor screen, but it was the right design.

"This is a dove."

"All right. Then what's a dove to you? Is it part of your tribe, does it menace your existence, is it something you want to eat, or do you not care about it at all? An animal will put you in one of those four categories."

"It's none of those things."

Would it be something she didn't care about if she was so positive about her answer?

"It's something I don't care about," Mio continued. "Since it looks like I can't eat it and it's so gross. I totally don't care."

"What do you mean by 'gross'?"

Ayumi faced the fencing.

"It's because you don't see doves in there but humans shaped like doves."

"What? Human-shaped doves?" Mio ripped into the synthetic meat. "Why would I think that? That's no bird."

"It's only gross to you because you're thinking of them in human terms. Same thing when something is cute." As Ayumi spoke, in exactly the same way she would normally, she handed Hazuki a bottle of mineral water. Hazuki took it without a word.

"Pitying and adoring animals are both acts of human arrogance. In fact I see no big difference between protecting and hunting them. Human logic is only understood by fellow humans."

"Feeling sorry for animals is arrogant?"

"Not your arrogance, Hazuki, but humanity's arrogance," Mio said.

"Hazuki's a human, remember?" Ayumi said.

Hazuki felt like she'd been cast off or something.

Then all of a sudden, Rey Mao spun around. Mio was no doubt stunned, coughing up a little water. "What's wrong with you?" she said. Rey Mao crumpled up the food packaging and said *all done.*

"Did it move?" Ayumi said.

Rey Mao didn't answer, saying instead "I'm going home."

Ayumi looked outside and grumbled, "You'd know."

"When it sounds. Went east."

"East—that's the opposite direction. But it's really an animal-like feeling, isn't it? I'm fed up."

"Hey, Kono. What do you mean *did it move?* What moved? What sound?"

"On our way here there were some area patrols on the street ahead."

"Area patrols? I didn't notice. Makino, did you notice anything?"

Of course she hadn't.

"Then you, Catwoman. You gonna go like that?"

Rey Mao opened the door without responding, turned around and gave the room a once-over, then pointed her gaze at the entrance to the next room.

"Be careful," Ayumi said. Rey Mao lifted one hand and took one step outside.

"See you, Mio."

There was a very short pause.

Just then, as Hazuki stared at the fingertips Rey Mao lifted, just in that brief moment, Hazuki felt unsure and looked to Mio for reassurance. Mio had no sort of reaction, and with food bits still on her cheeks she just sat there looking dazed. While Hazuki was looking at that small dazed face, the door slammed shut.

Hazuki looked for Rey Mao's back, though the shut door hid it.

Needless to say, the door—a quadrilateral affair with no decorations—broadcast not one piece of information on Rey Mao's current location, distance, or speed of departure. Nonetheless, Hazuki knew implicitly that Rey Mao was going farther and farther away.

She looked at her monitor. It was already eleven o'clock.

Hazuki stared briefly at the doves and then left Ayumi's house along with Mio. She said *goodbye* in a very soft voice, but Ayumi probably did not hear it.

For some reason Mio was silent as well and barely spoke to Hazuki until she reached home, where, thanks to Mio, the occupancy sign was lit even though no one was inside.

It's as if nothing happened.

Time stood still in her house.

No, it was like it continued to flow despite being stopped. No part of the configuration had changed.

Whether Hazuki was inside or not did not really matter.

On her dining table was the meal that came out while she was gone, in exactly the position it had been left, already cold.

She checked the kitchen monitor. Nothing. No visitors on the log, no items that warranted any special attention. There were two messages in her main monitor, but one was a notification of how many kilowatt minutes she'd used this month and the other was an announcement of a discount on opening new lines of electric wiring service.

There was no point looking at this stuff now, so she put her monitor on sleep mode.

As she stood in the dining area she saw a scene, a setting that had not changed at all in ten years. She began thinking every part of today had been a complete lie.

Of course she remembered the feel of Yuko on her back, the smell, the weight; but the memory had practically no reality to it.

What Mio had said was true.

The world in our monitors, the world displayed in numbers, was the truth, and what took place in actuality was all lies.

Hazuki thought.

One just had to repeat the pattern.

In the end, that was all Hazuki's past was. There was no such thing as truth in Hazuki's brief life. What she thought was her past was just an accumulation of patterns.

People misled themselves into believing they knew time or history because they could mince the repetition of patterns. They depended on their ability to measure the passage of time. They counted on their ability to count.

The digitized past was all the same.

A today identical to yesterday.

Last month, last year, last decade, the same.

In that case…

We are *the same as animals.*

Hasuki stared at her cold food and took three sips of her soup before giving up.

After hesitating for a long time she finally drained it into the garbage disposal.

The food looked like it was squirming. It made her lose her appetite.

Hazuki knew synthetic food that had never lived had no chance of moving, but she couldn't help think that meat and fish—that is, food that looked like meat and fish—looked like it was glistening, moving, fighting for its life.

Hazuki felt ill. She splashed her face with cold water and gulped down a large amount of mineral water.

This only made her feel woozier, so she took a shower and went to the room she was supposedly in this whole time—the bedroom.

She made her room pitch dark and got into bed.

She felt like she could smell just a hint of animal.

CHAPTER 014

THE NEW CORPSE was found the day after Shizue had visited Hinako. The victim, Asumi Aikawa. A fourteen-year-old girl from her lab class.

If it were one of the serial killings, Aikawa would be the sixth victim, the seventh if you included Ryu Kawabata, second if you only counted those killed in Shizue's residential district.

She was killed on a school day.

The communication session ended in the morning. That afternoon was a designated administrative break for faculty.

Even though there was no better foothold on the murder investigation, no clearer leads, and though the center still didn't know the whereabouts of Yuko Yabe, the center didn't seem any different. Not one person asked about the case. People weren't more nervous than necessary, and everyone was doing their job as usual.

It was someone else's problem.

The details of the other cases had long been returned to storage in monitors. Only the information newly delivered contained any controversy, and there was nothing unusual in the daily news. That was probably what everyone was thinking.

Shizue realized the police had probably finished processing the data on the community center's children.

For that reason perhaps, news of discovery of this dead body felt horribly unreal by the time Shizue heard it.

The news came in right after the area chief's regular communiqué had been deployed to everybody's monitors at the center.

These communiqués were sent from central and were supposedly meant to highlight model areas of health-regulatory environments, or something like that. No one read them.

This week's communiqué spotlighted the recent medical exams. Shizue's section happened to yield the highest percentage of children deemed of Triple-A health. Though 10 percent fewer Triple-A results would by no means be a bad statitistic.

Shizue should not have been thinking about her charges' performance in a health exam. The discrepancy of 10 percent fewer or more children of optimal health was hardly negligible. Instead of thinking of the 10 percent laxity she could get away with, she should have realized that the 10 percent her clients had over the average child was a feat.

A list of the children who made Triple-A status was sent to each area counselor. At the top of that list, coincidentally, was Asumi Aikawa.

Shizue didn't think that was a good sign.

The fact that Asumi Aikawa was at the top of the list was merely the coincidental result of an alphabetical order.

Still, she was the first recorded child of supreme health, only to have her second introduction to the world be as a corpse.

So.

It seemed like there were not enough people worried and too few people panicked.

Another communiqué was sent to each area counselor to make sure people went home, and after a little less than an hour on standby, the local and prefectural police were there again, another emergency meeting organized, and finally, almost everyone grasped the gravity of the situation.

Asumi Aikawa's body had been disposed of in the residential area right in the middle of Section A.

Wounds on her body were severe, and the corpse itself was dumped unceremoniously.

The area police explained the discovery in a tone neither resentful nor outraged but officious, describing the way the body was treated with a figure of speech.

"Treated like trash."

Shizue's thoughts drifted to refuse.

She'd never seen "trash" in Section A.

For ostensible upkeep of living conditions, all unnecessary and damaged goods were categorically hidden, because then it was unquestionably "clean."

In Section A, each household was held responsible for managing its own refuse. Any unusual trash that the household was not able to dispose of properly could be taken care of by the area municipality for a nominal fee. Anything the municipality could not handle went to the Prefectural Office of Living Standard Maintenance, and anything the prefecture couldn't dispose of could be collected by the National Special Waste Disposal center.

Collections were swift, clean, and expensive.

It was costlier to throw things away than to buy them.

Which was why no one threw anything away. Trash never left the home. Never left the city. Never left the prefecture.

Moreover, the fines imposed on those who illegally dumped trash were exorbitantly high. No one wanted to take the risk of throwing anything out at all.

The same went for Section B and the commercial district.

The establishments had self-imposed management.

Whatever waste couldn't be managed by individual firms was collected by the cooperative waste collection agency and dealt with periodically.

You couldn't see it from the outside.

Shizue had heard that the waste management problem was dire even in the last century, but as she had never seen mountains of trash, she had absolutely no feelings about it. No one threw anything away, and that was that.

Therefore, Shizue wondered what it meant to be comparing a corpse to trash. In a world without trash, would such an analogy work? The city was beautiful.

Still.

No, it couldn't be.

What made it dirty was simply not visible. The city was by no means clean. Shizue knew that. Since there was absolutely nothing dirty, it was impossible to know what was clean. There was no context.

The city just looked vaguely orderly. As a rule, everyone threw away their trash. That must mean that the city was overflowing with trash.

People thought the entire world was controlled, but there were things that couldn't be. Anything that couldn't be controlled, humans removed as unnecessary and then disposed of it.

Proof of this impulse to throw out the useless was in those other places—there was this so-called trash in Section C. Section C was by no means the type of slum you used to hear of in the past. It wasn't as though you couldn't set foot in it, nor was it like the area was full of the desperately poor. Section C simply couldn't pretend it was in control of anything. Because they couldn't pretend they were in control, the trash was visible. Illegally dumped waste was immediately collected in other sections, but not in Section C.

That was what came to mind when Shizue heard the word *trash*.

And generally speaking, Section C's rubbish was industrial trash no typical household would produce.

Tiles, ceramic bits, metal pipes, resin containers, wiring and tubes, magnetic film, needles...

In fact it wasn't just in households you'd never see these things. You'd just never see these things, period.

It was like a time warp.

And when the chief said *thrown out like a piece of trash*, this was what it meant to Shizue.

And all Shizue could hear when the area chief spoke were hackneyed platitudes and bureaucratic condolences, and in the end all she could think of was a corpse lying in a pit of industrial refuse.

There was no dignity in the image.

Broken things, useless objects—those were what got disposed of illegally. That stark image figured prominently in the back of Shizue's mind.

Arms, legs, the head, scattered on the sidewalk—even these graphic details did not seem real to her.

That notwithstanding, Shizue had never seen a dead body before. In fact, other than one specific group of people, no one in the nation would have ever seen a corpse in their lifetime. Like industrial refuse, no, even more so, dead bodies were painstakingly covered up and were always swiftly processed.

No.

Shizue had actually seen a dead body. Once.

Her mother's. She had been made up to appear as she did when she was alive. Not because Shizue's mother was in fact alive, but it was not *really* her mother's dead body either.

It was a replica of a human.

A fabrication.

The corpse that was destroyed and left by the side of the road was, to Shizue, the replica of a person.

And Shizue was unable to find that atrocious.

It was just *a body thrown out because it had no use anymore.*

Useless parts.

Deficient parts.

Something struck her.

Fuwa! Hey, Fuwa!

She saw memory hair float in her field of vision.

"What's wrong? Are you okay? I wouldn't blame you for being disturbed by all this..."

She was not disturbed. Just lost in thought.

"But we've got to keep a straight head on…" counselor Takazawa intoned with a grave face. She already knew what he'd want to say next.

You're so hard on the outside, but deep down inside you're still a woman. There was no doubt in her mind. Shizue shot him a scornful look.

Shizue was well aware that it was unjust conjecture. Even if she were right on the money, it would still be conjecture. She just wanted to loathe this guy.

"This killer is a real weirdo, a real nut job," the area chief declared. Shizue didn't even feel like explaining how problematic that word was today. Everyone in that room including Shizue, in fact, all of humanity, was weird.

There was no difference between normal and abnormal. All humans lived along a continuum. There might have been extreme cases, but be they vicious killers or church altar boys, there was very little difference in what went on in the minds of humans.

However, what scared her the most was that this was definitely some kind of aberration.

Arrogance was a weakness. It would be difficult to live your everyday life self-conscious of your peculiarities. You needed more than just a half-hearted emotional intelligence quotient. That was why humans were made forgetful. Shizue let herself believe it was typical to be pacing with anxiety about their abnormalities.

That was why humanity created concepts such as personality and character, which were indefinable and thus irreproachable. When people said that they were this kind of personality or had that kind of character, it was only because they didn't actually know themselves. Humans weren't that pure, and the brain was not so simple.

Shizue believed that people who spoke easily about their own personalities or whatever other kind of self-ascription were cowards who couldn't admit to the deception inherent in their beliefs. And those depressive people who couldn't be comforted by even this so-called understanding of their personality would slander failures as "weirdos."

Yes, criminals are all failures.

And of course, their actions were recriminating.

In a society based on the principles of a legal system, the criminals were the failures. Yet even after acknowledging the existence of such flawed individuals, Shizue believed no one had the qualifications to place blame.

Shizue knew better than anyone that people had feelings. Still.

"The victim's parents are really confused right now," the area chief said. "I mean, I understand their sadness and anger. Their daughter was savagely killed by a deranged criminal after all. I can even understand being perplexed, but they're asking what role the community center had in this ordeal." The area chief looked in Shizue's direction.

"This Asumi girl had been missing since two nights ago."

Th-that's right, a voice said from the back of the room.

It was Shizue's colleague Yuko Shima.

Asumi and the last victim, Ryu Kawabata, had both been students under her charge.

"It hasn't been announced publicly."

"The police intervened with the announcement."

"What does that mean?"

"I mean, they were afraid of prank calls, so the information was never broadcast."

"And?"

As if speaking as his proxy, the internal affairs officer spoke for the police chief.

"Why were the police informed before this discovery was announced to the center?"

"I did try to notify the center," Shima said. "As soon as I got the message from Aikawa, I forwarded it to the main terminal at the center, the chief's personal monitor, and even to internal affairs. And then..."

"Then what?"

"Message delivery failed."

"Failed? Why?"

"The police."

"The police stopped it? The police prevented your message from sending, is that it? That's a problem, isn't it?"

Of course it's a problem.

Shizue did not want to think too deeply about what made this problematic.

"That is, Aikawa had twice spent the night away from her residence without permission."

"She was a delinquent, was she?" the area chief said. Shima shook her head.

"Aikawa attended an evening course," Shima said

"You mean the training," the director acknowledged.

Shizue had no idea what kind of training he was referring to but thought it strange that any training would take place at night.

She examined Shima's composure.

She had no idea what Shima could be thinking.

"That's all we know for now," Shima mumbled. "I also, um..."

"You understand? No, wait a second. Why do the police have that information? Only counselors are supposed to be privy to that kind of information. Did you tell them?"

"But...they have the data files on all the kids, remember?"

The area chief rapped on his desk. "Aah!"

"But it was just yesterday evening that the data collection was completed."

"At 4:23 PM exactly," Takazawa responded almost inappropriately, to a question no one had asked.

"Though since the data is organized alphabetically—"

"Asumi Aikawa's student data classification ID number was 00002," Shizue said, impatient with this conversation.

Her information had been processed three days ago. Two days ago when Shizue had started her second batch of data processing, Aikawa's information had long been processed.

"You shouldn't be so satisfied with that answer," the area chief said, annoyed.

"I want to know how the transmission of a message can be stopped in the first place. Isn't that against the laws of privacy protection of personal information?" the director grumbled.

"Why is it that the transmission of a notice of an emergency situation to the counseling center gets tied into a vicious crime? It's information meant to prevent the crime, moreover. This might be the one instance when information works against us. This is bad. Really bad. Frankly, the fact that a message sent to a counselor—no, you can't look at the content of the data while it is being sent, and you can't choose and interrupt the messages, so there must have been a physical hack of the circuits. Why did you keep quiet about this, Shima? You should have seen the police's tyranny as problematic."

"Uh..." Shima stood up. "I immediately restored my system. So I just thought it was a server malfunction. Then, the police contacted me as soon as I restored my circuits, and the police told me that it wasn't decided yet whether it was related to the killings, and the murders were still under investigation, so I shouldn't bring too much attention to this kind of delinquency, and they told me to keep quiet and—"

"What's the meaning of this?" the area chief asked the administrative representative, who in turn looked at the director.

"Aikawa's parents reported their missing child to the police before you?"

"That's what it sounds like. No wait, I'm wrong…" Shima was being painfully elusive. "I was the first one to hear this news. I told them to let me know if anything happened. Then I cut off all vocal communications and immediately drafted a notice addressed to the center and was going to send it. But then it didn't send, and oh, this is what the police said. Once the communication was received, they'd assumed the center had been notified and forbade any further communication, but in the process they froze the network, so they had to take emergency measures and shut down everything. They were very apologetic, very polite…"

"I don't care if they're polite. You have a record of this interaction?"

"Yes."

Shima brought out her monitor.

Not that she needed to.

Until an individual went in and deleted the information, all communications were recorded in a mainframe, and even if they were erased, the communications were temporarily stored in regional databanks.

It was also annoying that they had to belabor the questioning.

"However…"

"This *has* ended up being connected to a murder investigation," the area chief said. More grumbling.

"There's a possibility we might face examination of this center's accountability in the matter. We'll need the representative counselor and even non-counselors to keep that in mind."

"You say accountability, but there's nothing we could have done."

"Well, except in that we had information before the murder, and local residents can't be interrogated. They have unlimited rights."

"Even that is limited to just data collection."

"Even if there was information, we don't know that it was obstructed."

"No, it's because we don't know that there is the possibility it was obstructed."

Something that didn't *seem* random could by default be considered highly plausible, sure. But Shizue thought that to bring up plausibility in a situation like this was meaningless. Of course one could also approach this situation and say it was imperative to exercise complete diligence with every possibility. Yet, "possibility" meant that the result of consideration would be the exact opposite of an original hypothesis. In the event that a thorough and time-consuming investigation yielded a satisfactory explanation, the problem then became whether the subject taking responsibility for this explanation could then adequately perform inevitable crisis management.

Shizue was fed up.

These people were not wondering whether they were responsible at all. They were neither defiant nor responsive. There was absolutely nothing commendable about them.

This was a meeting to ascertain who would take the blame. Had it been clearer who should take responsibility, there would have been no meeting. There was no victim or crime in a debate like this.

The core of the judgment.

That was probably a big issue for these people.

No one knew what lay ahead.

No matter how detailed the information upon which an opinion was based, no matter how astute the calculation behind a theory, there was absolutely no such thing as an absolute.

The assignation of an accurate interpretation only occurred when the results of the determination were considered good. When they weren't, it wouldn't matter how sophisticated the interpretation, it was considered a blanket failure. The core of the judgment always ran a risk.

"I see…"

Shizue ruminated on what the girl Hinako had said. That divinations were meant to assuage humans of their sense of risk. The core that took responsibility was God.

"So this is the fault of the police, am I right?" the director said.

"Well. I don't know about 'fault' but—"

"But it is. They're the ones who created this irresponsible gag order. If I recall correctly, isn't Aikawa known outside the prefecture?"

"She was an athlete. An aspiring pro," the administrative representative answered. *Okay, that's what he meant by* training *then*, Shizue thought.

It wasn't just that she wasn't responsible for the girl in question. Shizue didn't have an interest in sports news. In fact, no, she didn't care at all whatsoever.

Asumi Aikawa was already dead to her.

How accomplished this girl was in her life, what kind of legacy she'd left, shouldn't have mattered. At the very least, all that mattered in this situation was the meaning of her death. Weighing the facts of her death with the quality of her accomplishments in life would be a form of contamination in Shizue's opinion.

Shizue was bothered.

Idiots would continue to pass blame around forever. What could have been just an informal notice had now become something worse than that god-awful conference. With a notice, one simply announced a piece of information and it was over. There was no place for a debate. It was no place for half-hearted complaints or for plaintiffs to show their ire.

Shizue was starting to feel lightheaded, so she brought out her wet cloths and wiped down her desk.

The horrible smell of antiseptics stung her nose. That stabilized her a little. The antiseptic smell she loathed was still better than the breath these people pumped into the air.

Fourteen-year-old girl, disemboweled.

There were over a dozen stab wounds. All of them deep. The body was cut in half, her insides quartered. Her neck and all four limbs were nearly completely severed. It was easy to visualize it all. There were far more horrific images on the monitor, and if she'd really wanted to see them, all Shizue'd have to do was file a request.

But Shizue could visualize it.

But it wasn't accompanied by realism. The misery in Shizue's mind had no blood or flesh. She tried to actualize the replica, to make it an original.

What hindered her original was not having a clear idea of Asumi Aikawa's face. The image of the corpse in Shizue's mind had the characteristics of Yuko Yabe. Yet the more she tried to add realism to the image, the farther the image got from her, making it vague at best.

Then she saw her mother's face.

"Who was it that contacted you?" the area chief suddenly asked.

"Was it the police or an area cop? Or…"

"It was a prefectural policeman by the name of Ishida," Shima answered.

Ishida!

A sickly face. Logical diction. Disagreeable expressions. The image of Ishida wiped out that of her mother.

"Ishida…Isn't he the guy who was here the other day?"

"That was the officer in charge of the investigation, and Ishida's one step above that man," the administrative representative said.

"Meaning that's the man personally responsible."

"Vocal communications are obviously recorded. He knew it too. But if the director of this investigation himself contacted you, our not knowing about Asumi Aikawa's disappearance and as a result no one here doing anything about it is totally the police's fault, isn't it?"

The area chief asked if this Ishida character was in fact in a position of being able to take any responsibility.

"He *is* the director, so…"

"Director, yes, but the director of the prefectural police. I think it always comes down to the local responsibilites."

"That may be, but he's really high up in the chain of command. You could even say he's top brass at the prefectural department, and looking at his public profile, it seems that his record, his backers, and his connections are plentiful and very influential. Not to be overlooked, it seems. He's at central right now, but again, very high up even there."

"Hmm."

It sounded like he was impressed. But also relieved.

Shizue held her breath. Something was rotting.

"But why is this guy sticking around the area of the crime, then? Doesn't he have more to do up at central?"

"Actually, he's apparently an expert in heinous crimes, and especially in special cases like this one involving savage or brutal murders, and so whenever something takes place he inserts himself with the area patrol. Well, this isn't anything they've publicly broadcast at police headquarters. It's underground information."

That *Ishida*? *If he is in fact an expert, he is one incompetent expert*, Shizue thought.

These past few years there had been very few arrests made in connection with serial killings and especially not in the more heinous ones.

Besides, if you thought about the way the police were organized, the odds of such crimes taking place were low. There were certainly situations that required a specialist with focused talents be dispatched to a crime scene, but it was difficult to imagine a bureau superior assuming such a position. Even if that officer had prior experience with a similar case.

The problem here was the source of this information.

This "underground information" the director referred to was probably the nonpublic information supplied by crime fetishists. They collected information on crimes by various methods. Very little of that information could be trusted. It was just a kind of online rumor mill.

What they were saying about Ishida was conjecture based on his having been by coincidence at the scenes of these savage crimes. No doubt that was all it was.

If you looked at it realistically…

A case would be deemed unsolvable, and then after sending the case to the cold file another similar crime would occur. The police would fail once again to solve the crime and once again stop investigating. If that were the case it wasn't inconsistent with Shizue's appraisal of the murders.

She didn't know about his past record or his network, but Ishida was not remarkable. That much she was sure of. However, everyone above the area chief was convinced.

The area chief told Shima and the representative counselors to stay behind and work overtime. Everyone else should wait till the police made their statement about the crime and keep quiet until then. Finally, the meeting drew to a close.

"The police news conference is planned for six o'clock exactly. At the same time, Shima and her colleagues will be meeting with the victim's relations. Sometime after tomorrow we'll convene another conference. I will send details shortly."

That was really all he had to say from the beginning. No need for a half hour of nonsense.

That took all of twenty seconds.

Shizue looked at the clock on her monitor and reexamined what the area chief had just said, then confirmed the time required, shut off the power, and scrambled out of her seat. She had to admit it was pretty rude.

As she stood up and turned on her heel however, she ran into Shima, who had a severe expression on her face.

She didn't quite look sad or worried, but exasperated. Shizue couldn't really blame her. Even she was exhausted by all this. And if something had happened to Yuko Yabe, Shizue would be in this same situation. And in that situation, she would certainly make the same face as Shima was making now. Or so she thought.

Similarities.

Shizue called out, and Shima responded with only a weak glance.

"This might be a strange question, but this girl Asumi Aikawa, she didn't by any chance have an interest in deformée characters, did she?"

Shima narrowed her eyes without changing her composure in any other way. Now she looked annoyed.

"What's that?"

"Anything, really. Just anything like animation or…"

"*No*," Shima answered clearly and out of sync with how annoyed she seemed from her body language. "She expressed no other interest or hobby besides running. I think she *hated* people who were into animation. Her parents remembered hearing her say that too."

She seemed awfully knowledgeable. This was unusual for Shima, so Shizue couldn't help but ask again, at which point Shima said, "I like that stuff a lot."

"You...you mean you personally like animation?"

"Yes. I had to see Asumi Aikawa a lot because she had such a special talent for running and competed in national races. Once, when I mentioned deformée characters she abruptly cut me off. I'll never forget it."

Shima spoke as if there was nothing in her heart and continued to speak with no intonation before finally turning her back to Shizue and leaving. Then as if only to herself Shima mumbled, *Why'd you have to go and die*, and trudged out of the room.

It wasn't as though Asumi Aikawa had died because she wanted to.

In any case, Kunugi's hypothesized key connection—the shared interest all the victims had in deformée characters—did not apply to this victim.

No.

She could simply be the anomaly.

The exception.

Those who fell outside...

...were all missing something. Their livers.

It would be strange for Shizue to ask about something like that. It would be strange even for a police officer to ask about it, much less a counselor.

The autopsy results wouldn't be made public for some time. Plus, only people in the police department would have access to that information. Civilians would only have access to that information after the case was over—after the suspect had been prosecuted and sentenced.

Then there was the complicated process of obtaining consent from the bereaved necessary to get that all started.

The data would have a serious protection applied to it and couldn't be seen except on the monitors they were downloaded onto. Furthermore it probably couldn't be copied.

Unless Kunugi...

Nah, there was no way a dropout cop like Kunugi, who'd been relieved of any responsibility for this investigation, would have access.

What was I thinking?

That was when Shizue realized. The only thing she had to be concerned with was the disappearance of Yuko Yabe, not the investigation of this murder. That was someone else's job. If she was preoccupied with this murder it was only because she was trying to escape reality. She was thoroughly disgusted with her work, but she knew she ought to give some more thought to figuring out her own situation.

Shizue shook her head several times.

CHAPTER 015

NOTICE OF THE communication center's temporary closure came on a Saturday.

That day, her legal foster father came home with no warning, which was unusual and made Hazuki feel cloistered.

But that her foster father came without warning did not mean he came alone.

Executive secretaries, assistant secretaries, security details, and the like came streaming in, clearly having created time between duties to force this meeting.

So yes. They were there.

In this case though, it'd be more accurate to say they had come to this building where Hazuki, the man's foster child, resided, merely to pop their heads in.

He'd always say something nice to the people he met. He was a gentleman.

You seem well.

You're pacing through your curriculum well.

You'll only lower your achievement level if you work too hard.

The day's average study periods are too long, aren't they?

Hazuki's foster father knew a tremendous amount about Hazuki. Before he came home he would always examine the data collected on her. It was no doubt his commute read, prepared for him as her guardian.

In just one hour, this person could know what Hazuki had done in the past month.

She felt fortunate but not happy about it.

Hazuki's foster father had six children to his name. Not all of them were biologically his. Legally, Hazuki had one older sister and older brother, two younger brothers and a younger sister.

She'd met them before but couldn't remember their faces.

Each of them had been sent to a home, each of them had started a life there. Her foster father would take in and raise these children as his own.

You could have said Hazuki was lucky.

Orphans in this country were beyond numbers. Fifteen years ago when

Hazuki was born, the nation was at its peak in the number of parents who'd abandoned their children or else were denied the right to raise their own children, though both figures had waned over the years.

These parentless children lived mostly in welfare institutions. Though they were institutions, the environment was good and there was no real social stigma attached to living in one. Orphans weren't discriminated against as they were in the past and enjoyed all the freedoms every other child did. From the child's point of view, it was probably much better than living with impoverished parents.

Hazuki's life in the institution was not so different from the one she lived now.

You could have said the house she lived in now was like her own private institution.

But she had a father figure, at least legally. The person with kind words for her was not just a guardian or counselor, but a man who assumed the role of father.

Hazuki didn't know why her foster father did any of this. As far as his actions were concerned, Hazuki had heard that at one point he'd been criticized, but lauded at other times. Hazuki didn't really care one way or another whether he was a philanthropist or hypocrite.

All that mattered to Hazuki was that here was a man who invariably assumed the role of father over her, and that he was sympathetic and kind toward her. That was enough for her.

However, Hazuki's father was a sort of foster father and yet not quite a foster father. He'd not once ever called her by name. It wasn't as if she hated it or refused to let him. Just that having this gap in their relationship put her at ease.

Her foster father was saying the same thing with the same tone as he always did. Adding that she ought to pay particular attention to her surroundings now.

That was his reason for coming home. He had come for *real access* to assure Hazuki would "pay attention to her surroundings" since there'd been another murder in the area.

He could have just sent her a message, but it was very conscientious of him to go out of his way to engage in real access.

At times like this Hazuki realized that her foster father worried about her deep down inside. It was clear in his body language he was sincerely concerned, but if he weren't his actions were still pretty impressive.

Whenever she saw her father she recognized that she had developed an adeptness at expression comprehension, and she didn't see the usefulness of communication labs anymore.

It was difficult to learn an unquantifiable, uncodifiable skill. When you spent your days in front of a monitor you gradually forgot the power of communicating via your expressions, with your gestures.

Maybe not so much forgot as stopped being aware of doing so.

Hazuki would certainly laugh when amused and cry when sad, but she didn't know what she looked like to someone else.

For that reason she also couldn't tell when looking at a laughing stranger whether they were laughing because they were amused or for some other reason. She couldn't be sure. She couldn't imagine.

Everything outside the monitor really was fake.

Her foster father's power of expression and his ability to convince her that lies were true perplexed Hazuki.

She did think he must have been a good person.

She received the message about the community center's closure in the midst of this cloistered feeling.

Because of this, she evaded her father, who kept doling out statements of worry.

"I'm sorry."

Say it.

There was no way to verbally distinguish one sort of apology from another.

No, if apologizing for interrupting a conversation, it should sound different from when you apologized in earnest.

Though Hazuki didn't know why it was different.

When an apology was in writing there was no nuance to detect in the first place, and eventually you stopped using ambiguous expressions. Flat words with limited meaning became the language of choice. It was meant to prevent confusion. *Expressions with only one interpretation.* Writing under this rule was a mandatory condition of the era's uninterrupted communication style. Of course, it was no more than a pretense. Trouble couldn't be avoided, but at least this way it never surfaced.

Hazuki's generation derived 80 percent of its conversational communication from written language, so saying "I'm sorry" for any other reason than to apologize was practically obsolete. There was no use for the expression and no one knew how to say it.

"What's the matter?" her foster father asked.

Next week's communication sessions were canceled. All outside travel was prohibited, day or night. If you absolutely must leave the house, you had to take your monitor and set it on GPS mode so that if for example you were killed, the authorities would know where to find your body.

Hazuki's foster father grimaced as Hazuki read her message. Then said, "This is a serious problem."

He kept talking about something or other, but Hazuki heard none of it.

Hazuki's consciousness was focused on her monitor.

At the bottom of her screen was an icon she'd never seen before.

A turtle.

The shape of a turtle.

There'd been no stupid icons on her screen this morning.

She was pretty sure there hadn't been anything there till she got the message from the center, actually. Her foster father was still saying something or other, but her voice recognition was turned off.

Mindful of her foster father's gaze Hazuki deftly slid her finger across the tablet and moved the cursor.

OPEN.

No audio upon opening the file.

THERE WILL BE A POWER OUTAGE FROM 5:55:30 TO 5:56:00 PM.
LEAVE THE HOUSE DURING THOSE THIRTY SECONDS. WAIT AT THE DOVEROOM.
WE MEET AT THE PRIVATE ROOM.
DO NOT PASS YOUR FOYER UNTIL AFTER THE OUTAGE.
WRITE BACK RELEVANT INFORMATION ON BACK OF THIS MESSAGE.
THAT'S ALL.
--MIO

Mio. Mio Tsuzuki.

As Hazuki scrambled to close the file it closed on its own. It must have been programmed to do that. If the message were open for any less time she wouldn't have caught all the information.

Five fifty-five PM.

The clock on her monitor said it was 3:33. She had two hours and twenty-two minutes. The helper would be gone by then.

But...

Hazuki looked up.

"Just don't worry so much," her foster father said. "The security on this house is impeccable. Intruders cannot get in. You have no reason to go out anyway, so there's nothing to worry about. I'm sure the community center will reopen soon enough. I'll also tell the police to ensure the fool-proof safety of the house."

Intruders…

Intruders had penetrated this house several times now. It just hadn't been a crazy killer or some sly pervert. It was a little girl with some hacking skills.

Nothing would make her feel safe in this house.

Her foster father said, "I'll be off now," and placed a hand on her shoulder.

That hand was warm and soft. But it made her think of the sensation of Yuko Yabe's wobbly body.

She felt somehow odd.

"I'm thinking of dropping by your little brother and sister's. I don't think they have anything to worry about, but…I'm going to spend the night at my office tonight so I won't be far. If anything comes up please contact me."

He smiled. *See ya.*

"Okay, goodbye."

Soon the helper had arrived, and Hazuki went to her own room.

Wait at the doveroom.

Ayumi's rooftop.

Had something happened to Yuko?

She turned her monitor on. The turtle icon was also on her bedroom monitor, but no matter how many times she opened it the file would immediately close. She didn't know what was going on, but it must have been one of those things. Mio had made it, after all.

It sounded like she was supposed to reply by typing in "relevant information" on the "back," and she sought just enough time to jot something down. As long as she was typing it seemed the window would not close. She started to wonder what would happen when her voice changed, and while thinking about it she accidentally pressed the enter key.

> WHAT THE HELL

She meant to type "hell is going on?"

She tried once again to open the file, but this time at the end of the text her own additional sentence was tacked on and immediately disappeared. When she saw her incomplete sentence on the screen she went limp. She didn't feel like finishing it anymore and put her monitor in sleep mode.

Hazuki remained there till 5:55 PM, sitting in that chair doing nothing. She didn't put her hands on anything. At the fiftieth minute she left her room. She was going to leave her house as instructed.

She moved to the living room. The helper was gone. Her dinner was on the dining table as usual.

Two more minutes.

Those two minutes were long. Curiously, looking at the food on the dining table whetted her appetite, but she had no time to eat. *Why am I suddenly hungry now?* Hazuki thought.

Fifty-five and ten seconds...twenty seconds...thirty seconds.

Hazuki reflexively opened the door and went through the hall.

She hadn't had any intention of obeying orders, but there she was.

Through the foyer and out the front door. She stopped outside the door and took a gulp and spun on her heel.

The gate light snapped back on. The foyer and house lights all went back on shortly thereafter.

The occupancy light turned on.

She could not go back in now.

If she went back in now the security camera would spot her. Once in the foyer she would also have to use her ID card to get into the house.

But the house thought she was still in it. If someone ostensibly already inside entered this house, the system was sure to go haywire.

What a mess.

Oh.

Hazuki scrambled to get her monitor out. She made sure her GPS wasn't on.

It would be another system contradiction if her GPS showed her outside the house. Fortunately it wasn't turned on, but for some reason the monitor *was* on audio mode, even though Hazuki never listened to music.

Geez.

She deleted all the notices from the center.

No one was following the letter.

It wasn't that dark out yet.

Hazuki stared at the road leading straight ahead. The road went on forever. It made her uneasy. She couldn't get a complete view of it. She couldn't position herself on it. She didn't know where exactly she was.

Nothing changed in the frame when she moved, making it pointless to move at all. Maps were maps because of the delineations they made.

She looked at her monitor. Not being able to use her GPS also meant she could not use the navigator. It wasn't as though she'd forgotten how to get there, but…

At this rate she couldn't tell how quickly she was moving either. Nor could she confirm exactly where she was. No…

Hazuki was most definitely in her own home. The Hazuki standing on the side of the road now was a mere ghost of the real Hazuki. Hazuki's ghost moved around like a real ghost would. Aimlessly.

Even when she stepped on the ground it seemed insincere.

She checked the time.

She wanted at least to know how much exercise she was getting out of this.

If she couldn't measure distance she could at least measure how many calories she was burning.

She'd been walking for twenty minutes.

She walked past what used to be a burial ground for the dead.

Beyond the alleys was a wild forest.

There was a three-floor regulation-size building holding back the forest.

There was…

There was a nonregulation structure.

Ayumi's place.

Hazuki had walked for twenty-five minutes and twenty-two seconds to reach the doveroom.

After confirming the vacancy signal at the front of the building she walked around to the back.

She climbed the metal spiral staircase.

In the illegal structure built on the roof of this building a light was on.

Hazuki hesitated to move immediately toward the door and walked along the fence to where Ayumi had first been sitting. She sat down on the chair left there.

She sat down and looked up.

She looked at the sky the way Ayumi had. The world had gone dark. It was pitch black here and there. *Night skies are inconsistent*, Hazuki thought uselessly.

As she focused her eyes Hazuki began to see lights. Mio had said it was weirder to be able to see the lights than not, but even Hazuki could see a few. They were smaller than the pixels on her monitor.

After much concentration she realized the black part of the night sky was actually an obstruction—it was a physical object. She thought it was one deep black object, but it was actually a bridge. And as soon as she thought this, she felt like she could recognize the entire world.

The bridge was black and large.

There was a loud noise behind her.

"What are you doing?"

Two catlike eyes peered at Hazuki from behind the door.

It was Mio.

"You were supposed to come in when you got here. What are you doing?"

"Nothing."

"*Jesus*," Mio let out, leaning forward to grab Hazuki by her right sleeve and pull her into the room.

"Don't you think this is a bad work environment, Kono?"

Mio's hands clasped Hazuki's shoulders as she spoke. Mio's face was right in front of hers. She didn't have time to back away and was trapped looking straight into Mio's big round eyes. She was stunned.

Pupils. Iris. Capillaries. Eyebrows. Eyelids.

A living thing.

Mio thrust Hazuki into the room.

Hazuki took a few steps toward the dove cage with her eyes still open. Mio slammed the door shut.

Mio must have felt the same thing, Hazuki thought.

She was not used to making eye contact with humans either.

Mio looked over her shoulder.

"You're really weird."

"What do you want?" Hazuki said in a small voice. She looked away from Mio.

"What do you mean what do I want?"

"Your file."

"You didn't recognize that drawing?"

"I know what it was. That's what I'm asking now."

"You knew? I'm so bad at drawing."

"So?"

"It's a turtle! I don't know how to draw anything else. At least not animals."

"That's not what I mean," Hazuki brought her hand to the wire netting. "What *was* that?"

"Huh? Oh, well…an electronic message or voice message would leave traces. I had to think of a way to communicate without leaving a trace. It was really hard. I found a path no one in the general population would use and put out a weak signal on it. A signal of extremely random numbers, so if anyone did happen to pick it up it wouldn't make sense, but on a specially programmed monitor the code can be deciphered. That's how…"

"That's how nothing!"

"What's the matter?"

"*Why* did you do that?"

Hazuki looked around nervously. Mio started cackling. "I didn't think you'd come."

"I got…worried."

"Nah, I mean if we still had labs I wouldn't have called you out here, but it's canceled. They don't know when they'll solve the case, and I knew you'd be worried about it in the meantime."

"Worried about Yabe?"

Was she worried? Sure she was a little ruffled and generally uncomfortable with the situation, but as soon as she got home everything was normal, and as long as everything was normal she wouldn't think anything out of the ordinary. She was not worried about Yuko Yabe.

Yet, Hazuki had trouble identifying what she had thought or how she felt specifically during that time.

The unpleasant sensation of carrying Yuko Yabe's body?

Hazuki looked at the doves.

She would remember the smell and movements of the creepy animals.

What have I gotten into?

She heard Ayumi's voice.

The door to the room with the bed opened and Ayumi appeared.

"I'm sorry if we're causing any more trouble."

"We're not doing any such thing, Hazuki. Jesus, you're so weird."

Hazuki thought Mio was much stranger than herself.

"Tsuzuki's explaining it poorly," Ayumi said.

"Explaining what?"

"That message you sent, which made no sense."

"Yes it did. I sent just enough information to get Makino to come here. I got around the system just fine."

"Not that."

Ayumi pushed a chair toward Hazuki. "Then what?" Ayumi said.

"The plan?"

"I think so. Yabe's almost completely recovered. She wants to go home. Tsuzuki objects. That Chinese girl can't be caught. I don't care either way. Tsuzuki thought we should ask what you thought since you've been in this from the beginning. She thought you would be concerned. I don't know why you would be, but that's what Tsuzuki said."

Mio took the chair Ayumi brought to Hazuki, spun it around, and straddled it.

Ayumi grabbed another chair by the back and pushed it toward Hazuki.

"But there was no protocol for secret communication. Anything we sent you would have been recorded. And we couldn't guarantee any record of communication wouldn't get you in trouble. I told her to go see you personally but this one wouldn't have it."

"It didn't make sense for me to go to your place alone."

"So Tsuzuki came up with this weird coded message. I thought she was going to ask you point-blank what you thought we should do about Yuko, but then she made you come out here. If you ask me, I think she wanted to see you."

"What?" Mio's face scrambled.

Wanted to see her?

Mio dropped her chin to the back of the chair. "*What do you mean wanted to see her?* I don't know what you mean, Ayumi."

"I think you do. You went to a lot of trouble to hack into electrical systems and security systems, and you used unheard-of precision to design a way to get Hazuki to come out. So yes, I think you wanted to see her. If you can make such grandiose gestures, you can certainly make much simpler ones. If you got caught you'd be in big trouble. Hacking and illegal data transfers are serious offenses, even if you are a minor. This time you shut off the power in her house for thirty seconds on top of everything. I bet you'd have to pay restitution on that."

"Stupid. No one's going to think some fourteen-year-old kid would commit such pointless criminal acts. Most people think kids won't act against the system."

"It's because they're kids that they do. Do such meaningless things."

"I guess." Mio lifted her brow.

"Either way," Ayumi said to Hazuki, "this crazy one called you out here and wanted to talk to you face to face. I didn't think you'd come, but…"

"Sorry." Hazuki's voice was soft. She was sure this was the last thing Ayumi needed. It didn't occur to her till now.

"This one's always apologizing, isn't she?" Mio pointed at Hazuki. Ayumi didn't respond. She simply turned toward the other room and said, "She came."

Yuko Yabe stuck her head halfway out from behind the door.

"Sorry," she said.

"This one's apologizing now too!" Mio sounded entertained. She stood up and offered her chair to Yuko.

After looking at the chair for some time with her pink eyes, Yuko sat down.

She was wearing the same thing as when they'd first met. Ayumi must have had it cleaned. It didn't look dirty enough.

"I started to feel weird. I was a little…confused."

Of course.

You were violated.

You were about to be killed.

But, she said, she was also on her period, which made her disoriented.

It was a very matter-of-fact thing, but Hazuki was not used to hearing people talk about periods, and…she got a horribly raw, which is to say visceral, feeling.

"Yuko's assailants were Ryu Kawabata, who is now dead, and Nakamura, who's now on the run," Mio said. She leaned against the dove cage.

"On the run?"

"On the run. The police and the area patrols are looking for him. He threw his monitor away, so the investigation has just gotten more difficult for them."

"His monitor?"

"When there's a person of extreme interest in a level D crime, the courts are authorized to follow their GPS units. You can track everything by satellite nowadays. According to the police report, all they found was his monitor at the house. There was no money withdrawn from his account, so it doesn't look like he's used his ID card. He's apparently been on the run without food or water. I mean, unless he *is* a criminal he won't get that far. A criminal will get himself caught even before there are notices out for his arrest. It's just a matter of time before he's caught. It's best we wait till then."

"You really think so?" Ayumi said.

"The police are also looking for Yuko. If it's just a matter of time before Nakamura's caught, it's also just a matter of time for them to find her. Neither of them have monitors right now."

"Yeah, but…"

"It'd be stupid to think Nakamura would get caught and not Yuko.

If they can find him, they can find her, and if she can hide here indefinitely, then Nakamura can hide somewhere forever and not be caught either. I don't think we can say for certain one way or the other."

Yuko looked up uncomfortably at Ayumi. Mio looked unhappy.

"No one's going to find Yuko because she's got us protecting her."

"There's nothing to say Nakamura doesn't have co-conspirators too," Ayumi said.

"Yeah, but..." Mio said. She brushed against the wire netting.

The doves were startled.

"All the more reason to keep her here."

"Uh, the subject in question is saying herself she wants to go home."

Ayumi walked away from Yuko and sat in the chair in the corner of the room.

"Right, Yuko?"

"I don't want to keep being a nuisance," Yuko said.

"Well—"Ayumi started.

"The wider the window of opportunity to go home, the harder it is to do it. I think it's plenty difficult to send her home now," Mio said.

"Why...why were you attacked?" Hazuki asked.

Mio's eyes went wide. It must have been a bad habit. "Good question. Yuko, why *were* you attacked?"

"I'm sick," Yuko replied.

"What do you mean you're sick? Like you're carrying a disease?"

"No. Nothing like that. I have what they call an extrasensory defect. I think."

"Extrasensory defect," Mio pronounced slowly.

What did that mean?

"You're talking about *that*?" Mio said. "But that was never declared an illness or a handicap. It was just announced, right?"

"It's what I have though. I think."

"What is it?" Ayumi asked.

It was hard to ask what kind of sickness this was.

"You don't know?" Mio asked. "You don't know either, Hazuki?"

"I don't."

"It's kind of difficult to explain. The Academy of Perceptual Disabilities just announced it last year and said they were going to further research whether there was a relationship between aberrations in the olfactory senses or whether they were unrelated, and whether one could call them aberrations in the first place. Opinions were very divided."

"How do you know all this?"

"I heard from my friend's doctor. Well, 'heard' meaning I read something he wrote."

"A friend's doctor?"

"A twenty-eight-year-old German," Mio said. "He's taking the same session as I am. You know, statistics."

Hazuki'd completely forgotten that Mio conducted graduate-level classes in statistics. Mio was so genius she could talk circles around anyone.

"You know how there are people who are color-blind?" said the genius. "There have been people who've been unable to distinguish certain color frequencies since long ago. Now, there are people who also can't distinguish smells and tastes in the same way. They can't determine if something's bitter or sour. People with extrasensory defects can't tell shapes apart, er—it's not that they aren't capable of it. Oh, it's hard to explain.

"Okay." Mio drew a tablet from her pocket and connected the monitor and drew something with her fingertip. While drawing she started to chuckle.

"Ha! I'm so bad at this! Oh well. Okay, Hazuki, what is this?"

On the display screen was a drawing of something that looked like a bird.

"A bird."

"Ha ha ha. You can tell? I feel like it looks like a turtle or something. Okay, so it's a dove. I drew that guy over there sleeping in the corner of the cage. I drew it the way I thought it looked. See, you can tell by this bit here that it's a dove. See it?"

Now that you mention it.

"Thing is…" Mio started and got serious. "If that's what this is, then what's this? It's a little childish, but then…"

Mio drew erratically on the screen, then searched for something in the monitor and showed the new drawing to Hazuki.

"What about this?"

On the screen was a cartoon deformée image of a dove.

Even Hazuki could tell what *that* was. Some famous person had drawn it. It had been used as the logo of the international bird preservation society a few years ago. The lines were simple and the details were charming. For an animal lover like Hazuki the attraction was obvious, and she had even downloaded a whole picture book of drawings by the illustrator.

"This is a caricature of the dove. But a real bird?"

Mio faced the monitor toward the dove.

The monitor beeped.

"This is the real bird."

On the screen was an image of the dove behind a wire-mesh cage.

"People long ago used to call these photographs. This image and that bird are almost identical. The image was taken from the dove. And this cartoon character is also a dove, at first glance." Mio worked at the monitor and divided the screen in two, the drawing of the dove on one side and the picture of the bird on the other.

"But these two things are totally different."

"So what?"

"I can see that this image is the dove. It's not that cute. It's kind of gross, even. It's growing feathers. It has bumps all over it. I tried to draw all those details, but as you can see, it didn't matter how hard I tried. The result was this ugly drawing."

Mio divided the screen in three now to present her first drawing along with the other two.

"It's really bad. But it's because I don't know how to draw that it looks this way. What I *see* when I look at the bird is this picture. You following me so far?"

"Yeah, but…" Hazuki answered tentatively.

Mio turned the display toward Yuko.

"Yuko, which one is real?"

Yuko looked at the screen for a while, then turned and looked at the birds behind Mio.

"I'm not sure."

"Right."

"If I had to guess," Yuko said, and pointed at the caricature.

"There you go," Mio said, looking at Hazuki again.

"There I go where? What do you mean?"

"Yuko sees the world this way."

"What way?"

"In these *cute cartoon caricatures*," Mio said, annoyed. "*Deformée* actually means something that's been misshapen. Exaggerated or diminished visual characteristics in drawings. With abstraction and symbolism and transposition. Hard stuff. Anyway, this kind of art is an expression."

Mio turned the screen toward Hazuki.

"When I try to express it, it's shitty. When an expert does it, it's cute.

But that's just a difference in drawing skills. I'm sure the guy who drew this and I see something closer to that picture when we look at doves. Actually, I'm positive people think we are seeing the same exact thing. There are those who differ, though."

"You mean that the cartoonist might have seen the dove exactly the way he drew it?"

"I have no idea how *he* sees it," Mio said. "Only Yuko can know what she sees. Consciousness is a response and responses can't be embodied, so they can't be transformed or moved or transferred. Drawing what your consciousness responds to is about as close as we get.

"Look," Mio said once more and showed Hazuki the screen. "There's no way someone can draw exactly what they see. I thought I was drawing it exactly, but it's still closer to the cartoon of the dove than it is this picture."

"I see…"

In other words, you couldn't look directly into someone's mind. Hazuki suddenly got uncomfortable.

People couldn't connect to each other.

"But if we believe what Yuko's telling us, that means that at the very least she does in fact see the world differently than we do. But actually, even the world Ayumi sees is different from the one you see. It's just that the difference in perception between you two is a normal aberration. When the difference is much greater, it's called abnormal. Yuko's perception might be abnormal, but it doesn't affect her daily life or have a serious impact on the human workings. For now."

That was why they didn't call it a disability.

"It's hard to imagine this is congenital, but if it's acquired then there's no way to discern who's been affected by it. Cause unknown. Some people say it's the result of reality deprivation."

"Reality…you mean *real access*?" Hazuki said.

"It's like people who are tone-deaf. People say that it's a result of children being exposed to electrical noises while developing their sense of hearing. I don't really understand myself, but they say that you go tone-deaf when you're restricted from experiencing the broad range of natural sounds. Similarly, people are saying you have extrasensory defects from being raised from infancy in front of a monitor's limited range of colors and shapes. Like I said, I don't know personally. It's just someone's theory."

"That could be me," Yuko said. "Mom and Dad were really busy all the time. They bought me a fundamental guardian system."

"Ah…"

"We had that at my place too," Mio said. "I didn't use it properly though. I broke it and played with it like a toy. They were so pissed. I was pretty much raised by that Chinese family below us, anyway. But you, Yuko, you were much more obedient."

"Not obedient," Yuko said. "Just that if I broke that thing they would never buy me anything again. Then I'd have nothing."

"It *was* expensive. Well, cheaper than hiring someone, but still…"

"And…"

Ayumi had remained silent this whole time but finally turned to Yuko and asked, "What does your extrasensory defect and the attack have to do with each other?"

She didn't see how they could be related.

"Someone said I was blasphemous."

Yuko lowered her eyes.

"What do you mean, *blasphemous*?" Mio asked.

"Remember when we drew pictures of ourselves in communication lab? Was it last year?"

"Yeah. I remember. I was really bad at drawing back then too," Mio said and searched her monitor anew. "Look. Here. The instructor didn't say anything, but that damned counselor Fuwa straight out laughed out loud."

On her screen was a drawing of what looked like a human face, easily distinguishable as at least having been drawn by Mio, regardless of any resemblance to herself.

"That was a major failure on her part as a counselor."

To think of what you looked like; to imagine what your face communicated to others; to then know how people perceived you; to determine the difference between how you saw yourself and how you were seen by others—that had been the goal of that communication exercise.

Hazuki had hated it, to be honest. She didn't see the point in looking at herself for any length of time or in knowing how others perceived her. Hazuki never looked at anyone and didn't let herself be seen by anyone. She looked at no one.

"Can I see that for a second?" Yuko extended her hand. Mio handed over her monitor.

"Is it a problem if I pull up my public file?"

"Not really. Not if it's public data."

Yuko pressed the keys with her slim fingers. Her pink nail polish was badly chipped.

The self-portraits from communication lab were used through the year on everyone's public profile pages—with their consent, of course. Hazuki hadn't consented. Yuko, having accessed her own profile, turned the monitor screen toward the others.

"This is my self-portrait."

Pink hair, pink pupils. Pink piercing.

It was a splendid rendering of a young woman.

"You're good!"

"I don't know. I drew that looking in a mirror. Just like you did looking at the dove, I was drawing exactly what I thought I saw. I didn't think anything of it when I was drawing it. A lot of kids were drawing this way."

"It's a copy."

Mio kept looking at the screen in admiration.

"You can tell there's an original. Every expression is always just a copy of some kind of original. There's some originality in the process or method. But when it's a child, it's difficult to simplify complex patterns, so they mimic a method that's easier to understand. That's how they draw buildings and for that matter, animals. It's a copy of a drawing, but it's also an imitation of a thought process, because you're drawing something deliberately unlike the way it is in reality. The child adopts a method of abstraction. But after depicting things in this way for a while, you eventually learn the difference between what you see and what you depict. That's how you learn to revise and develop your own patterns. But these days we don't really have the opportunity to draw anything. Most homes don't have paper, for starters."

Hazuki's home had paper that her father had brought over once.

But she didn't have anything to draw with.

"That's why you don't get to practice the process. And more and more people keep imitating. We fix it in our minds that this is how we have to draw, so we never learn the difference between what we see and what we draw. It's all right since we hardly see reality. So there are some people who can draw themselves exactly how they look. But you're different, Yuko."

"Really?" Hazuki asked and Yuko nodded.

"But you can't know that. There's no way to know. So…"

They couldn't know, could they. In fact, Hazuki had no idea even now.

"I never thought that I was so different from everyone else. I was told I drew very prettily. I wasn't concerned with how differently I saw," Yuko said.

"I was laughed at," Mio said.

"But, so yeah, I got a strange message at the beginning of last month."

"Strange how?"

"An anonymous one."

"You can always find out the sender, even if it's anonymous."

"I didn't know who it was," Yuko said.

"What did it say?"

"Exactly what you just did, Mio. That it was a copy."

"Copy?"

"Yeah. Copy. As in, it isn't a self-portrait. It's plagiarism. They said it was extremely inconsiderate of me to pass off the drawing as my own face. So I responded that it wasn't a copy. I said that's exactly how I drew it originally, exactly how I saw myself. Then they said I was sick. In fact they said it was a blasphemous sickness. That if I really saw things this way I didn't deserve to live."

"That's *creepy*," Mio said.

"But what does that mean, blasphemous, anyway? What is it blaspheming?" Yuko asked.

"If anything's blasphemous, it's what Mio thinks a dove looks like," Ayumi said.

"Ouch! I won't disagree, but it's not my fault Yuko's so good at drawing. It's not about that anyway. Okay, so what's blasphemous about extrasensory defects?"

"Yeah. I didn't know then either. But I started wondering if it meant I was sick that I thought I looked that way, and then I started to feel weird. I knew a little bit about it. I did a little research. But I didn't really understand. Then we had that medical exam. You remember…"

"Did you talk to Fuwa about it?"

"I couldn't. I wanted to ask someone I knew."

It would be difficult to talk about accusations of blasphemy to a relative stranger, no doubt.

"So I tried divinations and things like that. I went to medical pages on my monitor. That's when I found the International Caricature Symptoms Academy's extrasensory defect recognition test."

"International what?"

"Caricature Symptoms Academy. I took their test and the results were positive."

Yuko cocked her head to one side. "It was bunk. It was baseless. It couldn't be. It was no more than a gag page created by some pervert to increase his page views. Total bunk."

"Well, maybe not bunk, but probably a website made by the guys who sent you the message," Mio said.

"What do you mean?" Hazuki asked.

"The original message came from them, right? They did a search on your self-portrait and found someone who drew a deformed character that resembled your drawing and sent you a scary message, then they said they'd kill you for having an extrasensory defect."

Then...

What were they planning on doing preparing such a test?

"In other words, they want to cleanse the world of people with extrasensory defects?"

Mio placed her chin in her hands and said with an unusually quiet air, "It has nothing to do with whether it really tests the abnormality but whether anyone will take the test. In other words the test is a trap, and those who take it..."

Are killed.

"I wouldn't have ever thought of that," Yuko said. "The results of the test were serious, and I got this reply from them saying that my abnormality was dangerous. That it was a problematic disease I should tell no one about. Then it told me to come out for the cure."

"Don't believe that crap," Mio said aloud. "Only a child would fall for that."

"*We* are children," Ayumi said.

"You can't make that judgment."

"Judgment? Well, I wouldn't buy it. Besides, it was nighttime, right? Weren't you scared to go out?"

"I was more scared of doing nothing about it. You know, because of that first message. I thought I would be killed if I really had this disease."

"Oh, right," Mio said.

"Mom and Dad couldn't know. They were too sensitive. I couldn't talk to them about any of this, so if I was going to be able to fix this, I figured I'd fix it as soon as possible. I didn't fathom..."

No one would have thought there'd be someone waiting to kill her.

"You know that old building by the bridge?"

"No, I don't," Mio said, put off.

"It's an old factory," Ayumi said.

"It's condemned."

"I didn't know that. I confirmed the location they gave me on my monitor and it didn't come up as a commercial building, a manufacturing building, or a residential building. It was…nothing. It was just a site off the middle of a traffic route. It was public land, but still…on the map the building was simply marked green, so I assumed it was a hospital. If it were Section B or C, I wouldn't have gone. But when I arrived no one was there.

"Just when I got scared and was about to leave, those guys came out with sticks and knives."

"Yikes," Mio said with a grimace. "That's scary. That's when they were like, 'Die!'?"

"They didn't say anything like that. But they were saying something about how God made man and something about an eternity of something or other…I didn't understand. They just yelled at me, and then as they attacked, I defended myself with the only thing I had—my monitor. Then my monitor snapped and broke. I didn't know what was going on. In fact I didn't realize I was set up until yesterday. So I started running with all my might and got to the bridge, when…"

Rey Mao was there.

"And that's when the fight began," Mio said, standing up. "What was cat girl doing? Probably practicing her *gongfu*, right? Then it got out of hand, and that's when she showed up, right?"

Ayumi.

For some reason she was staring through the floor.

"I was so scared," Yuko said. "I probably hung on to her when I saw her coming my way. I vaguely remember screaming, but I don't know what I said, and I don't know what happened. I don't remember anything after that. When I came to, I found myself following her."

Section C. The old red-light district. Rey Mao's neighborhood.

"Where's she living now?" Mio asked.

"Near your place. It was underground, but I knew it was Section C."

"How?"

"The smell. Back when I lived in the city, I had relatives in Section C. When I was little my parents would leave me there while they went on vacation. I hated it. There were all these weird people and gross smells, and it was all polluted. But when I complained about it they'd get mad at me. They told me the red-light district was just like that."

Mio made a confused look.

She was also a resident of Section C.

Yuko read Mio's reaction. "*Shit, I'm sorry,*" she mumbled softly. "But that's how it really was. I was only four or five, but I thought it was so much better to look at the district on a monitor. No offense, Mio, but I really hated it there. That's how I knew by the smell that I was there again. But I was scared. I couldn't stop shaking and I couldn't keep walking. Then she started bringing me food."

"The cat."

Rey Mao.

The undocumented girl with Chinese clothes.

"She didn't tell me her name. I answered all her questions. Then she said, 'You're the same as Mio Tsuzuki, then,' and she told me you lived nearby. She told me to go see you."

"Hmph."

Mio plopped down on the floor. *What'd that bitch say about me?* She sighed.

"Nothing bad, actually. She said you were friends...once?"

"Tch, friends. We played together when we were little."

Yuko looked straight at Mio with her pink pupils.

"But...she told me a lot of stories. I was crying the whole time and couldn't remember anything, but thanks to her I calmed down a little. But just as I stopped being so scared I realized suddenly that I didn't know what I was going to do. I didn't have a monitor, so I didn't have a sense of time and I didn't know where exactly I was. I was so confused, and when she left I went outside. That's when you two came by."

"Is that so."

That day in the rain...

Hazuki had had no idea of all the things going through Yuko's mind when they saw her there. Her talking with such familiarity about Section C, her knowing exactly where Mio lived, her standing there in the rain without an umbrella: there was a reason for all of that.

Yuko's not knowing about the murder and her strange reaction to news of it would all be normal in that situation. Everyone had their reasons for doing what they did; those reasons produced all kinds of emotions; and those emotions prompted action. The more Hazuki thought about it the more obvious it all seemed to her, and she became uneasy. You couldn't look inside a person's head. So?

There was no way of knowing anything about this.

None at all.

Wait. Ayumi might have known.

"After that I lost consciousness again," Yuko said. "The person that was killed was one of the guys attacking me. In which case, I had even less of an idea of what had happened, and I panicked."

"Then you broke into a fever," Ayumi said, still facing the wall. "You had a 105 degree fever."

"You're cold, Ayumi," Mio said as she approached her. "I mean, you knew, more or less, what was going on. And you didn't do anything."

"I didn't know what happened to her afterward. She was safe as far as I could see, and since she didn't ask for help I didn't offer it."

"Miss Kono did everything she could. See, I feel better and everything." Yuko looked up at Mio.

"And you too. I wanted to thank you and Miss Makino."

"What the..."

Mio walked past Ayumi to the other wall and said *she's so weird.*

"So I'm ready to go home. I won't continue to be a bother."

"But," Hazuki began and paused. "One of the assailants is dead and the other is on the run. Isn't it dangerous?" she said finally.

"The police will protect me."

"You sure you're okay?"

Mio let out a sound of uncertainty.

"The police are trying to establish a connection between your disappearance and the murders. Obviously they've looked into your communication logs. They're certain to have made the connection between you, Nakamura, and the now-dead Kawabata. They don't know how Kawabata died, but it's clear Nakamura is involved, and they'll agree you were being followed. So yeah, if you appeared now they'd protect you. But..."

"But what?"

"How will you explain the several days of disappearance?"

"I don't want to cause anyone any more problems," Yuko said, looking down. "Not for that other girl either."

"You mean Cat Freak? If you think about it though, if Nakamura is ever caught, they'll find out about her too. She helped you knowing that much, so if you were interrogated you could just tell them you were hiding out at her place the whole time. It's like you were anyway," Mio said.

"No. For the time being she should just not say anything about any of this," Ayumi said.

"Yeah..." Mio responded. "It makes no difference, right?"

"No, if Yuko talks about Rey Mao before they catch Nakamura, she'll be under suspicion."

"Oh, right."

The one who was killed was not the one being violated, but the one who was violating—the violator was the victim.

If someone saved Yuko knowing who her assailant was, Rey Mao would naturally be the first under suspicion.

"I don't think Nakamura will be caught so easily. There was another murder yesterday. I still think it'd be better for her to be protected by the police than to hide out here."

The latest victim—Asumi Aikawa. Hazuki couldn't remember her face.

However, Nakamura was on the run and wanted by the police. Would someone in that situation still be killing right now? Couldn't this be an unrelated event?

"But, Mio, you're the one who said that Rey Mao being questioned by the police would threaten the entirety of Section C and its residents. That may still be, but I doubt if Nakamura knows all about Rey Mao's situation. I mean, even Yuko didn't catch her name. There's no way she'd have given up that information accidentally," Hazuki said.

"So what's she supposed to say about the week she disappeared?"

"I'll just tell them *I don't know*," Yuko said.

"Temporary amnesia," Ayumi said

"Isn't that a little childish? It's so convenient," Mio said.

"That's not true." Ayumi stood up. "If she were lying—*if* she were lying, that would be the most productive answer. You just say you don't know anything if they ask."

"You mean she just lost consciousness for a week and magically regained it?"

"No, I mean that if she started to make up something she'd have to pile on more and more lies, details. Eventually she'd say something that would expose the lie. Why not just say 'I don't know' and be confused about the whole situation from the beginning."

"One answer for all of it then. 'I don't know,'" Yuko said.

Mio crossed her arms and started pacing. "What do you think, Hazuki?"

"I, uh, don't really know, but even if she decided to pretend she doesn't know, how's she going to get to the police?"

"Ahh." More of Mio's signature eye-widening.

"What do you mean *how*?"

"Is Yuko going to go home still having no idea what's what?"

"Well, she's not going to just waltz in and say hi to her parents, but let's say she's walking aimlessly around her neighborhood. The police would apprehend her then, right?"

"And what if Nakamura finds her first?" Just as Hazuki asked the question, Yuko hugged her shoulders.

She was scared.

"Where do you live, Yuko?"

"Huh?"

Yuko said her address.

It would take at least an hour to get there on foot.

"So you're pretty far from here. You think she should walk that alone? I didn't see any police or area cops in the twenty minutes it took me to walk here. I assume you didn't either, Mio."

"This is a safe area, so they never patrol here," Mio said.

"If I got this straight, a straight path from here to Yuko's house would lead through Section C. Even if she went by way of the community center she'd have to walk through Section B."

"There's that green preserve by the center. The police think Nakamura might be hiding out there, and they've focused their search to that area. So what about going to the community center? Guaranteed to be lots of cops there."

"But that means Nakamura might be there too," Ayumi said.

Shit! Mio spit out.

"Anyway," Hazuki continued. "If she's going to go to the police, this is the safest place for her to be picked up."

"But," Yuko lowered her pale eyes. "You all would be..."

"That's the safest way to go."

"Call the police here? Hazuki. What are you going to do when they come? Are you retarded?"

"Look, I know we can't do that. We can't explain why she's here. It'd be unnatural for us to say we just saw her milling around coincidentally and decided to protect her. We'd been told not to go out and all. If we obeyed the warning how would we have run into her, right?"

"Maybe we take her somewhere else and call the police there?"

"How? Yuko doesn't have a friggin' monitor." Mio scowled.

"She needs to borrow someone's monitor to get ahold of the police. What about the emergency monitor at the center of town?"

"Someone with amnesia using the emergency monitor? You'd think she'd have used it earlier rather than waiting a week."

"Then there's no other way for her to go to the police other than to have them find her. But sending her out alone is too dangerous. It's no less dangerous if we go with her, and if the police find all of us, it'd be the same as if they came and got her here."

"Hazuki's right," Ayumi said. "In the end, we're just kids. If we're thinking about Yuko's safety, the best solution is to call the police from here and explain everything. But then we'd be completely exposed—Hazuki's sneaking out, Mio's hacking, and my being up here at all."

Yuko's life couldn't be exchanged.

Ayumi didn't say it but Hazuki heard it.

Mio shook her hands through her hair frantically. "Yeah, I mean getting caught is one thing, but isn't this all really frustrating?"

"I don't understand. Frustrating?"

"Frustrating, meaning I don't like the way this feels. Do you understand *that*?" Mio said. Ayumi said, "No, I still don't understand." Hazuki had a feeling she did.

Though it was just a feeling.

Mio rubbed her head with her right hand and then stopped. "Wait a minute!" she said. "I know how we can call the police without actually calling them."

She looked around at everyone.

"*Cheer up!*" Mio said. "Okay, we all go to Hazuki's house."

"Huh?"

"It's near here, and it's in the safe area of Section A, plus no one's there, and it's secure as hell. Am I right?"

"You are, but—"

"You guys are no fun." Mio sighed. "Look. First I'll jigger the system to let Hazuki back into her house. Then Yuko will kind of wander past the gate of the house. The surveillance camera will catch it and notify the security company. Hazuki will say she was just studying when she looked at the screen, recognized her, and immediately called the emergency line. What do you think?" She looked around, trying to make eye contact with the others.

"The police will come flying to her place," Mio concluded.

"Is that...okay?" Yuko turned her painfully beseeching look over to Hazuki.

Hazuki nodded.

That should be fine, she thought.

CHAPTER | **016**

THE TERRIBLE NEWS was delivered on a Wednesday morning.

At the emergency meeting held over the weekend, it had been decided that the communication sessions would temporarily be put on hold. But that did not mean the counselors had no work to do. Though they didn't have direct access, the counselors had to monitor the surroundings of each child via messaging, and if there appeared to be a problem they would have to resolve it promptly.

Unlike administrators, counselor workloads increased in times of emergency.

What with her having to support Shima—who could not execute her duties due to her cooperation with the investigation—Shizue ended up working at the center three days straight.

She returned home Tuesday afternoon and finally got to bed at two in the morning after taking care of personal affairs that had piled up in the meantime.

However.

Sleep, which could hardly be called pleasant but was nonetheless welcome, was forced to end after a mere five hours.

Shizue received an emergency message. An emergency message replete with alarm.

Yuko Yabe had been discovered.

Not a recovery. A discovery.

Yuko had been killed.

This was terrible.

Shizue took a shower and went to her dresser. She looked horrible. It couldn't have been the result of fatigue. She looked way worse than Shima did last week.

Why'd you go and die?

It was what Shima had said. There was not a whole lot different between the two now. Shizue didn't need the words to come out of her mouth for the thought to be visible on her face.

She groomed herself because she had to.

It would have had more impact had she run out of the house without so much as a look in the mirror, but Shizue didn't like to present herself in that way.

Besides, all the time in the world wouldn't change the situation she had to confirm. If she were able to resurrect the dead, Shizue might run out barefoot, naked even, but desperate cries wouldn't bring Yuko Yabe back.

Dead children don't return.

She thought, though...

That just made her seem like a heartless woman.

Her countenance looked even more horrible than before.

She was a horrible person.

Her instructions were to be at the center as soon as possible, so she left.

Beginning with the area chief's and continuing with all her associates' were the faces of idiots, lined up and dazed.

They'd determined at the last convening the general stance the center would take toward the crime. Just because there were now more victims didn't mean that stance should change. It stood to reason then that they had nothing to say to each other, but then Shizue also thought there had to be something they should be doing.

Eventually Shizue was called into a special meeting room.

There were a number of men who looked like investigators, and Ishida.

"Miss Fuwa," Ishida voiced as soon as Shizue sat down. "I'm sure I don't need to explain to you that the situation has gotten worse. I know you provided all the information you had, and we for our part did everything we could, but regardless, let me start by saying sorry."

Ishida lowered his head.

The investigators lined up behind him also all bowed.

"I appreciate your apologies but I have no way to respond, since from the beginning stages of the investigation you made it clear my opinions as a counselor were totally impertinent. If you're going to go on about placing responsibility, I should be declared the victim."

"I'm apologizing knowing all of that full well. If the victim's survivors find a problem with this case, it will initially be directed toward you. In that sense...I am expressing regret in the fact that it didn't matter how much time we had; we were unable to prevent this tragedy from taking place."

He was talking in circles.

"So is there something I can do? I've submitted all the data on the children, even more information on the victim since she was missing. If there's anything else…"

"It's as you say," Ishida said. "But isn't there something you're neglecting to tell us?"

"What would that be?" Shizue answered unphased.

Ishida was expressionless. Shizue didn't typically like exuberant people, but in this case it was Ishida's metallic composure she found loathsome.

"Last week after our interrogation, you went to Hinako Sakura's residence, did you not?"

"I did."

They had been following her.

It could be Kunugi had told them about this.

Actually, his timing *had* seemed too good at the time. He'd made up some convenient excuse about having been on patrol or something, but he could have been following her.

"According to her family you were not there in your capacity as a counselor."

"It was a private matter."

"Meaning? If you don't mind, could you please tell us what you talked about?"

"I asked her about divinations. Miss Sakura gave me a whole lecture."

There was no point in hiding this information. It was half true.

Ishida's thin lips curled, and he tapped at his monitor screen with a fingertip.

"A counselor listening to a lecture by a child."

"Is that odd?"

"Not odd. I gather you've been lectured by other children in your charge before. However…"

Ishida stopped to look at the portable big-screen monitor.

"I can't imagine you had a personal interest in divination. Nothing in our records indicates you had any interest in the occult before. What's more, you don't strike me personally as someone who would believe in such superstitions—that's to say, you seem more like someone who'd reject those ideas."

"People are known to change, officer."

"You mean you suddenly took up an interest?"

Shizue asked *is that not allowed?* and Ishida said *of course it is.*

"Well, Hinako Sakura's testimony corroborates your story. I'm sure there are no problems."

"You interrogated Sakura?"

"We still are."

"She has nothing to do with this."

"We'll be the judge of that," Ishida said. "Actually, she is the very last person to have spoken directly to the victim. It was after the medical exam last month, but of course, you already knew that. There were several communication sessions afterward but she didn't speak to anyone off-session."

"It is not uncommon for children to refrain from any vocal communication with others. That's precisely why we have them attend these communication labs."

"Well, well." Ishida sat up. "Our records indicate Yuko Yabe was precisely not one of those kinds of children. She didn't meet with people privately, but you wrote in your notes yourself that she was very enthusiastic about talking to others during the labs."

What an asshole.

"There's nothing too out of the ordinary in the data we received for that month, but we looked a little deeper into it and discovered that for the month leading up to her disappearance she became uncharacteristically quiet. What do you have to say about that?" Ishida asked.

To be honest, she hadn't even noticed.

As far as Shizue was concerned, Yuko Yabe hadn't exhibited any noticeable behavior at all.

She replied honestly.

"Is that so?" Ishida smartly withdrew. "Well, I suppose there are things even a counselor wouldn't notice. I guess there's nothing we can say about this."

Ishida looked directly at Shizue. "Oh, I didn't mean for that to imply any deficit in your counseling abilities. You are an excellent counselor. It's just that we hear about children who aren't able to open up. I'm sure they've got to be a handful for you. We just discovered this bit of information after a careful reading of the data you provided us, but with that many children in your care I suppose it would be impossible to know everything."

"It has nothing to do with the number of children I counsel. It's not as if I were watching over more children than the law allows. If you're wondering why I didn't notice this change in the child's behavior it's because of my inattention to her."

"No need to get defensive. I want to say this again, but we hold your services as a counselor in very high esteem. If you didn't notice it, we think it's safe to assume there was nothing to be noticed. We thought maybe she had a medical situation, but she received Triple-A health status on her medical exam. No diseases or ailments. Her late communication deficit might just be incidental."

"Incidental?"

"An incidentally poorly placed bug as they say in divinations. That could happen to anyone."

Something was wrong.

Shizue knew it.

"However…"

At last there was what came after. Shizue turned away from Ishida's plastic-looking face.

"Well, I mean even a gifted counselor such as yourself can't be expected to grasp every single thing a child is going through. Just as we as police officers can't possibly grasp every single aspect of a criminal. There are some things only other children know. Isn't that right?"

"Humans aren't so pure that they can be easily grasped."

"Exactly." Ishida closed his monitor. "And that's precisely why you went to see Hinako Sakura, isn't it? That is how I understood it. That's the kind of person you are. You weren't going to be content to sit back and watch nothing be done about Yuko Yabe's disappearance. You knew Sakura was the last person Miss Yabe spoke to, and you wanted the information Sakura had, that only Sakura could have. Am I wrong? You said it was a private matter, but it was an action you took based on your duties as a counselor."

"That's…your own interpretation," Shizue said. "You can infer all you want, but I can't tell you more than the honest truth. Besides, even if you're right, haven't you already interrogated Sakura?"

"Like I said we still are. It's just…she won't answer any of our questions."

"Won't answer? What do you mean?"

"Sakura definitely spoke with the victim, but she said she's forgotten what about. She tells us it was probably nothing important. We just have a hard time believing that. According to the data we have on her, she has an incredible memory. We're pretty sure she remembers what happened a little over a month ago. Besides, unlike the victim, Hinako Sakura actually did not have many interactions with other children. Her *real contact* with Yabe would have been exceptional. Unforgettable, even."

Hinako was hiding something. The fact that Yuko had been worried about the illness she had.

"That may be, but...if that's what she said, that must be what happened," Shizue responded.

If she didn't want to talk, Shizue wasn't going to make her.

Least of all to Ishida.

Besides, she was sure Hinako Sakura had nothing to do with the murder.

"What about it then, did you hear anything?" Ishida sat up.

"As I said before, I went to Sakura to ask about divinations. I didn't hear anything. Aren't you guys supposed to be experts at getting information out of people?"

"If we're experts at interrogation, then you're the pro at figuring out children." Ishida intensified his glare.

"Any clues at all?"

"None."

"More importantly, could you tell me about how Yuko Yabe's body was discovered? I just received word this morning and haven't heard any specifics since then."

"Ahh," Ishida said. He pulled up his monitor again.

"Yuko Yabe's body...was in Section C...on the east side. She was discovered there. It was this morning, no, closer to last night, that she was found. Four fifty AM. She was discovered by a patrolman local to the area; he was there looking for another missing child, that Yuji Nakamura. The corpse was in a savaged state. You can think of it being in the same state we found Asumi Aikawa."

She didn't want to think of it at all.

"Estimated time of death is somewhere up to thirty hours before the discovery. We're still performing the autopsy, so we won't know any more till it's completed. It's possible she was murdered late Monday night."

At the very least, she wasn't killed immediately after her disappearance.

"You have no idea where she was while she was missing?"

"No. However, we think she was wearing the same clothes she was last seen in."

"Based on what? You have eyewitnesses from the day of her disappearance?"

"No. We don't have eyewitnesses from the day of her disappearance. That's why I can't say for certain, but we deduced that she hadn't changed clothes from looking at the wardrobe her parents had at the house. According to them, there is only one outfit missing, and it's the one she was found wearing."

She'd been wearing the same clothes for over a week.

"It does seem, however, that her clothes were cleaned at some point," Ishida said.

"The chemical composition on clothing is altered whenever it is cleaned. We determined from a test of a swatch of her clothing that she'd had her clothes cleaned approximately five days before she died. Meaning while she was missing."

"She had her clothes cleaned while she was missing?"

"I don't know if we should call it 'missing' anymore. It's more like she was hiding," Ishida said.

"You think she was in danger and hid herself?"

"Her parents were gone and all…"

"But wouldn't she go to the police for protection in that situation? Or at least the center, where I…"

No.

Yuko wouldn't have felt she could trust Shizue.

"Did you find her monitor?" Shizue asked.

"We didn't find her personal mobile monitor. She had her ID card on her, but it wasn't used once during her disappearance. You would need to use an ID card at some point just for the cleaning, but we don't know anything more about that."

"What about her personal communication log?"

Only counselors were privy to that information.

"With her parents' approval we were able to look into that as well. There is *absolutely no record* of communication."

"None? No communication sent *or* received?"

"Nothing personal."

Was it possible for there not to be any communication whatsoever? Knowing Yuko, that seemed especially implausible.

"The suspect…"

Yuji Nakamura.

"Okay, then what about this Nakamura then?"

"We haven't been able to trace him. There's this thing with the Kawabata boy too. It's a very dangerous situation. We're putting all our energy into this investigation."

"Are you saying you've changed your search status for him from likely culprit to possible victim?"

"I've said this several times now, but we never had any evidence confirming his guilt. He's a person of great interest, but in keeping with what you said yourself, we are treating him as a potential victim in this investigation. Besides…"

Ishida peered back as if to confirm the presence of the investigators standing behind him.

"Just between us, there have been some sketchy types coming forward. Eyewitnesses."

"Sketchy types."

"You know, undocumented residents in Section C. They have no citizenship. There are quite a few of them in this country, but then we run into issues of human rights. We can't just expose them all, and our department frankly doesn't know how to handle them. It seems Nakamura, Kawabata, and Yabe have all three been among these people."

"The undocumented residents?"

"About 20 percent of the area's juvenile population resides in Section C, am I right?" Ishida asked.

"If that's the figure the police came up with then I'm assuming it's correct. The breakdown of children's residential demography doesn't mean anything, so I don't bother to put it out there."

"Aren't you required to be concerned with the children's living environment?"

"All that means is that the area you mentioned has characteristics that don't meet the standard of residential environments. It's been a predominantly commercial area, and so it has no history of having been developed as a residential area. That's beyond me."

"But it's a nonstandard environment, then?"

"Yes. But, excluding the undocumented residents, for example, most of the people residing in Section C are what you'd call average citizens. Documented residents are using the residential area correctly, and so even if the environment is nonstandard, there is no reason to give it special attention. At the very least, we as counselors should be more concerned with individual homes."

"So you don't think that the nonstandard characteristics of a particular area might affect the quality of life in an individual household?"

"Unfortunately no," Shizue answered. "Households are independent within their neighborhoods. The people inside the household are independent of their homes. What connects individuals to each other is information; physical proximity has no real bearing. This is why we built community centers. Ours is a society where so long as they aren't coerced or systematized, people won't care who's in the next room."

"I believe it," Ishida said.

"Those who still believe in the primacy of geography are largely of the bygone century. They—well, if I had to pick a side I'd be one of them too—believe it imperative to maintain the framework of a nation-state. That's why we create borders. And building the framework means maintaining it. But categorizations and labels don't necessarily equate with control. It is irritating."

"Irritating?"

"Yes. That much is obvious from the fact that two-thirds of the police infrastructure is concerned with information supervision. But…"

Ishida drew a cloth from his pocket and wiped the frame of his monitor. "Still, we don't exist just on intake of information alone. We also live, eat, and sleep in this place. As long as *real access* happens, there will be crime."

Shizue wasn't going to disagree with him there. She was sure that was true.

But Shizue didn't believe in it.

"That's why we have epic mistakes such as investigation exhibit R," Ishida said. "Those undocumented citizens who have centralized in Section C, in particular, have built a life ignoring the framework we as authorities have taken many pains to build. These people have now formed communities with blood ties and connections to the land and established a lifestyle by means of illegal methods."

"So you're suggesting they are all criminals."

"In that someone who doesn't abide by the law is a criminal, yes. Undocumented residents are all criminals. Regardless, the reality is that they refuse to live under our rules and social mores. In other words, it'd be more accurate to say they live in their own country. Meaning that Section C represents their country and our country living side by side. I think it's impossible to say that living situation doesn't have an effect on the average citizen."

"You're really talking in circles, aren't you?" Shizue blurted. "To be sure, I have children in my care who interact with undocumented or foreign citizens, or else they used to interact with them. That goes without saying. I've given you all the data."

Shizue said *you already know this*, and Ishida responded matter-of-factly that he did.

"Then what else could you possibly want to hear from me? The worst has already happened, and so there's little need to hurry, but this is also no time for us to be sitting around at leisure. Stop beating around the bush and just tell me what you want."

Ishida's eyebrows, neatly matching in shape, lowered, and he smiled weakly.

Then he started tapping lightly at the screen of his monitor with an index finger and very purposefully said, *I see then.*

"Well, that makes it easier for me to talk as well. Actually, the undocumented citizen that came up in our investigation is a girl of about fourteen or fifteen years of age. Of course she doesn't have a family seal or anything, so we can't know her exact age or real name. But she is definitely very close in age to all the murder victims in our investigation. I suppose it could be said her proximity in age won't have anything to do with this, but—"

"You're saying she had interaction with the victim?"

"Not exactly, but we can't say she didn't at least run into one of the victims. We had this sketch made based on the eyewitness accounts of several people and ran it through the children's database, and..."

Ishida turned his monitor toward Shizue.

On the screen was the face of an unfriendly-looking young girl.

"Mio Tsuzuki. She's one of yours, right? Seems she's a very intelligent little girl. Looking at her developmental profile on the public server. Frankly, I was shocked. She's advancing at a stunning pace."

"She's probably the most advanced in her age group for the area."

"It's more than that. As far as I know, she is the most intelligent girl of her age group, bar none. It'd be safe to call her a *world*-class genius. Really, an exceptional specimen here. However, she's got emotional problems, doesn't she?"

"Not at all." Shizue responded arrogantly. "Mio Tsuzuki is clearly advanced. But beyond that, she's a completely normal fourteen-year-old. That's all. Sure, her intellectual maturity does not match her emotional quotient, but there are no real problems there to speak of. She has the same problems other children her age have, and she's growing in the same way that the other children are. There's no reason to see her advancement in education as a problem source."

"I understand," Ishida said. "She is a resident of Section C, yes?"

"Yes. She lives in the old red-light district at the center of that section. And?"

"We believe she has interfaced with what might be a suspect."

"Mio?"

This was an unexpected development.

"Miss Fuwa," Ishida said. "Mio Tsuzuki's parents, er—at least what looks like someone a generation older, shall we say, grandfather? Her grandfather did much for the expansion of the area when it was still a specialty business district. As the red-light district collapsed and the people deserted it, he stirred up quite a bit of action with the police and residents. Since her elder died off, she's been working in extremely specialized information production, and though not illegal, it's not the kind of thing we can exactly encourage. She's been involved with people with foreign citizenship or no citizenship."

It was difficult to say what either of Mio's parents did. She couldn't immediately say whether they were a problem or not. They were what used to be called *bankers*, but she didn't know exactly what kind of setup they worked in.

And as Ishida pointed out, Mio was in an area surrounded by a lot of people who'd never had interactions with average citizens. Mio herself was raised by a foreigner and could be said to be in a very special living environment.

However, it hadn't once occurred to Shizue to connect Mio with recent events, and even now though told there was a connection, she couldn't be forced to believe it.

"It seems you've had personal dealings with this Tsuzuki kid also?"

"She tutors me after the communication labs. As you said, she is a world-class genius. There's a lot to be learned from her."

"Have you heard of anyone referred to as 'Cat'?"

Cat. That was...

"If I recall, Mio used to play with a cat when she was little."

"So you remember this?"

"That there was a cat. I think it was a cat."

"You mean like the animal?"

"Is there any other kind of cat?" Shizue asked. "There are still a lot of cats in that area."

"It's the name of a human," Ishida said. "Seems she's of Chinese descent—alias, Cat, the Chinese character for which is pronounced 'Mao.' We don't have any details on her, but we believe she's an undocumented resident who's been involved in procuring illegal foodstuffs in what used to be a pharmacy."

"That's your suspect?"

"We have a report of someone having seen, last Sunday at the time we believe that Ryu Kawabata was killed, what looked like two males and one female minor fighting. Based on what they said about her attire, we're pretty sure it was this Mao girl. Furthermore they've said there was one other girl there."

"Another?"

"It's possible it was Yuko Yabe."

"You're saying Yabe was at the scene of Kawabata's murder?"

"Possibly. There's a possibility she was at the scene. However, this Mao girl was also seen later near Yabe's home. It seems she was near Sakura's residence as well."

"Sakura's? Really."

"This Mao was probably visiting the Yabe residence. Hinako Sakura was visiting the Yabe residence. It was shortly thereafter that you and our investigator were there, and after a short dispute Sakura was apprehended and went back home. We think maybe Mao saw this take place and followed Sakura to her home. It fits with the time our observations say Sakura returned home."

This girl had been watching Shizue and Kunugi at the time.

They were being watched.

Shizue's spine froze and sent a horrible chill through her entire body.

"We don't know what Aikawa has to do with this, but Kawabata, Nakamura, and Yabe all had some kind of exchange with Mao, and their lives were in danger thereafter. Kawabata was killed, and the other two, fearing for their physical safety, went into hiding. However, Yabe was discovered, and…"

"Killed?"

Really?

Something was slightly off in this interpretation. Maybe not off, exactly, but it was too simple. It seemed too convenient the way it all made sense.

"But the circumstances have suggested the interpretation for us," Ishida noted. "In that case, you can assume there's a criminal organization amidst the undocumented resident community and that it is behind these murders. In fact, it'd be prudent to assume—"

"You're saying it's easy to understand. You really think an average city resident, a minor for that matter, is capable of organizing a criminal organization like that?"

Ishida laughed. "Do you recall a case from fifteen years ago in which a group of foreigners organized a huge sale of drugs? The targeted drug buyers were all between the ages of ten and thirteen. The reason that case blew open was because of a skirmish between the teenage buyers and the selling organization. Sixty percent of electronic crimes are committed by minors, and half of them are involved in some kind of criminal activity online. I don't know what's going on in this case, but it's not impossible."

"Really..."

Something somewhere was off. Shizue couldn't shake the feeling.

"We discussed this at the first conference, but the rate of crimes among minors has decreased over the years. But that's a number our Investigative Unit R produced. If you include the figure produced by Investigative Unit V, that number is hugely skewed. Moreover, even in the figures Unit R produces, it doesn't figure in the attempted crimes, and we've determined that the number of people involved in crimes has gone up. So..."

"I understand," Shizue said.

But this wasn't one of those situations.

"The only official record we have of this possible suspect, Mao, is her interaction with Mio Tsuzuki. This Mio and the victim were in the same communication session. And you were the counselor for both of them. That's why we—"

"I'm sorry, but I don't have any information I think will be useful to your investigation."

"It seems that way," Ishida said half seriously. "Well, seeing as how you didn't even realize we were talking about a human, I guess it's only fair."

Ishida refreshed his monitor and read something on the screen. "This is our thinking. The cat print is similar to the old art of China. This description has been our lynchpin."

"The cat print."

"Yes. There are actual cats in Section C, and felines have...well, prints. So unless you are hunting for them, it's no sort of description. However..."

"The art of China."

"That's right. We actually did a search on the keyword 'cat' in the kids' files. As you can imagine, we got a lot of search results, but when you search Section C and Chinese people, Tsuzuki comes up. When we looked into it, we found out her residence was located near an area where there was a catlike person. Then we filtered our results. When we reviewed the information, we could only infer that the 'cat' that popped up so frequently in her data was not an animal but instead referred to a human. If you read her descriptions carefully, the word for the animal 'cat' was frequently spelled in katakana. And the cat pattern she referred to was a costume print, or rather, embroidery. Most of this is from descriptions from her early childhood. After she turns ten there is suddenly no more mention of cats."

"Is that so? I mean, so it is."

It had been five years since Shizue started seeing Mio.

It wasn't just that Mio possessed an unusually high intellect. She also had an incredible centripetal force. Her perspective and interpretations were unique and always stood out in comparison to the other children. Still...

Shizue knew nothing about the cat.

What else didn't she know about Mio's earlier years?

As a counselor, this could be a huge missing piece.

What a child saw, heard, ate, underwent, undertook in his or her formative years...

The advice and counseling one provided a child could change drastically based on these curious details. That was why Shizue had taken special care to check the historical data when she took over Mio's file from her predecessor.

But.

Her predecessor probably hadn't noticed references to the "cat" either.

By the time Shizue had been handed Mio Tsuzuki's file by the girl's previous counselor, Cat had probably long since passed into memory.

But there was no changing the fact that Shizue had known nothing about this.

Nothing.

Shizue knew better than anyone that there was no knowing a child.

Ishida had been staring at Shizue but eventually turned an ear toward the investigator at his back and then said *understood*.

"What did you find out?"

"We know that for now, there's no more information we can obtain from you. However, we'd like to be able to follow up with you. You'll be working here along with Miss Shima. Is that all right?"

Shizue didn't feel like responding.

She just nodded and left the room.

The spotless hallway seemed somehow smudged.

It was only a tentative straight line.

Shizue felt the wall against the palm of her hand.

She had not once in her life run a hand against a wall.

It was smooth.

And even though it was a different texture entirely...

It felt like when she had held the hand of her deceased mother.

Shizue took her hand away from the wall and wiped her palm with her wet wipes.

Repeatedly.

When she closed her eyes she could see Yuko Yabe's imploring face.

But it wasn't quite a face. It was more like a vague image, by no means clear, but definitely Yuko's.

Yet no sooner had she tried to remember the details than it devolved into a different being altogether.

That being was her dead mother, or Mio Tsuzuki, or Ishida, or the horribly exhausted self in the mirror.

The Yuko inside Shizue was...

All made up of borrowed images.

Why'd you go and die?

Shizue turned the inorganically placed corner of the building into the unpopular entrance hall and walked through to the counseling booth. It was the private office they'd designated hers.

In a room like this she could do her work even if just on standby.

She swiped her ID card, and the door made an unpleasant sound before opening into the room.

Everything in the room was painted in a green theme to calm the nerves.

Her private office was a bright, well-lit space. It was conceptually relaxing. But there was no way Shizue could relax in that environment.

Whatever the structure or the color of the room, it was a workspace for Shizue. Tension, yes. Relaxation, no. Countless children entered that space to unravel their inner thoughts, to express their minds, cry, and get angry. Shizue received any and all of these nonuniform communications and had to process them like a bureaucrat while seeming to care.

She got to her desk and took a deep breath.

She turned on her monitor and called up Yuko Yabe's face. There was no meaning in it. She'd wanted to see a real picture of her in order to clear away the vague one in her head.

Pink pupils, small frame.

"Color."

There was no color in her visualization.

Adding the color pink quickly and permanently materialized the real Yuko Yabe for Shizue.

Now there was no confusing her image with anything else.

It still might have been a borrowed image, but at least the Yuko inside Shizue now had her own existence. In the middle of completing the image, Shizue felt suddenly like a hole had opened in her stomach.

This must be what they call being sad.

Just then.

Shizue noticed that the growth pattern in the field outside swayed unnaturally.

The counseling booth's window faced the inner courtyard of the center.

The inner courtyard connected to the green area surrounding the center. Though they were connected physically, the yard and the green area were cordoned off by laser sensors designed to prevent outside intrusions.

The security at public institutions was unsurpassed. In other words, this wasn't a place for ordinary civilians. Maintenance personnel came in throughout the day, but the days were different, and they usually had finished their work by very early in the morning.

That reminded her...

Shizue looked down at the windowsill.

A few days ago, four days maybe, they'd announced a search of the green area on the center's periphery for Yuji Nakamura, who it was believed had been hiding in the area. At the time of the communication, Nakamura was a person of extreme interest, practically a suspect, so it made sense they used the word "hiding" to describe his disappearance.

It was different now.

The investigators must have deepened their search into the courtyard.

Or it could be Yuji Nakamura himself crossing into the courtyard.

Shizue placed her hand on the window.

She turned off the security.

She focused her eyes again.

The natural makeup of the greenery.

It was swaying.

Shizue put her hand on the window lever.

The glass window slid open with a low buzzing sound from the internal motor. The outdoors broke in. Temperature change. Temperature change. Then natural sounds. Smells. The smell of damp earth. The scent of grass and trees that had grown out of decayed nutrients. A pungent and dirty scent Shizue detested.

A swooshing sound in the grass.

Shizue grabbed the security line receiver by her window.

Regardless of whether Nakamura was the culprit or the victim, whether that was him in the grass in the first place, she would need to notify someone. There was definitely someone out there.

"Who's out there?"

Her voice was hoarse.

The person in the shadows wasn't Yuji Nakamura.

"Hello?"

"Oh thank God it's you. I thought I was done for."

The man brushed away the leaf in front of his face.

"Officer…Kunugi? You…"

"Actually, I uh…"

Kunugi looked at the security receiver in Shizue's hand.

"Are you going to call them?"

"If that's what I should do."

"It isn't," Kunugi said. "They'll dismiss me from the force if you do that. They might even add immediate punishment."

"Punishment?"

"Yeah, punishment. On top of committing an offense while in uniform, I've trespassed in an area of prohibited entry."

"Offense while in uniform? But aren't you investigating this area?"

"Investigating, sure. The investigation here ended yesterday at ten AM. Right before they announced withdrawal from the center I lied to the guard at the entrance and came into this courtyard."

"Lied? Lied how?"

Kunugi's clothing was well soiled. He was covered in dirt and leaves.

If Shizue were to believe what Kunugi had just said, he'd have been camping out in this forest for over a day. Of course he was dirty.

"I told you I was on disciplinary leave, didn't I?" Kunugi said. "I have no authority to do anything right now. My police privileges have all been revoked. During my disciplinary probation they monitor the usage of my ID card. It's like I have a criminal record, so I'm treated worse than the average citizen. I had no choice but to lie. So I just came in here and said I was on the investigation without showing them my ID."

"Why would you do that?"

"It's a long story and if I tell you, you'll be involved," Kunugi said. "Given your position, it would be prudent to activate that security line."

It would be prudent.

Shizue remembered the way she looked in the mirror before she left. The face she envisioned transformed into Ishida's. *Prudent action*. What a nasty phrase. If there was any time to act stupidly, unnaturally, it was when someone had just died. It would probably be okay.

No, definitely.

Shizue replaced the receiver into the wall unit.

"Why didn't you call them?" Kunugi asked.

"I'm reconceptualizing the truth."

"That's a nice way of putting it."

"Are you really on disciplinary leave?"

"Why would I lie about something like that?"

"Maybe you're pretending to be informal so you can trap me into giving information off the record."

"Ishida…" Kunugi said. He puffed his cheeks. "Ishida's questioning you, so now you're doubting me."

Shizue didn't respond but examined Kunugi's expression. He'd furrowed his brow. *So listen*, Kunugi said. He took a deep breath and spoke again.

"This is what I meant when I said our talking to each other would cause you problems. I wasn't following you for them. They were following me. It's because I came to you that those guys started following you."

"What do you mean they were following you?"

"That's a good question. I don't know myself. I just knew I was being tailed. I was positive after we left that restaurant. My pursuer let up as soon as I noticed him, but now they have a tight GPS track on me. I know that much. Even after I turn off the screen on my monitor there is a slight noise, and when I receive my news bulletins the color is slightly off."

"You're totally marked, then?"

"That's right. With my movements monitored I was unable to go anywhere, but after a week of lying low I couldn't resist anymore."

"Resist what?"

"No, it's just that being watched made me feel imprisoned," Kunugi said. He laughed. "I could have stayed home and played old role-playing games, but knowing everything I did was being tracked made me antsy. I had no choice, so I left my portable monitor at home and came out."

"Your monitor?"

"They're going to know something's wrong when I don't move for this long. That's why I came here early yesterday morning, but then I got stuck when the investigators left. What a joke, right? Surveillance cameras everywhere, I couldn't move. Even if the police didn't find me, eventually that skinhead woman guarding the grounds would realize I hadn't come back out. I had just about given up."

Kunugi shrugged and laughed anew.

Shizue was confused. Why was he laughing?

"You've been here for over thirty hours."

Shizue wouldn't have lasted ten minutes. All she saw when she looked out at the forest were breeding grounds for microbes and insects.

"I'm pathologically filthy, remember?" Kunugi said. "It's relatively safe out here. Despite my looks, I'm actually not that great in the outdoors. You're not going to believe this, but when I was a kid they said I was a clean freak. Toward the end of the twentieth century, kids still played in the mud and stuff. But not me. They used to have these personal game units. They were like toys. I played with that thing all the time. I didn't realize till I got to this age that it's important to play in the mud too."

Kunugi showed off his mud-caked hands to Shizue.

Shizue withdrew and pointed her left hand to indoors. Kunugi made an incredulous face.

"What are you thinking?"

"There are no children here today. In fact no one's here."

"Still. I can't go in there!"

"The security system is turned off and the surveillance cameras in counselor offices are shut off to protect the privacy of children. As long as no children come into the room the cameras won't move. Once we leave this room together I suppose the cameras will go back on."

Kunugi was astonished. He laughed uncomfortably and reached out a hand for assistance. This man was just as capable of reconceptualizing the truth as Shizue.

"I'm...dirty," he warned.

"I can tell."

A visible mess was always better than an invisible one.

Kunugi carefully made his way to the window, removed his mud-caked shoes, and stepped into the room. He made a thudding sound. He smelled like mud. Shizue immediately closed the window and returned to her desk, turning on her air filter.

"There's no need for that," Kunugi said. "Why are you saving me if you have to hold your breath?"

"Because I don't know why you are running around. I'm having a hard enough time figuring out why you were put on leave. Moreover, why is a police unit tracking one of its own officers with GPS surveillance? I find this all very hard to believe. It'd be another thing if you were suspected of the murders."

"If that were the case..." Kunugi had been facing the window looking out and turned to face Shizue. "You would be in serious danger."

Kunugi put out both his hands toward her.

"If I were a murderer, it's possible this mud on my fingers would get all over your neck."

"Strangulation is it? If it's at all up to me, I'd like to be stabbed to death like all the other victims. Anything but strangulation."

I don't like it, Shizue added softly.

Kunugi lowered his hands.

"I'm sorry, but I'm actually not strong enough to kill you with my bare hands anyway. It's an optical illusion, all this. I may be large, but I have no physical strength. I ranked a C at my physical. So not only did I get bad grades I'm not even strong enough to be a jock. I'm able to eat because I'm a public servant, but I'll never amount to more than a local beat cop. I'm so stupid I once Tasered myself by accident."

"Can I sit here?" Kunugi asked. He plopped down into the counseling chair without waiting for an answer. "So Ishida called you?"

"Yes, he did."

Shizue leaned against her desk.

"Yuko Yabe was killed, huh?" Kunugi said. "This morning," replied Shizue.

"She'd been on the run for a good week. If the police had somehow gotten to her sooner her life could have been spared. If only..."

"Nothing we say now will bring her back. If you want to talk about what could have happened, I'm the one who delayed reporting her disappearance. Even if I'm to blame for negligence, repeating what's happened would just be backwards."

"You're cold," Kunugi said. "I feel real remorse. I feel bad."

"I feel exactly the same way in that regard. But, Kunugi, what were you thinking this time?"

Kunugi's eyes widened. They were unusually large eyes.

"What do you mean what was I thinking this time?"

"That's about as direct a way as I could think of to ask why the police would be following you around."

Shizue stood up, dispensed some flavonoid beverage from a push-button machine, and handed it to Kunugi. Kunugi savored the drink.

"Thank you. For bringing me this, I mean. Ah, I'm sorry if this will seem indelicate. I wasn't going to collect morning dew or anything, so my throat was totally parched. I never thought in this day and age that I'd find myself in this kind of situation. And I'll have you know I haven't done anything or thought of doing anything. Since I spoke to you last week, I've just been thinking about that theory I have."

"That one of the murders in this serial killing spree is unrelated?"

"Yeah. Going back to last year's murders, the murders that took place on the butsumetsu and the ones in which the one organ was never discovered are unrelated, I still believe. And then this newest case…"

"Another deformée character–related incident?" Shizue asked.

"Actually, Asumi Aikawa didn't seem to indicate any interest in DC." She'd confirmed with Shima. Kunugi agreed.

"But that just isn't going to fly."

"What does that mean?"

"Asumi Aikawa was also *missing a piece*."

"Missing…"

"Missing a part. So if she were into DC, it would actually not fit with my theory. This is one of the other thread of murders."

"You mean one of the murders in which an internal organ was removed."

"Her liver was missing."

Shizue was stunned.

The broken replica of a human had in fact not been complete.

"I did a little search on Sunday on a colleague's monitor. He's a good cop. Unfortunately he thinks I am too. He'll never move up. So what did Ishida tell you?" Kunugi asked.

"Aikawa wasn't one of my kids, and the notice we got at the center said nothing about missing livers. Just that the body was found severely damaged."

"I suppose there's no reason to point out something like that. The cops don't think the criminal made off with the liver or anything. I doubt if there's such a thing as an organ-takeout murderer."

"Made off with…"

Kunugi took a wet wipe and wiped his face and neck. "Making off with doesn't mean anything. Maybe forty or fifty years ago, but there's no way someone in this age would need a live organ transplant. Cloned organs are cheaper and guaranteed. One can't know the quality of some random girl's internal organs, and no doctor would perform a surgery that low-tech. A live organ transplant is actually quite difficult. I don't think anyone would do something that arcane. So then what would they do with the organ? That's the question.

"There are those people who fetishize certain body parts. There are cases from long ago of murderers who saved a certain part of the body, even those who collected those parts."

"Even internal organs? Unfortunately I don't know of anyone who collects internal organs."

"Well it wouldn't be strange if you did," Kunugi said, and brought the blackened wet wipe to his nose before throwing it into the trash chute. "There are so many kinds of perverts out there. There's no rhyme or reason to them. Depending on how you looked at things, we could be considered perverts too."

"I agree," Shizue said.

"But we don't have this weirdo's—I mean, I'm not being prejudiced here, but...we're talking about someone who's committing criminal acts in order to satisfy his idiosyncrasy. I don't think this is the kind of thing that an individual does."

"You have a basis for this theory?"

"Sort of. Think about it. If you believe what I'm saying, it's been a two-year streak of serial murders if you combine the butsumetsu killings from last year and the deformée character killings of this year. I haven't looked into serial murders from before that, but if you did—*if*—the pattern could go back forever. And if *that's* the case, we can't keep saying these murders are just a pervert fulfilling his whims."

Kunugi was probably right.

It was too calculated. Actually it wasn't even a matter of it being calculated. This kind of crime wasn't necessarily an emotional one. Emotional inclinations had nothing to do with the intellectual quality of crime. Motives, ones fueled by sexual inclinations, minutely trained, painstakingly conceived sex crimes...There were too many of them.

"You mean the scale is too big?" Shizue asked. Kunugi nodded.

"I think this goes beyond one person's criminal file."

"If your theory proves correct, I believe you're right that we're dealing with more than just one perpetrator."

"An organization," Kunugi answered hesitantly.

"What kind of organization would be doing this though, right?" Shizue said. "Lieutenant Ishida indicated the possibility that it was the undocumented residents of Section C."

"Undocumented residents?"

"They aren't really an organization, but they have certainly grouped together and created a life for themselves and their kind by unlawful means, so they would be capable of pulling off something of the scale you were talking about."

"Yeah, but…where did that come from?" Kunugi asked.

He scratched behind his ear.

"You don't know?"

Kunugi stopped his fingers and said, "I don't. We weren't considering undocumenteds when I was on the investigation."

"There's apparently witness testimony that the night Ryu Kawabata was killed, the victim along with Yuji Nakamura were both fighting a young woman. That young woman is an undocumented resident. Yuko Yabe was also apparently there."

"I didn't hear any of this. Ryu Kawabata and Yuji Nakamura were spotted within the vicinity of the scene of the crime. No one's out on the streets there even in the middle of the day. It's hard to believe there was an eyewitness. If there were, it has to have been Nakamura or Yabe."

"But that's what Ishida told me. That there's some fourteen or fifteen-year-old girl called Cat who runs with some kind of medicine-seller or something."

"You mean the organic food products people. They definitely have a wide network of connections. Still, it seems a little out of nowhere." Kunugi made a severe face and resumed scratching behind his ear.

"This undocumented resident was apparently watching us when we went by the Yabe residence. After we apprehended Sakura, who was also there, the girl started following Sakura."

"How did they get that evidence?" Kunugi crossed his arms. "Certainly after the request for questioning was made, the police investigated the goings on around the Yabe residence. But she hadn't been killed yet at that point. It was a *disappearance*. Of course, it was possible she was tied up in the murder, so they could have been looking for suspicious types. Typically in the investigation of a disappearance they will look first into what the victim was doing at the time of the disappearance and what they were doing right before."

"Obviously," Shizue said.

"Right? We were there two days after she'd been declared missing. Given that, whatever they heard in the area had to have been incidental. I doubt that they went as far as patrolling Sakura's home. When I was attached to the case, Sakura wasn't believed connected to any of this."

Shizue had heard the same. Hinako was under interrogation now, but that was only now, after Yuko Yabe had been discovered dead.

Kunugi shrugged his whole body.

"Overheard evidence is tricky. These days, nobody just sits outside and observes. No one walks through town. Everyone's reading their monitors. When officials ask to make real contact most citizens deny them. You can't force them. Everything you say to them is recorded. Not like back in the day. You can be charged for saying outrageous things now. They're always saying your statements will remain anonymous, but if you say anything they think reveals accountability, they'll shut you down.

"That's why I doubt they were able to obtain such perfectly compact and convenient evidence. Even this bit about Kawabata accompanying Nakamura on his outing was evidence submitted by a cohabitant and local cop."

"In that case, how should we interpret what Lieutenant Ishida has divulged? You don't believe he actually obtained this information?"

"No, if the lieutenant divulged this information in a circumstantial interrogation, it's got to be at least somewhat accurate. There were other investigators present when Ishida questioned you, yes?" Shizue asked. "No matter where the conversation took place, all statements made under questioning are a matter of public record. Besides I doubt if the lieutenant would start lying to you now. So this is what I think: they got to the girl they suspect of being the criminal first."

"First?"

"Yeah. If you take into account that business about Mao being suspicious, the story changes."

"You mean they've dug up information targeting the undocumented residents?"

"I'm sure they got *some* information. There are a lot of people out there who harbor negative feelings toward the undocumented residents. If you go to any anonymous tipline on your monitor and enter anything about potential criminals and input features of that young girl, I'm sure you'd get tons of information in less than an hour. Most of it will be useless junk data, and there's no credibility to any of the information, but some of it will seem useful," Kunugi said. "Even if it's anonymous there's a source for everything, and that means you can always trace it. If you know what you're looking for, odds are good you'll find it. It eliminates a lot of the labor."

"In that case."

"So..." Kunugi crossed his legs and balanced an elbow in his lap, then put his chin in his hand. "I'm wondering where this first bit of information came from. We have to figure out the connection. Before the police knew of Cat's existence they couldn't have started anything. Who's the source? Until we know that, the evidence can't be collected. Because you can't wring it out of her. I'm positive someone was spilling information."

"Spilling?"

"Secret information, I mean. Someone must have been leaking info on Cat to the police. Moreover, it's very sensitive information. If it wasn't, the police wouldn't go that far. Regardless of whether they were bewildered or not, there was a suspected culprit—Nakamura, who after your little suggestion went from suspect to potential victim—so something happened to make the direction of the investigation change."

Direction, meaning that even after what Shizue had said, the police were still suspicious of Yuji Nakamura. But then...

"I was under the impression from what Lieutenant Ishida said that Yuji Nakamura was no longer under any suspicion at all."

"I'm sure he isn't." Kunugi sat up. "I think Yuji Nakamura is already in police custody."

"What?"

"The search around the center's premises ended Monday night. But it's not like they found who they were looking for, so normally they'd keep a few people on. This was considered the most likely place he'd hide. But then suddenly everyone is taken off duty yesterday. It's just a hunch, but I think Nakamura is the one who provided the information on Mao."

"Nakamura?"

"Nakamura's testimony would be rock solid. If Nakamura himself states that he and Kawabata were attacked by this girl, they'd stop at nothing to find her. So—"

"Why wouldn't they announce that they'd apprehended him, then?"

"Because..." Kunugi was forced silent with his mouth open as the monitor on the desk lit up with a message.

Kunugi's hunch was wrong.

The message on the monitor screen was a notice of the discovery of Yuji Nakamura's body.

CHAPTER 017

"WHAT'S GOING ON?" Mio yelled.

Surrounded by cables and particle board, Mio appeared strong.

"Why? Why'd she get killed? What the hell is this *fatal wounds to the abdomen? Abrasions all over both her legs? A section of her viscera missing, including her liver? Severed carotid artery?!* Hey, Makino!"

Mio kept gesturing at the different monitors lined up in front of her. Over and over.

It was...

Hazuki couldn't look directly at them.

"Look! Look at what they did to Yabe! Why?!"

"I..."

"This wasn't Nakamura. So who did it?"

"I don't know, I..."

Hazuki was at a loss for words.

She had no idea what was what anymore.

It was another turtle icon on her monitor. Another series of directions followed that had led her here to Mio's.

And as soon as she'd arrived, Mio showed her the images of Yuko Yabe. She had been torn apart.

"The area patrol came where we left her. They came, right?"

Hazuki kept nodding. It made her nauseated.

But she worried she'd get yelled at if she sat down, and just as the thought occurred to her she felt tight in the chest, and then before she knew it the bridge of her nose got hot. It reminded her of her early childhood.

"Stop crying!" Mio barked, and glared at Hazuki. "Why are you crying? This is the first time I've seen anyone cry. You're pouring liquid from your eyes."

"I am?"

She wouldn't have known unless someone told her.

Tears.

Mio turned her back.

"Our plan failed. No, that's not it. It went as planned. Right? Did we screw up somewhere?"

No, we didn't.

Saturday night.

Hazuki and Mio, along with Ayumi, had taken Yuko toward Hazuki's house. First, Hazuki had gone inside, walked to her bedroom, and turned on the monitor. Then after ten minutes, she started to pretend to do schoolwork. Then another ten minutes. The alarm went off. An image of the area leading up from the front gate to her foyer appeared on the monitor. She confirmed it was the image of Yuko slumped over and made the emergency call on her security receiver. Five minutes later the area patrol showed up with the security company and made vocal confirmation.

We've secured the trespasser on your grounds.

Could you please verify for us?

Yuko's face appeared on the screen.

Do you know this young woman?

No, I don't, Hazuki had replied.

If someone had really just suddenly appeared on Hazuki's front step, Hazuki wouldn't immediately recognize who it was on the screen. To play it safe she'd decided to pretend she didn't know. To avoid suspicion.

It would have been strange for Hazuki to know that Yuko Yabe was supposed to be missing.

The Yuko on her monitor screen looked lifeless. It was a ruse, of course. Hazuki thought she saw Yuko form a faint smile as she turned her face away from the screen.

Even if she did, who knew what that smile meant. Hazuki didn't.

That was the last time she saw a moving image of Yuko.

And today, the image of Yuko.

Torn apart.

"I confirmed everything too," Mio said. "Yabe definitely got into the squad car. I told her to tell them who she was as soon as she got in the car, so she was sure to have let them know. There was a request for questioning out for her, so once they knew who she was they would have immediately taken her into protection. Even if they needed to verify her identity they would have at least kept her in custody. She would have been totally safe. But…"

Why'd she die? Mio said again.

Just as she was about to holler something again the door slammed open.

Beyond the ocean of black cables stood Ayumi.

She was totally calm.

"Why'd you call me out here?"

"You're late."

"I don't really use my terminal. I don't even look at the monitor."

"You should at least look at your monitor. Look, Ayumi…"

Her eyes narrowed before Mio could say anything. She'd noticed the image on her screens.

"Yabe…?"

"Yeah. Cut up into pieces."

"Who…did it?"

"You think *we know*?" Mio said and turned around with her chair. Mio was crying too.

"Where did you go after we dropped off Yuko, Ayumi?"

"I did like you told me and followed the car for a while."

"Till where?"

"You know I can't very well chase a car on foot. I'm pretty sure they were headed to the center in that patrol car. They'd gotten too far from me to confirm, so I gave up."

"That's right. That's it. The area patrol squad car unit G02254 definitely went to Makino's residence, picked up Yuko Yabe, then headed to the protective services of the administrative center. I checked. They even called in to headquarters. They reported that they'd apprehended a young woman they believed to be the one for whom there was an interrogation request still pending. Look at this."

Ayumi closed the door and walked past Hazuki straight to Mio's side.

"This is the news I got."

On the monitor screen was a list of notifications.

"The same emergency message was sent to the prefectural police investigative unit. But…"

Mio tapped at a key.

"It was never received. In fact, there's no record of the transmission, even."

She tapped again.

"Look. There's no record of the transmission from car G02254. It's just disappeared. In fact it was erased. The only record of it is in my hands."

"What do you mean erased?"

"It's been made to look like it was *never there*. Everything's been made a lie. Do you understand, Makino? We've been denied by someone. What we did that night has been completely erased! Who would turn us into a lie? Who would rip Yabe to pieces?"

"Calm down, Tsuzuki." Ayumi had been reading the information on the various monitors and then settled down on a duralumin case.

"This is police data?"

"Yes. It's a postmortem report. Though the autopsy results aren't posted yet."

"What moves are they making?"

"I don't know. I don't know, but the murderer isn't Nakamura."

"Probably not," Ayumi said quietly, but with certainty.

"What's with you?" Mio glared at Ayumi with her now red eyes. "How would you know, Kono? Nakamura *was* going to kill Yabe, you know."

"But he couldn't."

Still... Mio rubbed her bloodshot eyes.

"You wouldn't think that normally. You'd think Nakamura did it."

"Not really. If it was in fact Nakamura I saw under the bridge that night, there's no way he could attack Yuko, who was being protected by area patrol, by the way. Besides, the police say he's a kid. About your age, Tsuzuki."

"Yeah, but...the reason *I'm* saying Nakamura couldn't have done it isn't the same!" Mio wiped her nose and tapped at her keyboard again. "Look."

This time Ayumi quickly jolted her head away after just a quick glimpse at the image.

"What the hell was that?"

"Look closer." Mio pulled up the monitor. "Yuji Nakamura was killed too."

Killed?

There was in fact an image of a male body torn apart on that screen.

"Even I was surprised. This was released just before Hazuki got here. He'd been tossed out of a deserted house here in Section C. A local cop found him, and there's been no autopsy performed yet. Now you ready? Look. Look at this. It says he's been dead *for at least three days*. It says so right there."

"Three days since they found him? Wait, what?"

"*Three days since he died, you idiot!*" Mio screamed, hysterical for an instant. She took a deep breath.

"Until the final results of the official autopsy are released we don't know for sure, but they're saying that Yuko was probably killed on Monday night. But Nakamura was killed on Saturday or Sunday. Yabe was found first, but Nakamura *died first.*"

"Him too…"

Hazuki, like Ayumi, had to turn away from the monitor.

Mio huffed through her nose.

"Similar methods. Their throats were cut with a dull weapon. Deep wounds in their chest, stomach, and right arms. You can't really tell from this image, but it's the same as the others…especially Kawabata. What does all this mean?"

Something's not right, Mio kept muttering to herself.

"This screws up everything. I thought this whole time Nakamura was the one who killed Kawabata. They had a falling out. They both attacked Yabe. That much is certain. They were going to kill her. Kono saw that too."

Ayumi said *yeah* in a small voice.

"Then, Rey Mao appeared, saved Yuko from being killed, got pulled into the fight, and Nakamura ended up killing Kawabata, right? Now everything's uncertain!"

"What do you mean uncertain?" Hazuki asked.

"I can't sort any of this out. It's all just so nonsensical. Maybe Nakamura wasn't the culprit of the other murders either. So I looked into it."

"What did you look into?"

"The reason they supposedly attacked Yuko. It was hard to tell from just what Yuko was saying. So I looked into it. I got a better idea. They had a motive."

A motive to kill Yuko.

To curb the spread of this extrasensory defect Yuko had.

"Kawabata and Nakamura were apparently big followers of that old-fashioned style of moving image."

"Following what?"

"No, like they were maniacal fans. To the point where they started to believe in those images."

"Believe—you mean those old pictures?"

"Something or other movies. It's a special kind of moving image."

Belief in moving images? It didn't quite come to her.

"You don't know what I'm talking about? They're like those antiques from forty or fifty years ago. What was it again, you know, you take a roll of film and draw directly on it and then transfer it to transparent film, and then roll the images. There's stuff that's not stick figures either. Kawabata collected old machines to tune up and watch this stuff from antique real shops. He would apparently try to convert it to soft files. Nakamura collected paper versions. Paper! Can you imagine how expensive that would have been?"

"So what?"

Well, Mio placed her fingertips on the tablet this time. "Okay, so one of the directors of these something something films—he's obviously been long dead but let's see…Here it is. And this too. This is a movie by a different person. There are apparently a lot of people who still collect and talk about these two guys' work."

On the screen were several images of a girl in fascinating clothes.

"This, and then this is a little different…These were made by various directors, but these two happen to have died within a day of each other. I mean they were born a year apart, but what do you call that? The day you die?"

"*A death anniversary*," Ayumi replied. "It's called a death anniversary, the day they die."

"Okay, death anniversary. Well, their death anniversary is a holiday for these guys. They call it their AM-versary, but it was started by a group of old people. It's at the end of March. They have events and stuff. Let's see. So people from all over the world, yes, from abroad and everything, were summoned by this group. I mean it's just a message from a crazy fanatic. I don't know what purpose they have in sending messages to dead people, but there's a pretty substantial amount of mail that gets sent."

What appeared to be a monument appeared on the screen.

"There's apparently a data stocker at this commemorative statue, where every year the messages get transferred. It's a complete waste of time, but that's where these people write to."

Mio entered some code into the search window and pressed return.

"'Ryu Kawabata/Everything begins with you/The world you created is majestic/The imbeciles who pass off their replicas of your work as their own originals, they forsake you, but I will not forgive the jerks that refuse to acknowledge your work/These retarded idiots…' How do you say this word? I've only ever read it."

E-rad-icate, Ayumi said.

"'…*shall be eradicated*,' it says. 'These retarded idiots shall be eradicated.' Doesn't that sound like he's going to kill them? No one talks that way. He's totally nuts."

"No one says *totally nuts* anymore either."

"Shut up. Nuts is nuts. But look. This is the next message. 'Yuji Nakamura/This world is a facade/That which transforms and decays is not the truth/The world you guys have created is absolute and unchanging/You are the truth/The idiots who try to make their filthy reality appear true must die/I will not forgive such blasphemy...'"

"Blasphemy," Hazuki repeated.

Yuko said she was accused of being blasphemous.

"You think this is why she was targeted?"

"*Yes*," Mio answered. "She had an extrasensory defect. In other words she saw even her own face this way." Mio returned the screen to the image of the deformée character illustrations.

A beautiful young woman from long ago in the monitor, and they didn't know her name or what she was doing in there.

It did strangely resemble Yuko.

"Kawabata and Nakamura thought this chick was their god or something. But to Yabe, this is actually what she thought she looked like. *This is what I look like*, she thought when she drew it. It does look like her drawing, right? The eyes and nose are the same."

I see, the whole thing is based on a pattern. It is reduced and adapted the same exact way.

Only the color of the pupils was different.

"If you look carefully, you'll see Yuko's father also wrote messages here. Nothing extreme like that other guy, but just how he was really into this stuff as a kid, and how he's still into it. Typical fan mail. Yuko had probably looked at stuff like this since she was really little. Maybe not shown it *per se*, but she had definitely seen it. Someone with her kind of perception disorder might be affected by early exposure.

"They wouldn't forgive her," Mio said in a loud exhale and snapped off the power on the monitor farthest from her.

"But...aren't there tons of people who do these kinds of illustrations?"

"You saying it should be okay to copy?"

"Copies *are* okay. There are originals, and someone makes a copy. The copy could never be as good as the original. Except in Yuko's case. To her, the world really looked like this. She lived in a world made of deformée images. These fanatics couldn't forgive her. They had to confirm that she really had this defect, and when they did, they promptly eradicated her."

Eradicated.

"That's their reason? Because she sees the world like it's illustrated?"

Should people be killing each other?

"The first girl who was killed…" Mio continued. "The first victim won the grand prize at the Deformée Character Biennale. The DC Biennale is where everyone exhibits their original DCs. The character that wins the prize is obviously praised as an original, but her work apparently looked a lot like something that appeared briefly in these guys' moving image work. None of the judges noticed. It created a big stir but eventually they dropped it. It was just similar looking, and no one really thought it was a direct copy. But these fans wouldn't forgive it."

"Blasphemy again?"

"Yeah, you know, 'the idiots who pass off your original work as their own have to be eradicated.' That's what they did."

She had a point.

"But that's not all."

Mio drew up another image on the monitor next to the one she'd just turned off.

"You know this? It's been popular lately. Deformation Idols. I prefer the old monsters and stuff, but…"

Even Hazuki had seen this character before.

It was the star of an explosively popular fiction series from last year.

The series was about a girl from no country in particular, from no era in particular, going on some kind of adventure.

Hazuki remembered downloading a few episodes because there were so many rave reviews.

But she'd never actually watched them all the way through.

The story was mediocre and it unfolded too suddenly; there were too many unexposed elements and subplots for Hazuki to follow. Eventually the show got to be boring for her.

Earlier this year, people had begun broadcasting their own daily lives twenty-four hours a day by connecting onto a special network.

It wasn't as though something were happening all the time—mostly it was just people asleep—but that meant you had a different episode every single day for a year. You'd wonder who on earth would want to watch something like that, but daily life shows were apparently really popular, especially among the middle-aged to older viewers.

"Doesn't this look like her?"

"What do you mean? This older DC character?"

"The one that looks like her and this other illustration. Look alike, right? The face and the hairdo?" Mio asked.

"Ahh"

Now that she mentioned it.

"The creator of course acknowledges being influenced by old DC artists. However there were some extreme fans who wouldn't let it slide. They said this was the original, and what do you call that moving illustration thing again? A..."

"Anime?" Hazuki suggested.

"Yes! Anime. What's *anime* a redaction of, I wonder. What language is it? Anyway, it was an original work having nothing to do with that ancient anime. People agreed it bore a resemblance, but you know, they were a little defensive. There are lots of fan sites for this show. So here's this hotshot on one of the biggest fan sites for the show defending it, and she became famous for actually speaking out about it a lot. Well, she was killed too."

"Really?"

"That girl from the neighboring section. The second victim. Also, you know those people who dress up like their favorite characters? There was that one girl who was famous for wearing identical clothes to and doing her hair exactly like these DC characters. She was the fourth victim. She was on the daily life channel and garnered her own fans. The crazies probably didn't appreciate that."

"Didn't appreciate..."

"*Kawabata and Nakamura* didn't appreciate it," Mio said impatiently, then turned off that monitor. "That was probably blasphemous to them too."

"You're saying Kawabata and Nakamura are responsible for all these other murders too?" Ayumi said. She looked at the palms of her hands, then brought her nails up to her nose. "Serial murderers, huh?"

"Vicious murders." Mio stood up from her chair.

"No mistaking it. Right?"

"They were definitely the killers!" Mio yelled. "No doubt about it! But then if they were, then..."

"*Wait a second.*" Ayumi lifted her face. "There are others."

"Others?"

"Aikawa was killed too. And there were others killed before her."

"Yabe makes it seven. Those guys had motives to kill four of them. The remaining three...suppose they all had this extrasensory defect. Aikawa from our district? Aikawa could have. It's hard to find out, right?"

"It's speculation."

"Still."

"Still nothing. Besides, at the very least, Nakamura and Kawabata couldn't have killed Yabe. Yabe was also killed by someone else," Ayumi said.

"Like I said, I don't know what that means!" Mio pounded her desk with force.

"These crimes had to have been committed by them. The other murder victims don't have anything in common with them. Even though..."

"Everyone except Yabe."

"So?"

"Wait." Hazuki waved her hand through the air. "Yabe was definitely targeted by Nakamura and definitely attacked by him. That's a fact, but she was killed by someone else. Then isn't it possible that in the other cases too, a different person killed them than the one who taunted them? Aren't there, like, a lot of these animation fanatics?"

"You saying they have more partners?"

Hmmm, Mio said and withdrew, dropping her body back in the chair.

"Kawabata and Nakamura failed at their assignment, so they were—what's that word again? Era..."

"Eradicate."

"They were eradicated."

"I don't know about that," Ayumi said with her hands cupping her mouth and nose. "You have a better explanation?" Mio said.

"No..." Ayumi said softly.

"According to what Mio said, there are old animation fans all around the world."

"See, I told you!"

"So then let's say there are many others like Nakamura and Kawabata who are fanatics about this stuff. If there are, it's possible they're placed all over the world, right?" Ayumi said.

"I guess," Mio said.

"Perversion doesn't have borders. So. If they are all over the world they could form a unit."

"An organization that would eradicate from the world all those who blaspheme ancient animated illustrations? Huh?"

"I'm sure there are serial murders taking place all over the world at this moment, but I think this is the only part of the world where the murders are motivated by anime. You think that means the homicidal anime fans all live in this region? Or you think this area is full of the kind of people that would want to start a murdering club?"

"That's not what I meant," Hazuki said.

"Then why are all the murders taking place only here?" Ayumi asked.

"Are you saying there's another motive?" Mio said.

"No." Ayumi looked suspiciously at all the machines in the room, then glanced at Hazuki and faced Mio. "There are other murderers," she said.

"Other…"

"Those two aren't the only killers."

"You think there are others with motives to kill?"

"Motive doesn't matter, really," Ayumi said expressionlessly. "*What do you mean* it doesn't matter?" Mio responded. "It can't not matter."

"Well it doesn't. No matter how sophisticated the reason, a murder is a murder, and similarly, it doesn't matter how great the motive is, if you can't kill, you won't. But someone who can kill definitely will."

"That may be, but…"

"There are killers nearby."

"Nearby?" Mio spun around and did a once-over on her room and said, "No. There are not." Then, "What are you talking about? Or wait…are you suggesting that that Rey Mao bitch is the other killer?"

Ayumi didn't say anything.

"What is it? Did you see something? Did Mao kill Kawabata?"

"No, not that. I've told you already, she took a punch and got knocked out. I'm saying—"

"*What is it?* What are you trying to say?" Mio pressed Ayumi.

"Just that we shouldn't single out Nakamura and Kawabata."

"But we should. They killed people."

"You don't have to be special to kill people."

"That may be, but these guys are. I don't know if it was for anime or animism, but…What do they take humans for?" Mio kicked the steel legs on her chair. "What kind of monster values invented characters over real human beings? Even when people used to kill cows and pigs, they knew not to kill each other. People have been picketed and even punished for catching fish and killing sharks! These guys killed *humans*! Are humans less important than sharks? Less important than these damned illustrations?"

"Humans aren't more or less important." Ayumi looked straight at Mio. Mio widened her eyes.

"What did you say?"

"We're not bigger or smaller or even better or worse. Humans and fish *are the same*," she said, and took a deep breath.

"Neither of them has special value," she said finally.

"No value?" Mio walked over the cables on the floor and raised a fist to Ayumi.

"Are you saying Yuko's life had no value?"

Ayumi lifted her face. "No. I'm saying that to crush a bug or to murder a human is all the same. You take life. If we can't kill people, we shouldn't be allowed to kill bugs. That's why today we no longer eat murdered animals."

"Yeah, but…"

"I'm not saying Yabe's life had no value. Just that hers wasn't any more special than another's. There's no such thing as a life that's too big or too small. Our lives are perfectly suited for the bodies we inhabit. And none of us has a more special life than the other."

"And that makes it okay to murder people, Kono?"

"I never said that." *I never said that*, she repeated, and clenched her thin white fingers into fists of her own. "It's probably not okay to kill."

"Of course it's not! It's a serious crime. I mean, *this* is a drawing. It's not a fish or a turtle. It's a fucking drawing. They're suggesting the drawing is more valuable than a human life. I can't understand that. And this drawing…it has no value whatsoever."

Click. Mio turned off another monitor.

A snapping sound reverberated through the walls and ceiling as she powered down the last monitor.

"Those guys didn't care one way or the other about human life, right?"

"I don't think so."

"Then what was it?"

"Nakamura and Kawabata didn't view human life lightly. The animation that these guys cherished—I've watched some of it too—and the message was always that human life is incredibly valuable, that the human life force is weightier than the earth. The plot was always some humanistic mumbo jumbo. So there's no way they viewed human life lightly. I just think they didn't realize a human's life was as sacred as a fish's life. In fact they thought human life was infinitely more important than that of any other animal. However, they killed one person, and nothing happened. Then they knew even less the value of life."

"How so?"

"They got away with killing one human, and nothing in the world changed," Ayumi said. "It's different from the world in the monitor."

Yes. This was something even Hazuki understood.

If truth lay only in the monitor, then what lay outside it was all false. In that case not even murdering a human would be real. You murder, get caught, go to court, get sentenced to jail. Thus was born the *murder case*. Until all that happened a killing was just a fantasy.

But...

Ayumi glanced at Hazuki and said, "This is different from what you think, Makino. Killing people is real. Like eating food."

"Eating."

"Sure." Ayumi looked at her palms again. "No matter how immersed we get in our world of numbers, no matter how deep we escape into our monitors, we still have to eat. Even if it isn't life that we're eating, we take something, put it in our mouths, chew, digest, and defecate. That is all real."

"Okay, and...?"

"You can say you ate but still be hungry. That's because we're living beings. So that's real too. Similarly, they can record your death, but as long as you're alive, you are still living. The records can say you were born, but until you come out of the womb you are not human. Your Cat friend doesn't exist according to the government, but clearly she's no ghost. I've seen her with my eyes and even talked to her. She exists. Makino is supposedly at home, but she's not. She's right here."

Right.

According to the record, Hazuki was not here.

But right now, Hazuki was right here.

"Right?" Ayumi said to Mio. "Am I looking at the ghost of Makino? A false Makino?"

Possibly false, Hazuki thought. But.

I'm right here.

"You see, humans are made of these squiggly innards that they stuff with food and turn to mud, which they then excrete and regenerate. They are born bloody and die bloodless. That can't be digitized. So killing humans is *real*."

"But..."

Then why... Hazuki thought.

"Reality is much more of this nothing than we think. Nakamura and Kawabata didn't understand that."

"Nothing. *It's all nothing*," Ayumi said. "If a player does something wrong in a game, he or she may lose and even risks being ejected from the game world. Game over. In real life there is no game over. The world doesn't end. Even if you kill someone, even if you do something you're absolutely not supposed to do, it's not like you won't be able to use your server anymore or that information will no longer be transmitted. The world will not end if you kill someone. Yabe was killed, Kawabata was killed, and tomorrow still came. So...

"They were *confused*," Ayumi finished.

"Confused, eh? If they were killed for being confused then I can't stand for it," Mio said quietly.

Ayumi passed a look straight through Mio's profile.

It was incredibly natural.

"Tsuzuki...you're a regular do-gooder."

"Don't tease. Whether anyone dies or gets killed is not my business. It's someone else's problem. But I'm just frustrated. I'm pissed off because I don't know what's going on. What *is* going on? I wanted to observe everything taking place in the world. That's why I built these special monitors. But some guy I don't know has squirreled his way around the system and killed Yabe. I don't get it."

"You're amazingly straightforward, Tsuzuki." Ayumi sighed and walked toward the door that wouldn't open.

"Are you expecting someone?"

"No. Why?"

"Nothing..."

BAM! From the hallway. Like someone had kicked at one of the doors leading to Mio's room.

Then the door in the middle and finally the door that could open, did.

"Mao..."

With straight long hair and her Chinese clothing, Rey Mao stood there. Rey Mao stood silently, then entered the room with a serious air and grabbed Mio by the collar and pulled her up from her seat.

"*What the hell what the hell?!*" Mio tried to scramble away.

"What the fuck did you do?"

"What the...Were you injured?"

"*Shut up!*" Rey Mao barked. Mao's clothing was torn and dirtied. There was blood on her face. The black clump by the side of her mouth also looked to be dried blood.

"What kind of arrangement was that?"

"It wasn't an a-arrangement! Cat, you're choking me."

"Don't you dare call me that!" Rey Mao dropped Mio.

Mio fell hard onto the chair and then onto the floor.

"I knew it. You killed them. You're here to kill us now too."

"Me, the killer? Then it *was* you who sold me out. For a second there I..."

Rey Mao went quiet and shook her shoulders.

"What do you mean for a second? What do you mean sold you out?"

"Stop fucking with me."

Rey Mao raised her arm.

Mio craned her neck.

"We don't like it when we're betrayed. We hate it more than anything."

Hazuki had been curled up, and now she was being pushed back to the corner. Ayumi proceeded forward and took Rey Mao by the arm.

"That's enough. If you hurt her... Your strength is a deadly weapon."

Rey Mao looked at Ayumi.

"You..."

"What's this about?"

"It's about that night. You told the police about me."

"We didn't."

"Then why did they snoop around, looking for me?"

"I don't know anything about that," Ayumi said.

Rey Mao shook off Ayumi's hand from her arm.

"You want to go at it?"

"No. I've told you before I don't know how to fight. I hate getting hit."

"Stop talking nonsense."

Rey Mao grabbed Ayumi this time. Mio flew up from behind her.

"Stop it, Cat."

"Let go." Rey Mao released her arm. The three of them fell against the wall. The case Ayumi was sitting on fell onto its side with a thud.

"You can't do that. It's dangerous!" Mio said loudly, throwing her body over the case. "You morons! W-what do you guys think this is? This thing could blast us a kilometer into the earth!"

"Blast us?"

"It's the turtle I was telling you about, the turtle. My second attempt at it, anyway."

"You mean your plasma weapon. That movie with the turtle—"

"I'm not planning on using it on anything...or anyone." Mio shrank and sat back on the floor. She looked up at Rey Mao. "Just because you aren't documented doesn't mean you can do whatever the hell you want. *That really hurt*," she said, rubbing her arms.

Rey Mao stood in a coil of cables set up by the wall, tense all the way down to her fingertips. Ayumi was leaning against the wall just a few paces from her and shifted her eyes from Rey Mao's arms to her face and said calmly,

"This weird girl did not sell you out. Not even I am interested enough to cause you trouble. If I'd reported you, I'd be questioned too."

Rey Mao's look at Mio relaxed a little, and then she turned her face to Hazuki.

"You're that politician's daughter, aren't you?"

"I'm..."

"She has nothing to do with this either."

"How do you know? She's on the side of the authorities."

"So are Tsuzuki and I, then. What did you call it again? *Caged?* We're all caged."

"Well then..."

Rey Mao picked up a cable and let go of it angrily. She said to Hazuki, "Why'd you send Yuko away?"

"She wasn't sent away. She was killed." Mio stood up abruptly.

"See, this is why you need to get connected. Yabe is dead."

"Dead..." Rey Mao slumped into the wall. "She died?"

"She's wrecked."

"You...*weren't you there?*" Ayumi said.

"When?"

"We thought maybe when the area patrol came to pick up Yuko, you chased after them."

Rey Mao didn't respond and instead looked sternly at Ayumi.

"Hey, were you there or not, Cat?" Mio asked angrily. "Why were you hiding from us then? Help us out! You seem good at physical labor. And Makino, if you knew she was there, why didn't you tell us?"

"I didn't know. I just...thought I did," Hazuki said.

"Why?"

"She's not supposed to know Hazuki is the daughter of a politician. They were never introduced," Ayumi said.

"So?" Mio took a second to understand and then turned her neck.

"I see. So she knew because she was at Hazuki's house that night. Her full name is on the front gate. And if she were there, it can be assumed she followed us there. And she wouldn't have known anything had happened to Yuko. We didn't, after all."

"*I* did, though," Rey Mao answered.

"You were worried, were you? Well isn't that nice," Mio said.

"Nothing like that. This was a matter of life and death. Of course I was concerned," Rey Mao said. "I thought of calling you, but of course I can't."

"You guys are so hard to deal with." Mio sat back down in the chair.

"Then you really have nothing to do with this?" Rey Mao asked Mio.

"None. If the cops are after you it's because you screwed up somewhere, or someone else has been giving them information. We have nothing to do with this."

Rey Mao painted the wall with her back as she slid down onto the floor and sat. She was very badly injured. It must have hurt.

Ayumi held up Mao's left arm. She winced.

"You got hit pretty hard. Was it the cops?"

Rey Mao shook her head. Her hair fell to the sides.

"I lost. Again."

"Lost?"

"To the guy with head art and the foreigner in the metal suit."

"What are you talking about?" Mio scrunched up her face and scratched at her head.

"The guys who abducted Yuko."

"Abducted?"

"Yeah. Kono, was it?"

"Call me Ayumi," Ayumi said.

"Ayumi, eh?" Rey Mao said. "You gave up on them at that intersection, right? Well, after that the patrol car stopped one more time."

"Stopped in the middle of the route?"

"Yeah. It looked like they got some kind of message. I was hiding behind the shadow on the sidewalk, so I decided to stop and watch a little. Then, after about five minutes, the head art guy and the foreigner in the metal suit showed up. They knocked out the local cop and the security system rep and carted Yuko off with them. So I..."

"You went to save her...again. Can't say you're bored, I guess."

"Those *fuckers*." Rey Mao looked at her left shoulder. Mio went over to her and took a look.

"Holy shit! They cleared a hole into your shoulder."

"They had...guns."

"Guns?! Like a pistol? You lie!"

"I'm not lying."

"But the only people who have guns in this day and age are in

Africa or the Middle East. They've been totally banned everywhere else. They're inefficient for killing *en masse*, they're too powerful for use in self-defense, too ridiculous to threaten with and so difficult to handle most of the time they injure people by accident. Nothing good about them."

"They're *great* for killing people," Rey Mao said.

"That's *all* they're good for," Mio said. "No one's making money making them. Everyone's stopped making them, so it's only the secret organizations that have them now. Even the guns being used in Africa are rusty old pieces. I've only seen them in movies from ages ago."

Hazuki hadn't seen them even there. In her history courses she'd perhaps seen an image of one. Even when they were mentioned in fiction it came with a disclaimer.

"What do you call those guys who just scare you into things? Goons? Those guys don't exist anymore, right? I mean, what would they threaten you into doing these days? You can't even kill animals. The only thing a pistol is good for, like you said, is killing people." Mio went quiet all of a sudden and stared back into the hole in Rey Mao's left shoulder.

"Hired hit men?"

"I know I'm in no position to call them strange, but these are some strange people. Ayumi." Rey Mao called Ayumi.

I can't get used to hearing her say that, and it's a name I hear a lot. Hazuki was startled.

"It's like you said. In the end, my fighting method doesn't stand a chance against someone who is out to kill. I dodged him and went for his vital points. It should have brought him down, but that skinhead didn't even flinch. He came at me with his survival knife... It was scary," Rey Mao said. "Because *I* wasn't trying to kill him. But that was his only motive. There's a big difference there. I was scared so I ran, and then they didn't come after me anymore. I just ran away. Then they shot me. I think it was a silent gun."

Hazuki couldn't even imagine being shot with a gun.

"You kept running?"

Could she have been running with those injuries for the last four days?

"I was in Section B for a solid day. Partly because the bleeding wouldn't stop, but also because in the daytime I couldn't move. After a day I was able to come back here to Section C, but this time the cops were here. What's more they were asking around for me by name. I just assumed that meant..."

"You assumed that we had told on you."

"I couldn't think of anyone else who knew about me. And the area patrols were everywhere. I couldn't go back to my place. The pharmacists on the west side hid me for a while, but then the cops showed up there too."

"What about your injuries?"

"We got a doctor who sees us. He sees us for injuries and illnesses. Nothing fancy though. Just twentieth century medicine."

"I can't believe…*you made it out alive*," Ayumi said. "Not even the police can go up against guys with guns. These days not even cops get weapons."

"It took everything I had to protect my life. That girl is another story. That girl…"

Died? she asked and Mio said *yes, she died*, without emotion.

"Who are these people? What's going on?" Mio asked.

"Tsuzuki, you're so full of questions today."

"It's because I have no idea what's going on!"

"I do," Ayumi said.

"What do you know?"

"Don't you see? The guys who killed Yabe—they have guns and weapons and are out for murder. They can intercept police and government information and alter it. I don't think they have anything to do with those old anime and DC guys."

"You don't get it at all, Ayumi."

"But I do."

"What do you get?"

"That these aren't the kind of people we kids can go after. That's all we need to know," Ayumi said.

Ayumi faced Mio.

Mio sneered at Ayumi.

"You're giving up?"

"I'm not doing anything. We're just kids. We're not cops. We aren't do-gooders. It's more weird that we are doing anything at all."

"Yeah, but are you content to let this go, Kono?"

"Sure," Ayumi said, and looked for Hazuki's backup. "We've made it this far without worrying about other people. I hate interacting with people. Makino's the same way. But…"

But that all changed.

They'd never even made eye contact before.

Now they'd looked right at each other, yelled, and grappled.

It was all weird. It was weird, but...

"I think," Mio started, then repeated *I think*. Mio must have been thinking the same thing.

"I think I don't like the way it was. I hated it. What about you, Cat?"

"I'm running away."

"*Running away!*" The sound came out of Mio's throat at a high pitch. She advanced on Rey Mao. "You're running away?"

"I don't want to get killed."

"You're running away, Cat?"

"Stop it, Tsuzuki," Ayumi grabbed Mio by the shoulder. "She's seriously injured. She almost died. Do you have any idea what it's like to have escaped an attempted murder?"

"What?" Mio rubbed her eyes and looked with disbelief at Rey Mao's black and red bloodstained shoulder. Hazuki looked at it as well.

The pain had burnt black.

"We grew up not knowing any pain. We can't know what it's like. We can't really empathize. We couldn't possibly tell anyone not to run from it or to be less selfish. Listen, Tsuzuki. The next time this girl is attacked she *will* be killed. If not her, someone else. None of your magic computer programs can bring a person back to life. I for one don't want to have to deal with any more *real contact* life or death situations."

"I don't either," Mio said and extended a finger toward Rey Mao's open wound.

"Does it...hurt?"

"Yeah. I've never hurt like this before. Totally different from taking a punch."

"That bad..."

Mio touched her forehead to Rey Mao's shoulder and looked at the floor.

"It would hurt to die, wouldn't it, Cat?"

"If you died quickly, it wouldn't hurt at all."

Mio remained motionless.

"All right." Ayumi, who'd been looking at Mio's back, turned her face toward Hazuki. "Let's just stop now. Makino goes home. We can't keep doing this."

Yeah.

Of course that was what they wanted. At home time stood still. It would be like it was yesterday, last year. If Hazuki just went on repeating what she did every day, the world would do the same. Her feelings would have nothing to do with it.

"And you, Mio—you need to stop snooping around."

"I can't leave Rey Mao alone."

"She's strong. You'll only make things worse by trying to help her."

"What if Rey Mao is—"

"Caught by the police?" Hazuki asked.

"What about it?"

"I mean, the police won't kill you or anything because they know that those two guys saw you and are after you. Even if your relationship to us is exposed."

"It hasn't been." Rey Mao peeled herself off the wall. Mio lifted her face too. "I don't have any proof of identity," Rey Mao said. "My life here is a crime. I might not get killed, but I won't get off without a conviction."

"But there are other murderers, right?"

"Yes. People I've never seen in these parts. Guys like the skinhead with the peacock tattooed on his head, and the one who looks like an old soldier in a metal suit. I think those guys were hired."

"You can't beat guys like that," Ayumi said. "So, like you said, running away would make the most sense. The more we try to help, the worse your situation gets. You understand now, Tsuzuki? Your friend gets killed."

"My friend…" Mio said.

"Unlike Makino and me, you actually have a friend here. You should value that."

Mio widened her bloodshot eyes and sharpened her mouth. She looked like a pouty child put off by having been scolded.

"It's just that…" Rey Mao leaned forward and got up on one leg. "Makino here," she said, gesturing toward Hazuki, "she's in danger now too."

"Danger?"

"These guys know that Yuko was secured at her house. The police officers that secured Yuko after processing her, and you, both recognized Yuko. They know that. They might come after you. Be careful."

"The security at her house is *ridiculously* thorough," Mio said. "An insect would set off the alarm."

"Insects are flying in and out of there all the time. A child could break in. Don't underestimate these guys."

Hmm, Mio groaned very purposefully, and moved over to Hazuki. She examined Hazuki's face. "That's it."

"What?" Hazuki said.

"Make the first move. Makino, have your father call the police and see what ended up happening with the so-called trespasser."

"What's that going to accomplish?"

"Everything. That cop who was attacked by the skinhead and the metal soldier didn't die, right? He's probably scared of the skinhead and was threatened not to talk by the metal soldier."

"*Not to talk?* You mean threatened to keep quiet?"

"Right? Like Cat said, the records can be tampered with but not the memory. That's why Makino could be in danger too. In that case she should talk first."

"Right, but to say what?"

"Make a statement. Something like, 'The girl apprehended by our security system for invading our house looked a lot like the one they're saying was killed.' Hazuki, they made you look at her on your security screen, right?"

"Yeah, but I told them I didn't recognize her," Hazuki said.

"That's normal. But they're going to start broadcasting her face all over the world tonight. The face of a savage serial killer's victim. You're going to see that and think it bears a resemblance."

"And tell the police?"

"No." Mio was suddenly upbeat. "You tell your father. You're going to have your politician dad tell the police."

"I see…" Hazuki thought of the expressive face of her foster father.

She hadn't thought about it before, but he was certainly a powerful figure. And more importantly, he would never harm Hazuki.

"Imagine. Information brought in by a prefectural suit. Not even the police would ignore that. And the security company's records might have been erased but not the mainframe security data from your house. The system set up in your house can save all kinds of images. There's about a month's worth of incoming records that get saved privately. If Yabe appeared on your home monitor for even a moment, there will definitely be a record remaining."

Remaining.

A record of that fictitious night.

"If you leave it alone the system will erase as it records new material, but it'll still have records of just a few days ago. You should pull it now and save it on a flash drive or something. If you compare that data against the data saved by the security system people, you're guaranteed to turn up some discrepancies. Then the police can't keep quiet and the officer that took Yabe in can't keep hiding behind his fear of the skinhead.

"What do you think about that?" Mio said to Ayumi. "You have a problem with this? This is a complete offensive campaign devised by a child, as you'd put it. It's a citizen's duty. If all goes well, doubts about the murder will be exposed. I mean, it's not like the guy will get caught, but Makino will be safe. After that…

"She's at the mercy of the authorities." Mio tied it all up.

CHAPTER | **018**

SHE SET HER monitor on voice-recognition mode. *Initiate call*, she inputted in a soft voice, and called *Shima*.

The face that appeared on her monitor screen was haunted.

Shima was located just four rooms away and in the same standby mode as her cohort Shizue. As soon as she appeared Shima said, "Not *again*."

"This is being recorded. You should watch what you say."

"I'm not in any state to be careful about what I say. You should know that as a counselor," Shima threw at Shizue.

Shima's voice, transformed into a signal and then reconstructed by Shizue's monitor, lost most of its bite.

"What are you saying I did? They died anyway."

"I'm in the same situation. Don't lash out at me. But let's talk about Nakamura."

"How can you be so calm at a time like this, Fuwa?" Shima sneered at Shizue.

Shima wasn't really sneering at her, she knew, but at the lens.

"I'm not calm. But—"

"You're pissing me off. They're going to call me in soon, so I'm turning this off now."

The image on Shizue's screen disappeared, and the disconnect signal came up.

"She's really been through the ringer," Kunugi said from behind the screen. "She's closer in age to me, your cohort."

"Is she?"

"What she feels about what's happened is more important to her than what's taking place right now. She basically understands that the world she controls is subjective, but that means she can't see the other side. We were all like that when we were young."

"That's a sort of truth, isn't it?" Shizue answered. "I don't fault it."

"Well, it isn't bad. Just, it makes it impossible to lie. Your judgments are all subjective. To be honest with yourself involves a devotion to what others don't know. Then the more others don't know, the more you become indistinguishable from criminals. It's a given that you can't know exactly what someone else is thinking, so if you stop pretending to know, there's no reason to ever lie. Then the foundation of society begins to crumble. You were raised in a world separated from that fundamental behavior."

"You make it sound like we're bad people," Shizue opined coolly.

"Are you objecting? Objecting would be about as useful as that dust box on the monitor. It's just about knowing whether there's something of use in there. Well, it doesn't matter," Kunugi said and added after a thought, "*No, I guess it does matter.*"

"It might be a serious problem. I say that, but then again most of the guys at the center of the police department are about my age," he said. "The guys at the top of the prefectural police are probably about ten years older than me. I'm not saying they're done for like I am, but it's a troubled generation. We're all being moved around to accounting or administration or office direction.

"They probably decided about ten years ago that that was the way to go. You keep ascending the career ladder and there's some old man squatting on the top seat, so the organizational flow has been bad. If you look at the numbers, there are a lot more people joining the senior population, so it's inevitable. When you reach a certain age it only makes sense that you'll get sent back to the bottom of the ladder, but to change every assignment…The elderly are smarter than that. It's something to think about, a generation of people with the right to speak. It's not like these young guys can just go in and take their places."

"Ishida's still young."

"*No way*," Kunugi said, sincerely doubtful. "Ishida's about the same age I am. Maybe just a couple years off."

Interesting. Shizue thought Kunugi must have been about the age of her father. She didn't think Ishida could possibly be the same age as Kunugi, but to be even within a handful of years of him was still unbelievable.

"I thought Ishida was much younger."

"It's because I look old."

"You look your age."

"Thanks," he said. "Though I don't remember ever telling you my actual age, ha!" Kunugi stood up. It was just an observation—couldn't have been false flattery.

Kunugi disinfected his hands with a cleaning solution and stood up by the drink dispenser, put down the rental cup he'd been fondling, and hunched over the touch-screen display.

"I'll help myself to another cup. That Ishida is one wise fellow. I mean it's a career that dates back. He doesn't talk about it that way now, so you wouldn't know, right?"

"I do get that sense. I'm not that young either."

Kunugi raised one eyebrow toward Shizue. He filled his cup with the flavonoid drink and walked over to the window. "Me and Lieutenant Ishida see, we're from the same region. The east side, three sections away from here. So we'd never worked face to face, but I knew him by name. We're both from a bygone generation. Still had schools. I was barely getting by, but he was top of his class. He was a real straight-A student. And it wasn't just his grades. He was raised in a really cushy environment. From the starting line, there was no comparison."

"Cushy?"

"Rich." Kunugi savored his tea. "Ri'ichiro Ishida has noble ancestors."

He didn't look like it.

"He's a direct descendant of the founder of SVC. He's the son of the current chief or something. You remember SVC. I was talking about it over dinner that night. The whole bioengineered food industry? SVC is at the center of that whole industry."

"You mean *that* SVC?"

"Yeah. I don't know any other companies with the same name, but I'm sure it's that one. They pioneered the whole man-made alimentation industry. They used to be called Suzuki Food Sciences."

She didn't know about the original company name, but even Shizue had heard of SVC before.

According to what Kunugi had been saying before, they had a vested interest in the execution of the complete crossover from organic to man-made foodstuffs.

"Food ingredients were their main product, and they exchanged technology with foreign companies and were the first to come up with a good meat alternative to living animals. They were the first to push the export of food from Asia at the end of the twentieth century. It was established in 1975. It's a long-established corporation."

Shizue didn't think biotechnology dated back so far. When she voiced her doubt Kunugi shook his empty teacup. *No no, it doesn't.*

"It wasn't called that," he said. "But even the development of wheat grains is a sort of biotechnology, no? Humanity has always had a voracious appetite. As you can tell by the old name of the company, SVC has always been interested in producing food products. You know, when the company's pioneers grew up after the war when food was scarce, food substitutes were really popular. Do you remember food substitutes?"

Shizue had heard a lifetime's worth of history of the war growing up, but surprisingly, this was the first she'd heard of substitute food products. There was no mention of the phrase in any of the published information about that period. Shizue's generation had learned all about the country's way of life at the time. International ethical issues and conceptual problems were important, so when it came to learning about the two world wars, Shizue had only learned to recognize the numerous examples of man's inhumanity toward man in the past. These were especially terrible ones that had directly involved her country.

"Well, there was such a thing," Kunugi said. "At the time you could eat tuna without a thought. But then you couldn't, and then we were eating shark the way we used to eat tuna, but if you think about it now it's all screwy. Well, the idea was to make readily available foods seem like unavailable food. That was the source of this whole idea."

"To make sharklike tuna? That's definitely screwy."

"Isn't it, though?" Kunugi chuckled. "Well, SVC was concentrating on food products and never made a priority of medical products, so they escaped pretty much unscathed by the whole DNA information registry hoopla. And then other similar companies lost out their vested rights to that market. SVC stirred up their fighting spirit and vehemently opposed the regulation, you know. That was how SVC gained the trust of the industry and became the biggest player in the bioengineering game.

"They got ahead by holding out," Kunugi said. "At the end of the day it was a fish in troubled waters. I guess we don't say that anymore though. The nuance is a little off. Anyway, they avoided direct attack, so they saw great returns in the end. Whatever could fuse best with the existing system would win."

"You seem to know a lot about this."

"The SVC headquarters are right by where I was born. The company's presence really brought up the standard of living out there. Seventy percent of the residents had been receiving some form of relief. My father worked there. So yeah, I know a lot about them. There was a monument to the founder, Yutaro Suzuki, built in front of the community center. So Ishida is a direct descendant of that guy. His mother was Suzuki's granddaughter. Quite a little prince he was."

"And he became a cop?"

"Strange, I know." Kunugi looked out the window. "Well, inherited jobs are sort of rare nowadays, but who would have thought he'd go into the police force? He could just keep playing. Besides, there are so many other more relevant industries he could work in now. The area patrol out here are an enterprise of SVC."

"Is that so?" The area patrol was a unit of citizen volunteers that had formed fifteen years ago.

At the time the area patrol unit was formed, the police force's administration was undergoing changes, and the ubiquitization of security systems made single-handed police processing even more complicated. Eventually, the traffic, security, patrol, and crime prevention units were separated and turned into citizen initiatives, making them self-managed entities that developed into what they were today.

The mother organization was still the old police unit that oversaw the breakoff, but they were managed by designated security companies in each area.

"The company that manages the area patrol in this prefecture is D&S, right? The old company name was Ishida Security."

"Ishida?"

"Exactly. It was founded by Lieutenant Ishida's grandfather. The son of the founding Ishida got married to the daughter of the second-generation president of Suzuki Food Products. I don't know which came first, but one of the companies got subsumed in the other and they merged to form D&S. There are other companies like this. Like that company I told you about before, Shikida Enterprises."

"Yes, and wasn't one of the victims of last year's serial killings employed by them?"

"Yeah. That's also a member of the SVC group. SVC has quite a reach here and going west. That's why I figure it'd be even easier for Ishida to just take on a higher-up position in one of those companies. No need to go into the police force."

"But he's supposed to be the region's expert on bizarre murder crimes."

Shizue had heard that from a questionable source.

Kunugi made a strange face. "What did you say?"

"Is that incorrect?"

"Not that it's wrong—just who exactly told you that? It couldn't have been Ishida himself."

"I think it was underground information," Shizue said.

"Underground, eh? Well, Ishida was definitely working in the bizarre crimes squad when the killing spree occurred last year. Before that...No, I can't know without looking at my server. It's unsolved anyway, so for the lead detective on the case to be suddenly replaced...I guess it's not unheard of. His moves have all been deliberate and upward. He's advanced very steadily."

"Without solving any of the crimes?"

"If he's advancing it must be for a reason, sure. It could be just that he's economically endowed, or that he has some leverage with central administration, or that...If you started conjecturing it would never end, but there's no doubting he's a stand-up man with real qualities, and if you skim the cream from the crop, there really is no need for him to stay in the police."

This was true. There were plenty of better jobs for him.

"But still..."

Shizue understood what he was saying, but Kunugi himself shut his mouth and went quiet, like he'd suddenly run into a system error.

"What's the matter?" Shizue asked. Kunugi, this beat-up old failure of a cop, practically the opposite of Ishida, was gnashing his teeth. *This is no good.*

"It's nothing. Just..."

Kunugi's face became still and gazed at the empty cup.

Shizue became aware of the fact that she was getting used to an existence divorced from normality. Perhaps she'd come across so many situations that ran counter to the law that she couldn't help say things that she'd normally reject.

No.

This was all one big evasion of reality. She'd just completely stopped thinking about anything related to Yuji Nakamura or Yuko Yabe. That was why she was entertaining this useless conversation. She hated wasting her time, but every time she thought about doing anything related to the case, she'd make that horrible face she saw in the mirror that morning.

"I can't stay here forever."

Kunugi popped up and placed the used cup back in the holder.

"If I get caught here it's your job on the line too. I'm sure you're in no state of mind to be making idle chitchat."

He wasn't wrong, but...

"You're right, but you're in the best place possible for hiding. The rooms can't be viewed from the halls for the sake of the children's privacy, and the sound protection is complete. The courtyard beyond the window is, as you know, off-limits. As long as there are no children in the room nothing will be recorded, and unless myself or a child inside the room makes an emergency call no one can open the door from the outside. The only drawback is how we're going to get you out of here when I leave the office."

"The sensors turn on when the room is vacant. Then…"

Kunugi looked at the ceiling. There were five cameras.

"I should leave as soon as I can to avoid causing any more problems for you."

Kunugi took deliberate steps toward the door. "But I can't check the area. I can't see or hear what's going on out there."

"That's true. You could open the door into the hall and find people walking there…That would be bad."

"Yes, it would." Kunugi stood motionless at the door.

"You couldn't just say I came in disguised as a cop and threatened you, could you?"

"I couldn't lie like that. Besides if I said that you'd be…"

It wouldn't just be that he'd be suspended. They'd send him to trial.

"It's not a lie, though." Kunugi furrowed his brow. "It's half true."

"I don't remember being threatened."

"Even if you didn't feel it, this is plenty threatening. I snuck into a no-entry area and illegally came in through your window. Besides, you shouldn't worry about what happens to me. If I get caught anywhere in this neighborhood they'll take my badge for good."

Kunugi extended his arm toward the door shield.

"Wait. Even if you get into the hall, how do you plan on getting out of the building?"

"I guess I can't just go out."

No, you can't. You can't go out if there's no record of you having gone in.

"These past few days there have been several police officers and area patrols coming in and out, but even they have had to pass their IDs through."

"Of course. Even zero-year-old infants have to have ID. The only way to go in and out without an ID is to break your way through the glass doors. However, the glass is reinforced, so it'd be difficult to break with your bare hands."

"Yeah. Even if it weren't reinforced, I couldn't break it. Even if I broke it I doubt I'd get through it. I should just get caught."

"Get caught..."

"On purpose," Kunugi said. "I'm just going to cause you more trouble if I stay here."

"It won't matter where you are. Be it at the front of the building or in my office, wherever you get caught they'll ask how you got in. If you refuse to answer they'll figure it out when they find that the only place where security was compromised was my office. They'll suspect me of helping you anyway."

"In that case, I'll just go out through the yard. That's where I was to begin with."

Kunugi went toward the window. "If I leave through here, it'll be as if I was never here. I mean, unless you count the two cups of tea I had, but you could say you drank them."

"What about the sensor?"

"Sensor? Well, there's no limit to barriers on my way to freedom. I'm sure they'll send someone to find me eventually, but out through the courtyard will be better than busting through a glass door. I don't have any upper body strength, but I can run fast. Because I'm a coward."

"If you run at full speed at your age, you'll get hurt."

"That's age discrimination if I ever heard it," Kunugi said. "Eh, I guess it's okay because we're talking privately."

"It's also the truth. I'm just telling you as a cautionary measure. Even if you run, where would you run to?"

"Where..."

"You aren't possibly thinking of going home and playing your old role-playing games, are you?"

"Actually, that's not a bad idea, but my server has been totally inactive for the past few days, so it's highly likely someone's there surveilling my house. With my monitor in the house but the house itself showing total vacancy, they'd know there's trouble. Police officers are required to keep their monitors on them, even when on leave. Not that they'd be contacting me or anything. I'm not going to find a way out by being buttered up by your hospitality, and besides, I won't get anything done just sitting around here."

"Does that mean you had something you wanted to do in the first place?"

"I didn't have a concrete mission or anything, but with Yuji Nakamura dead now too...I'm not satisfied just sitting around anymore," Kunugi said in a low voice.

"As if you were ever just sitting around," Shizue said, as if she had been either.

"This latest theory that the undocumented resident is the culprit doesn't sit well with me."

"It might have some validity though. It's questionable where the police got their information, but if the lieutenant is spouting it, it's possible it's true. However, if this girl and this undocumented pharmacy her family runs are the supposed criminals, the police can't say Rey Mao did everything herself. If there were an unknown partner..."

Someone *under the radar*, as it were.

"Well then," Kunugi said and reached out to the door panel again, when just at the same moment, a beeping sound went off and her desk monitor turned on.

"Wait."

Kunugi turned around.

Shizue put an index finger to her lips as if to say *be quiet*.

"Yes, this is Fuwa."

On the display was a female employee at the center's entry.

"There's a child here requesting to see Counselor Fuwa."

"A child?"

"Did you not have an appointment to see a child privately?"

"No, I didn't."

"I see. This is a *real contact* request. The child is presently here. Insists on seeing you—given the circumstances I felt I ought to call the director, who asked that the child be apprehended at your office."

"Apprehended...either way I'd like you to see the child. I can't turn her away. Since children aren't allowed to be out right now anyway."

Shizue shifted her gaze from the monitor screen to Kunugi.

Kunugi received her look and moved away from the window toward the desk.

Shizue's face was being watched by one of the cameras, so she couldn't make any facial gestures to express what she wanted to say to Kunugi.

Kunugi came up to just behind the monitor and opened his mouth to speak. Shizue quickly uttered, "I understand, I'll be with you in one second," and closed the dialogue.

"What are you doing? I told you not to make a sound."

"Yeah. I thought it would be easiest if someone on your monitor saw me attack you. Then Lieutenant Ishida would arrive immediately. Otherwise—"

"I'll figure something out. Just sit still."

"Figure something out? Isn't there a kid about to show up here? Then what?"

"These aren't normal office hours. Something's wrong."

Shizue called the reception desk.

"This is Fuwa. I apologize for abruptly signing off. I was slightly confused. Now who did you say was this child that requested to see me?"

"Uh, one Ayumi Kono. She's in your session for age fourteens."

"Kono?"

Ayumi Kono. What kind of child was she?

After thinking about it, Shizue gathered herself.

"She lives alone, if I'm correct."

"That's right. We have received a notice of long absence of her guardian. In case of emergency our center takes over as her guardian, which is why I thought the director's judgment..."

"I see. But this girl..."

Her older sister was a member of the environmental cleanup development project and living abroad. That much Shizue recalled, but that didn't help her remember anything else about the girl herself. She couldn't remember any characteristics. She left her sentence unfinished and searched for her file, whereupon a picture of Ayumi Kono came up on the display.

Very short hair and a refined-looking face.

Ahh...

"W-where is Miss Kono now?"

"It was dangerous to be outside the building, so I let her through the entrance gate, but she's not yet in the hall. If you give me the cue I can open the hall gate."

"The child in question has a fear of strangers and will not like seeing people she is not acquainted with. Are there any police-related personnel in the East C road between the entrance hall and the counseling booth?"

"Please wait a second while I check."

Kunugi waited with bated breath. Shizue looked at the still image of Ayumi Kono on her display. Something about it...

Something about it troubled her.

There is no one there, the display answered.

"Is that so? In that case please block the East C road from the entrance hall until the visiting minor has gone through. Obviously if there is an emergency you can lift the block, but this child is particularly frightened of police and authority figures. Please advise."

"I need the director's permission to block the road, but I can tell you what the odds are of this child running into anyone. As of now all the police personnel are in the south corridor, and all the center personnel short of the director are in separate meetings in the west corridor. You and Ms. Shima are the only counselors here as the rest of them have been asked to return home. Right now in the east corridor it is just you and Ms. Shima."

"That's fine. In that case please open the hall gate for Miss Kono and ask her to proceed to counseling booth C0045."

Shizue was about to close the dialogue when the attendant said, "Wait, there's something else. The police have instructed to have the minor escorted back to her house by a guard brought in by the area patrol after the interview. You will have to contact me again about the pass-ersby in the East C road anyway, so please contact me as soon as your interview is over."

"Understood."

Shizue turned off her communication, turned her chair around, and faced Kunugi.

"What do you think?"

"What do you mean? What are you going to do?"

"The minor will be headed this way. Right now there is no one between here and the entrance. You just need to leave before the child arrives."

"Into the hall?"

"The only sensor in the hall is one for body temperature. There is no visual surveillance. I will tell the child that you are the bodyguard as-signed by the police—that's not technically a lie. Stay outside the door and flat up against the wall until our meeting is over."

"You mean like a bodyguard."

"Yes. If you're in the middle of the hall they'll know you're a human. When the interview is over I will escort the child out, so at that point please follow us to the entrance hall. I can open the gate from inside. Once it's open we'll appear on the management department's scans, but there's a brief interval before the scan begins. I realize I said you're old for the exertion, but you will have to run as fast as you can to outside the center. The area patrol will send someone for the child immediately, so you need to clear out before they arrive."

Go anywhere, Shizue would have normally said.

"You could go to your parents. You can say you lost your monitor in the house and went home to your parents. They'll buy that, won't they? Losing track of your monitor is a minor violation."

As Shizue finished her sentence she stood in front of the door and brought her hand up to the sensor panel.

The door opened.

Kunugi moved uncharacteristically correctly from the window to where Shizue stood, and said, "I owe you one, big time."

"I don't expect anything," Shizue said.

Kunugi stepped into the hall at almost the same time a small figure appeared on her floor.

She looked just like the girl in her monitor.

Her gaze looked somehow pained and forced Shizue to look down.

It was immoral.

Shizue still didn't know what compelled this girl to come to her.

She'd come out to make a real contact conversation in the midst of a warning not to leave home, so it must have been a serious issue. And yet the whole time, Shizue was thinking of how to use this opportunity to help Kunugi escape the center. This was unforgivable as a counselor. Not only against the counselor's code but her own personal code of conduct. She was behaving…recklessly.

"I'm Ayumi Kono," the girl said.

"Miss Kono…" Shizue still couldn't recall anything about her. "Please come in. This is the police…"

Shizue gulped. Ayumi was looking at Kunugi's hands. Kunugi must have noticed as well. He put his hands behind him. In those hands were his mud-caked shoes.

"I am your bodyguard," Kunugi said. "Please come in."

"Wait a second." Ayumi stood her ground.

"Wait…wait for what?"

"Please don't close the door. When you do and I swipe my ID to come in, the room starts recording. I came to tell you something I don't want recorded."

Don't want recorded…

Shizue's heart started racing. This girl…

What was she doing here?

"But as I'm sure you're aware then, what gets recorded here can't leave the center without your permission. So…"

That wasn't true.

Recordings might be abridged, but they all got handed over to the police.

Shizue was lying.

So…

She couldn't tell her *not to worry*.

Shizue turned her eyes away again.

"In any case don't worry. As long as what you say doesn't have to do with a crime I don't—"

"It does have to do with a crime," Ayumi said.

"What did you say?"

"It does have to do with a crime."

"What do you mean?"

"The police report clearly indicates a criminal."

"What?"

Shizue stopped Kunugi from coming forward.

"Not just that, but the police distorted the information on the criminal," Ayumi said.

"Th-that's ridiculous."

"Please, Mr. Kunugi." Shizue had to speak harshly to Kunugi. This was probably not just childish fancy.

"Do you have proof?"

Ayumi didn't respond but instead swallowed Shizue's look.

She was not the kind of child to play a joke like this.

No child would play this kind of prank at a time like this.

Besides.

Her gaze was totally fixed. Uncomfortably so.

Shizue pressed a button on her monitor. "All right. The security is turned off now. If you come in now, the sensor won't go off, so you won't be recorded. Just say you forgot your ID card."

"I had to use it to get into the center."

"Oh, right. Then…"

"This is fine," Ayumi said.

"I understand. So what did you want to tell me?"

Ayumi looked up and down the hall and, having confirmed no one was around, began to speak.

"It's about Yuko Yabe's murder."

"Is there information about her murder already out in public?"

Ayumi didn't respond to Shizue's question.

"Yuko Yabe was being threatened by Nakamura and Kawabata. They lured her out and beat her up. Did the police know that?"

"That Nakamura and Kawabata were after Yabe? Well…"

"Lieutenant Ishida had said there was no record of communication from them in Yabe's monitor," Kunugi said.

"I heard from the victim *herself*," Ayumi said.

"The victim... you were in contact with Yabe?"

"If there is no record of the messages, then they were erased from her monitor."

"You're saying the murderer was also erasing personal information?"

"Did you also know that Yabe trespassed into Representative Makino's home on Saturday night and that the area patrol apprehended her?"

"Makino..."

Shizue looked to Kunugi for a sign. Kunugi was petrified.

"S-Saturday night?"

"An emergency call was placed, the area patrol came to secure her, and the patrol car took her away. That much is certain. But then the car was attacked by two men, and Yabe was abducted."

"Hey! Stop talking nonsense. This is ridiculous. The police would have..."

Overcome with emotion Kunugi blurted all this out but then suddenly exhaled.

"Did you see something, kid?"

"Is that true, Miss Kono?" Shizue asked.

"Did you see someone?"

"I can't say," Ayumi said. "That undocumented resident saw it."

"So *that's* what this is," Shizue said, emphatically.

Ayumi didn't respond.

Shizue's imagination ran with a new ferocity. "Did this undocumented resident happen to kill Kawabata while rescuing Yabe from him?"

"That's *false*," Ayumi said. "The undocumented resident has not killed anyone. Your suspicions are misdirected. There is another killer."

"You know who? The killer?"

"I don't know who killed Yabe," Ayumi said. "But I do know that the information the police have is all useless. That much is certain."

Shizue looked at Kunugi anew. Kunugi's brow creased even more deeply and his face expressed discouragement. "You're saying that there's been tampering with evidence regarding the crime."

"*Ms. Fuwa*," Ayumi said. She was almost never called that by her children. "I have a favor to ask. You need to keep Mio Tsuzuki and Hazuki Makino in a safe place."

"Tsuzuki and Makino?"

"Both of them know everything I know. Makino knows that the

trespasser at her home was Yabe. So she knows that there is something wrong with the information about this case. Through her father she is making this statement to the area patrol shortly. But...

"We can no longer trust the area patrol," Ayumi finished.

"If there is an information leak, there's a possibility that we may have disadvantageous information going out to the murderer."

"But, no, if information is in fact being falsified, the police will still only depend on the information on record. They won't simply trust anything they're told."

"Not even if it's from a prefectural assemblyman?"

No, that wouldn't be ignored.

Still, there was no way to know for certain if recorded information was being falsified. In which case all they had to depend on was the informant's memory. Obviously...

That's why she would be threatened.

"Miss Kono..." Shizue stared straight at Ayumi's face.

"We don't know who killed Yabe. All we know is that she was attacked by Kawabata and Nakamura, that she was at one point secured by the area patrol on Saturday, and that she was then abducted. But neither Tsuzuki or Makino are suspicious of the cops."

"And you are, missy?" Kunugi asked. Ayumi looked back at him.

"It is not that I suspect the police. I just don't trust anyone right now."

"But you trust this counselor?"

"I do."

"Miss Kono...why would you say that?" Shizue asked.

"It's not a good thing to murder people, right?"

"Huh?"

How cavalier. That was what Shizue thought before she could think of a response for Ayumi. Ayumi Kono struck Shizue as a cavalier girl for some reason. Her short haircut, her thin neck, the way she stood completely still in the same posture, all of it meant to be exactly that way. Totally different from the diminished face Shizue saw in the mirror. Shizue was made up entirely of useless parts.

"It's not good," Shizue answered.

"Why isn't it?"

"Because the law has determined it so."

She would leave it at that. Kunugi looked perplexed, but Ayumi let out a little laugh.

"I think it would be bad for any more dead bodies to surface. But

I can't do anything about it. I don't know Makino or Tsuzuki very well. But you know them better. Plus you're an adult. Slightly better for this...than me."

"But I'm with the police," Kunugi said. "Remember, you don't trust us?"

"I think the kind of bodyguard that doesn't even have indoor shoes and has to hold his dirty outside shoes while waiting in a hallway is probably not trusted by the police. Whether I trust you isn't an issue anymore."

The young girl's smart comment caught Kunugi a little off guard. He brought out his shoes from behind him. "All right, you have a point. You got me."

"Please." Ayumi lowered her head.

"All right. I'll see what I can do."

"What should I do?"

Kunugi said, "*Don't worry*. We won't let them kill any more people. But adults are cunning. They may betray you. You're not safe."

"I'm fine."

What a girl.

Shizue was a little scared of this purposeful girl with nothing out of place.

Was she always this way?

She was definitely one of her original kids. They'd had several meetings. Countless communications. But she'd never seen this face before. She'd never received this straight visual line.

It was as if she were a wild animal setting her sights on prey.

There was a sound behind them.

What was it?

A slight noise.

This sound...

She'd heard it before. What was it? It wasn't out of place. She'd even gotten used to hearing it day to day. But it stood out. It was a sound she shouldn't have been hearing here. Not now.

No, it was...

Shizue, thinking only of what the sound was, pushed Kunugi to the side.

Did they see her?

As soon as Shizue moved her body to push Kunugi, there appeared on the glass wall of the hallway a pinpoint red dot. There was no mistaking it. The *tally lamp* was reflected off that wall.

That sound was of the surveillance camera turning on. Security was in motion. No...

"Oh. Really, you don't say. Okay. I understand," Shizue said aloud and purposefully, and motioned to Ayumi to walk back toward the entrance. "I'll send her out, so don't worry," Shizue said into her office in a loud voice again and closed the door.

She swiped her ID card.

The room signal indicated vacancy.

"What's going on!" Kunugi said. "What are you trying to pull? Hey!"

"Some of those cunning adults...seems they've already betrayed us."

"What?"

"The surveillance cameras."

"What?!"

"The surveillance cameras on the ceiling..."

"Did they move? Are we being recorded?"

"The security was turned off, so the recording system wasn't supposed to activate till the door closed and the room was in counseling mode. I can't believe it was recording."

"The conversation in your room was recorded then..."

No, it couldn't have been.

"At the very least it wouldn't activate till the door was opened. It's not made to operate at all times. So..."

Even if it weren't recording...

"Was the camera trying to *observe* you?" Kunugi asked.

"That must be what it was doing."

Why did Shizue need to be surveilled? Or did they suspect Ayumi?

Maybe they knew to expect she would have some information related to the murders.

"I've said this several times now, but the space inside the counseling room is very strictly protected. Barring only the extreme cases, there is no outside observation into the room allowed. It's forbidden. As long as the central control system program itself isn't altered, it's unthinkable."

"This is the work of the police."

"Even if the request came from the police, if the director of the center doesn't acquiesce...no, not even a police order would do it. It's what your lieutenant likes to refer to as a situation that supersedes the law—center consent would be needed to conduct such surveillance."

Why. Why did everything have to get so messy?

"Did I get caught in the surveillance?"

"Who knows?"

"I'm sure they couldn't have known I would be here."

"In any case we can't stay here. Let's go."

"Go…go where?" Kunugi said.

"I'm the one being sought. You don't have to…"

"I'm the one who was illegally surveilled."

Right. Because superseding the law was the same as breaking it.

The line that separated good from bad was not ethics or morality or common good, but the law. Just as there were crimes that could be forgiven by human empathy, there were noble acts that could not be justified by ethics. The data collection performed last week was an example of those charged with upholding the law instead ignoring it. It was as Ayumi had said.

The police couldn't be trusted.

Shizue pushed Ayumi down the hall.

Frustrating didn't begin to describe it.

The walls zigzagged but were designed to look straight. What was with this clean, flat, functionless wall?

Shizue struck the wall with all her might.

Her hand hurt. It was neither soft nor warm.

"Hey, slow down," Kunugi said. "You were given explicit orders, weren't you? Not to leave this center?

"There's no reason for the police to restrain someone who's not even a suspect," he said.

"If I can't wait for my chance then I can't not cooperate either. There's no logical reason for my being held here. I have a monitor and a GPS if they need me.

"I can't stay here!"

"That's not what I mean. I meant your job here…"

"My job here was crushed this morning."

"But…where are you going to go?" Kunugi asked.

"Like you, I'm not sure," Shizue said. "We need to get out of here. As soon as the attendants realize there are three people in here they'll send someone. Then you won't have time to worry about me anymore."

The sound of her feet running reverberated in her head.

Things like discretion and prudence all shattered one after the other.

She pulled Ayumi by the hand into the entrance hall.

"Miss Kono, at this point you're in danger too," Shizue said without looking at her. "I noticed when the surveillance camera went on, but I don't know when the audio surveillance started. I don't even know where they could have been listening from. If it's as you said, that the police fabricated information on the murderer, you're in danger too."

Now.

What do we do?

Shizue passed her ID card through the reader that opened the entrance hall to the front gate. She took Ayumi and went into the entrance.

Shizue stopped Kunugi in the middle of passing the gate. As long as someone was standing in the doorway the gate wouldn't close. There, nothing would be recorded.

Shizue went forward to the entrance camera with Ayumi.

"Surveillance team." As she spoke the lamp on the camera went on, and the female attendant from earlier appeared on the screen directly under the camera.

"This is Fuwa."

"Oh, uh…"

"I have Ayumi Kono here. I'm seeing her home."

"But as I mentioned, she's to be escorted by the area patrol," said the attendant.

"I told you already. This child cannot be around unfamiliar people."

"But—"

"I know what they said. There's no need to get in touch with them."

The attendant looked dismayed. There was nothing in her manual about this kind of situation.

"Just wait, please, Ms. Fuwa…Hello, calling Counselor 458321."

The entrance gate opened. The monitor screen blinked off.

Kunugi started running.

Kunugi passed the building at exactly the same time the monitor screen reilluminated.

"You may not leave the building. Wait right there."

"Go."

She pushed Ayumi out.

"Miss Fuwa, you may *not* leave the building."

"Run, fast."

"I'm closing the gate, per instructions from the director."

The reinforced glass gate started to close.

"Both of us have to go." Ayumi yanked Shizue's arm from the other side of the entrance.

"Ms. Fuwa!" Shizue tripped forward from the impact of Ayumi's pull.
Ayumi embraced her.

The gate closed.

Shizue, collapsed, took in a deep breath of the scent of Ayumi's arm
that now held her up.

It was the smell of a beast.

CHAPTER 019

HAZUKI HEARD BACK from her father not thirty minutes after sending her message.

At the moment Hazuki sent her message, her foster father was in a meeting with an influential person—the president of some big corporation Hazuki didn't recognize.

She was sure he would be surprised, since she'd never sent a message to her father before, and though her foster father was in this big important meeting, he read her message nonetheless.

Perhaps because the message reached him in the midst of work, his reply was curt. And yet it was clear he was worried. It was different from the kind of message Hazuki would send—direct language meant to avoid any misinterpretation.

Hazuki was sure she'd understood exactly how her father felt, but conversely it was *his* interpretation of what Hazuki was going through that was now uncertain.

Her foster father was not so much concerned with whether the intruder Hazuki had identified turned out to be the latest murder victim in this killing spree, but that there had been an intruder at his house so shortly after he'd just come in to check on his daughter. Normally in a situation like that the guardian would be alerted directly. He was not only going to send a message of complaint to the security company for not having received any notice, but he would also ask for a detailed account of what took place.

He'd sent a message, received a message, made a vocal communication, and his communication duties were completed.

That should about do it.

It wasn't as if he needed to be apprised of the situation in detail.

Besides, what her father was doing or thinking were all the assumptions of a child, from a child's point of view. It'd be impossible to conjecture. Hazuki herself hadn't grasped the circumstances she'd been put in. What the problem was, or how to resolve it, were practically unknowable for her. She just couldn't relax. Her feelings wouldn't settle.

She was probably sad.

This was probably what it was like to be sad.

She'd done something out of the ordinary, so it followed that she'd feel out of the ordinary.

If this was what happened when one dealt with other people, she did not want to interact with people anymore, or so Hazuki, for a moment, thought.

She faced her terminal and started to do homework as a matter of habit.

As long as she was studying she wouldn't think about Yuko or Ayumi or Mio.

It was nice to be moving automatically.

Not even nice. It was a state of no feelings at all.

An hour later she received a vocal prompt.

"Are you studying?"

It was her foster father on the monitor.

"How did you know?" Hazuki asked.

"Because you answered so quickly. You must have already been facing your monitor. Besides, you are always studying at this hour."

"Yeah, but…"

He was like a dog. Animals only knew how to recognize patterns, Mio had said. Hazuki didn't like that.

"I went ahead and asked D&S about it. I mean, the security company. The meeting I just came out of just happened to be with the new president of the company."

"Oh. Is that right?" She didn't voice any opinion on the matter. Should she have found that a relief?

"So I was able to confirm right there," her foster father said.

"You mean you confirmed that she was…"

"A different person."

"Different? What was different?"

"The girl who was caught climbing onto our property and that groupmate who met her untimely…I'm sorry, she wasn't a groupmate, was she? She wasn't even your age. According to their report the girl was an eighteen-year-old life preservationist. One of those who believe even antiseptic cleaners used to kill bacteria are inhumane. Actually she'd been harping for antiseptics to be called floracides."

Who *cares*?

"She just wanted politicians to acknowledge that it is living beings we kill when we approve antibacterials," he said. "One of these people who believed we have to be aware of all the murder we commit in order to lead healthy lives. Anyway, the girl who tried to break into our house was in one of these organizations. She was there to petition something."

What planet was he on?

"Normally they're supposed to make appointments to see me and make *real contact*, but you know, those guys are impetuous."

"Those guys..."

I don't know those guys, Hazuki thought.

"You're lying."

"I'm not lying," her foster father said politely.

If this wasn't a lie, then it was Hazuki's story that was a lie.

"I have it on record, so it can't be a lie," her foster father said. "They even showed me the record themselves, and just to be extra sure they let me talk to the security personnel that apprehended her, along with the area patrol that accompanied him. I confirmed their patrol car ID and everything."

Car ID. Hazuki didn't remember it, but she knew Mio would. She thought about asking for it but realized it would seem unnatural and was probably a waste of time at this point. Mio had said that the patrol record was erased.

In which case all of this was bullshit.

"As for why I didn't get notice of this myself, D&S is not to blame. They are doing their sincere best to fulfill their duties. You weren't harmed, were you?"

"No, I wasn't," Hazuki said. *Should I have been?*

"Well, I know it was probably unpleasant, but nothing happened. They even responded to your call inside the time they guarantee. They were apparently just held up in processing the data from the night's report."

Hazuki didn't doubt that. The data was being rewritten.

"In the case of an intrusion, after the target has been secured, the security company is contractually obligated to contact the police as well as the security client within twenty-four hours with a detailed report. In this case, myself and you should both be receiving a report."

Hazuki didn't want that report.

That wasn't the problem. There was no point in announcing that the person apprehended was Yuko Yabe. There was no point. She was dead.

On top of which, being told this story about some girl she'd never seen or heard of was only confusing.

"This time, they were apparently having difficulty identifying the intruder. She didn't have an ID card or portable monitor on her. That was probably to protect accomplices who helped her get on our property."

Lies. This was all made up.

"Furthermore, they were having a hard time processing the data. They don't know why, but the information chain got stopped up somewhere. I own three properties in just this area alone and many more in the whole prefecture. It could be because of that. The security in this entire prefecture is managed by D&S alone, so you can imagine it gets confusing. Still, they've apologized," her foster father said.

"They assured your safety but didn't protect you after all. The president, the CEO, and our security liaison all expressed great regret. They wanted to come and apologize to you personally at the home, but I figured that would be a nuisance for you."

Nuisance was right. There was no reason to come visit the home.

"Usually I'd announce this publicly and make it a problem, but I've decided to leave them alone since they did inspect the system so expeditiously and assured resolution of the problem. Oh, but of course if this isn't enough for you, I will definitely take punitive measures against them."

"It's not that it's not enough, it's just..."

It was all wrong. Someone was fabricating the truth.

The past was being tampered with. Hazuki's experience had been negated.

"Do you know the name of this girl?" *A made-up girl like that couldn't possibly have a name*, Hazuki thought. It was a lie, after all.

But her foster father uttered a name.

"It was technically illegal entry, but she didn't get past the front gate, so we can't really sue her. It's not a criminal case, so there's no police report to file. But if you're still feeling scared, that's reason enough to place a fine on her. Do you want me to do that?"

That would be pointless.

This woman was probably not real. A girl who existed only in a terminal, only as a fragment of data. Since data was truth, and what was in the terminal was evidence of truth, then this person probably existed. But if this girl existed, that made Hazuki the phantom.

Hazuki was the lie.

"I don't want a lawsuit."

"You're right," her father said. "Taking this to court would be difficult. But if you don't think D&S adequately looked into the bug or demonstrated sufficient good faith, I will turn this incident into a worldwide spectacle and demand proper resolution. Fortunately nothing bad happened this time, but there must be times this kind of thing yields much worse outcomes, so I can certainly take extreme measures. This is a precarious situation to be put in for anyone living in this prefecture, no, in this country. In a more serious situation this would have to be dealt with by central. This might force a reassessment of everything from the relationship between the area patrol and security companies to system license standards."

These words meant nothing to Hazuki.

He was probably exactly correct. *Words so exacting that other adults who spoke this way would understand easily*, she thought. She thought, but she knew the words and the reality were disjointed.

"Anyway, I'm glad you brought this to my attention," her foster father said. "To be honest, I was really surprised, then worried, when I received your message, but actually I was also glad. This is the first time I've heard from you in a while."

Glad?

Hazuki didn't understand why receiving a communication from her would make him happy.

"Oh, and as for the murder case, well the victim count has gone up, but this incident doesn't help solve the case at all. It truly pains me not to be able to be there with you, honestly. Unfortunately I just can't. But I've requested a special patrol tour of the premises. A patrol officer will be regularly checking in on the house, so please don't worry."

That was…

"Father." It was the first time Hazuki had called him that. She didn't know why.

Maybe because she was feeling so desolate. Her foster father made a seemingly happy, seemingly sad, difficult-to-interpret facial expression and said, "It's going to be all right."

The monitor went blank.

All right.

Would it be all right?

"Dad…"

Her body was sunk, but her mood was floating. Her body and mind were not in sync. It made her uncomfortable.

Was she scared?

Yes, scared.

What was she scared of? She'd never felt this way before.

Hazuki took the disc out of its case and put it in the desktop computer on her table.

Recorded on that disc, per the workings of Mio, was another truth that had been pulled and copied from the house's main terminal data bank.

But it was actually not a fact anymore. It was a lie.

She ran the recording.

It displayed the time.

A girl appears before the gate and collapses.

It displays the fact that a security transmission is sent.

Five minutes later the screen freezes.

Then the patrol officer and security representative arrive.

Voice.

We've apprehended the intruder.

Could you please verify?

Her face appears on the screen.

That sullen face.

Hazuki's voice.

I don't know her.

Their voices.

Really?

Could that have really been someone she did not know? She said she didn't know who it was, and that was what was on record; that was now the truth. The past could only be verified by records like this.

No.

The girl she didn't know that appeared on her monitor smiles faintly. It was Yuko. It was definitely Yuko Yabe.

Hazuki froze the image of Yuko smiling, because it was the only frame in which Hazuki was certain it was her. A girl she'd never seen or known before wouldn't smile like that. Would never smile *for her* like that.

Then she slumped, got serious. Hazuki remembered the warmth of the touch of flesh. The *feel* of a human.

The smell.

That was the unrecorded memory of Yuko Yabe.

Those things were not recorded on this disc. Therefore, this disc would not be able to prove anything. This so-called life preservationist girl probably had a face very similar to Yuko's. No way to distinguish them from just a grainy monitor image.

If there were no record of Yuko, there was definitely going to be problems.

They just had to make a copy of this moving image.

It all becomes a lie.

Hazuki noticed something blinking in the corner of her vision.

A turtle.

Another message from Mio.

OPEN.

JUST ONE HOUR AGO, THE PATROL COMPANY RE-ENTERED THEIR DATA.
THE ENEMY IS A STEP AHEAD OF US. THE IMAGES AND THE MOTION
RECORDERS APPEAR TO BE A FABRICATION. ALL THE DATA IS BUNK.
FABRICATION 800. COULD BE BAD. I WANT TO DRAFT A COUNTERMEASURE
PLAN. MEET AT THE DOVE HOUSE. THERE WILL BE A POWER OUTAGE AT
EXACTLY 1900 HOURS.

--MIO

Seven o'clock.

Her monitor said it was 6:48:38. She had less than twelve minutes.

Hazuki closed the image of Yuko smiling and ejected the disc from her drive. Then she changed from her house clothes to a tracksuit.

The suit was made of a new material that could measure body temperature and regulate moisture absorption and release. It was light and easy to move around in but didn't feel like anything when worn. Hazuki just liked the way it looked.

Then she put on the walking shoes she hadn't yet worn.

The power had been out for a mere thirty seconds the last time and the time before that. She didn't want to get stuck in the foyer still putting on her shoes when that time was up.

She remained still for five minutes.

Then she left her bedroom, the monitor still on, and locked the door.

Just as she descended to the living room, a visitor's call rang.

Who was it?

Hazuki ran to the living room's main terminal to confirm.

There were two men in area patrol uniforms standing in front of the gate.

"Miss Makino. We're local area patrol officers. We've come to talk to you about last week's incident with the unannounced intruder and to check in on you."

This was bad.

There were only five minutes till the planned outage.

"I've already spoken with my father about this. There's no need for a follow-up."

Go away. Go away!

"Ah yes. But you see, we have a special police matter here. Plus it's in our private surveillance contract with you to come by…if you could just spare us a moment of *real contact*."

Real?

"That is, as part of our duties we'd just like to assure you by meeting face-to-face on at least this first occasion."

"That's all right. Really—"

"It's a rule. We've seen the layout of your home, but if for the record we could just assure your security personally…We just need to see the interior of your home. It will really only take a minute."

Only four minutes left.

What to do.

"We're not here to harm you. I'll run my ID card now so you can see."

The two men slid their ID cards through the reader, one after the other.

On her screen appeared their headshots, names, and ID numbers.

She couldn't keep denying them.

"All right, one minute," Hazuki said. She switched her security system to visitor mode and unlocked the front gate.

The door clicked open.

"Employee ID DV320054, DV321886, now entering the Makino residence, in 122 Section A 5035-62."

Hazuki stood in the hallway. Two large men appeared in the hall.

One of them was skinny for his height, but the other looked enormous, like he was from a foreign country.

"If we could just check the windows by the doors, then. Oh, and you should confirm our IDs. Protocol."

"Your IDs…of course."

Hazuki turned on the main monitor in the foyer.

The last images of the two of them popped up.

Hazuki assumed they wanted her to compare their ID images to their real faces.

The skinny one was definitely himself. The helmet made him look a little bigger, but…

The other one.

Huh?

This can't be.

"What seems to be the matter?"

"Oh nothing."

The other face on her monitor, the headshot of the other man.

Peacock tattoo on his head.

"Is there a problem?"

"N-no."

Her heart was racing. It pumped and squeezed. The blood in her veins raced, and for a split second her vision went completely black.

What do I do. What do I do. What do I do.

These were the guys.

These were the guys that had killed Yuko.

"Do you mind then if we come in?" the skinnier one said.

Hazuki shifted over against the wall.

She couldn't say a word.

Her tongue was glued to the back of her mouth and her voice would not work.

"The back entrance is over there, then? And I'm sure it's usually kept locked."

The skinnier man took off his shoes and came into the house. Hazuki walked around him.

Then...

The larger man took off his shoes. Her heart. Her heart.

He silently walked past Hazuki, slowly. Very slowly.

They walked past her.

She stopped right at the door to the living room.

Her fingers.

Her fingers were trembling. No.

No no no no no.

"What's the matter?" The bigger man looked back.

"Why are you shaking?"

Go. Go to the back.

"What's the matter?"

"Uh..." This was bad. She didn't want to look at his face. She was scared. Scared. Very scared.

Hazuki turned her face away. She looked at the monitor.

If only she could go into the monitor. In there, she was never scared.

"You don't seem well. Perhaps you've come down with something?"

They were moving.

The time. 6:59:05 PM.

Fifty-five more seconds.

Hazuki closed her eyes and started running.

She caught the larger man, who stood there mouth agape, off guard as she whisked past him and made it to the living room. She closed the door.

"What's going on?" The large man opened the door. The other one ran toward the hallway. The larger man entered the living room. The thin one followed him. Hazuki rounded halfway around the room along the wall.

"What's the matter, Miss Makino? Miss Hazuki Makino!" the men said loudly. They followed her. One more corner till the door. She was in front of the door.

"What's the matter? Hey, you don't think—"

"She knows about us!"

Her hand was on the doorknob. The skinnier man...

Pulled out a knife.

Its reflection splintered through the air for a flash and then.

Lights out.

Hazuki lowered her head and ran with all her might down the hall, opened the door to the foyer, and shut it hard.

She ran till she made it outside the gate.

If they were still putting on their shoes in the foyer when the power went back on they would be locked in the house. They needed a code to get out of the house. And if the number of people inside the house before and after the power outage was different, the system would read an error. The security system would initiate a check. Then...

Hurry. Hurry. Hurry. Hurry. Thirty seconds.

Hazuki ran.

Slam.

They'd run after her without putting on their shoes.

They were coming. They were coming at her fast.

Whoosh. The sound cut through the wind.

Something incredibly hot sped through the space under her earlobe.

She heard the sound of something thudding on the ground. She turned back. A fan of blackness spread across the ground.

The thin man's arm was aimed forward like a spear. His weapon flew from the tip of his hand and gleamed in the air once.

Then the black night behind them lit up through her windows. The electricity went back on.

Something quivered. It spread like it was riding the wind.

Ggg, the man's voice.

"Get up. Hurry."

That voice.

Rey Mao.

Rey Mao's straight hair whipped about again.

Those long arms were wrapped around the skinny man's throat.

"Run away, now. When the other guy gets out we're both in trouble."

Another blow. The man collapsed on the grass.

"It's no use. I can't kill him with *gongfu*. Hurry now. Run."

Hazuki couldn't respond.

But.

Her arms and legs started moving. She couldn't tell if it was her or the world moving.

She couldn't see anything before her. Her head was empty. There was no inside or outside.

Hazuki had not normally thought about the fact that she was alive. Every day she felt half dead. So why was she so scared of death now? If Hazuki alive was the same as Hazuki dead so far as the world was concerned, why did she fear death so much now?

She turned down an alley and ran up a hill.

Ayumi!

Her body moved involuntarily.

Behind Ayumi's house, at the foot of the metal spiral staircase, Hazuki had a fit of dizziness and collapsed. Her equilibrium failed her, and the world started to turn. Hazuki turned over on the ground once. Then somehow she got herself up, braced herself against the wall of the house, and wrapped her arms around herself. Her teeth wouldn't stay still.

Rey Mao silently appeared before her.

"It's all right. We got out of there before the other guy got out."

"Haaa…"

"Calm down. Mio called me out here. She said our enemies were onto our movements. The data we were trying to send was being rewritten, and she worried you would be attacked. What a pain in the ass."

"Pain in…"

"You know what I mean," Rey Mao said. "She means well but she causes trouble. That's all. Now get up. Can you stand?"

Long arms. Hazuki fell into those arms. They were colder than her father's.

The girls wound up the spiral staircase to the roof.

"I doubt if they know about this place," Rey Mao said. "No one would suspect an unmarked room like this to be in Section A. It's a great hideout."

The sky was black and large.

There was no light on in the dove cage.

"Ayumi must be out. I wonder where she's gone at this hour."

Rey Mao scoped the area out before opening the door. It was unlocked.

"Mio's not here either. We got here at a good time. Well, let's just go in."

Hazuki floated in.

It was dark inside. The window to the dove room looked like a floating cutout.

"This is weird," Rey Mao said. She told Hazuki, who just stood by the door, to sit down.

"Th-thanks." That was all she said for a while.

Rey Mao let out a deep sigh.

"I thought you might get attacked on your way here, but to think they actually went into your house. Those were area patrol. Or did they disguise themselves as area patrol to get in?"

Hazuki shook her head.

"What does that mean?"

"They were real."

"Real? What do you mean real?"

"I checked their IDs. They were both real area patrol guys."

"But that was definitely the guy the other day who apprehended Yuko in the car. The other one..."

"Yeah. The guy with the peacock head art."

"Then it was definitely them. They're real...patrol? Then our enemy is the area patrol..." Rey Mao said. "This is no good. Maybe Mio's also..."

No.

Hazuki didn't want to hear the rest of that sentence.

"Uh..."

"Hazuki. My name's Hazuki Makino."

"Ha-zuke-ee..." Rey Mao sat down in a chair. "What kind of girl is Ayumi?"

"Huh?"

"She's weird, eh?"

"Well..."

"Aren't you friends?"

"We're not...friends."

What are *we? We're definitely not friends, but...*

"I'm not sure," Hazuki answered. She really didn't know. She didn't know much about Ayumi. Just what everyone else could find out about her on the public data server. The only undocumented fact Hazuki had on her was this illegal room on her roof.

"Hmph," Rey Mao said. "You guys are so complicated."

"Complicated?"

"Never mind. Hazuki. Just hide here for now."

"Here?"

"You can't go back home, you know that." Rey Mao stood up.

"Where are you going?"

"I'm going to follow those two guys."

"That's dangerous."

"Of course it is," Rey Mao said matter-of-factly. "For us, *living* is dangerous." She stood in the middle of the room and looked all around her. "There's nothing here."

"Nothing?"

"Nothing of use," Rey Mao said looking up at the ceiling. "Oh by the way, Hazuki. You should turn off your monitor. We don't know exactly what it can do, but it does indicate that you are at the *terminus*."

Hazuki had not once ever thought of it that way, but Rey Mao was correct.

"You all are connected one way or another. That might make you feel safe, but it's restrictive. You can't run with a thread tied around your waist."

But.

Without it...

"If the area patrol is your enemy they will find out where you are."

Certainly so if Hazuki's monitor was in GPS mode.

Even if it weren't, the police could force a search.

She stuck her hand in her pocket. The disc with Yuko Yabe's record. That was all she had on her.

Hazuki frantically patted her body. It wasn't there. Hazuki didn't have her monitor on her. This meant that her location, her coordinates...

She had no idea where she was.

A harsh flapping sound caught Hazuki by surprise. Rey Mao grabbed one of the doves. The small creepy-looking animal with eyes that looked almost as though it understood its captor shook violently in Rey Mao's long arms.

The dove was just like Hazuki.

"If anything happens, I'll let this dove fly back."

"Let it fly?"

"They know *exactly where* they need to go, so it'll come back here. So don't go anywhere till it comes back."

The dove was nothing like Hazuki.

"Don't get yourself killed," Rey Mao said, then she disappeared into the night.

CHAPTER 020

"IT'S LIKE A shitty action flick," Kunugi said. "I used to watch those things as a kid. Vulgar stuff."

Ayumi silently looked down the road. Shizue was trying to digest everything that was happening.

Without so much as sorting or organizing, abstracting or finding symbolic meaning in it, Shizue was trying to swallow what had just happened, whole.

This indescribable, complex, dirty, potent odor. It was the smell of earth, water, grass, and trees. Those things alone were already too much for Shizue. But she had learned that children needed those things.

Shizue herself was raised in an environment where such odors had been completely extracted. Shizue knew full well the negative effects that an environment without nature held for people. She had a vast amount of information on the subject. Still, there was nothing she could do about the way she'd been raised.

There was no turning back time. She'd thought seriously about what was called a "resocialization," but Shizue was already completely developed. So she had given up on the idea.

She couldn't take it anymore.

"Maybe you should have stayed back after all," Kunugi told Shizue. "There was nothing they would have held you for. You shouldn't be hiding in the bushes like this. You could say you escaped an abduction, no?"

"I became plenty suspicious before you were brought in."

"Even so," Kunugi rubbed his nose. He got dirt on himself. "Now you've made one hell of a criminal of yourself. Not a prosecutable criminal, but one that's clearly guilty. You just ran into the woods with this stupid middle-aged loser who just kidnapped a minor. Even if they didn't press charges, you'd be hard-pressed to get your job back, I'm sure."

"Thanks for reminding me."

That was enough.

Shizue stared at Ayumi's profile.

"I trust you," said Ayumi. That admission made Shizue feel like her job as a counselor was done.

If she dilly-dallied any further no one would trust her.

"This is all just hearsay anyway, and there's no evidence to speak of. You're still a good counselor."

Kunugi, tired from squatting, collapsed into a seated position on the ground. "If you were my counselor, I'd be set."

"I'm sorry."

"Hmph," Kunugi let out through his nose. "It's getting darker and I'm starving. But we can't move. If I keep quiet I'll lose my nerve. They didn't see me in their surveillance cameras, right?"

"I don't think so. By the time I fled the gates, several area patrol officers had gotten to the entrance hall and possibly a few police officers. I ran as fast as I could and didn't look back, so I can't say for certain, but they're sure to have at least seen your back."

"I saw," Ayumi said.

"Saw? Who?" Kunugi asked.

"They were probably police. They weren't wearing uniforms and they weren't area patrols."

"You saw all that while running in the other direction? That's something else."

"I was pulling Ms. Fuwa's arm, so I was already facing the building."

"Oh, right. Then why aren't they chasing us?" Kunugi asked stupidly. "Don't they think they should chase us? Or is that how futile it is for us to hide?"

"They're probably waiting for us to come out to arrest us."

"That's definitely one way to get us, but...now we have no idea who the enemy is." Kunugi threw his hands behind his head. "Role-playing games are so much easier to decipher."

"You really should have stayed home with your games, you know."

"I can play the old ones from memory, I've played them so many times. The newer ones are actually a little harder," Kunugi said.

They saw a light go on in the distance.

Probably street lamps.

Shizue had thrown her portable while on the run and now had no idea what time it was. If they'd placed a GPS tracker on her they'd know with one search where they were. She had had no choice but to throw it away. Yet without her coordinates, she didn't know exactly where she was. How inconvenient.

They were on the west side of the green area surrounding the center; that much was certain. Yuji Nakamura had been suspected of hiding out here. Turned out he was not hiding out here after all, but now Shizue was.

It was getting darker.

Kunugi's already nebulous profile became hazier still and eventually disappeared into obscurity.

All they could hear was their own breathing.

In a room, the sound would seem strange. In their new setting it sounded natural.

"Someone's coming," Ayumi said.

The sound pierced through.

"How do you know?"

"It's the area patrol and Hinako Sakura."

"You can see them?"

"Yes. Two area patrols. They're holding a flashlight."

"That's some incredible vision you have," Kunugi said, incredulous.

Sakura.

She'd probably finished being interrogated and had now been released. They'd been questioning her this whole time. To her it probably felt like torture.

"Oh no."

"What?"

"Sakura saw me."

"Liar. Where is she?"

"On the main road."

"The main road. The one leading out of the center? Don't be stupid. You couldn't see that road in broad daylight, much less in the dark of night. It's too far from here. Why do you think we hid here?"

"I don't know. She noticed me though," Ayumi said.

"The area police have stopped."

"Are they coming this way?"

"No. It looks like they got an emergency call. One of them is running off. The other one and Sakura are walking again."

"Can she really see all this?" Kunugi asked Shizue.

"I'm sure there are things children see that adults cannot."

"Because they're innocent."

"Because they're ruthless."

"You mean adults are nice?" Kunugi asked.

"Adult vision is fogged."

Hmph, Kunugi let out through his nose again.

"Miss Kono," Shizue called Ayumi. "How's it…err…" What was

Shizue supposed to say?

"I'm fine," Ayumi said.

"Miss Fuwa." This time Ayumi addressed Shizue. "I want to ask again, but killing people—it's wrong, right?"

"Yes. It's bad. One should absolutely never murder. It is against the law."

"Nice and simple," Kunugi said. "It was so much more sticky when they explained it to me back in the day."

"What do you mean, *sticky*?"

"You know…" Kunugi leaned to one side. "We talked about morals and ethics, about being an upstanding citizen and the importance of humanity. Whether it was important."

"Of course it is."

"Right. Of course. My feelings as a concerned citizen, improving the human condition—humanism, is it? Obviously I learned all that. I know it, but *hmmm*, I don't know how to explain this. When I was young, those words were all somehow meaningless. No, I mean I knew a lifetime's worth of sadness and pain and fear. I got mad at the really flagrant criminals. I'd get unreasonably frustrated, enraged. You know, social order. I used to believe in social order so much more than now. But then, I sort of…"

"You weren't satisfied with it," Shizue suggested.

"Kind of…" Kunugi answered. "Even I don't understand why I'm not satisfied. I just knew this was not the way a police officer should feel."

"These emotions and humanist theories are not why we must not kill. Those are only the reasons why we *created laws* against killing humans. Confusing one for the other has led to our discordance, no?"

"Hmm?" Kunugi made a strange sound. "The reason why the laws were created?"

"Isn't that so? When a friend or relative is killed you become sad, angry, hurt. That's only natural. Therefore it is universally understood that any violent attack on one's right to live of healthy mind and body is a bad thing. That's why laws forbid the murder of humans."

"That's probably true, but doesn't it amount to the same thing?"

"No, it doesn't," Shizue said.

"How's it different?"

"Well, let me put it to you this way. If no one was sad about the death of a particular person; if no one felt anger or vengeance or hurt from the death of someone who would have caused more suffering to others alive than dead—is it okay to kill *that* person?"

"N-no. I mean, of course not," Kunugi said, sounding defeated. "No one should ever be murdered."

"In that case, all those complex feelings and ethics and teachings don't constitute reasons for forbidding the murder of humans. Even if you are sad, upset, or for that matter happy, you cannot kill. The law is blind. It doesn't matter who you are."

"Ah," Kunugi said smartly. "That's why you insist on saying that murder is wrong simply because the law says so. Morals and ethics in and of themselves can't explain the reasons behind the law. Of course, it's axiomatic that laws are created on the basis of morals and ethics, and if you can't believe that, you will most certainly be confused, but I just don't think the same way about the question of whether committing a crime is ever justified. As it stands, the thinking is that morality is attained as a result of abiding by the law *and* that it also leads to our emotionally comprehending the meaning of good, right?"

"You mean why one shouldn't doubt the law."

"No. Doubting the law and disobeying the law are different. If you believe a law should not be abided by, you should do everything in your power to change it. There's no rule that because the law is bad it should be disobeyed. That's an infringement of the rules. You can't get along that way. Even breaking a bad law is a punishable crime."

"But changing the law is difficult," Shizue said.

"That's something only lawmakers say. It's humans who've created the laws, and if they follow the right procedures it's humans who will change the laws. However, so long as the majority keeps acknowledging the law, it will not change. Even if the laws are not correct. Even if the law looks wrong to everyone. But of course, no one's going to abolish laws against murder."

But.

"But a long time ago in this country, vengeance killings were forgivable. Even in this century, murder was publicly sanctioned. The death penalty, I mean. Those laws were eventually changed by people, right?"

"I see," Kunugi said.

Now they couldn't see anything.

There wasn't enough light for their eyes to even adapt to the dark.

"When I was about the age of this young girl here, murder was popular," Kunugi said.

"Popular?"

"By that I don't mean that it was a free-for-all of everyone killing each other. But kids my age were committing these crimes one after the other. I don't know if they thought killing someone would improve their own lives, or if they were thinking at all. Well...I had nothing to do with it. Kids knew the consequences of things like that, I'm sure. It's only the idiots that ignored the consequences. But..."

It felt like Kunugi had stood up.

"When I was in elementary school...That is, back when there was such a thing as elementary school, that would be about when I was about seven to twelve, kids were grouped and separated into classes to learn things with other kids the same age."

"I had that when I was growing up as well," Shizue said. "Obviously it's been banned since, but elementary schools existed until pretty recently."

"Is that right? Well, it was elementary school, then junior high school, and throughout that whole time I had this one friend. A boy. He was serious and didn't like to play outside, so we got along. That kid came over to my house one day and asked a favor of me."

"Favor?"

"Yeah. He asked me to record an emission on what you kids call an on-air entertainment channel now. Back then we still used magnetic tapes. Anyway, it was not uncommon back then, so I agreed. I taped this thing and brought it to his house the next day. But when I got to his house, there was a tarp stretched around it," Kunugi said.

"What is a *tarp*?" Ayumi asked.

"A blue sheet. I thought maybe they were renovating the house. But then it turned out to be the police."

"Police...what was going on?"

"It was a crime scene. There had been a murder," Kunugi said nonchalantly. "He'd killed a girl from the neighborhood, and his parents found out. He then killed his parents and siblings."

"That's—"

Kunugi started laughing. "That fucker beat the girl with a stone and then went home covered in blood. He was scolded right in front of the house. I guess that was when he decided he would kill his entire family. He knew that the only time his whole family would be in the same place was when his favorite show was airing. Obviously he wouldn't be able to watch it, so he asked me to record it for him. What do you think about that?" Kunugi said. "When he came over with the blank tape, he'd already killed the girl. While I was watching his show, he was stabbing his mother in the throat with a kitchen knife. I didn't know what to do."

Kunugi seemed to lean to one side again.

"I got angry. Even sad. But I didn't know what I was sad or angry about. He was totally normal. He didn't cry, yell, scream, or act frightened. So I didn't think to bother asking him to confide in me or to tell me anything. He didn't look like he was thinking about anything at all."

"That's..." Shizue couldn't find the right words.

"I just thought 'hmph.' It must not be a big deal to kill people. Then I was scared of myself for thinking that. That's why I asked an adult about it. Just like this young woman did. *It's wrong to kill, isn't it? It's not right to kill, right?* I learned that it was wrong. No, I *knew* it was wrong. Any brat knows that. My heart aches when I see a child crying over murdered parents. When I see parents who've killed their child, I want to kill them with my bare hands. But it's like you said before. It would be wrong for me to kill even the parent who murders his child. So then what? What's the difference between me and that kid?"

"What *was* the difference between you two?"

"Nothing at all," Kunugi said. "He was a minor. Back then, unlike today, minors were protected unconditionally, and on top of that, they got psychological assessments. *Behavioral disorder*, they decided. Certainly thinking about it now, it was a typical behavioral disorder, but at the time, I was totally unsatisfied. I guess I still am, actually." Kunugi laughed.

"I mean if he was guilty of behavioral disorder then I was too, I thought. It's the same. I couldn't forgive him for being a murderer. I was really torn up. I was confused and frustrated. By the time I realized what was going on I was the washed-up old man you see before you today."

He sounded defeated.

"It turned out we're no different," he said with the same voice. "I just discovered that. It's really all about whether you can learn to abide by the laws as a matter of fact, or not. It's that simple, but it took me thirty long years to figure it out," said the voice in the dark.

"I didn't have any adults like you around to tell me the straightforward truth. So I got to thinking. And I kept thinking...and thinking...and then became a cop. Even after I became a cop though, I didn't fully understand. Just that it was bad to kill people, but that just because someone had killed someone, the crime didn't make them a bad person. Humans are stupid, so they make mistakes easily. They won't even notice that they did. By the time they do it's too late."

"Too late?"

"Yes. There are such things as do-overs, but when someone dies it's forever. It's too late," the darkness said in Kunugi's voice.

This was something Shizue had been saying herself for a long time. Shizue extended her arms out on the ground. The warm earth felt cool despite its real temperature.

Like a corpse. Like her mother's dead body.

"When someone dies it's forever." Ayumi's voice. "They don't come back."

"Kind of like us now," Kunugi mocked himself. "Good adults like us, stuck here now. It's stupid."

Really stupid, Shizue thought.

They were silent for a moment.

"What time is it, I wonder. How long have we been sitting here?"

"Probably about twenty minutes." Ayumi seemed to have stood up.

"Miss Kono, you sure? You said you left your monitor." When Shizue had thrown her portable terminal away Ayumi had said she didn't have hers to begin with.

"I don't carry that thing unless I'm going to the communication session. Even though you all tell me to."

"Then how do you know how long—"

"The position of the moon," Ayumi said.

"The moon…"

In the sky the moon hung large.

"The moon…"

Of the ten thousand lux light waves emitted by the nearest fixed star, a mere 0.5 lux was feebly reflected in the earth's only satellite, which hung 384,400 kilometers from earth.

"The moon's out?" Shizue asked.

She hadn't seen the real moon in so long. Just when she was a kid. This inorganic and aimless 0.5 lux star was quiet and calm, cold like the skin of a dead body.

The clouds had obscured it.

The reflected light was almost a complete circle, like a hole in the sky. It was a weak pale blue color, but it provided plenty of light to counterpoint the outline of dull humans.

Shizue looked at the sphere of light in the sky. Kunugi probably did too.

"You can tell time by that, eh? Can you also tell where we are?" Kunugi said sarcastically. It looked like Ayumi's silhouette had just nodded.

Her head was pitch black with the quiet light of the moon behind her.

"Did you train in this kind of thing, or are you one of those stargazer types?"

"Animals always know exactly where they are."

"Hmm?"

"They know where they are between the earth and the sky. In other words, they know exactly what they are. I didn't know what I was before. I was envious," Ayumi said. She then waded her way through the grass ahead of them.

Shizue stood up.

All of a sudden...

In the path of the pure and mysterious spotlight of the moon appeared another silhouette.

The figure's entire body, jet black, was basking in the moonlight.

"You're a man-eating being," the pitch-black human form said, its voice thin. "A woman-eating, child-eating being..." It was a voice that sounded like song, like weeping.

"I beg of you, embrace the blood. Give human blood. Embrace it tonight..."

Kunugi stood up.

The small black shadow slowly advanced toward Ayumi.

"Are you a wolf?" the shadow asked.

Wolf?

This voice. Hinako Sakura.

"Is that you, Miss Sakura?"

It was indeed Sakura, dressed in black mourning clothes.

"Wolves are extinct," Ayumi answered.

"I beg your pardon," Sakura said in characteristically over-polite language.

She lifted her face.

Straight black bangs.

Gray eyelids. Gray lips.

The face that floated in this moonlight was completely different from the one that tried to explain the meaning of a word like *occult*, seated uncomfortably in the counseling room chair. Her monochrome make-up didn't feel out of place here. It was probably very difficult for a girl like this to lead an existence under the power of sunlight. In this weak moonlight she seemed more alive than ever, Shizue thought. She was very pretty.

"Why did you come back?" Ayumi asked. "Didn't they escort you home?"

"I've come to warn you."

"Warn?"

Hinako shifted her gaze from Ayumi to Shizue.

"Another girl has gone missing."

"Huh?'

"Just as you and the police officer over there were fleeing the entrance hall a message was fielded at the center by a guardian reporting his charge missing. She's been missing since last night, and the center's director then ran to meet the head investigation officer, acting very confused."

That's why no one came after us.

The police had no time to waste looking for the likes of Shizue and Kunugi.

However...

"Who's missing?"

"Another fourteen-year-old girl from our class. I have never talked to her myself, though I'm sure we've met. I have no memory of her," Hinako said. "Someone by the name of Kisugi."

Kisugi.

At least this wasn't one of Shizue's children.

What is this? Why do I care if she's one of mine?

Even in such a confused state, Shizue couldn't help thinking that.

How could she be worried about whether this was her problem or not when she should be worried about the girl's safety? At least she should act shocked.

I'm really a coldhearted woman deep down inside, Shizue thought.

She couldn't accept the facts.

No, it was probably just that she did not want to hear about any more people she knew getting killed. That was the truth; Shizue was sick and tired of all this.

Yet if Shizue turned her feelings around it meant she didn't care if someone she didn't know got killed. Either way one thing was certain. Shizue was a horrible woman. She was horrified at herself.

It was like she couldn't face herself.

She was depressed.

"And then," Hinako continued. "Half the investigators left to go to the source of the call. I was left to finish my interrogation with a remaining investigator when we were interrupted by a call from the security company. He received an area-wide alert to the patrol and director. An emergency call. I overheard what they said."

"Did something else happen?"

Something was happening as they spoke.

"Yes. At exactly 1900 hours, something went awry at the residence of Representative Makino."

"Makino," Ayumi reacted.

"Then almost all the remaining investigators at the center fled to that scene, and they decided to release me, but on my way out of the center while on the promenade, my accompanying bodyguard from area patrol suddenly got an emergency notification."

"That's what that was…" Kunugi looked over to Ayumi.

"And then?" Ayumi asked curtly.

"Ms. Hazuki Makino was then kidnapped by the alleged suspect of this serial killing spree, one undocumented resident."

"What the hell?!" Kunugi bolted upright.

Shizue couldn't move.

She was one step behind…again.

"But I'm sure these were all *fabricated truths*," Hinako said.

"You're saying they lied?"

"I believe so."

"Do you have proof or is this…a premonition?" Kunugi asked.

"I inferred it from the way the director of investigations behaved and how he reacted to all the news."

"You mean Mr. Ishida?"

"When the notice was received, it wasn't yet known if Representative Makino's case had something to do with the serial killings. That's to say, it wasn't yet determined if his call was in fact an event," Hinako said. "At the very least it could have been a mere security system bug, and that could be resolved by any area patrol or security system representative without involving an investigative director. However, this investigator instructed his men to be at the Makino residence and assure the daughter's safety at once, *before* the area patrol had sent him any official report on the matter."

"That's…"

"Normally, the area patrol would go there first, no?"

"That's true, but circumstances are circumstances. If something was reported from the home and it's known that there is a girl there the same age as a bunch of murder victims, you'd worry," Kunugi said.

"Representative Makino has *several* homes in this area alone," Hinako said.

"Oh…that's right."

"The fourteen-year-old girl lives alone in just one of those houses. Even a police officer wouldn't know which house she was in just from hearing the registration number from a security company, would he?"

"No, I suppose he wouldn't."

"Also..."

"There's something else?"

"After this police officer told his men to go to the scene, after the investigators had left his side, he contacted someone and was given instructions himself. His personal camera was on, and he got a voice message. He said into the camera, "*It's Mao again.*""

Rey Mao. The undocumented resident.

"Then he said to do as they'd been instructed in the handbook and contact the D&S Processing Center immediately."

"And what about that?"

"The director of investigations, he's with the police, correct?"

"Of course. He's the lieutenant chief of Division R investigations in the prefecture. What..."

Shizue was struck by the prominence of the sinews on Kunugi's neck as he spoke.

"What about it?" he finished.

"Do the police always give instructions to the area patrol directly?"

"No. Not normally. We have different protocols for alerts." As soon as Kunugi said this he relaxed the muscles in his neck and said, "Good point. If he told someone to notify D&S, that means Ishida was talking to an area patrol, as you suggest. In other words, the message sent to all the patrols afterward was written by Ishida himself."

It was all made up.

A truth made of lies.

"I do not know what is transpiring in this region," Hinako said. "All I know is that something ominous, something wicked, is about to take place. Earlier when I was passing by, I was able to see all of you. I...it was decided you could be trusted, and so I came to tell you of what has happened."

"Decided...by whom? God?" That was how Shizue heard it, at least.

"No, I decided myself," Hinako said.

"Thank you," Ayumi said to her.

With the moon behind her again, Ayumi faced Shizue and Kunugi.

"Miss Fuwa. Mr. Policeman. I have to go now."

"Go...go where?"

Ayumi stretched her thin neck toward the moon.

"I hate talking to strangers."

"Everyone does. Including me," Kunugi said.

I don't care about anyone.

That was what Shizue wanted to say.

"That's why I don't like this kind of thing. But I can't go back, either."

Ayumi's gaze pierced through the moon.

It was no use.

They weren't going to be able to stop this girl.

With the full moon behind her, the girl was frighteningly brave, refined. Shizue felt a strong sense of futility in the face of that image. She had no intention of stopping this girl. She couldn't even think of a reason why she would try to stop her. Weak and baseless, Shizue had no way of intervening.

"I'll be fine," Ayumi said. She lithely walked off, disappearing into the woods.

Hinako prayed quietly and then followed after her. The shadows seemed to waver behind them.

The tired old beat-up cop and the totally exhausted counselor looked into the darkness of the forest that had just swallowed up two little girls for quite some time after.

"What do you think?" Kunugi was the first to speak.

"I don't think anything."

"You think this is all okay?"

"I don't, but…no, I do." Shizue stepped forward to where Ayumi had been standing. "What are we doing? Running away, hiding in a place like this…Isn't there something we should be doing? This is no good. That's what I was thinking. But we don't know who we're up against. I don't even know what I'm angry at. All I can see in the darkness is my own face. I am most angry at myself."

Kunugi lumbered forward the way he always did.

"That's not very like you."

"It is though. This is me. I'm a horrible woman."

"That has nothing to do with it. But sitting here, I've finally figured out who the enemy is."

"Huh?"

"I wasn't even thinking about it at first. Then I doubted several times. But each time I doubted, I denied the implications of my doubts. It couldn't be, that was stupid. I second-guessed myself. I've been able to go on over twenty years this way as a cop. If my theory is right, I've been had, I think. That's why I deny it."

"I don't understand. You need to explain."

Kunugi turned his back to Shizue.

"You don't think Ishida is suspect?" he said. "If we buy what that girl was saying, this last call was connected to the deformée character serial killings. The culprits are Kawabata and Nakamura. Embroiled in this is an unrelated event. It's structured exactly the same way. The reason an unrelated event has been connected to the serial murders is because the police saw an intangible connection no one would be able to make. A fact only the police have access to is a fact the police lieutenant has to know."

"That may be, but—"

"All these investigators after the killer and somehow the killer keeps evading arrest. But what if it's because the lead detective is throwing them all off…What do you think?" Kunugi said. "Of course they're not catching him. The director has no intention of catching the killer. And why does the director have no intention of catching the killer? Because he wants to take advantage of the victims of the crime," Kunugi said.

"The director…"

"Yes, the lieutenant," Kunugi said. "If you're gaining something from the victims, you'd want to draw out the crime spree. Make it a long ordeal, let the killer keep doing his thing, and throw your own crimes into the mix. Make unrelated events seem related. The real criminal is going to go on committing those crimes, so the investigation will obviously point its head in the right direction. But they will still not be able to catch the guy. But no one's going to doubt the internal workings of the police. A lot of people dislike the police, but no one would do such a thing. The police will continue to suspect various potential culprits but never actually arrest them.

"It takes a special kind of nerve to do something that awful," Kunugi said, practically spitting. "After the crimes, you dump all the sins on that original criminal and catch your breath, but if like last year the suspect has an alibi making it impossible for him to have committed all of the crimes, then you're in trouble. Weapons can be tied to a crime anyway."

"That's awful."

"You got that right." Kunugi tied up his thought with the word. "Awful. Indeed. So I've thought this over. But rethinking the situation made me softhearted."

"To cover up one's own crime, you mimic the pattern of another criminal, then overlook the original person's crime," Shizue said. "No, you actually force them to commit another one?"

"That's right. However, this time something went wrong. In any case, a part of the criminal group ended up dead. But…"

Meaning there were several criminals?

"Even with one dead, there was another still living. They had no choice but to use him. That's why the police approached the Nakamura crime with only one theory. Until you said something about it, Nakamura was going to be the criminal. But they'd lost him, even after proclaiming it was him for so long. Even I didn't buy that, but there was no way not to believe it."

"They let him go in order to continue committing crimes?"

"I think they might have even been sheltering him as a fugitive."

"Nakamura?"

"Nakamura's investigation was staffed with an unusual number of people. And if you believe he was the one who provided information about Mao, you can see the thread here. Nakamura was after Yuko. However, he couldn't get her. She was probably protected by Mao. Then Kawabata died. But in order for the reverse-victimization to continue, they needed Nakamura to continue killing people."

"That's why they hid him?"

"They probably brought him in. Nakamura's next target was Yuko Yabe, so they needed him to kill her. That's why they were so fierce in their search for her. That's also why they acted so quickly when news of her capture was sent in."

"The area patrol aided in killing Yuko?"

To borrow Ayumi's terminology, they whisked her away.

"According to what the young woman was saying earlier, the news was spreading too quickly. It's hard to believe the culprit was outside. Besides, an actual patrol was attacked. Someone from the outside couldn't have approached him. But—"

"Ishida could have."

"Could have. He's a direct heir to the SVC corporation, which is an affiliate company of the area patrol and directly linked to D&S, which manages the area security systems. What's more he's the lieutenant of the prefectural police department. In one sense, he can get away with anything. Look. It's not that the police or the area patrol leaked information to the outside. The enemy was on the inside the whole time. Inside the police operation. The enemy was getting information directly."

Kunugi spun around and faced Shizue.

"This one time, it didn't go as planned."

"Nakamura was killed before Yabe could be apprehended, you mean."

"That's right," Kunugi said. His eyes were wide now, visible in the dark. "Once Yuko Yabe was whisked away, obviously Nakamura had to go to work. That's why he was apprehended. However he was killed before he could kill. That made it impossible for him to have committed all these other killings in the serial crime spree. That's why Ishida created a new culprit."

"Mao," said Shizue.

"Yeah. All those who believed Nakamura was the criminal now believe it's this Mao. Ishida no doubt knew of Nakamura's death before discovering the body. He trimmed all the branches so he could transplant just the root of his story. He'd already decided that Mao was a bother to Nakamura and his own crew, so if he could make her out to be the criminal, he'd be killing two birds with one stone."

"But…" *The story works. But…*

"Why?"

"How the hell should I know!" Kunugi yelled. "Look, you said it yourself. These serial murder cases crop up every year like clockwork, and the only people who deal with the cases are the police. The reason I was suspended was because I suggested we weren't dealing with a single serial killer. You were under suspicion because of your doubts too."

"So what are we supposed to do?" Shizue was yelling now too. "A good-for-nothing middle-aged cop and a high-maintenance counselor with a spotless record, hiding in these goddamned trees. What are we going to do? We're going to get caught and arrested!"

"That's fucking right," Kunugi said in a louder voice. "That's why I tried not to bring you into it." Then, quietly. "I'm sorry I yelled at you."

"This could all just be my imagination. In fact it almost definitely is. But either way, we're stuck here in this forest and it's the middle of the night. So what do we do indeed. Should we surrender?"

"Huh?"

She didn't want to think about the future. But it wasn't like they could stay there forever. There was only so much putting off she could do with reality.

If today was any indication.

She was like a child. This was not how adults behaved.

But Shizue was an adult. As long as she behaved like one, she would have to assume responsibilities like one.

But…

Kunugi wasn't telling a fiction. He was right about everything.

Shizue couldn't imagine anything beyond that.

Kunugi on the other hand looked like he was actually relieved after having said everything he did. But…

"I for one," Kunugi started, and scratched his temple with an index finger. "I for one thought I'd sit out my life till retirement bored every day—no fun, no excitement, then one day die. I never thought I'd be in this situation. Look at us! This is like a novel. First of all, that I'd ever be talking to a beautiful woman like you for any length of time…

"I hope that's okay. This is about as private as it gets." Kunugi let out a weak laugh. "Since my marriage failed, I haven't been able to interact with anyone correctly. I don't know how much distance to maintain and so I end up alone. Well, I've certainly gotten older but when it comes down to it I'm as wet behind the ears as I was when I was fourteen. I'm practically a child. Inconsiderate and imprudent."

"If what you've said is not a figment of your imagination but the truth, then what?"

"If it's true…"

"If we decide everything you just said is true, then what do we do? What course of action would a prudent and considerate adult take?"

"There is no course of action. Yeah," Kunugi said. He dropped his head a little.

"Someone's coming again." There was a flashlight behind Kunugi. It was close by. Ayumi was able to see so far into the dark, but here Shizue didn't notice until the light was flashing right behind Kunugi. The grass rustled loudly.

The bright light shifted into the shape of a cross. Shizue's eyes couldn't get used to it. Her vision went completely blank for a moment, and then a flare burst in four directions.

"Boss? Is that you, Boss?"

The light shone on Kunugi.

He blocked the light with a hand and suddenly his filthy appearance was completely revealed.

"What are you doing here, Boss?"

"Is that you, Takasugi?"

The light moved over to Shizue.

"Shit. Did I walk in on something?" said a young voice. "Get a room, will ya?"

"That's not funny. This is no time for jokes. This is—"

"I know," the young voice said again.

He turned off the light.

An awful kaleidoscope of bright shapes floated in Shizue's pupils.

"But aren't you relaxed, Boss. Something bad must have happened. It's a good thing I'm the one who found you."

"What's going on?"

"They're not saying anything to us yet. The brass is going crazy, calling this an unprecedented ill, but we're in the middle of the crime spree now. This is the last thing we need, Boss. A scandal."

"So what are they saying I did?" Kunugi asked.

"Don't ask me what *you* did. But seriously. They said that you behaved inappropriately with a female employee at the community center, that you trespassed into the center during a forced leave of absence, and then you kidnapped both her and one of her kids during a counseling session."

"Whaaat?" Kunugi let out in a strangled voice.

As Shizue's vision returned, the silhouette of the officer disappeared and was replaced by the master of the man's voice.

He was probably the same age as Shizue.

He had a boyish face for his age. He was wearing a stretchy training suit and had a flashlight in his hand.

"This guy's one of my kids from Investigative Unit R I was talking about this afternoon. Takasugi."

He'd probably been told he'd never get promoted working for Kunugi. The young cop said, "I'm Takasugi," with an expression either humble or sweet, then snickered at Kunugi. "Geez. I'm sorry but there are some wild rumors running out there. To an old bachelor, a beautiful woman is certainly a sight for sore eyes. But I thought your type would be more uh, voluptuous. I guess you can go *intellectual*, huh?"

"Hey. Shut up. I don't have time for jokes right now," Kunugi said.

"I know. Whatever anyone else thinks, I don't buy it. Anyone who knows you knows you wouldn't do any of that. That's why I went looking for you off-duty."

"Looking for me?"

"Both of you," said Takasugi. "Lieutenant Ishida...he's acting really strange."

"Strange how?"

"Everyone in the office has noticed too. Even in the way he's treating you...it's strange."

Kunugi's face fell as if he'd lost his nerve, and he turned to Shizue.

"In any case, let's go somewhere safe. I have my vehicle ready," Takasugi said.

CHAPTER 021

JUST THAT, SOMETHING smelled.

She didn't know what time it was. Didn't know where she was. Didn't know anything.

She was scared of the dark.

She was scared of the dim.

She was scared of the sinister.

Without an accurate count, one minute and one second felt exactly the same.

Latitude and longitude and height...where those axes met was where she was.

Points had no mass.

Therefore, even a slight deviation would make her unsure of who she was. If there weren't numerical values, she'd be as good as naught.

So if only someone would look over her, if only someone could assure her she was in fact there, Hazuki would not disappear from the world.

Rey Mao was right. The terminal was a terminus. But a terminus is also a concept. It too had no mass.

It was a terminus because it was connected to something behind it. No...

Not a terminus, a terminal.

The terminal was at the very edge of a space. In other words it was distinct from the body it terminated.

Being linked was what gave one a sense of being alive.

This world with another reality; Hazuki was only able to see through her monitor.

She didn't know if she were dead or alive.

If Hazuki's heart stopped, if her breath ceased, if her brain waves quit, nothing would change. It would be just one of countless terminals turning off. It would be the disappearance of something already without mass.

So why was she so scared.

Just thinking about it made her sit up straight, sturdy. Her fingers were shaking. Her throat dried up.

That man was carrying a knife. With that knife, with that sharp metal object, that man was going to cut her body. He was going to stab her.

Ow.

It hurts.

If she was going to feel this way, she would rather not live. This.

This was awful.

A creepy moaning voice.

The doves.

A sound that evaded description. It was the sound in their throats.

Nails clicking on the floor as they walked, feathers brushing up against feathers.

It was all disgusting. Animals were not cute. They didn't look cute. Hazuki was a little jealous of Yuko Yabe.

Yuko.

Yuko was dead.

It didn't feel true. Nothing was real. And yet if it weren't true why was she so sad.

Hazuki wrapped her arms around her knees and lowered her head and started to cry.

The doves started flapping around.

I want to die.

And just then.

The doors flew open.

The first thing Hazuki saw between the doors was a black silhouette set against a quiet.

Round.

Moon.

"Makino..." it called. "You're here."

Ayumi.

"Ayumi," Hazuki uttered for the first time.

She wouldn't listen to her body.

Or rather, times like this, Hazuki didn't know how she was supposed to react, if she was supposed to at all.

She just lifted her face.

Tears fell one after the other.

They didn't relieve her of her feelings.

Where were you? I was so scared. They tried to kill me. Why don't you tell me anything? Why don't you listen to me? Are you okay? I was worried.

Were you worried?

She had a mountain of things she wanted to say, ask. But none of them would express how she felt, what she thought—what was in her head was all expelled, and whatever a stranger might casually think of her could be right, could be wrong. So she said nothing and concluded after some thoughtful hesitation that she was sorry.

"I'm sorry."

"For what?"

Ayumi was being her same old self.

Ayumi looked in on the doves behind her wire cage. Where Rey Mao had broken it.

"For coming up without permission."

"I don't mind. Did Mao do this?"

"Yeah," Hazuki said and held her knees in again.

"Who chased you?"

"The area patrol." Somehow, Hazuki was able to answer easily. Even though it was a horrifying experience.

"Real ones?"

"Real. But the same ones who kidnapped Yuko Yabe."

"Ahh." Ayumi stopped her hand on the wire fence. She looked up once.

"I didn't know where else to go."

"This place can't be very safe either."

"Really?"

"Apparently. That's what Ms. Fuwa said. I think she's right."

"Fuwa? The counselor?"

"Yeah."

"You met with the counselor?"

"Yeah. I wanted to leave you and Tsuzuki to her."

"Leave?"

"I thought it would be dangerous to call the police or area patrol. Remember I didn't let anyone call them before, either. You guys said it would be okay and called them anyway. So I thought I'd make myself useful."

She was right. She'd been opposed to Mio's plan to call the area patrol by way of Hazuki's foster father. She'd said it would be dangerous. Mio had said she didn't know why it would be.

Hazuki…

…didn't know either.

But eventually had agreed to it.

Pretending nothing had happened with Yuko made her sad, somehow.

But Ayumi's conviction was correct. The patrol assailed her through the terminal through which she obtained the story.

"Fuwa...What did Ms. Fuwa..."

"She's on our side," Ayumi said.

"Our side...you mean we can rely on her?" Hazuki asked.

"I can't honestly say if we can rely on her, but she will definitely not hurt us. I know that much."

"You know that?"

Hazuki had no special feelings or thoughts on Fuwa. It was just that she didn't hate her.

Fuwa had once said to her that there were things about children that a counselor would never know. She couldn't remember when, but it left an impression on her, and since then, Hazuki'd felt positive about her. It was thousands of times better than the counselor pretending she knew more than she did.

"Adults are wise. Not like us. They're good at telling lies, and have stature. But because she ran into us, now she has nowhere to go either."

Had something happened to her?

Ayumi applied her weight to the wire frame and brought the sides together, re-establishing the barrier between the doves and humans.

Then Ayumi just looked at the doves for a while.

"I tried going to your house."

"Mine?"

"There were lots of cops. The door was torn open, so anyone looking in could see what happened. Looked like your dad was there too, though I didn't actually see him."

Father.

I bet he's worried.

Because he's a nice man. But that could be one of the well-told lies Ayumi suggested adults were so good at, and it could just be adult nature too. Still, Hazuki thought he'd be worried.

She thought it, but couldn't confirm it. She'd never felt like wanting to see him, but now, if even just slightly, she did. She wanted to see that he was worried about her, right in front of her. Otherwise.

She didn't know.

"I just took a look at my monitor downstairs."

Monitor.

The window into existence.

"There was a turtle icon on the screen. When I opened it there was a message from Tsuzuki."

"Tsuzuki…"

Mio. What was Mio doing?

"Is she all right?"

"After she called you she said the police came. They're suspicious of her because of her connection to the Cat. She's being followed, so she couldn't come here, and her house is being watched, so she can't go back."

"So…she's okay."

"I guess," Ayumi said.

"I mean, if you're surrounded by the police, you're probably safe."

"But you were attacked by the area patrol, right?"

"Yeah, but…"

"The police are not to be trusted at all. Even what happened at your house wasn't reported correctly. They just made up some story. And that's the story they're telling your father. They're saying the culprit was the same person who tore this metal fence."

"Rey Mao? That's wrong. She—"

"Rescued you, I know. She's a champion of justice or something like that," Ayumi said. "Sakura's the one who saw through the lie. I heard from Sakura."

"Sakura?"

"Funeral Girl."

She was the one who'd come by Yuko Yabe's house, according to Mio.

"She noticed something amiss in the information they were publishing, so she came over to my place to let me know. Then I went to your house, but it was dangerous, so I left. I was worried."

"Worried, about me?"

Ayumi turned her head to Hazuki and nodded.

"Why?"

Ayumi had no reason to worry about Hazuki. And as Hazuki said as much, Ayumi turned and said, "You didn't have to worry about Yuko either but you did."

"Yeah, but…"

It didn't feel the same. They'd never interacted with Sakura.

"Tsuzuki, Sakura…weirdos apparently worry about strangers. Don't sweat it."

"I'm not."

She didn't really understand.

"Did you respond to Tsuzuki's message?"

"No. I don't like sending messages."

"I wonder if she's okay," Hazuki said.

"Look, now you're worried."

"Aren't *you*? Don't you worry about people?"

"No, I don't," Ayumi answered.

"But you came looking for me."

"I came looking for you instead of worrying."

Ayumi brought a box out from under the table and lifted the lid.

"People die, even though other people worry. And people live despite not wanting to anymore. It doesn't matter what goes on in your heart; it won't make a difference in this world. I don't believe that praying or begging or concentrating on something will make it come true. So instead of worrying, it's better to actually do something."

"Do?"

"Worrying and thinking about something is all personal. Do something. I'm not good with people." Ayumi brought out something heavy from the box.

"I know that much."

"Right? Say for example I was really worried about you. But I don't have the verbal strength to tell you that. Then you don't know that I worried about you. And if we were separated, then you really don't know that I worried. Then I have no choice but to do something. The heart doesn't communicate."

She closed the lid on the box.

"People's hearts are kept in boxes like this. One can only make up what goes into it. People make up what goes into one another's hearts and get the sense that they've communicated. Whether they're right about what went in...can also only be made up. So," Ayumi pointed to the lid. "There are people who learn to give names to what lies inside the box. People who notify others. Some people put labels on their boxes. But no matter what you write or what the label says, you can't open the lid, so you'll never know if it's true. Whether or not to trust someone is something you have to imagine."

Ayumi put on training gloves.

"I can't pretend to know how to label the lid, and I don't like trying to imagine what's inside the boxes of others. That's why I'm alone."

There was a swishing sound.

It was the sound of a shock-absorbent life vest being fastened onto Ayumi's body.

"Am I cold?"

"I don't know."

No.

Hazuki knew exactly what Ayumi was saying.

But Hazuki was unable to carry herself like Ayumi. She didn't think it was about strength or weakness.

Hazuki's previous counselor, the one before Fuwa, had told her she needed to be stronger.

The counselor had told her not to depend so much on others, to be independent. Told her that at the end of the day, everyone was alone, so all one could do was protect oneself, the strong female counselor said. She thought that sounded correct.

But five years ago, that counselor had committed suicide.

She didn't think the counselor was wrong. Someone so good at protecting herself from the outside was probably able to destroy herself too.

Her foster father would say that no human could live alone.

He'd say that people always helped each other, rescued one another, and somehow made do. So he taught her to be nice to strangers. Hazuki thought that sounded correct. It was always other people doing the things she needed in life. Hazuki could only exist in that setup. She would also have to one day take on a caregiver role. She knew that without a doubt. She accepted that way of thinking without consequence.

But.

At the end of the day, was it that a person is always alone, or unable to live alone?

These statements were diametrically opposed. Hazuki knew that. She accepted them without contradiction.

Usually this didn't bother her. It was not a nuisance. But thinking about it for any amount of time made it all confusing. Whatever was correct, whatever was incorrect, she felt like a failure in life for not picking a single sentiment. Then she was unsure several times.

There was no way she should know.

"Forgive them," Fuwa had said.

The counselor.

The counselor had no way of knowing how kids like them thought.

"You don't know yourself, do you? It's pointless to try to know. Even

I don't know. So just forgive them."

Forgive them.

That was right.

That was what Fuwa had said.

People can't live alone, can't survive alone, that's true. But everybody's alone in the end. That's true too. You're not wrong about either. But I don't think you need to go out of your way to be strong. I say those guys who tell you to be number one or give it your all, or not to lose…can all scram.

It's because humans kill themselves over ratings and whether they've won or lost at something that they've become useless. Those things shouldn't matter…

What's wrong with me.

What.

What's wrong?

That was what Hazuki had said. She remembered everything Fuwa had said clearly now.

It made her slightly happier.

She had thought counseling was just a sham, but it really worked.

"I bet you're hungry," Ayumi said.

"I'm thirsty," Hazuki said. Ayumi handed her a water pack.

"Haven't you eaten anything, Makino?"

"I ate, but didn't finish."

It was true. Before getting the message from her father she had had some soup.

Her throat felt like it was being painted over. She choked up a bit.

"You should eat."

Ayumi brought some junk food over to Hazuki. "You'll get weak unless you eat. You won't have to be attacked if you die of illness."

This was true. She did as Ayumi suggested and put the synthetic food in her mouth, chewed deliberately, then swallowed. She wasn't hungry to begin with, but the food felt like it was sticking to her.

She looked at the food in her hand. There were bite marks where she chewed. Man-made meat made to look like dead animal flesh. It said on the packaging that this was what the real thing tasted and felt like, but Hazuki didn't know the real thing. Of course she also didn't know what it was made of. This unknown material was going to turn into her own blood, her own flesh.

I'm made of things I know nothing about, Hazuki thought.

"After you eat you should get some sleep. Sitting won't help you relieve fatigue."

"But…"

"You shouldn't go home yet. I don't think you'll get killed, but they'll ask you too many questions. And it's possible they won't believe a thing you say. They already have a script."

"You mean even if I tell them the truth, they won't believe it?"

"Probably not."

"But they suspect Rey Mao."

"Not suspect. They're positive it's her. No one looks more like a criminal right now than her."

"That's wrong. The killer is that big man. The guy with the head art and—"

"Makino."

Ayumi put her hand out. Hazuki grasped it.

"Listen. The more you say Rey Mao isn't the killer, the greater the disadvantage you put her at."

Hazuki stood up and sat on the chair.

"Why?"

"Why would an undocumented minor rescue you?"

"Because…"

"No matter how sincere she was in rescuing you, she still attacked an area patrol. There's already a bulletin out about it. The story's been written."

"But it's a lie."

"There are a lot of things you have to do to change a finished story. You can't explain without explaining everything that happened. If you explain everything that happened, they'll know she was also in a fight with Nakamura and Kawabata. Both of them are dead. She may not be the killer, but the police sure think so."

"There's nothing we can do."

"*That's not true.*"

Ayumi opened the door to the bedroom.

"Get your rest first. When you get up, go to your father."

"What?"

"It's okay. He's your father, isn't he?"

"Foster father," Hazuki said.

"Blood relation doesn't matter. At all. At the very least, your father won't kill you. And we can't trust the area patrol or police right now."

Ayumi looked straight at Hazuki. Until recently, they hadn't ever made eye contact.

Hazuki stood up.

"What are you going to do, Ayumi?"

"I'm okay."

"No you're not. Where are you going?"

Ayumi wordlessly walked toward the doves.

"Don't go."

"Are you going to worry about me?"

"It's not that. I'm scared. Please don't leave," Hazuki said.

She grasped Ayumi's arm. She felt like a child.

"Don't go. I don't want to be alone."

"I won't. It's okay," Ayumi said. She led Hazuki to the bedroom and sat her down.

"I'll be here till you wake up. Just get some sleep."

"Really?"

"I told you already, it's not safe here either."

"So?"

"I have to be on the lookout till morning," Ayumi said.

As she listened to these last words Hazuki slipped off her shoes and slept in the same bed Yuko Yabe had slept on.

She stretched her arms. Her joints were aching. She stretched as far as she could, and the back of her head started to feel fuzzy.

Ayumi left the room.

There was a round monitor gleaming on the rooftop window. That was...

No. It was just reflecting light.

"Good night." Hazuki heard a voice, and before the doors closed she had fallen into slumber.

She dreamt that Yuko Yabe was sleeping next to her.

In the room next door were Ayumi, Mio, Rey Mao, and...

Herself.

Who was she, then? wondered Hazuki in her dream.

They're talking about something she can't quite hear.

They're eating. So they're alive.

Yuko was...

Something rustled. An unfamiliar sound. Had her helper come?

She rubbed her red eyelids and opened weary eyes to see a light coming through the ceiling window.

That's weird. A window in the ceiling.

Morning.

Hazuki opened her eyes and sat up.

It was bright. *Where am I?*

Ayumi.

Don't leave me alone.

Hazuki flew to the door. Her body hurt. It was slow. It wouldn't move. But to leave her behind? *I'm here now. I'm alive. Don't leave me.*

When she opened the door she saw Ayumi standing in front of the cage of doves.

"Ayumi."

"Did I wake you?"

It wasn't such a tremendous amount of light, but it blinded her.

"Have you been up this whole time?"

"Well, 'this whole time' is just four hours. It's only four."

"Four in the morning?"

Ayumi was holding one of the doves.

"What is that dove?"

"It's the dove Rey Mao took from here. It just came back."

I promise the dove will be back.

Don't go anywhere till then.

"Something happened to her."

Ayumi said nothing and simply extended her arm.

At her fingertips was a small object.

It was a pink neo-ceramic stone.

"That's..."

"It was tied to this dove's foot. Yabe's piercing."

The pink piercing belonging to pink Yuko.

"Where did...I mean, where was the dove?"

"That..." Ayumi pointed at a cloth on the table. "This was attached to its leg. A piece of natural silk fabric. Rey Mao's. It had writing."

"Writing? On the cloth?"

"Writing in blood," Ayumi said simply.

"Blood? I don't understand. Blood on the cloth?"

"She didn't have anything else to write with. No paper. She's used to bleeding, so she used some of her blood to write with. She wrote Area 119 SVC Memorial Building."

"What was this piercing doing there?"

"Rey Mao...she went after the guys who attacked you. This is where it led her."

"I still don't understand."

It was the piercing Yuko'd been wearing in her ear.

It'd gotten stuck on Ayumi's bag.

It'd fallen in Mio's house.

Because of this piercing, because they'd found this small pink stone…

"This is probably where Yuko was *murdered*," Ayumi said.

Murdered…

Now, Hazuki finally understood. Everything.

"Ayumi…you don't think…"

Ayumi released the dove inside the cage. It flapped its wings and flew to the edge of the window.

"I guess there's no convincing you to go back to sleep now. You should go downstairs and shower or something. When you're ready, I'll be leaving here. You go to your father's. It'd be best if you contacted him from the main terminal downstairs."

"If I do that they'll know I sent it from here."

That would cause a nuisance.

"Don't worry about me anymore. I'm fine."

Ayumi faced the door. Hazuki stepped in front of her.

"No you're not. What do you think you're going to do?"

"It's none of your business."

"It is. Ayumi, are you going to that address?"

"I am," Ayumi said.

"Why?"

"You saying I shouldn't go?"

"Why are you going?" Hazuki asked. "It's just dangerous. You said you hate dealing with people. That it's not for kids. You said if it's none of your business, not to interfere."

Ayumi looked up at Hazuki with sad eyes.

"I have a *responsibility* to undertake."

"Responsibility?"

"Because it's *wrong*." Ayumi hesitated. "To kill people."

"But *you're not* a superhero do-gooder, remember?"

"Right. I am no superhero. But I'm not going to let Rey Mao continue to be put in these screwed-up situations. She didn't do anything wrong. Now hurry up and shower so I can leave." Ayumi took out her ID card and handed it to Hazuki.

"If we go in there together the main terminal will identify two people, but if you go in with my card the sensor won't know who it is. I didn't lock it and there's no security PIN code. Just use the card and leave it by the door or something."

"No!" Hazuki stood up and blocked the entrance.

"Move, Makino."

"N-no. I don't like being alone."

"Like I said, contact your dad from the terminal downstairs."

"I don't want to!" Hazuki was throwing a tantrum. "What if I can't get ahold of my dad? And if I did, I don't know if he'll be able to come home. He's always traveling. It'll take time for us to meet. And by then my dad's sure to contact the police. He won't think that the police or area patrol are untrustworthy, that they might be killers. He's not a child. He couldn't possibly believe something that fantastic. He'll just laugh at everything I say."

Ayumi looked at Hazuki, amazed.

She was probably surprised. Hazuki surprised even herself. Hazuki had never yelled at anyone before. Never stood up for anything. She wasn't going to let up now.

If I don't do this, Ayumi will leave. And then she will die.

"Anyway, go shower. You're dirty."

"Stay here. Till I come back. Promise me you'll stay, or I—"

"I get it," Ayumi said. Hazuki looked into her eyes. She was trying to stare out the truth.

She wasn't lying.

Hazuki didn't have any reason to believe it, but she did. But she didn't really know. No, it wasn't just that Hazuki didn't know, but she had to believe Ayumi wouldn't leave her behind.

"I'll be quick. Just wait."

Hazuki hurriedly put on her shoes and ran out to the rooftop.

It was white, red, bright.

There were clouds. It was bright. Shining.

It was enormous.

The sky was so big her eyes spun and threw her off a little. She went past the side of the house and through the foyer. She ran the card, opened the door, and went into the unfamiliar house. She wanted to take a shower, this was true, but she became anxious.

She scanned the room.

For now she would pass the monitor and go to the bathroom.

She looked at the monitor on her way back.

A turtle icon.

There was a message from Mio when she clicked on the icon, just as

Ayumi had said.

I have to tell her.

I have to tell Mio, at all costs.

YABE'S PIERCING FOUND AT 119--SVC MEMORIAL BUILDING RECORDING
CENTER. CAT FOUND IT.
--HAZUKI

Just as she depressed the last key the window closed.

Dad. To think I was going to contact you.

But maybe I should.

She hesitated a moment.

Ayumi had said she wouldn't mind, but Hazuki knew a message sent from this terminal would cause Ayumi problems later. But she knew they couldn't do anything alone. Honestly, calling her foster father in might help. At the very least, to protect Ayumi.

She went into communication mode on the monitor. And just as she did...

"What's happening?"

Access denied? No.

The screen looked funny. Hazuki immediately quit the communication program.

This is not right. Is it broken?

Oh no.

Hazuki cut the electricity and force-quit the monitor.

Shit.

Hazuki flew off the chair and out through the foyer, grabbing her shoes and running out the door, leaving it open as she ran to the back of the house.

"Ayumi! Ayumi!"

She hurried up the spiral staircase. The way it wound up she felt like she was climbing to heaven. The sound of her kicking up the stairs was loud, and then there was Ayumi in front of her. Practically running into her, Hazuki came to a dead stop.

"What's wrong?" Ayumi asked. She was holding a backpack and had a waist pack snapped around her hips.

She was even wearing boots.

"It's not working. The communication line."

"Locked?"

"Probably."

"You can't gain access?"

"It looks like I can, but when I tried, suddenly..."

"I see. Let's go."

"Together?"

"Yes, together. You'll be safer that way."

Ayumi stood at the topmost step of the staircase and looked straight out as far as she could. In the direction she was staring the first time Hazuki came here.

"We're going to take that traffic route."

"What? You mean the overhead speedway?"

Where Yuko was attacked. The road above it.

"Are we even allowed to walk on that?"

"It's for freight drivers only, but there's a tunnel that runs underneath the entire length of it, and it connects to the commercial zone of the next section at one point. No one's allowed on it from six in the morning to six at night. It's the fastest way to 119. We'd get there by evening." Ayumi peered at Hazuki.

"Are you going to be okay?"

"I can walk it."

"Let's go."

I don't want to die. I don't want to die crying, in a dark lonely place.
I don't want to die anymore.

"Another kid's been kidnapped. Ms. Fuwa might be arrested too. I don't know if Cat or Mio are still alive. You and I are in danger too. You still want to go?"

"I do," Hazuki answered. Sitting here and doing nothing would be at least as dangerous. She knew if she stayed there and started crying, with her arms wrapped around her knees, she would feel like dying again.

"All right then. Grab that water. Let's go, quickly. They're probably already on their way here."

Ayumi turned back once. One hundred thousand lux of sunlight rose from the horizon.

There was no hope there.

CHAPTER 022

THE RIDE WAS by no means pleasant, and she was in a terrible mood, but compared to being pasted with wet grass and being sucked down into the mud, the backseat of Takasugi's old-fashioned electric car was infinitely more pleasant.

Takasugi's rescue only reaffirmed the gravity of Kunugi's fate.

When Takasugi had come across Kunugi and Shizue, the area patrol had been searching the public roads adjacent to the forest. Thinking he'd try to get ahead of the patrols, he chanced getting out of his electric car and walking onto the promenade.

There, Takasugi had noticed two children running off. With the mandatory curfew in place he'd wondered what they could be doing out and followed them. That was when he'd noticed the two adults.

Of course, Takasugi had heard the report—its validity notwithstanding—that Shizue had been kidnapped along with one of her kids.

"If I tried to protect the child right then, there's no mistaking it—you would have been arrested, Boss. Anyway, you guys weren't hard to find even in these woods, getting in each others' faces like that," Takasugi said.

He was right. Neither Shizue nor Kunugi realized where they were or how loudly they'd been speaking. Or rather, it was because they realized what was going on that they'd started yelling in the first place.

I wonder what happened to Ayumi? Shizue thought.

Everything about her was so composed. Where had she gone? *Was it the right thing to do, letting her go off like that?* Shizue thought, and thought it over some more. Being with them was probably not the best thing. But to leave a helpless young girl in the night city when there was a killer on the loose; that was even dumber.

And what about Hazuki Makino? And Mio Tsuzuki?

Those girls...

Shizue was unable to protect or save anybody after all was said and done.

She couldn't forgive the world or forgive herself. She was an incompetent counselor, and there was nothing anyone could do about it.

She got depressed. She just wanted to get into a hot bath. Her clean but astringent body soap was one of the only perfumed products she allowed herself.

They stopped at an electric parking station.

There were very few manual recharge electric cars out on the road anymore, so there wasn't a soul in the lot.

There was a pay toilet and real shop in the parking structure. Neither Shizue nor Kunugi could use their cards, so both of them used Takasugi's. Shizue would have rather died than ever use a men's bathroom, but she really had no choice. The real shop required Takasugi to make purchases himself also, and despite Shizue's serious but futile objections, she had to let him buy her stockings. If it were up to her she'd buy a complete new outfit.

She ate food she didn't think humans could eat and drank a bottle of water that for some reason was chilled to just above freezing. Despite the strangeness of the meal, it was something in her stomach, and she finally felt like she was going back to normal. Shizue was convinced now that humans were mere animals.

"All right then," Takasugi said over his shoulder from the driver's seat. "So I've driven us up to here, but...what do you want to do now?"

"What do we...What can you do for us?"

"As you can see, I am on break."

"You idiot! You were just taking a break in the middle of this huge case?"

"What are you talking about, Boss? You're a public servant, not some has-been salaryman, you know. You can't talk to me like that! You've got the times confused."

"You know, I've been yelled at for being old-fashioned for thirty friggin' years. But you know what? What you think is natural was all set up by us. From where I stand, you're the old-fashioned one. From now on, you gotta work harder."

"This is a problem." Takasugi backed down and looked at Shizue. "Can't you counsel this old man or something? Boss, if anyone's not working, it's you. I'm the one who ignored his break and decided to come rescue you. This is a clear violation of the uniform. If I get caught I get canned too! I don't want to be demoted."

"That's why I've been saying not to worry about me!" Kunugi started to flare up. "There's nothing easy about this."

"I know that. You tell me not to worry about you but then you ask to see the data on Asumi Aikawa. *You* say those things. I mean your moves are my cues to understanding what's happening in the case, but...the way you go about it."

"That's it." Kunugi stepped up. "Weren't you saying that Lieutenant Ishida was acting weird?"

"I did. That guy is...weird."

"Weird how? I always thought he seemed suspicious, but it was just the way the evidence built up. I didn't think he himself was a weird guy."

"Really?" Takasugi said in a casual voice. "I see. I guess you haven't really been in the know with the management team."

"What's that supposed to mean? You're just a policeman. I'm a patrol director. Is that not good enough?"

"It's not that. But what I mean is that there are board meetings. There's even data that only the uppermost levels of the police chain of command get to see. Anyway, besides responsibilities, his distaste for you was really obvious."

"I knew that he hated me," Kunugi said.

"He was hysterically damning you. Look, you published that memo about last year's case, right? Ishida's the one who censured it. He was at some other prefectural post before, right? He was the head of Investigative Unit R. The one who made claims on that lieutenant post? Him."

"Really?"

"Yes, really. Look, the old lieutenant was getting up there in age. If Ishida played his cards right he'd get promoted there, but one missed step and he'd be sent down a level to Investigative Unit V. Everyone always ends up at the bottom of the chain, but you may as well move up the totem pole while you can. So under the guise of inheriting that position, he had you demoted."

"All Ishida has to do is make beef and you're demoted? It's not like the successor to a post also gets to run staffing."

"Boss," Takasugi said in a strange voice. "You came from the 119, same as me, right? Then you know who Ishida is. He's not just some elite cop."

"I know that," Kunugi said. "He's the prince of the Yutaro Suzuki enterprise, his great-grandchild."

"Yutaro Suzuki isn't just the father figure of some big food production company." Takasugi narrowed his brow. "He's like a god to a certain population of people. He created a way for humans to create animal proteins without ever killing animals, so the animal rights activists love him. So do the life preservationists. He built food production facilities in underdeveloped countries and made cheap nutrients widely available. This has gotten him a substantial amount of clout."

"I know this. I read somewhere how he's the ultimate benefactor of the food industry. It was some foreign journalist's bullshit article though."

"No, his contribution to employment and nutrition problems has been highly regarded. Suzuki isn't just lauded for his service to the betterment of living standards. There are all those people who don't eat beef or pork as a religious matter. Now they can actually eat versions of those things."

"They're allowed to eat things that look like beef or pork?" Kunugi asked. "Even a replica of a cow is a cow."

"No, it's all completely synthetic. There's not one naturally occurring molecule. It's not like there's any pork mixed into beef. I'm sure in the beginning even a clone would have been sacrilege to them, but hunger was king. If you stop thinking about it being so much like beef or pork, it's just a scientific creation. Besides, because of this dummy meat, we've stopped killing cows and pigs the world over. It's for the sanctity of those animals. That kind of connection can't be made by just idiots," Takasugi said.

"I'm sure that because this country was able to convert the whole world to a synthetic diet, through the power of SVC—well, second and third generation SVC leaders had political clout. SVC didn't just gain influence in political and business worlds because of their work, but because of Yutaro Suzuki's charisma."

"He's really that special?"

"I'm sure he is. He's supposed to be awarded that world-famous something-or-other prize this year. It's a tremendous honor, but it's not going to the corporation or the president. It's going to Yutaro Suzuki himself."

"So they're giving it to a dead man," Kunugi said.

"He's not dead," Takasugi said. "Yutaro Suzuki is still alive."

"In the hearts of the residents of Area 119, right? Yeah, I've heard that whole eulogy. People say that whenever something big happens in the neighborhood. Give me a break. He was old a hundred years ago!"

"Older than that. But Yutaro Suzuki isn't just living in the hearts of the people. There are people in government who also hold him in the highest regard. Anyone now working for the environment got their start because of him. And Mr. Ishida is a direct descendant."

"Neither of us is a resident of Area 119 anymore," Kunugi said. Ishida was turning out to be a much bigger deal than even he had believed.

Conservationism was such a given these days you didn't hear the word much anymore, but fourteen, fifteen years ago it was an important buzz word. Just when everyone had thought there was no going back, no fixing the environment problem, that we'd come to the precipice, the government finally recognized the problem.

The problem of conservationism went beyond just the issues of natural resources and food. It was a crisis. It had to be resolved by any means necessary. Any measure, no matter how trifling, was taken without question.

That was one kind of boom. At least that was how Shizue thought of it now.

The era's dangers were like a kind of fever. If it passed, you forgot it. At the time, conservationism had been the fever everyone caught.

Environmental destruction was still a serious problem but seemed laughable nowadays. Shizue was still young when the boom swept the nation but felt unusually cold toward the subject.

Governments were always a little late in reacting to popular demand. It was the same back then. Transportation technology and manufacturing regulations were strategically developed, but by the time the final synthetic food conversion was completed it had been close to ten years. Still, for a country as slow in responding as Japan was, a decade was probably one of the more swift responses. The measures had been adopted with the intention of preempting international judgment. It seems this country, so bad at making decisions, executed one excellent one—the complete conversion of the human diet to synthetic food, and this new diet had become the world standard.

Behind this excellent decision was Yutaro Suzuki, they said.

"There are people inside police headquarters who are Yutaro Suzuki believers too," Takasugi said. "Die-hard believers, as they say. Ishida's a special kind of being to them. That's why no one will go teeth to the wind against him."

"You mean because if you contradict them you end up like me."

"No, not that. If you really contradicted them…*this wouldn't begin to approach what would happen to you*," Takasugi said.

"Hmm."

"I'm not kidding, Boss. What's dangerous is dangerous."

"That doesn't mean they can just do as they please."

"Of course," Takasugi said and faced forward. "I didn't say Ishida is weird just because of what's going on with you, though, Boss. Even with this whole data transfer ordeal over the children's files, he's the only one who saw a need for it. There were quite a few members of the brass who saw a lot of problems with it. Look, I'll get you out," Takasugi concluded.

"What do you mean?"

"If we stay here you'll be arrested by morning. If you're going to move it's gotta be during the night. We're done with interrogations for the night at headquarters. No one thinks you have access to any transportation. We've wasted enough time as it is," Takasugi said. Shizue noticed the time on the control panel of his car. It was 2:50 AM.

"We have nowhere to go."

"Let's get you to another area for now. How about my parents' home?"

"You mean in Area 119?"

"I can shelter you there for a bit. Then you can be off to your own homes."

"I haven't gone home since the divorce," Kunugi said. "I can't seem to face them. My mom keeps bugging me about seeing her grandkids."

"This is no time for pettiness," Takasugi said. He started driving. "Can't you just pretend and introduce Miss Fuwa as your new spouse?"

"Of course not. If that gets processed my family gets in trouble."

"Ahh, okay then. I guess it's my house after all. I have one younger sister, but she's a shut-in, so she won't bother you."

"A shut-in, huh?" Shizue asked.

"Yes. She's twenty-three but she hasn't been out since the age of eight. That's fifteen years. But nowadays you can have all your needs met in-house without stepping foot outside, can't you? Especially in that neighborhood, where everyone's wealthy."

"Is that all thanks to Suzuki too?" Kunugi asked.

"Yeah."

"What a hero. And to think his great-grandson's the way he is..."

"Yes, well. Yes."

"What's the matter?" Kunugi asked.

"No, it's like you said, Boss. Ishida's collusion with the area patrol has been whispered about."

"Just as *I* suggested?"

"Didn't I tell you? There are rumors he's using them for personal business. He's the grandson-in-law at SVC, but he's a direct descendant of D&S. He's extremely close to them. Seems he's using that relationship to his advantage. Area patrol is supposed to be a public industry. They need a certain amount of secret interaction with the police, but collusion is unethical, and besides, it's no good for one individual to be moving all the pieces."

"No use, certainly. Hey, Takasugi."

"What?"

"Why did you save me?" Kunugi asked, oddly.

"Because I trust you. Though you've said so yourself, I won't ever get ahead if I keep trusting you."

The car sped up.

"Don't go over the limit."

"It's already past three. We're almost there. Let's get there before dawn."

"Get where, exactly?"

Takasugi wouldn't answer.

The car took a wide turn.

"How about you sleep a little. You both must be tired."

"Sleep...right. And snore it up a little?"

"What are you saying? Ms. Fuwa, seriously, can't you counsel this guy?" Takasugi said. "Who on earth does this because they want to? I'm doubting Lieutenant Ishida. He's used his position at the police department to wield the area patrol for his own use, while letting the serial killer go unapprehended."

"You believe that?"

"What are you saying?" Takasugi said, as it turned orange outside the window.

They'd entered the tunnel. A strange sound filled the transport. Shizue hated moving vehicles.

"You think so too, right? That's why you left your house during your suspension, and why you're on the run now? You plan on denouncing Lieutenant Ishida, right?" Takasugi asked.

"The reason I left my house isn't because I doubt Lieutenant Ishida. I was suspicious, but I was just unsatisfied. You noticed?"

"Well," Takasugi said.

Shizue couldn't hear very well.

The tunnel's structure was old, so the acoustics were off. The car window passed one warmly colored streetlamp after another.

She started to feel dazed, like she'd been drugged.

The silence continued.

It was an awful silence.

Shizue hated the soft-colored lights. Her breath became short. She wanted to open the window. The smell of the synthetic resin, the smell of mud on her shoes, the smell of sweat. It was hard for her to breathe. But if she opened the window now in this tunnel, she'd let in the dusty, dirty air.

Shizue dealt with it for approximately twenty minutes.

As soon as they'd exited the tunnel the car regained some quiet.

It was bright out.

Shizue looked at Kunugi's profile.

He was haggard. There was mud on his face. His beard was growing in, and there were dark circles under his eyes.

His bloodshot eyes glared at the driver's seat.

"Hey."

"We're in Area 119 now," Takasugi said. "The sun'll be up soon."

"That's good," Kunugi said.

"What's wrong, Boss?"

"What kind of work were you doing yesterday, Takasugi? Were you at the center?"

"Well, sure. There was a lot going on, what with Nakamura killed and then the discovery of Yuko Yabe's body."

"You got it backwards. Yabe was discovered first."

"Oh, right. I heard the news from a little girl yesterday. While Ms. Fuwa was conducting her own interrogation I was in a different room with another girl."

"Hinako Sakura?" Kunugi asked.

"Yeah, yeah. Her. She had that weird way of talking. It was hard to understand what she was saying. She had nothing for us in the end. Must be tough being a counselor." Takasugi glanced behind him.

"Did you investigate the Kisugi girl's case?"

"No, I didn't."

"Why not?"

"What are you talking about? That's right when you cleared out of the center and created that noise. I was confused. I made up something and asked to leave. It was time for me to take a break anyway."

"Really," Kunugi said in a low voice. "So when the call came in about the commotion at the Makino residence, you were with Ishida, interrogating Sakura?"

"Yes. I wonder what happened with that anyhow. I wonder if they found that undocumented minor."

"What time did you clock out?" Kunugi's tone was blatantly accusatory.

"Like I said, after the report about the Makino security breach we took Sakura home."

"You're not saying you got to us at that point?"

"Yes, I did," Takasugi said. "I was worried about you. At that point I clocked out and went back to area headquarters to change, then I started my electric car and came out looking for you."

"Is that right. That's strange," Kunugi said.

"Strange?"

"You said I told you I had suspicions about Ishida's relationship with the area patrol."

"Yes, I did. And?"

"I've never said anything of the sort to you, ever."

"Really?" Takasugi said, his voice a squeak.

"Listen, Takasugi. I'm not like you. I'm an average cop. I'm not smart. I'm just realizing that you're not telling me something about last night. To be honest, what you're saying I said didn't come from me. You got it from your investigation of Hinako Sakura."

"Is that right?"

"You...you were following her."

"W-why would you say that? I—"

"How did you hear about us?"

"You're talking crazy. What are you saying? I told you, I passed by and heard you two arguing, then found you. Boss, you were talking about Ishida's relationship to the area patrol. I overheard that and probably thought you'd said it to me before."

"I was talking in a low voice at that point. There's no way you could have heard all that from the promenade."

That was right...Shizue didn't come out of the brush until after Kunugi had expressed his doubts about Ishida.

"Is that right?" Takasugi replied. "I must have just mixed up the details."

"There's no way you just arrived when you did. So how do you know that Representative Makino's home was broken into by the undocumented minor?"

"I heard that in the briefing."

"That information wasn't yet available at the time of the briefing. The area patrol didn't get that information until after Hinako Sakura was processed. It would take time for that information to get processed, so the investigative unit wouldn't have heard anything until even after that.

You were already out by then, right?"

Takasugi wouldn't answer.

"How do you know what Ishida communicated via memo? Huh, Takasugi?" Kunugi yelled. He reached forward to grab the back of the driver's seat.

"I know!"

"What?"

Kunugi poised to attack.

Shizue, suddenly.

Awakened. This man.

This man was...

"You tricked us, Takasugi!" Kunugi yelled and climbed toward the driver's seat.

Snap. A blue light ignited.

Kunugi dodged Takasugi.

It was a stun gun.

"Hey, now. I'm driving!"

Kunugi jutted his arm out. The sound, again.

"Agh!" Kunugi howled. He curled back into the rear seat.

"You're scaring me. Now be a good passenger and sit quietly like the counselor!"

Shizue wasn't being well behaved; she was simply shocked. The black fear in her head boiled to a tumult.

"Shut up! Shut up shut up shut up. You're one of Ishida's goons!"

"Why, you..."

Kunugi grabbed at the driver's seat again and started shaking it.

"Whoa there. That's dangerous, Boss," Takasugi said.

"You fucker! Why are you doing this?"

"I told you—there are believers, even in the police department."

"Stop the car. Stop it now!" Kunugi went for his door, practically yanking the handle off. Simultaneously the car swerved hard, sending Kunugi toppling over Shizue.

"Shit." Kunugi kicked at the door.

"It's no use, Boss. You can't open it from inside. Besides, we're almost there," Takasugi said as he twisted his neck, sending an ominous look back at them.

The sunlight pierced through the windshield.

Before them was a large building. But in the glare of the sun they couldn't see it.

Where were they?

The car slowed, then poured down a slope into an underground garage.

"I told you. No one gets away with contradicting us." Takasugi laughed, joyfully.

CHAPTER 023

HER CHEEKS WERE throbbing.

To think mere sunlight could do something like that. She didn't know it got so warm in the afternoon. It wasn't just that it was bright out.

Hazuki marched one foot after the other. She walked the endless freight overpass, empty and macabre, one foot after the other, repeatedly. The bridge looked clumsily constructed, and even though it was suspended in the air, the ground was hard and the whole thing was just ugly. The crack-ridden surface resembled an aging animal's skin.

She looked out as far as she could.

The bridge continued to the vanishing point.

She'd never seen anything like this before. Hazuki learned for the first time in her life that the world was so big, that space had so much depth. The world up close was full of cracks, but viewed from afar the road was flat, even smooth, and the background was all beautiful, even lines.

Her view became distorted.

"It's the vapors," Ayumi said.

"You mean the snake?" Hazuki asked.

"No," Ayumi took a gulp from her water pack. "The sun's beating down on us with no obstructions. The temperature of the road steadily increases. The heated surface warms the air above it. That's the haze."

"So it's the air that wavers?"

"The air is simply moving. What's behind it looks like it's wavering. How are your feet holding up?" Ayumi asked.

"They're fine," Hazuki answered. Her outfit happened to do the job. Another more constricting outfit would have made this road impossible to walk.

"It being difficult to walk here and all."

"I mean this is a freight road for transport vehicles, right?"

"It didn't used to be for freighters only, but it was never designed for people to walk on."

"So the road was for moving people too?" Hazuki didn't understand the appeal of moving on such a fierce-looking road.

"It was a long time ago," Ayumi said.

"It's pretty decrepit, right? The bridge would collapse in an earth-quake."

"This road? Collapse?"

"Sure. Most distribution takes place in underground tunnels now, so they'll probably tear this overpass down soon."

"Rocks won't work," Ayumi said. Hazuki didn't understand what she was saying. She didn't understand but wasn't about to ask why rocks wouldn't work.

The sky was blue. Brighter than a blue screen. It was crystalline, deep, strong, clear.

A large cloud floated by.

It was so big it made Hazuki dizzy.

She couldn't grasp the scale. She saw trees swaying in the green zone where the old-fashioned fencing was interrupted. Hazuki opened her eyes wide. The wider she opened them, the clearer the world was, and she felt like she could see all the details. Images not composed of pixels would stay focused no matter how closely you zoomed in.

The wind blew against her face.

The invisible air reminded Hazuki that she was here.

"Let's take a quick rest," Ayumi said, and sat down in the middle of the road. She lifted her water pack high, turned it over, and poured the contents over her head and face.

The spray glistened in the light.

"I like this air. It makes me want to go...anywhere."

Because there was no one around.

Ayumi looked down the road.

"Anywhere..."

Hazuki sat too.

The surface of the road was extremely hot.

"What's out there?"

"Another similar kind of city."

"Does this road go anywhere?"

"It does," Ayumi said. "It does, but it doesn't change. Up ahead is another city, and beyond that another city. It repeats itself. Nothing changes. The road is finite but the world endless. No beginning, no end. We are simply lights that turn on and off in this place. Just going down the road is useless," Ayumi said. She took some junk food out of her backpack. "Let's eat. We should eat now while we can. I don't know if we'll be able to find food ahead."

"Ahead…"

Out where it was useless to go.

Hazuki took a rice bowl and then some canned drinks out of the bag she was carrying. She handed one to Ayumi and chose a flavonoid drink for herself.

"Are we safe here?"

"No one thinks there will be kids here. And we don't have any personal terminals on us."

Hazuki thought to herself again that this meant they were not the terminus of anything.

"And I doubt if there's some big machine in the sky watching us from overhead."

"Sky…"

Hazuki took her rice bowl and flavonoid drink and stood up, walking over to an opening in the fence. She saw a city peek through the dense wood.

It looked like a map.

Is this how birds saw the ground?

Hazuki forgot she was in such an unusual, incomprehensible, and dangerous situation. She ate her junk food and stared at the landscape. She chewed, she swallowed. It was the most satisfying meal she'd had in several days for some reason. The flavors were strange and she didn't know if it was delicious, but she felt like she'd really eaten.

The sun was bright.

"There's a deserted real shop ahead thirty minutes on foot. It's dirty but there's a bathroom. There won't be any running electricity or water."

"You've been down this road before?"

"Yeah. I was walking on it *that day*."

"The day Yuko was attacked?"

Ayumi nodded.

"Yeah. I went as far as I could and then the sun set. Off-hours were over and freighters started rolling along. So I edged along the side of the fencing, unnoticed, and headed back. Getting down off the overpass was almost impossible. I would have been apprehended if anyone saw me, naturally, but no one did because they were driving so fast. When I got to where we climbed up, Yuko was there. We weren't supposed to meet," Ayumi said.

"But it's too late now."

Ayumi compacted the now-empty backpack and stuffed it into her waist pack. She stood up and extended her arm to Hazuki.

"My load's lightened. I'll carry the water."

Hazuki handed her the bag.

"Thanks."

"We have to make it easy for you to escape."

Escape.

Will I be in a situation I need to escape from?

Up ahead, perhaps.

"We have to walk at this pace for another three hours. The building Mao told us about is three neighborhoods away, on the edge. You won't be able to run if your legs are tired, so tell me if we need to slow down or rest. In this heat you can also get exhausted."

"Where are we?"

"We're almost in the commercial district of Area 121."

She knew.

Ayumi was different from Hazuki. She didn't need to get an overview, be connected to anything, to know where she was. She could calculate her distance from the sky and the earth.

They kept in deep pursuit of the untenable haze emitted by the heat and walked wordlessly for some time. Sweat ran down Hazuki's temples. She'd wipe her brow and sweat anew, repeatedly. Had she been indoors she would have felt intolerably filthy. What she was excreting was bodily waste. It was gross.

But she didn't mind it so much.

What she did mind was the sweat dripping into her eyes.

She felt swampy and hot around the nape and throat.

The haze was blowing into the space between her hair and flesh, staying there. She pulled up her hair and tied it with her kerchief.

It wouldn't quite hold up.

While Hazuki tried to tie her hair, Ayumi advanced.

Ayumi.

This must be why she didn't grow her hair.

Or so Hazuki thought.

It's useless, she thought.

She also decided she might cut her own hair when she got back.

If she got back?

Where would she go back to? Ayumi was right—there was nowhere to turn back to.

What awaited them ahead on this road was not hope.

But somehow Hazuki felt like she wasn't going to die.

The fear, the pain, the fact that she had felt like she was dead in that dark corner of a darker room, arms wrapped around her knees notwithstanding. Circumstances being utterly dire, without a ray of hope notwithstanding. The girl in that room last night and Hazuki today being the same person notwithstanding.

Why was everything different now?

They stopped to rest at the abandoned real shop.

The building was incredibly old. It looked like something from another country. There were remains of old gas-fired moving machines left behind. She sat on an extremely uncomfortable chair made of hard material and retied her hair.

When they stepped outside the sun was behind a cloudbank.

This made it easier to be on the edge of the road.

They rounded several curves.

The road running through the commercial district was not fenced but covered by a half-dome shell held suspended in the air by thick poles.

The material was invisible but totally impermeable. The light did not shift when they walked under it but made the shell feel like a bright white tunnel.

The view opened up when they exited the tunnel.

What had been a forward view opened to both the left and right.

The fencing was shorter now, and greenery could be seen above it on either side.

"Hills."

"These are the hills we see from the city."

"They're shaped differently. It's not like this."

"They look different because we're looking at them from a different position. We're inside the hills now."

"Inside…the hills?"

Hazuki couldn't fathom it. To her, hills were something she only ever saw in the background, a distant vista behind the city, no different from wallpaper. Now she was in that vista.

"This road was cut out of the hills. The road on the ground circles around the hills and takes twice as long."

Ayumi touched the fence with her fingers as they walked.

"This is it."

There was a chain-link door in the fence. Some kind of ivy or vine packed the holes. In the middle was a square steel plate prohibiting entry and trespass.

"It says not to open this. Isn't it dangerous?"

"It's coming onto this road that's dangerous. We're doing the opposite."

"You're going to open it?"

"Of course. The only reason people don't is because they have no reason to."

The fence screeched as they opened it.

Ayumi slipped through the doorway casually, as if she were returning home. Hazuki followed after her.

On the other side of the fence was dense tree and grass cover.

"Beyond this hill is Area 119."

"This is the hill?"

It didn't look any different from the green area surrounding the community center.

"It is," Ayumi said. "We're at a really high altitude now."

"Altitude? Oh...altitude."

"Yeah. The distance up from sea level."

Altitude. Her own height.

Ayumi changed her direction.

Latitude and longitude. Her own positioning.

Ayumi knew exactly where she was. No need for a monitor.

"Over here." Ayumi waded through the brush.

"We just climb a little more and then it's all downhill."

The grass was wet though it hadn't rained since they set out. The ground was squishy. She looked at her feet. The brand-new shoes she'd put on were thoroughly muddy.

The tree shade swayed in the wind. Drifting shadows, clear shadows, distant shadows, nearby shadows. Large shadows, small ones. All kinds of shadows all moving in different ways. Light passing through the leaves cast complex patterns on the ground.

Replicating this on a monitor screen would be difficult even for Mio.

"Are you having trouble walking through this?"

"Not...really."

There was no rebound in her step.

"This is better to walk on than asphalt."

Ayumi didn't slow her pace.

Hazuki was deliberate in her movement across the earth. She felt unsure of the ground under her shoes.

"It's soft."

"It absorbs all your reflexive movement, so you can't get as far as fast," Ayumi said.

Hazuki certainly felt like she wasn't getting very far, though the scenery changed with every step she took. The trees all looked the same but none of them were the same shape or color. The texture and shape of the trees were all slightly different. Even the quality of the light changed. The viewpoint changed because the ground was higher. The temperature seemed to shift as well.

And...

The smell.

The smell of grass. The smell of tree moisture. The smell of water. The smell of the earth.

And...

The smell of herself.

This was...

"The descent should start right after this last incline," Ayumi said, as she pointed forward. "We should be reaching the building somewhere in the middle."

Ayumi rested an arm against a large tree and looked far in that direction. Hazuki hurried up to where Ayumi stood.

She felt like she was flying.

The trees were packed into the sloping incline.

There was a gray block beyond it, spreading as far as she could see. That must be the city. Further beyond that was an unusually small stick-shaped building, as if part of the new wallpaper of buildings.

"Is that 119?"

"Yes," Ayumi said.

Hazuki had been in this code region two or three years ago.

But she didn't remember it being so flat. She had no special memories of it. Other cities she'd seen in this linear perspective were no different from her own. It was the only memory she had of such a view. In other words, the city of Hazuki's residence would also probably appear this sparse from afar.

That had been for...a communication session field trip. Yes, in fact they'd gone to see a food-processing factory. She was pretty sure Ayumi had been there too.

Ayumi had transferred to their area five years ago, so she must have been there. But she couldn't remember anything about her from then.

Hazuki only knew Ayumi transferred five years ago because she'd read her profile.

I didn't remember it.

"On a magnetic multi-passenger vehicle this would have taken forty-five minutes, and even in a transport vehicle on the surface roads this would have taken three hours. The vehicles that run on the freight route we took are faster at night, so they would have taken just thirty minutes. But for humans on foot…it takes a whole day."

On a monitor this would have taken one second.

I see.

Hazuki realized she had a filter over her eyes. The reason this view looked flat was because she couldn't help comparing it to the image on a monitor screen.

She widened her eyes.

More vividly. More clearly. There was a depth to this world.

"There's the building," Ayumi said, pointing again.

A short distance from the gray city, in the middle of greenery, stood a pointed white building.

"When we came here three years ago it was still being built. That's the SVC Memorial Building."

So she was with us on that field trip.

"You came on that trip?" Hazuki asked.

"I was with you," Ayumi said. "The building must have twenty floors. It was built after the skyscraper boom. We have another hour of walking, so let's take a rest," Ayumi said and sat down. Hazuki followed suit and sat down behind her. The way they always sat together.

Very short hair. Between her black hair and dark brown vest, a perfectly white nape.

Only what lay ahead of her foreground was different.

Usually Ayumi could sit like this for hours, but a brief moment felt like forever today.

Ayumi looked at the building at length, then turned her head to one side.

And ahead, a large round stone.

Ayumi faced that stone and fixed her gaze on it a long while.

All Hazuki could see was the pale nape of Ayumi's neck. She didn't know what kind of expression Ayumi had on her face.

"Ayumi."

"What."

"What's going to happen?"

"Probably...something I can't come back from. I've put you in a terrible situation."

"That wasn't your fault."

"No. It is," Ayumi said, still looking in the same direction. Then she motioned toward the building again. Hazuki looked over to where Ayumi indicated.

"Mao is probably nearby. She's still alive."

"Really?"

How does she know?

"Look," Ayumi pointed. "There's a bunch of area patrols out there. Something's wrong."

"Those are area patrols?" They looked like bacteria in a microscope movie.

"Must be around two hundred of them. I wonder if it's a squad."

"Two hundred area patrols?"

Area patrol. Uniforms. The thought of uniformed men awakened fear in Hazuki. Just a day ago, the image of the uniform carried with it a sense of security. It was different now.

They were all enemies.

A green wind crossed the surface of the wood and blew past the hairs on the nape of Ayumi's neck.

"The people in there must be really scared of Rey Mao."

"No, they probably need her alive. They want to pin all the killings on her, so they want her alive till they're through creating the case. I wonder what they plan on doing. Deploying such a big patrol squad is countereffective. There's no way she would storm into that compound. She might think she's a superhero, but she knows her limits."

Ayumi stretched and stood up.

"The main gate must be over there. What's that?"

"Where?"

"It must be an annex facility."

"That's the waste-processing facility."

"Ahh," Ayumi let out, as if understanding. "Then Mao must have been checking that out. It won't burn."

Ayumi extended her palm out over her shoulder to show Hazuki something without turning around. Her pale white hand. In it she held the pink piercing.

"It's neo-ceramic, so it's okay."

Didn't Mio say that too?

"It was stuck on my bag. It fell off Yuko easily and all the time. Yuko was kidnapped and brought here, and then the earring fell off somewhere in the building or got stuck on one of her kidnapper's outfits. Anyway, this piercing got caught in the refuse coming out of the building and was processed along with it. In other words, Mao has to be in that building."

"In that refuse annex?"

"Yeah, and they all know she's in there, I'm sure. That's why they have the place surrounded."

"So those patrols aren't there to capture her but to prevent her escape."

Still, it seemed like overkill. Rey Mao might have been strong, but she was still just a fifteen-year-old girl, just like Hazuki. Two hundred people was too many.

"Cat's really gotten herself in a mouse trap. How ironic. Still, why hasn't she come out yet, I wonder?" She paused. "I'm going in," Ayumi said.

"What are you going to do, Ayumi?"

"For now, help Rey Mao get out. I don't know what she's up to, but at this rate she's just walking straight into the enemy's trap. She's not the culprit. They can't make her one."

"Wait." Hazuki stood up. "There're two hundred of them."

"I know. I'm no match against even just one of them. I'm not planning on fighting them."

"Yeah, but…"

"You stay here."

"What?"

"It's safer here. It's even safer than my house, your house, or even Mio's house."

"I can't stay here forever. I can't be alone."

"It's better than being dead."

Her long eyelashes touched with green light, her eyes were like those of a fawn. Ayumi set the bag of water on the ground.

"No, Ayumi. I want to go too."

"You can't."

"I will."

"Why?!" Ayumi said in probably her first emotional outburst ever.

"Because I'm your friend."

"No you're not."

"What?"

"I hate human interaction," Ayumi said. She turned her back to Hazuki.

"You lie. Then why are you going into that building? Why don't you just ignore this?"

"They started it. I'm going in to stop this so I never have to deal with them again."

"Then why did you bring me here?" Hazuki said.

It took her till now…now, to ask that question.

To wonder.

"Because it's dangerous." Ayumi returned to speaking in her usual voice. "This place…"

"What about this place?" Hazuki looked around herself. What was it about this place?

"This is where *I stopped being human*."

"Stopped being human?"

"Thank you, Hazuki," Ayumi said, and she fled down the slope.

Her figure soon disappeared, swallowed by the living brush.

Hazuki felt slightly defeated.

"No."

Hazuki started after Ayumi.

As soon as she set out she felt dizzy. The strength of her legs had been sapped, and her arms wouldn't do as she wanted. She was sure she'd just lost self-awareness and that her body was exhausted. What kind of body wouldn't listen to the commands of its master? Whose body was this?

This is my body.

This body is mine.

Hazuki slid down the slope covered in dead leaves and then tumbled. She hit a tree root. She inhaled the tremendous scent of mud and earth. She choked on the odor and clapped a hand over her nose. The smell intensified.

"Ayumi!"

Hazuki was momentarily stuck in the brush. She cut through it, pulling out grass from the roots, caked with dirt. She jettisoned it.

Calm down. Breathe. Stand up. My body won't do what I tell it to. My feelings are ignoring my body. It's my feelings that won't listen to me.

I can do what I can do. I can't do what I can't.

It would be wrong to want to do something I can't.

I can stand up.

It's still there.

The building is still there.

It was obvious, but when she faced it she didn't know what was what.

To get to that building, she had to continue down the slope. By descending, Hazuki would find herself at a lower altitude.

The distance between herself and the building was shrinking, so the building *should* appear larger.

But then the blanket of tree cover should appear larger as she approached as well.

The trees in the distance were probably the same size as the ones growing right in front of her. Hazuki fired her imagination. The building probably stood as high as Hazuki was now. If only the building were on the same plane as her. The space between her and the building...

In other words, the forest...the green area surrounding the center...The building was just past it. It was much bigger than the community center.

I can see it.

As long as she could see her destination she was fine. It couldn't be very far.

It was about the distance between Hazuki's own home and the community center. If she calculated the height correctly she could divide the distance in measure. If she calculated the time it would take the distance would grow. That was okay so long as she was going in the right direction.

It shouldn't take more than an hour.

Still. She could still make it. Hazuki could make it.

Just don't rush.

The human body lives by moving. Hazuki had learned that.

The ability to see outer space, to see foreign countries without being there, to communicate with people whose language you did not know, these were all illusion. What sat in front of the monitor was an animal, and animals only knew the world in the context of its own size. The reach of your arms. That was the extent of your movement.

Hazuki climbed another slope, carrying the bag of water Ayumi left behind, and confirmed her orientation. She couldn't situate herself. She had only her compass. She looked up. The sun was bright.

This was how she would find herself.

She descended the hill, one step at a time.

Just descend.

Lift the leg. Lower the leg. She pressed her foot into the earth.

The self she left at the top of the hill somewhere eventually caught up with her body.

Now she couldn't see much more than half the building. This meant

Hazuki had descended to a lower altitude.

She looked up. She could tell the sun had moved.

She eventually reached something like a road.

The kind of road people used to travel on, she thought.

She got on this road and started moving.

Did Ayumi take this road?

How far ahead was Ayumi?

Was Ayumi still alive?

There were flowers abloom.

It was like in the pictures of nature preserves she'd seen.

The road curved wide. One side of it was walled by a cliff held back by a flimsy metal fence, painted white. It was rusted brown in patches. She could reach its edge, which made it a short fence: of no real use.

The asphalt under the fence had deteriorated; grass grew through the cracks. *Roads made of asphalt become unsightly with time*, Hazuki thought.

There was a fork in the road ahead. One side kept curving and the other kept along the side of the hill.

Which way?

Hazuki looked at the sun again. The hill was shaded. The shadows had lengthened significantly. Would she make it to the building before it set? The rays were certainly descending. Hazuki thought about how her shadow moved and stretched, comparing it to the sky.

This way.

She had walked straight toward her objective but got turned around by the curving road.

This curve would probably lead her to the city.

Hazuki chose the road that branched off.

Not ten meters into her decision did she stop. There was a metal beam.

A DO NOT ENTER sign. An indication not to go forward. A sign insisting that there was no farther to go.

But the road kept going.

This is the right road.

Hazuki placed both hands on the bar and climbed over, trying to hop over as quietly as she could.

She tried to follow Ayumi's scent.

Hazuki had learned that an animal's sense of smell was very advanced. She was not smell deficient, but she wasn't able to distinguish all smells. For starters she had no reason to have to distinguish between smells. All noxious smells were erased. The food her helper prepared was simply to be eaten, and all scent of it was simply the scent of food. She'd never made distinctions.

Anyway the smell of synthetic food was added after the fact. Without the smell, the food would all taste the same. That was all Hazuki ate.

The blocked road did not end, nor was it demolished. In fact it turned into a new road, one still well maintained. It was made of newer compound asphalt, no different from the regulation transit roads in Section A. There were street lamps and they were all lit. The greenery on either side of the road had been tended, looked almost man-made.

That the road was blocked meant it was private.

This must have been a private road used only by SVC.

Hazuki rounded a curve in the road and raised her face, then gulped.

A giant white building thrust up from the green landscape.

She suddenly lost her sense of direction.

She could contextualize where she was now to where she had started, but barely. Her position had turned with the road and was now completely confused. Losing all sight of her objective for a moment was certainly one cause. She tried to remember what the building looked like from atop the hill. How was Hazuki positioned in relation to this building now? Any guess on the matter was just that. She couldn't remember the image.

Refuse processing center.

That was where Ayumi had said Rey Mao was. This road probably went all the way to the building.

But though this road may have been connected to the building, she shouldn't be walking dead center down it.

There were two hundred members of the area patrol waiting.

Merely thinking the words scared Hazuki. Her legs trembled.

Up ahead. Up ahead were two hundred enemies.

In the green.

She'd probably be safer walking in the greenery. She'd be better hidden there than on the road. If she stayed on the road and ran into a patrol officer it would all be over. With her eyes still on the building, Hazuki took several steps back and moved to the side of the road, entering the brush.

A sensor.

Hazuki hurriedly withdrew her leg.

It was too late.

Definitely.

On either side of the road were laser sensors with cameras.

No.

What am I doing?

And that was when Hazuki stopped thinking.

In her blank mind, fear crept in.

The self and the body that had finally gotten in sync suddenly broken, her self taking flight with tremendous speed.

Hazuki's body screamed and took off at full speed toward the white building and the two hundred-strong area patrol force surrounding it. Reason and judgment had fled.

Hazuki, disjointed, was sending her self and her body straight to their deaths.

And for some reason this calmed her.

CHAPTER 024

SHE LOOKED AT the edge of the desk.

There was nothing for her to look at.

Neither amazed nor frightened, Shizue's gut was full of a terror about to drive her insane.

A black metal body. A metal tube sticking out from it. Facing it was Shizue, with Kunugi beside her.

She smelled high-quality leather. It was made to look exactly like the real thing, so the smell was, no doubt, just like the real thing as well. It was perhaps even real animal hide. She wanted to vomit.

She had to flee this sense of evil.

A soft voice murmured near her.

"How was your nap?"

It was an articulate voice, very serious.

"We let you stay in our finest guest suite. Only important people who've come from very far have stayed in that room."

"It'd be a lot nicer if we weren't bound and watched," Kunugi said.

Shizue looked at her hands.

They were still bruised.

"A little room service and permission to leave would be nice too."

"You're staying here free of charge, so consider the loss of these luxuries…a compromise."

Sitting in an expensive-looking chair behind the large lacquered desk was a man of weak constitution.

It was Ishida.

Standing to his side was a man wearing a surgical mask and white clothing. Next to the desk was Takasugi, who had changed into something more formal. Standing next to him was a man too thin for his great height. He wore an area patrol uniform and pointed what appeared to be a gun at Shizue.

Standing behind Shizue and Kunugi was a man with a tattooed head, looking ready to do harm.

The room felt antiseptic.

The ceiling, the walls, and the floor were all polished. There wasn't one speck of dust.

"Well, I was polite enough to have this wait until I personally arrived."

"Real polite. I'm sitting in this nice chair and everything. No complaints here, Lieutenant."

"How's it feel? Those are chairs we reserve for VIP residents, you know."

"It doesn't suit my ass," Kunugi said. "Probably because my ass is caked in mud. Oh, shoot. See how I'm ruining the chair?"

"Yes, I do," Ishida answered.

Such an awful voice.

"Not even children are this filthy anymore."

"You're right. But you know how old I am. I'm close to getting my pension and everything."

"That's all right. We're allowed to exchange the chair in the event it gets soiled. A lot of people come through here. Children, the elderly. We can't be worried about things getting dirty all the time."

"Where the fuck are we?!" Kunugi yelled.

"You don't know? I thought you grew up in this region," Ishida said.

"Of course I don't know. I haven't been here in fifteen years. I don't remember anything like this from back then."

"That's really no good. This is the central database center for SVC headquarters."

"SVC? Here? When I lived here there was nothing this pretentious. It was just bronze statues and factories. It was a dead-end town."

"Well now. The way you talk about this city I wouldn't figure you were from here," Ishida said, shaking his head. "It was here that my great-grandfather, Yutaro Suzuki, built the first synthetic food processing factory for SVC, which was then known as Suzuki Food Science Laboratories. This building commemorates the thirtieth anniversary of the new corporate identity, and also honors my great-grandfather. It's a hybrid intelligent building, equipped with the same technologies as the community center."

"Did you say the community center?"

"Yes. The first floor is designed to house a community center agency. Floors fifteen through nineteen are dedicated to the latest advanced medical research."

"I see. It's a high-class hospital for upper-income individuals."

"You're wrong. Anyone who lives in this area is allowed to use this facility for free."

"Free, eh?" Kunugi said.

"Only those from outside the area have to pay a fee, but we seem to be prospering. The rest of the building is filled with the archives of the achievements of Yutaro Suzuki. There is a museum, a relaxation area, an amusement space, sports facilities of all kinds—even lodging. And of course, a restaurant. We have the best quality foods crafted by the people of SVC themselves. In this age of little human interaction, it's priceless. We're proud to be able to provide these facilities for even those coming from other areas. Though you won't see anyone here today because we're closed to the public," Ishida said.

"Well thanks for coming out on your day off then," Kunugi said.

"Oh no, early this morning, Takasugi informed me of your arrival, and I immediately came over. Area 122 of this region is in a state of panic, what with the death of Yuko Yabe, the discovery of Yuji Nakamura's body, the disappearance of Ritsuko Kisugi, Hazuki Makino's kidnapping, and of course, Ayumi Kono's disappearance. The police are up to their necks. We actually had a schedule, but look how it's gotten late already. It looks like we had you waiting ten hours."

"That's probably right. You are doing the job of both police lieutenant and the criminal you're supposed to catch."

Ishida laughed smartly through his nose.

"Whatever makes you think that?"

"Don't give me that shit. Just do what you're going to do. You're famous around here. I've known I didn't fit in here ever since I was a little kid."

"I don't remember you from childhood. Still...I find that hard to believe," Ishida said, bored. "Kunugi, you're a public figure, an upholder of the law. A police officer. And..."

Ishida looked over at Shizue.

"Miss Fuwa, you are employed by the state to protect and raise healthy children. You are the apogee of adulthood. I'm not impressed with the fact that two civil servants that ought to uphold the law have blatantly ignored it. Your actions are completely antisocial. This is reckless behavior, even for children."

"Shut up!" Kunugi yelled. "Beating an innocent girl to death, letting a serial killer do his work, protecting him. That's what's criminal. You're the one who's antisocial."

"You don't understand, do you?" Ishida turned his chair out halfway and stood up. "Listen, let us say for example that we're in a situation where if one person leaves the room, the rest of the people in the room are in a bind. And there's only the one exit from this room." Ishida lifted a bent finger and motioned toward the large ornamented door behind Shizue. "The only way out of here is through that door. This means that in order to get in one needs to pass through that door. It's a rule. The law is simply a rule, just like that. I haven't passed through that door. I know how to get out without having to. If I leave here without having to use the door, no one will know I was here in the first place. I have not broken any laws. You, however…"

Ishida slammed his hand onto the desk. "You are found at fault for trying to enter through the door, for trying to *break down* the door! I don't know what exactly you did, but in other words, you broke a rule."

"That's just sophistry." Shizue was tired of hearing Ishida's voice. "This is all stupid wordplay. I have not done anything to violate the law. I certainly went outside after the police enforced curfew, but the investigation effort was marginal at that point, and the police had no basis to apprehend me as I was not even a suspect."

"You still don't understand."

"What?"

"I'm the one who determines whether you are a suspect or not."

"Pardon?"

"We're the ones who determine whether you are a criminal or not."

"The justice department assesses the crime, not you."

"You're right. I'm not the one who decides that. However, I am the one who allows the judgment to be made. That's what I'm trying to tell you."

Ishida slowly turned his face toward Shizue.

"The courts base their case on the data presented by us in order to make their judgment. Listen, Miss Fuwa, you are not the one who creates the data on yourself. We are. Your behavior patterns, your habits, your criminal past—that's all created by us."

"That is itself a crime," Shizue said.

"You're slow to understand things, aren't you? It's not illegal. I'm not suggesting that our judgments are made according to modern law. You are the ones disobeying the law. Did you think you'd get away with it? I can't imagine you did."

"I knew getting caught by the police was inevitable. I just didn't want to be caught by you. And to think that idiot was throwing me under the bus." Kunugi glared at Takasugi. Takasugi bowed slightly.

"He didn't throw you anywhere. He's one of my best men."

"Tch," Kunugi spit, and clasped his hands behind his head.

The man with the handgun visibly strengthened his grip. His fingers were tense.

"I'm not going to do anything. I'm a weak fighter."

Kunugi narrowed his eyes and focused on the weapon held out by the man.

"But, Ishida. You've been on this whole pompous rant about how you haven't broken any laws, but then what do you call what that man has in his hand? He's been pointing that thing at us from the beginning. It's too big to be a police-issue weapon, and I doubt that what comes out the end of it is a spray or resin."

"Probably not. The weapon he's holding certainly has lethal power. Bearing any kind of weapon like that is, as you know, strictly prohibited in this country by international decree. It's a Z model, 2010."

"What's he—"

"But it's the strangest thing. I don't actually see it."

"What?!" Kunugi raised his voice.

"I can't see what I don't see. There's no way something like that could be carried around in this country. As far as I'm concerned he's just extending his arm. There's nothing in his hand. Do you see it, Takasugi?"

"I don't see a thing," he said.

"You bastards!" Kunugi nearly rose out of his chair.

"Oh no no no. You really shouldn't make sudden movements like that. This man with his arm extended is very sensitive to people's movements. He might accidentally pull the trigger."

There was suddenly a straight red line from the end of the handgun to Kunugi's forehead.

Laser sight.

"If he moves a finger, that light guides—"

"Something that doesn't exist out of something else that's not there, I get it, I get it."

"This is what's called an overwhelming disadvantage, Kunugi. Miss Fuwa seems more sagacious. She seems to understand the situation."

"You're saying that what you say isn't there, isn't there. What is there, is."

Ishida clapped like a child. "Bravo. There's the lauded child psychology specialist, daughter of Yukie Fuwa. You're correct."

"My mother..."

My mother has nothing to do with this.

"That was some shocker four years ago, eh? To lose someone so important to you—"

"She has nothing to do with this," Shizue interrupted. "With you."

She didn't want to have to say it.

"I've read many of her books, Miss Fuwa. I quite respect her work."

"Respect?"

The dead don't return.

It's because of your attitude.

"Oh no. You're making a face," Ishida said as he looked into Shizue's eyes.

She turned away.

Who was this man?

"Did you not respect her? That's not right, now is it? You should honor her. Yukie Fuwa was your mother, after all."

What's going on? What is this?

"What would you know about it?"

Just as Shizue raised herself, the beam of the laser sight moved over to her forehead.

Her breath stopped.

"I'm sorry," Ishida said. "That stuff doesn't matter anyway. Now where were we?"

Ishida turned on a heel and sank into the chair again, laced his fingers, and rested his chin on them.

"What shall we do?"

His cold stare darted from Shizue to Kunugi. "It's quite easy to punish two troubled individuals. We can make them criminals, or kill them. No, not just kill, but completely eradicate the records of your existence. It wouldn't be very difficult. Still, I hate to create unnecessary deaths."

"Unnecessary deaths?"

"Unnecessary, sure. Your death would have no productive outcome."

"Productive outcome?"

Ishida turned back.

"What say we bargain?"

"Bargain?" Kunugi said.

"It's not a bad idea, I don't think."

"Hey hey, I don't think there's anything about this situation that's not bad. I'm not stupid."

"No, it's not bad. Listen. Right now according to our records, your crimes are minor, Kunugi. In other words if we processed and released you now you'd get off with a slap on the wrist. I mean, you'll probably have to be dismissed from the force, but there won't necessarily be a need for police action. Depending on the circumstance you might even go unpunished. But in about twenty-four hours you will be considered a kidnapper and murderer and prosecuted as such."

"Who are you saying I'm going to kill?"

"First, Ayumi Kono. It's been established that she ran off with you and Miss Fuwa. Then—"

"Wait," Shizue said. "You don't have her, do you?"

They got even her.

"Please don't worry about her right now," Ishida said. "That Kono is an amazing child. She was seen with Hinako Sakura on the grounds of the Makino residence, but we haven't been able to seize her just yet. It's just a matter of time though. I have the entirety of the D&S Security corporation on my side, after all." Ishida laughed. "This is information that just can't be parsed by idiots. Unfortunately, we weren't able to effectively use the data internally, but I have been able to use it personally."

"Kono has nothing to do with this. Nothing!"

"That too is something *I* determine."

"What's wrong with you?! Who do you think you are?"

"He's the great-grandson of Yutaro Suzuki," Takasugi said. Ishida cocked his head and laughed again.

"Unfortunately, after punishing Miss Fuwa, Kunugi will kill the child to unload his burden. And after chasing him for a while, let's see, for three days, shall we say? In three days, Miss Fuwa's body will be discovered. She will have been violated. It will be an unusual sex crime. And demographically speaking, only a man of Kunugi's generation would carry out a sexually violent murder. Probably the result of an inferior education," Ishida said.

"We all know that in your youth, child porn and other obscene materials flourished the world over. Adults would flaunt arcane words like 'immorality' but were still sex-obsessed buffoons. Then they'd shamelessly brag about it. It was clearly a mental disorder. Even prostitution or acts resembling prostitution were silently condoned. The phenomenon of sex enthralled all of society. It was a truly foolish time."

"I think on that one point alone we are in agreement," Shizue said. "Social delusions regarding sex reached their peak between the end of the last century and the beginning of this one. It was, as you state, a foolish time. But you can't say it's scientific to declare an entire generation of people as categorically problematic. You yourself are of the same age group as Kunugi, for example."

"You're right. We're only three years apart. However, I have nothing to do with this. I won't commit police crimes."

"Won't? You mean you will and cover it up."

"Cover it up?"

"Yeah. Make it look like someone else did it."

"What do you mean?"

"You've lumped your own murders in with the serial killing case. You've already tried to frame the undocumented girl for Kawabata and Nakamura's deaths."

"I haven't killed anyone," Ishida said. "I've done nothing. I'm a lieutenant, the chief of Investigative Unit R at prefectural police headquarters. Why would I commit such a heinous crime? Please don't say things like that. Also, it's strange to say that random murders are being assigned to the serial killer. It's a serial killer, so of course the killings are going to be random. There's no cover-up here."

"Sure," Kunugi said and shook his head over and over. "Yeah, I get it. Shit. You don't want to get your hands dirty. I'm sure you even have an alibi. You have a place and a person to verify your whereabouts. You're in the clear. I'm going to puke." Kunugi shook without moving. Like a restless child. There was an irritating, useless, endless anger boiling up from inside him that he couldn't chase down. Shizue knew the feeling all too well. "Shit, I'm so pissed off I'm going to go crazy. Hey, if you're going to kill me, do it now."

Ishida smiled and effortlessly shook his head. "You really are stupid."

"I know. That's why I'm here."

"I told you I'm willing to bargain. You could be the next generation. Miss Fuwa, you could go unprosecuted. Return to work, even. Kunugi, well, you will probably be dismissed from the force, but we can take care of you anyway. What about a post at the area patrol in your hometown? I can put you under consideration for a section chief position."

"What the hell would we have to do for you to be offering such a deal? What the fuck do you want us to do?" Kunugi was yelling now.

"It's simple. You admit to doing the things we suspect you of. Miss Fuwa can claim she was forced to do what she did by you. You are the culprit. She is the victim. What do you think?"

"You mean I'm going to be convicted of stalking her?"

"Precisely. Then at least we won't convict you of murder."

"And Kono? You'd also protect Ayumi Kono?" Shizue asked.

If this protects Ayumi…

Ishida shook his head again.

"I can't do that. That girl, Miss Kono, along with Miss Hazuki Makino and Mio Tsuzuki, will have to die. Speaking of which, Takasugi!"

"Sir, it's possible Ayumi Kono communicated some information to Hinako Sakura while she was at the community center."

"Then yes, I guess we'll have to kill her too," Ishida said.

"Are you not right in the head? You said a second ago that you don't like useless murders. What are you going to accomplish killing all these little girls?" Kunugi yelled as he stomped his foot.

"I said I don't like producing useless corpses. Those children would die for a great cause. Ayumi Kono is…"

Ishida put his hand on a touch-screen on his desk.

A digital screen appeared, upon which information on the child they were discussing popped up. The display furiously scrolled through reams of characters and images for Ayumi's data, and then eventually an image of her face appeared on the screen.

"Interesting. She's a triple A. And Makino…"

What was he saying?

"Hmph, she's an A-minus."

"That won't be a problem," said the man in white.

"Her base strength is inferior, but her organs are disease-free, and she is fed on D&S-produced food products prepared by a domestic with a premium contract, so there won't be any problems with her nutritional balance. As long as it's nothing like the last time, I think it might even be better."

"I'm looking forward to it," Ishida said, and he started another search.

Mio Tsuzuki's image appeared.

"She's a B."

"Ooh, we *must* get her," said the man in white.

Get?

"Hinako Sakura is, well, she looks like she's unhealthy but she's a double A. Wow, Miss Fuwa. All your children are so healthy!"

They were looking at the data from the childrens' medical exams.

These men…

"What are you doing?" Shizue was overpowered by an indescribable rage.

"W-what on earth are you doing?"

Ishida didn't answer, but simply laughed.

"What's so funny? What are you doing?"

"Miss Fuwa. You're not in a position to be asking questions. I was the one asking you questions. Now, Kunugi, what are you going to do?"

"I'm sorry, but I'm stupid, like you said. I'm so stupid I don't understand the position you're putting me in. What was it again? I'm supposed to choose between being a convicted murderer or pervert?"

"Yes. That's an astute way of putting it," Ishida said with a smirk. "So what's it going to be?"

"Don't kid yourself."

Kunugi looked at Shizue.

"Call me whatever you want. A pervert, an aberrant. But don't think I'm going to be part of any scheme that requires killing children," Kunugi said.

He leapt at Ishida.

However.

He was quickly stopped from behind by the large tattooed man and slammed into the desk, where he was immobilized. Shizue was toppled over in the process, chair and all.

As she started to stand up the laser was once again directed at her forehead.

Kunugi's arms were pulled up behind him, his face pressed onto the surface of the desk. He hollered, "You assholes! How dare you act so cavalier about killing children!"

"Kunugi!" Ishida looked down at Kunugi's squirming face as if it were filthy, his look full of disgust. "Yes, yes. We've seen your data, Kunugi. You were friends with a convicted killer. That bizarre murder of the perpetrator's entire family. That took place a long time ago, in Area 119 even. I seem to recall reading somewhere that you defended him. It's in the domestic violence archives."

"I have never protected a criminal. All murder is criminal. A great crime."

"However, I do remember saying something about how we shouldn't hold a murderer in contempt at some point in the past. You're recorded as having defended the killer."

"A crime is a crime. A human life is a human life," Kunugi said. "I never said that murder was excusable, much less the murders of one child after another."

"But, Kunugi, I never kill anyone without a good reason."

"W-what did you say?"

The muscles on the arms of the large man bulged.

Kunugi howled.

"That hold looks painful," Ishida said scornfully. "You just can't mind your manners, can you? You deserve to rot with those senseless perverts. The ones that murder without reason."

Kunugi struggled. "You saying it's okay to kill people if you have a motive?"

"What on earth is he saying?" Ishida said, incredulously. "And you call yourself a cop. *Motives?* What is a motive? Are you talking about an overwhelming urge? A loss of sanity? Baseless excuses? I can't forgive anyone who would take a human life in such meaningless circumstances."

"Then what noble cause can you come up with for justifying murder?"

"I don't have a noble cause. That's just more antiquated talk."

"I'm old. I was born in the twentieth century, just like you."

"Choose your words more carefully, Boss," Takasugi said.

Kunugi started to yell at Takasugi but it turned into a shriek halfway through as his arms were twisted even further behind his back.

"No one uses the term 'noble cause' anymore, Mr. Kunugi. The country is no more than an extension of the individual. Our generation knows that better than anyone. The foolish masses chose nationalism as a noble cause because it was easiest to understand. But it's ineffective. Ideals and morals and laws are no longer a function of national unity and protection. Their function is only to give the illusion of safety to a society."

"S-so what? Explain that in small words to this stupid old man."

Ishida disdained Kunugi's appearance—the squirming in the grip of the large man, the strained face.

"Poverty, stupidity…crimes wrought by lack of attention should be eradicated. Of course we can say that eradicating poverty and stupidity isn't just for the benefit of the country but for the overall good of humanity. People pillage because they're not of means, they don't have enough space so they invade other people's places, they have different beliefs so they start wars, they fight because they've been defeated for so long in the past. They steal because they're poor, they kill because they fight, they take revenge because they hold a grudge. It's all the same. In the past, some of the most unforgivable crimes were allowed under the auspices of nationalism. This ideological sophistry perpetuated by the masses is precisely what we used to call a noble cause. This kind of thing no longer exists."

"And so what?"

"Killing people is never right. That's why countries fight wars. The death penalty was outlawed. No one objects to that. And now it's illegal to kill animals. At least in this country. Right?"

"This was also one of Suzuki Senior's achievements," Takasugi said.

"Yes, Kunugi, I'm not killing people. Those girls are going to die anyway. There's nothing we can do about it."

"What do you mean there's nothing you can do about it?" Kunugi tried hard to face Ishida while twisting in the grip of the large man. "Like you said, most motives for murder are meaningless. But that doesn't mean the poor or uneducated are more likely to kill. I actually understand that people kill for no reason. Of course, it's unforgivable. It's absolutely unforgivable. Still, I understand. Pathological murder is just some phrase someone made up. It's unrelated."

"Hmm," Ishida said like an idiot. "And?"

"And I don't get you. I don't get even a molecule of a hair on your nose. I don't understand what kind of person uses stature and resources to create an organization, a safe place, to commit serial murder for who knows what purpose. And I don't want to know."

"Organization?"

"What else would you call it?" Kunugi yelled.

"Unfortunately, though in my position I do handle data accumulation in a specific industry, I don't have my own organization. I *am* a member of the police organization, but—"

"You've created your own organization. Don't pretend you haven't."

"Well, well, well. I do in fact collect data and maneuver the police force and other organizations. I help the courts make judgments, sure, but these are just things I do to maintain civil order. I'm not trying to make the police organization my own."

"You're puppeteering them. What about him? I'm talking about you, Takasugi."

The large man twisted Kunugi's arm even harder. Kunugi made an awful yelping sound.

"He is my underling and confidant. I didn't force him to cooperate with me."

"I'm a believer, sir," Takasugi said with a serious face.

Kunugi kicked his legs ineffectually.

"I can't look at this anymore. Arvil. Could you remove that disgusting face from my desk now? I don't want my floor dirtied either, but...Mr. Yudani, would you mind so much disinfecting that area?" Ishida said without so much as looking at Kunugi. The large man threw Kunugi to the floor and planted a foot on his chest. The man in white clothes wiped the desk with some moist towelettes.

"Oh by the way, this is Mr. Yudani. He's been responsible for the Suzuki household kitchen for over thirty years and is a special chef at our home. The one with his foot on your back right now is Arvil. He's French. He works only for me. I pay him quite well, so you can imagine how loyally he obeys my orders. The one holding that unsettling object is Lao, and he's an undocumented resident from China. He's got an interesting collection of guns. I made this family. These people are not the kind of people you think they are."

"It's nothing like in the old fictions, Boss. No low-class criminal gang. Gangs don't exist anymore, do they? It was a different time," Takasugi said to Kunugi. Then he approached Shizue, offering a hand. "Here, Miss Fuwa."

Shizue took that hand and stood up.

She couldn't believe how normally she was behaving.

She tasted blood.

In the midst of falling over along with her chair she must have cut her mouth. She felt the corner of her mouth with the back of her hand.

It was that taste of humanity that she hated so.

It smelled so human.

Shizue stood right in front of Ishida, her feet wide apart.

"Why, you look so brave, Miss Fuwa. Not like your friend here, cringing and wincing. Your kind of people are a necessity, working with kids and all, I suppose. It's too bad. It's really too bad."

Takasugi approached her. She gave him a look filled with contempt.

"This Kunugi character. He embodies what you hate most in a man—filth. As you've just heard yourself, he's denying my wonderful offer. Actually, you will meet an unnecessary death in three days as well if you find my offer disagreeable. So, what do you think? Can't you convince your friend here?"

"U-unfortunately, no. I am in complete agreement with the filthy man pinned to the ground," Shizue said.

"Well. That's a surprise," Ishida said. "Here I'd let myself believe that you and I were made of the same cloth."

"If you think you can compare yourself to me, I'd be better off committing double suicide with this filthy middle-aged man."

Shizue swept her hair back. She didn't usually ever touch her hair. She thought she saw Kunugi smile from the floor.

"We've changed tastes, have we? Still, can't say it isn't a change for the worse. But aren't you happy, Kunugi?" Ishida said, looking down at him. "It's been what, fifteen years since someone of the opposite sex liked you?"

Takasugi laughed, satisfied.

"Mr. Ishida." Calling out his name disgusted her. "Y-you. You all are crazy."

"Is that so? There's no data to support that. At least not technically."

Takasugi, while laughing, extended his hand to Shizue.

Shizue recoiled. She didn't want to be touched by any of them. It was worse than germs. "If you're going to kill me, please do it now. Please shoot me now with that gun."

"We can't do that. Listen, the data is all going to be rewritten. If there is a dead body, that's physical evidence. We can file an investigative report, but we can't really write it with a dead body around, and an autopsy would be unavoidable. It's all just such a hassle. We'd prefer you died exactly the way we say you're going to."

"Besides, Kunugi's not holding the gun yet," Ishida added with a laugh. "You know, they were still handing out guns to cops when Kunugi joined the force. But I'm sure he never fired the one they gave him. Your body can be tidied up completely without equipment, but it's impossible to make all traces of a human being completely disappear. It won't add up."

Ishida stood up and made clicking sounds with his shoes, walking toward Shizue.

"If he's going to do it, he's going to strangle her."

"Strangle…"

"Just like your mother."

"Stop it."

Her mother's throat. The marks left by the fingers.

The broken pieces of a human image on a screen.

Shizue screamed at the top of her lungs.

Mother.

Mother, you.

Mother, you idiot!

"Don't worry, we won't kill you right now. In three days."

No, no, no, no.

Shizue shook her head violently, sending her hair thrashing about her face. It was the same color as her mother's hair.

"It's hard for me to watch you acting so deranged. I was wrong about you, Miss Fuwa. Takasugi."

Takasugi grabbed her by the shoulders.

Just then.

The image on the screen on the desk suddenly changed.

"Hmm? What's this?"

"There seems to be an intruder," Yudani said.

"Intruder? From where?"

"From the rear gate. We're getting an image shortly."

"Ooh," Ishida raised his voice, almost chirpily. "Look here. Could it be? This girl. It's Hazuki Makino."

"Makino…"

Hazuki.

Shizue fell apart.

She was bisected. Into one self that wanted badly to escape this room, and the other self still a counselor.

"Hazuki Makino…"

Why?

"That was lucky, wasn't it?" Takasugi said.

"If Ms. Makino was being harbored by undocumented residents through the help of Mao, she probably realized she would get in real trouble. Yuko Yabe was the same way. They're coming forward on their own. It all works out so well."

"Lieutenant Ishida's so virtuous," Takasugi whispered to Shizue.

Don't kid yourself.

Shizue whipped herself away from Takasugi's side and walked over to the desk, where she looked at the screen from behind.

It was an inverse image of Hazuki Makino, who seemed from the angle to be floating.

"Makino…"

I don't want to see any more children murdered.

Those were her mother's words.

Those stupid, naïve words.

"Run! Don't come here, Hazuki!" Shizue screamed.

Not like Hazuki would hear her or anything.

"She can't hear you," Ishida said.

She knew that.

Shizue turned her head.

"I won't let you kill another child. I won't let you lay one finger on my children."

"*Your* children? Well, well, well, I'm surprised to hear such an old-fashioned sentiment from you. Weren't counselors the ones that banned the teacher-student, priest-parishioner dynamic once and for all?"

"That has nothing to do with it. Nothing at all. I know that child. She's my child. Don't kill her. That child...that child can't be killed. I can't watch that happen!" Shizue shouted.

"I don't want to hear this!" Ishida said. "It's no use listening to this illogical nonsense. It's unconstructive noise. Take this deranged woman and that idiotic man to...ah yes, to the microbe room. There is no need to soil this VIP room any further with them."

Shizue felt a strong hand on her neck and hands.

She was pulled away from the desk. It hurt.

The inverse screen image of Hazuki Makino grew more distant.

No. This couldn't be.

Don't kill her.

"Don't kill..."

The large ornamented door opened and Shizue and Kunugi were dragged into the hall.

Everything was clean. This floor was probably sterilized.

They heard the sound of an alarm and the doors at the end of the hall opened. There was yet another set of doors past it. When Takasugi put his hand up against the panel, the door slid up. They pushed Kunugi through the doorway. Next, Shizue was dragged in. They no longer had the strength to resist.

They were thrown out.

The door shut.

Through the reinforced glass door they saw Takasugi's face. Yet another door closed, and finally they could no longer see anything.

Shizue crept toward the door and felt around.

Even exhausted of all energy, what disgusted her still disgusted her.

A feeling, close to anger, even frustration, which belonged nowhere, burned in her stomach.

She pounded on the door.

There was almost no sound.

"Please don't kill her...don't kill her," Shizue said, crying.

"I'm sorry," Kunugi said to her back. "Nothing good happens to people who stick by me."

Shizue listened to the enfeebled voice behind her, but she did not want to turn around.

"My ex-wife said I was like a child. I'm beginning to think she was right. I'm about to turn fifty. And I'm still not going to be an adult. I wondered about why this was. And realized..."

Shizue turned around.

Kunugi was collapsed in the corner, his shoulders heaving with each breath.

Half his face was blackened and swollen. She thought he must have internal bleeding. His left hand was facing an unnatural direction, so it must also be broken, Shizue decided.

"I never had a proper childhood. That's why I can't have a proper adulthood. Kids have to be kids. I have all these issues because I never got to live out my childhood. That's why somewhere inside me I'm always thinking that I want to be a kid, that I want to do childhood right. Or I'll never become an adult. I'm an adult who longs to be a child. Things might have been different if I'd had my own children, but I suppose a child can't raise children." Kunugi lowered his face. It sounded like he was laughing.

"Kunugi…"

He looked up.

He must be in so much pain.

"Are you okay?" Shizue corrected herself and sat upright.

"You can't really have thought of committing suicide with a dirty middle-aged man like me. I'm filthy and thoughtless."

"Kunugi."

"It's all right. My ex-wife always said the same thing. I know it. I'm sorry I brought you into this."

"I chose to be here."

"But if you'd never met me, you might have been able to save your children."

"I don't know about that."

She didn't think so.

In reality, Shizue was powerless.

Shizue wasn't able to do anything. Someone who couldn't even save herself couldn't save others. Reason alone couldn't change the world. It just made her hate herself.

Previously, if Kunugi hadn't been around, she wouldn't have noticed.

"I'm a terrible woman."

"That's not true," Kunugi said to soothe her. "I mean, I don't think you are. To be honest, that last thing you said, about how Ishida isn't moral, really made the most sense. In your words. It made so much sense to me," Kunugi said.

She didn't want to see any more children being murdered.

I hate it. I don't want to see any more children murdered.
Mother.
"Those were my mother's words."
The last thing she heard her say.
At the time, this was how Shizue responded.
"The dead don't return, Mother."
"Ishida was suggesting," Kunugi tried in vain to start a thought, "that your mother was famous, but I've never heard of her. You know, poorly educated and all."
"My mother was, as he mentioned, a famous child psychologist and doctor. She had an ideological dispute with my father, who was a sociologist and feminist, and divorced him. I went to live with my father. This wasn't court-ordered but my own choice. I didn't like the way my mother talked when I was a child."
A despicable woman. That was what she thought of her.
Shizue had liked her father.
"My father was refined and rational. But still a man of the twentieth century."
"My generation, then."
"I suppose," Shizue answered. "I eventually grew up to be offended by my father's ideals. Half-purposely, I developed a communication handicap. And the person who ended up saving me was the mother I loathed. I left my father's side and filed with the courts to return to my mother. Though really it was just a lot of paperwork."
"Yeah, no kidding," Kunugi said, sarcastic.
"I wasn't dependent on my mother or anything. She may have saved me, but I didn't start liking her because of it. Her human interaction skills notwithstanding, she achieved a lot in her life. In that sense I respected her."
"And she passed away?" Kunugi asked.
"Yes. One of her sixteen-year-old subjects with a behavioral disorder. He killed her. He strangled her."
He strangled Shizue's mother for her own sake.
"This young man…he killed six people while under my mother's care."
"During treatment?"
"Yes. He was arrested and then they uncovered murder after murder—as his physician she was held accountable."
"Oh," Kunugi raised his voice. "That happened in Area 312, didn't it? A bunch of teens were killed, four or five years ago."

"That's right. My mother insisted on his innocence. The teen definitely had a behavioral issue and had committed violent acts. He was still in treatment, so he wasn't completely recovered yet. Behavioral disabilities are not easily cured. However, everyone asked my mother why she didn't recommend such a dangerous person be locked up. She kept insisting there wasn't sufficient evidence."

And then her mother, Yukie Fuwa, was destroyed.

"Mother, my mother, died along with the convicted teenager during a psychological assessment."

"Died together? Wait. I remember hearing that this boy lashed out during the psychiatric assessment, killed his psychiatrist, then committed suicide. Was that not true?"

"No."

He didn't kill her.

"He didn't kill her. She made him kill her."

"I don't understand."

"By insisting on defending this young man, my mother lost her confidence in the world. She said she would go insane if she found out he was guilty. She would go insane if she learned that she was responsible for any of the children's murders."

They would have died because of me.

Were they right? Tell me. Was I wrong?

Weakling.

"I hated this weak image of my mother. I couldn't forgive it. If she'd had any conviction she'd have pushed through. I told her coldly. That's what you're supposed to do as an academic, I said to her."

The dead don't return, Mother.

"But the evidence was overwhelming, and she started to think maybe he was guilty. If they could prove definitively that he'd committed these crimes, my mother's life as an academic and as a human being would have been over. That was the situation. My mother brought out the young man. It was her escape from reality. I received a voice message. At my house."

This boy...

He keeps saying he didn't do it.

Of course I believe him.

But it's clear he was the culprit.

His judgment is normal.

I can only determine that he's normal.

He's at no risk of temporary insanity.
Therefore he's totally culpable.

"To be honest I was shocked. Yes. I was shocked before I was surprised. No normal person would let someone undergoing psychiatric evaluation go free. It's not standard. I rebuked my mother. I told her to stop being insipid. This boy was already charged by the police, who filed with the public prosecutor, so short of any trial misconduct or aberrations in the last psychiatric assessment, her career as a psychiatrist would be over. All that would be left was a conviction by the court. 'Those dead kids weren't ever going to come back, so stop being stupid,' I said. I said it over and over.

"I saw my mother crying on the other end of the monitor in the hotel. She cried that she didn't want to see any more children die. She was going crazy. That was the first time I ever saw her cry. I didn't like it. 'I don't want to see any more children murdered,' she kept saying. I kept telling her: 'You can cry all you want. The dead don't return, Mother.' 'He's guilty. Don't you see?'"

It was right then that her mother fell apart.

Shizue noticed it. She also noticed that even though it made her feel bad she pretended it didn't.

That must have been the exact moment her mother totally fell apart. It wasn't the world that broke her. It wasn't academe. It wasn't the police.

It was Shizue.

Shizue's words broke her mother.

"And so my mother asked the young man to strangle her. 'You're going to be convicted of murder anyway, so kill me,' she said. He was crying as he strangled her. And then the monitor went blank. He fell to his death."

"Then…" Kunugi widened his cloudy eyes. "You watched…"

"While she was killed, yes. On that monitor I threw in the bushes yesterday."

The broken pieces of a human image on a screen.

"That's…" Kunugi couldn't finish his thought.

"This was a kind of double suicide. But the police decided the public wouldn't appreciate the truth. A famous child psychology expert and a young man believed to be a serial killer escaped from a psychiatric assessment only to end up committing double-suicide would be too messy. So they released a report along the lines of what you were just saying. Therefore…"

"Wait." Kunugi made a pained expression and tried to move his body.

"Wait. It might be a false charge after all."

"What are you saying? I saw with my own eyes…fingers wrapped around her throat. Tears streaming down her face."

"That's not what I'm talking about," Kunugi said. "Listen, Fuwa. Listen good. I'm finally remembering what I was trying to tell you yesterday and forgot. Look, until four years ago, Lieutenant Ishida was assigned to a prefectural post presiding over Area 312. I'm sure he was in charge of that particular case."

"What?"

"Maybe that boy was innocent after all? Your mother could have been right. You remember what he said. Data can be rewritten. He can create all kinds of evidence. Tampering with evidence in order to maintain social order—after all, video shown on monitors is the easiest thing for people to accept. Right?"

"That can't be…"

Somewhere, Shizue, who was bisected, suddenly became whole again.

"All six of those victims were treated in the same medical center, right?"

"Yes. Where my mother worked."

"If I recall correctly, that hospital was run by SVC. The company that operates it is an affiliate company of SVC."

"Then…"

My mother. The young man. Everyone, all of them…

"Shit."

Kunugi adjusted his position on the floor. "Ouch. Dammit. He can't get away with this. I want to kill him. Ow ow ow ow."

No.

Shizue stood up and looked around.

It was an empty room. Not just a figure of speech. There was truly nothing in there. No windows. No objects.

No textures. The walls, the floor, the ceiling, were all bathed in a dim blue-white light.

Only the mud- and blood-caked Kunugi stood out.

"They called this the microbe booth, didn't they?"

"Yes, they did. Because we're both dirty."

There was no opening in the ceiling. A purplish hue shone from flat planes of light. There were a few open holes, but all that came out of them were nozzles. They must have been for antibacterial sprays.

"There don't seem to be anything like surveillance cameras. No sensors, instruments, or switches either."

Just a touch screen by the door.

No card reader, even. They couldn't know if it was PIN entry, voice recognition, fingerprint recognition, or even an iris scan.

It couldn't be opened, in other words.

"You thinking of escaping?"

"You're not?"

"Hmm."

Hazuki Makino. Ayumi Kono. Mio Tsuzuki. Hinako Sakura. Ritsuko Kisugi. And Rey Mao...

At this rate everyone would end up dead. Why? What for? What were they doing right now?

There was no other outcome; those girls were going to die. It was out of their control now.

But it wasn't out of their control. That was just silly. Damned if Shizue would let herself be killed.

"I am not going to die here!" Shizue screamed. The echoless room swallowed her voice.

CHAPTER 025

AYUMI CAME RUNNING.

Her efficient muscles moved in sync.

She was graceful like an animal.

Several men came running toward her from left and right.

They were wearing uniforms.

They were patrolmen.

They were saying something she couldn't hear.

At that moment, Hazuki was in the middle of a wide road slightly higher up looking down at the scene. What was Hazuki going to be scared of now?

Would her legs collapse and stop moving? Maybe she was scared and nervous and resisting internally a little, but she was going to swallow all those fears, swallow them and be okay and think nothing of this. That was how useless she was.

Ayumi came running at her.

She hit Hazuki on the head.

"What are you doing?!"

"I was—"

"Come here!"

She grabbed her arm. The touch of a human.

"Run!"

Hazuki screamed.

The area patrol approached.

From the front and from behind.

Hazuki was yanked by Ayumi, her body falling from the sky, and she ran.

She ran around to behind the building annex.

They came from all sides. Hazuki was thrown against the wall.

"Ayumi!"

A large group of area patrol officers gathered around Ayumi.

This is my fault.

Because Hazuki had come here without thinking.

"Stop it!" she yelped. Like a child.

Several area patrols ran toward Hazuki.

Please, no!

Something moved above Hazuki's head.

She looked up.

Cat.

On the ledge above them was Rey Mao.

Rey Mao flew off the wall to avoid hitting Hazuki and kicked the closest patrolman on her way down. She quickly spun around.

She brought her arms immediately back up and drove her fists into the patrolman's face.

"What are you doing here, Hazuki?!"

Ayumi slipped past her.

"Rey Mao!"

"Ayumi!"

Ayumi rushed to Hazuki's right to lure in her pursuers, and Rey Mao stood to Hazuki's left, fighting off several officers at once.

They stood nearly back to back, Hazuki in the middle, to protect her.

"Why did you come all the way here?"

"You got the message on the dove, right?"

The patrolmen regrouped, and the girls were now trapped against the wall.

"Now we're surrounded," Rey Mao said. "I was so well hidden in the corner too."

"You were exposed," Ayumi said. "They only thinned out the personnel here to lure you out. Their plan was to go after you when you slipped through the crack to escape. The area patrol is probably not allowed into the building. That's why I thought it would be easy to make contact."

Hazuki had gotten in their way.

"And do what then?"

"Trade places. There was something I needed to talk to you about."

"Trade places?"

With their backs still to each other, Rey Mao looked to Ayumi.

The lights on the officers' belts clicked on.

Those were their monitors.

Finally, one of the officers broke through the ranks and approached.

"Hey, you kids," he said with no nervousness. "What are you doing all huddled up? These are just a bunch of girls. Who's responsible for this?"

"I am," said one of the patrol officers. He showed his badge to the other one.

He read the badge with his own monitor and said, "This is no good. Obviously, protocol is to call the police. And I have to come out here to check out the scene? You've gone totally overboard. All these patrols for a few kids who've gotten lost on the grounds. Were you planning to intimidate them with your batons?" he said, slapping the baton one of the patrols was holding. "You've gone too far. Too far. I need to file a claim with D&S from prefectural headquarters. Are the employees under review? This is child abuse. Report it to the administration."

"But this girl, she was resisting us."

"Of course she was. I'm sure she's scared. Look at all of you. How many of you are there? At least thirty. Three kids versus thirty adults. What about your posts? What if terrorists attacked the main entrance?"

The man turned to the group and looked at the patrol officers with disdain. "There's been no burglary or violence. You say things like, 'We come in peace,' but what kind of patrol officer attacks a lost child? I'll take care of these kids," he said. He approached Hazuki and the others.

"Hi. I'm...oh, wait." He pulled up his card on the monitor and turned his display toward the girls.

Investigative Unit R Section Chief, Police Division, Shoji Takasugi.

He was the real thing.

"Now, what are you doing here? Where did you get in? The premises are vacant today for maintenance. I apologize, but could you explain your situation in brief for me? Our intruder alert system picked you up on the sensors. We saw you on our security cameras, and whenever that happens we have to get statements from whomever we apprehend." Takasugi spoke very politely.

He seemed normal. Unusually normal.

Yes, police information could very well have leaked. The two men who attacked Hazuki were also dressed like area patrols, and he was certainly no different. Even so...

It couldn't mean they were all bad.

That was impossible.

This couldn't be a police-wide, area patrol-wide conspiracy. In which case...

Hazuki looked at Ayumi. Ayumi was looking straight at Takasugi.

Rey Mao was looking for an out.

The police had an arrest warrant out for her.

Of course it was best for her to try to escape.

Ayumi grabbed Mao's arm as she made the slightest movement with her body. Rey Mao looked at Ayumi in her peripheral vision. Ayumi didn't take her eyes off Takasugi and pulled in Rey Mao even closer.

Ayumi was…What was she going to do?

Takasugi looked perplexed and turned his head slightly.

"Well, I'm sure you were scared. Let's just go inside for now, shall we. If you just tell me what happened I can release you quickly. Let's have something to drink. Is that okay?"

"Sure," Ayumi said.

Rey Mao widened her eyes and glanced at Ayumi's face, then turned her gaze toward Hazuki.

Hazuki felt the gravelly texture of the wall against her back and looked down.

"Let's go then," Takasugi said. He then turned to the thirty-odd patrol officers and barked at them to go back to their posts.

The patrol officers all lowered their heads and went away without a word. One rubbed his neck and walked with a limp, probably thanks to Rey Mao.

"Like I said before, we're doing maintenance today. Everyone in this area knows that, but you see, tomorrow is the anniversary of our founder's birth. There will be celebrations and everything, so we're fixing up the place today and tomorrow. You girls are from another area, aren't you?"

"Area 119."

"Ah, well, that's too bad," Takasugi said.

The patrols lined up at strategic points.

Takasugi and the girls climbed low neo-ceramic stairs with a mid-century tile pattern and passed a large terrace. They traversed a well-groomed garden on a walkway to an open courtyard. There, the path continued on a slight slope with stone steps.

"Normally the escalator is running. It's stopped today. You should be okay though. You're young," said the officer as he descended the stairs.

Rey Mao stopped for a moment.

Ayumi, sensing Mao's sensitivity, turned her head.

There were area patrols lined up along the steps. Hazuki and the others were still surrounded.

"The main entrance is over there. Now how did I make a wrong turn?" Takasugi said in a loud voice, then beckoned the girls forward.

"It's all right. You aren't in danger anymore. I just want to hear your story. Depending on the mitigating circumstances we might even let you go without having to contact the community center or your guardians. I mean, really, depending on the situation."

At the bottom of the stairs was a sign pointing toward a hall on the other end of which stood the main entrance. It was a ridiculously extravagant entrance made of neo-ceramic and reinforced glass.

They looked up.

A bright white structure appeared to burst upward through the air.

It looked very different from up close. It was grotesque.

"This is normally where you arrive when you come here from town. There's even a solar transport shuttle that runs directly from the residential district. But as I said, today's a day off. So…" Takasugi kept talking to no one in particular and showed his ID to a patrol officer.

"Good work. The intruder alert has been taken care of. We just need to process their surveillance per the usual. Oh, why don't I just process these girls?"

"Officer Takasugi, I still need them to show ID to enter the premises."

"Ah, that's all right. If we just let them in unregistered I can contact the security office myself. It'll be a bigger hassle to start up the system when everything's shut down. And just to process tracking devices."

A tracking device.

As if he'd heard her thinking that, Takasugi looked at Hazuki and smiled.

"The ceiling is not very high here, but the space is wide open. There are usually a lot of visitors on working days. Therefore simply swiping an ID doesn't suffice. We have to set a tracker on everyone's monitors so we know who is where throughout the compound. There's also a hospital. If an elderly visitor collapsed somewhere unattended, for example, or if a child gets lost. Just that when we're closed like this, the system isn't operational, and if you don't have your monitors, it becomes a real hassle to set the tracker. We have to get you special rental units. And on an off-day it's not just people like you but even the patrols who go around the grounds without these tracking units. Shall we go in then?" Takasugi had the patrol move to the side, passed his ID card against a hidden card reader adjacent to the large door in the middle of an even bigger gate, and finished by very deliberately pronouncing his name: *ta, ka, su, gi*.

The gate opened soundlessly.

"This is a voice-operated gate. Now go in, quickly. You can't get in or out without me."

Ayumi entered.

Hazuki also entered, prodded forward by Rey Mao.

Rey Mao then went in and Takasugi closed the gate behind them.

He turned around and said, "Keep it up," to the guard.

The entrance hall was at least four times as wide as the community center's racetrack.

The space was ventilated from very high up.

It was a wide-open space.

Still, the floor and the beams were all polished bright. In the middle of the hall was a marble statue of an elderly man in old clothing.

How tacky, Hazuki thought.

There were six wide glass pipes running up the face of the wall. They must have been capsule elevator shafts, but shafts weren't usually as long as these pipes were. Takasugi took them directly to the elevators and pointed up.

"Look, you can see. Up there. On the fifth floor is the interrogation room. Let's go there. We have beverages and...oh, I hope the dispenser is working today."

Takasugi pointed his hand above his head and the gate to the third pipe elevator opened.

Ayumi went in. Rey Mao went in. Then Hazuki.

The elevator let out a short melody and closed the doors. A faint G appeared and the girls glided up as if slipping. The floor of the entrance hall quickly disappeared.

After all that climbing and descending the hills. To think of how much energy Hazuki used to raise her own altitude. Now she was ascending in a matter of breaths.

"What time is it right now?" Ayumi asked Takasugi.

Takasugi nodded smartly and pulled up his terminal.

"It's 5:05 PM and twenty seconds."

"Thank you," Ayumi said.

They came out to what looked like a lounge.

There were tables, chairs, and drink dispensers lined up around the space.

Takasugi said, "This way," and proceeded to the rear of the room, swiped his ID card and uttered his name again, which opened a golden door.

"Please, come in."

It was a glossy hallway.

There were several doors.

Upon entering the hall, the golden door shut behind them.

"Let's see. Where shall we go..." Takasugi said as he playfully looked at each of the doors and finally chose one.

"Let's go in here."

The doors inside the hall were apparently not voice-operated.

"Please, enter. What would you all like to drink?"

It was a simple but classy-looking greeting room.

Takasugi stood by the door and gestured toward the room.

But Ayumi wouldn't move.

As if suspicious of her movements, Rey Mao, who had until then been initiating all the moves, gave Ayumi a curious look and then looked over at Takasugi. He was smiling. Rey Mao turned her face away and walked into the room. Hazuki too. It was just as she entered the room that Ayumi spoke.

"Mr. Takasugi?"

"Yes?"

It was just as he turned his head.

Takasugi disappeared from before Hazuki's eyes.

The door closed.

"What the?"

Rey Mao pushed Hazuki away.

She slammed her hands against the door.

Of course it wasn't going to open.

No door was going to open without an ID card.

"Ayumi! Ayumi!" Rey Mao yelled as she banged on the door.

"Hazuki, what just happened? What happened to Ayumi?"

"I didn't see anything. Just heard their voices."

"What did you hear them say?" Rey Mao said and grabbed Hazuki by the shoulders just as the door reopened.

Standing at the open door with her back to them was Ayumi.

She stepped into the room, and the door closed.

"Ayumi! What happened?"

"Nothing."

"Nothing? What about that patrolman?"

"He's over there."

"There?"

Rey Mao looked to the door.

It was closed.

She couldn't see anything.

Rey Mao kicked the door.

"Shit! We're trapped in here. What the hell were you thinking, Ayumi? He's a police officer. If we get stuck here there's no getting out. You guys might be all right, but what about me?"

"This is obviously a trap," Ayumi said at the door, her back still to Rey Mao.

"Trap?"

"That officer, Mr. Takasugi. He already knows all about us."

"He knows...all about us? But..."

He looked so normal.

One could say that Hazuki and the girls were clearly conducting themselves in an unusual manner. Anyone from the police who hadn't any idea what was going on would come into this situation and behave exactly like Takasugi.

"No," Rey Mao's face soured. "He's prefectural police. There's no way he wouldn't have known about me."

"But what if it were someone who just looked like you?"

"Huh?"

"That man said it would be a hassle to assign trackers to us without terminals. No girl walks around without a monitor these days. If they did, it would have to be because they are unregistered or just ran from home without their monitor because they were being attacked or something. Like us."

"But it wasn't like we told him we didn't have monitors. That's only *if*."

"When I asked him for the time, he pulled out his monitor without any questions. He didn't think anything about it. Normally if someone wanted to know the time they'd look at their own monitor. No one asks other people what time it is. If they did you'd ask them why they didn't have their own monitor. He told me the time because he knew I didn't have one."

"Then..." Rey Mao narrowed her eyes. "You walked into the trap on purpose?"

"I couldn't do anything unless I got inside. Besides, we're safer in here than outside."

Rey Mao and Hazuki called her out. "Ayumi?!"

"Watch out for Makino," Ayumi said.

"Watch out? What are you saying?"

"She thinks we're friends but we're not."

"Ayumi," said Mao.

"Just stop it." Ayumi sighed with her back to them.

Hazuki was at a loss for words and just stared at the white nape of Ayumi's neck.

"You can be her friend, Rey Mao. You're strong and can look after

Hazuki."

"What the hell are you going to do?"

"I don't know," Ayumi said. "But I can't stay here. I can't get saved with you."

"Can't…Why can't you? I don't understand what you're saying."

Ayumi stared at the door without answering.

"Ayumi. You aren't possibly thinking of taking on all the bad guys alone or anything stupid like that, are you? That's the dumbest thing I've ever heard. You think you're a superhero now?"

"No," Ayumi said. "I don't know who the bad guys are. I don't know what's supposed to be right or wrong. I don't believe in anything and have nothing to protect. I've never felt the need to defend anything."

"Then what is it? What the fuck are you going to do?" Rey Mao yelled.

"Ayumi, are you planning on rescuing the kid who got arrested?"

"Is there someone else in here I don't know about?" Rey Mao asked.

"Kisugi. It also sounds like Mio's been apprehended as well."

Are they all right?

"Mio? That idiot." Rey Mao sat in a chair. "She's always been weird."

Ayumi looked back and glanced at the girls, but said nothing.

"Ayumi, you talk about rescuing them, but we're about to be imprisoned. You know how many of them are outside. Who knows how many are inside? This is a war. It was hard enough just to hide from them. If someone really is being held captive here, of course you'll want to rescue them, but don't think *you* are the one to do it. Not alone."

"I didn't say I think I can do anything about it."

"What?"

"It's not like I don't want to rescue them."

"Ayumi," Hazuki said and reached out to touch her. Ayumi backed away.

"You have it all wrong."

"Wrong?"

"I, I can't be with you. I have no intention of being friends with you two."

"Why not?"

"I'm a *murderer*."

Ayumi kept looking forward and raised a hand.

In her hand was a knife.

From the knife dripped red blood.

"What? What did you just say? What did you just say, Ayumi?"

Hazuki looked at the floor. At her feet, it was red.

"I am the killer."

Ayumi turned around.

She was red from the neck up.

"I'm the one who killed Ryu Kawabata and Yuji Nakamura. Just now I killed the cop too."

"Idiot!" Rey Mao said. She rushed to the door.

It wouldn't open. She turned around.

Ayumi was holding the knife up by her face.

"A-Ayumi. Hey…"

"You might die if you stay with me."

Rey Mao's eyes widened, and she looked past Ayumi.

"Hazuki…"

Hazuki didn't understand what Ayumi was trying to say. "What *is* she saying?"

"That night. After I was attacked and blacked out, you killed that boy?"

"Yes. Afterward, I killed Kawabata."

"You're lying."

"I'm not. I spilled a lot of blood that day. I washed and I washed but the beastly smell wouldn't go away."

I smell like a beast.

"Then that day…Ayumi, you…"

That day, at that hour, Ayumi was…

"I'll be all right. I'm the killer. Just don't get me wrong. I didn't do it to protect Yabe or anything like you did. I didn't kill Kawabata to punish him either."

"They attacked you first, right? They had it in for you? Because you were a witness? Right? It was self-defense," Rey Mao said. "You had no choice."

"That's not what happened." Ayumi lowered her knife. "Kawabata noticed me and started to run away."

"R-run away?"

"Nakamura actually ran off. I had no intention of following him. I was just going to go home. But Kawabata tripped and fell. Then he said to me, 'You saw it, didn't you? Listen. Don't tell anyone. If you do, you'll be the one arrested,' Kawabata said. Thinking about it now, he probably already knew someone in the police force. Even if they killed Yabe, they couldn't be tied to the murder without a witness. That's how he spoke."

"They had a collaborator in the police?"

"I…killed Kawabata and decapitated him."

"Why? Why?!" Rey Mao screamed.

"I don't know either. I was scared, that much is certain. But it wasn't to protect myself. I had a clear motive to kill. I knew that if I took him on he'd die. Even a child would have seen that. But at the moment, I could think of nothing else."

"Nothing else?"

"I couldn't think of anything other than killing him."

Rey Mao gulped loudly and stepped back.

"It was the same with Nakamura," Ayumi said. "The night Yabe went to Makino's house, you followed the area patrol after they'd taken Yabe. It was then. I didn't lose the trail of Yabe and her patrols. It wasn't that I couldn't keep up. It just happened that I ran into Nakamura."

"Nakamura was there?"

"Yes," Ayumi said.

"The police were probably sheltering him. Mao…"

Rey Mao didn't respond.

"He's probably the one who ratted you out to the police. He would have told them about me too, but he didn't know I existed. You stood out because you're already an undocumented resident. I had no distinguishing characteristics. I was fine."

"As soon as they secured Yabe, the police insider probably informed Nakamura. On the other hand, they could have sent an area patrol car to the people who attacked Makino and apprehended Yabe. If she ended up in police custody, they couldn't kill her. I don't know why but whoever sent those guys wanted Nakamura to attack Yabe. Nakamura was scared when he saw me. He turned pale and ran. I chased him."

"Were you planning on killing him?" Rey Mao asked quietly. "Did you chase him down so you could kill him? *Answer me, Ayumi!*"

Rey Mao was crying.

Hazuki was tearless.

"No. I wanted to hear his story. I didn't think of killing him. But he was…"

Ayumi looked down at her blood-covered knife.

"He disappeared into the abandoned building in Section C near where Tsuzuki lived. I figured he was hiding in there. When I entered the building he screamed, 'Don't come in here! Don't come in here!' I…"

These aren't the only killers.

Killing people is real.

There's a killer right beside me.

"Am I really that frightening?" Ayumi asked.

"Ayumi…"

"Nakamura practically looked like a small animal who'd just encountered a bloodthirsty predator. I wasn't menacing him or anything. I didn't even take out a weapon. But…yeah. He was begging for his life and I killed him." Ayumi spoke in exactly the same way she always did. "I'm a murderer. I kill people that cross my path. I'm a man-eating wolf."

Rey Mao crept backward and sank into a chair.

"You still want to be my friend?"

Rey Mao turned her head away.

"Yes. That's the right response, Rey Mao. Don't look at me." Ayumi sounded sad. "You understand too, right, Hazuki?"

Hazuki just stared at Ayumi's clear eyes. She had no response.

"Ayumi, you…"

"I cast doubt upon you by not speaking up. I'm sorry about that. That's why I had to take your place. You didn't do anything wrong," Ayumi said as she drew an ID card from her pocket.

Takasugi's ID.

"So I'm going now. I don't know what's going to happen, but I have to go."

"Wait," Rey Mao said, still looking down.

"You can't leave now. I don't believe you," Rey Mao said.

"Even with this?" Ayumi held up the knife again. "I'm a murderer."

"Ayumi."

Hazuki stepped up to Ayumi.

"You rescued me, Ayumi."

"I did. I did rescue you, but I'm still a murderer. It won't matter. Not all the good deeds I've performed. I still have a stink on my hands that can't be scrubbed clean," Ayumi said, and raised her blood-drenched hands. "Look. These are the hands of a killer."

No.

"But Nakamura and Kawabata were killers too."

"That's no reason to kill them," Ayumi said. "Even if they were killers, villains. Whoever kills them is already worse than the killer himself, Makino. Murder is never right. I don't know between right and wrong or the difference between truth and falsehood, but I am certain of one thing. I am not a good person."

"That wasn't your first time, was it? Kawabata wasn't the first," Rey Mao said. "Who was it?" Rey Mao said quietly but distinctly. "What about it, Ayumi?"

"Stop it."

Hazuki stared at Rey Mao. "It's a lie. Ayumi's lying."

"Hazuki, she's...I'm sorry, but she's not lying," Rey Mao said.

Ayumi quietly started talking.

"The first time was in those hills."

"Hills?"

"Here. It's here I stopped being human."

"There? In those hills?"

"I used to walk along that freight road. I don't know why. When I moved to my new house I started walking on that road. I'd walk all afternoon because at night it would be trafficked with freight transporters. I'd spend the night in the hills and walk back the next morning. Then last summer, I was attacked by a man there."

"Attacked?"

"He happened to fall on top of me. I didn't think anyone else was there, so I was caught by surprise. That was stupid. Thinking no one would be out that far. But when I thought about it, it was only far from my home. It wouldn't be far for someone who lives in the area."

"Then what happened?" Rey Mao asked.

"I tried to run away and he hit me. Then he kicked me. He held me at knifepoint. I was scared, so I fought back with all my might. I even screamed. I didn't know what was going on. Then, suddenly, he stopped. He apologized."

"Apologized?"

"Yes. He got on his knees and lowered his head, said 'I'm sorry I scared you. That was wrong. I'm sorry.' He was in his mid-forties."

"Was he a pervert?"

"He said he was wrong in the head. Thirty years ago he'd killed a girl, and when he was found out, he killed his whole family, was arrested, taken to a hospital, and released several years later. He was examined, treated, and told he was okay."

Killing people is wrong.

"That's what he said to me. I told him I knew plenty well that it was wrong. *I've reflected upon it, regretted it, thought many times of killing myself.* He kept talking. Kept apologizing to me over and over. I was just scared. He was..."

They had been under the light of the full moon.

"He said there were times he couldn't get over it. Times he felt like breaking everything and nothing he could do about it. That's why..."

Ayumi looked at her knife.

"He bought this knife and started walking around with it, and the unfulfilled dreams, the dreams he couldn't satisfy, would be tempered. That's what he said. Then, with his head still lowered, he handed me the knife. I killed him," Ayumi said plainly.

"That was my first time."

"Why did you do it?"

"I don't know."

"Why did you kill him?"

"I told you, I don't know. If I knew, I wouldn't have done it," Ayumi said. "All I know is that I was being attacked and that I was scared. I was annoyed by his sorry way of explaining himself. But I didn't have any destructive motives. I wasn't trying to break him. I wasn't mad at him, and it wasn't spiteful. But when he handed me this knife..."

Ayumi held the knife up close to her face.

"With his head lowered, crying, yeah. It was a full moon. The round moon was high up in the night sky. And then...and I knew that was *the moment*."

"The moment?"

It was a brief moment.

A thousandth of a second. The slightest of openings.

"The very next second he was dead. A lot of blood spewed from the gash across his throat. I was confused and didn't know what to do, and for a whole day I just sat there staring at the dead body. Finally, I dug a hole, buried him. You saw it, Hazuki."

"That stone?"

That large stone.

Under that large stone.

"That's his grave. The grave I made for him. Since then I've been going back to the grave all the time."

"You were feeling guilty."

"No, I wasn't. The time of guilt has passed. Even a child could tell you that. There's no point in apologizing to a grave. That's just selfish. I just...I kept wondering why I did it. I decided to go to the police when I figured it all out," Ayumi said. "And I'm not just saying that. At the time, I wouldn't have been able to explain anything if they'd arrested me. If they'd asked why I did it, I wouldn't have been able to answer. It's the same now. I wasn't taking revenge against bad people. But at this rate,

I'm becoming a serial killer. I didn't do anything for the good of mankind. It wasn't to make up for lost friends. I'm just a murderer," Ayumi said, and let just a single tear fall.

"I talked with Miss Fuwa and gained some perspective. I finally understood that killing people is indeed wrong. That's why I…"

"You're not planning on killing yourself, are you? Because that would be unforgivable," Rey Mao said. "Don't make this some beautiful self-realization. That would be tacky. What about it, Ayumi?"

"I don't think about wanting to die."

"But it sure as hell sounds like you're prepared to die." Rey Mao lifted her head and slowly stood up. "I don't care if I have to use brute force, I'm not letting you go."

Ayumi looked at Rey Mao with a sad face. "You're a friend."

Rey Mao moved swiftly to the card reader to block it.

"Stop it, Rey Mao."

"No. You asked once if I liked protecting the weak. I couldn't answer then, but I want to now. I do. I am a petty humanist for narcissistic reasons. It's just like you said. I like rescuing cats, taking care of them. I'm a teenage braggart. I knew it as soon as you called me out. That's why I consider myself your friend," Rey Mao said. "Though I realize what a nuisance it must be for an undocumented resident to be saying that to you."

"Nuisance is right."

"Ayu…"

There was a knife at Mao's throat.

"You can't stop me."

"A-Ayumi."

"I'm going to say it again," Ayumi said. "I'm a weak fighter. I don't know how to fight. But I do know how to kill. All you can do is punch me. All I can do is kill you."

"Ayu—"

Hazuki approached.

"Ayumi."

"Don't come any closer, Hazuki."

"But—"

"I…I might kill you too."

"No. I don't want you to do that," Hazuki said.

"If I end up killing you, what am I going to do next? So don't tell me we're friends. Let me go. I'm sorry," Ayumi said, and withdrew the knife and put her hand on Rey Mao's shoulder to push her away from the door.

The door opened.

"Ayumi…"

The blood-soaked young woman turned toward Hazuki's voice.

"I'll be all right."

The door closed.

CHAPTER 026

IT SOUNDED LIKE thunder in the distance.

Shizue became aware of her sensitivity to sensory input.

"What was that sound just now?"

"It sounded like something just exploded. Maybe that guy fired his gun."

With his left arm held up in a sling made of his shirt, Kunugi grimaced. "I don't know how loud a handgun is supposed to be, but I do know how advanced the soundproofing is in a room of this build. The walls in this room in particular are made of the highest grade soundproof material."

"Yeah? That was a pretty loud sound then."

"A big bang, yes, but also at a very low register, so there was certainly a large reverberation as well. Of the entire building."

"Reverberation, eh?" Shizue said. "Well if that's the sound of some terrorists storming in with an ancient piece-of-shit tank borrowed from some third-world country in a civil war, then I'm glad to hear it. Otherwise, I'm sorry, but no civilized country right now has the weapons necessary to take down a building of this magnitude. Not even a bombing run would do the trick."

Kunugi visibly restrained himself from making pained expressions as he stood up.

"What are you doing? You'll just exhaust yourself if you try to stand. Why don't you just sit down?"

"Just in case. I'm an old man with old habits."

Boom. This time it was closer.

"That just lowered the voltage."

"Voltage?" Shizue looked up. The purplish light started blinking.

"Something's wrong."

"The twenty-year-old lamp in my room does that." Shizue's glare was interrupted before Kunugi could finish his joke.

The lights suddenly went out. They were sitting in dark silence. The light...

"Power outage?"

"Not in a building like this. There's a medical center in here after all. They'd have a backup generator, by law. They'd have at least a backup battery or some kind of power supply."

The touch screen was lit up.

This wasn't a power outage.

Random numbers ran across the screen of the touch screen, which then went blank.

"We can probably open the doors now."

Shizue flew at the door with her eyes on the red digits left glowing on the screen, and pushed.

"Hurry. Help me!"

"I can't see," Kunugi said as he approached her.

Shizue felt a groove under the door.

"Here."

She tried first to get her nails under it, and then her fingertips. It was heavy.

The door moved slightly with a groan. Just as she thought. She applied all her strength in pulling it up.

A window.

One more pane. Kunugi applied his right arm.

A low groan.

The door opened.

"Get out, now."

Shizue pushed Kunugi through the half-open door, then followed him out.

The hall was also pitch black.

"Somewhere..."

"A hiding place?"

Two or three flashes of light coursed through the hall, lighting it up for a moment.

At almost the same time the door to the microbe room slammed shut.

"Over there."

Shizue went toward the hall she thought would lead directly to the room Ishida was in. Kunugi followed her, dragging one bad leg.

"Hey. Don't leave this old fart in the dust."

"I can't do anything with a dead old fart. Hurry."

For some reason Kunugi stopped and sank when they reached what looked like a kitchenette.

"How did we get rescued?"

"We haven't been rescued yet. Someone's attacking this building though. Probably."

"Attack? This isn't a game."

"No…"

The first sound was a physical explosion.

The power outage after that though…

It was a key-lock override.

All the doors in the entire building were probably unlocked now.

Why?

Was it to get in or to get out?

It couldn't have been done from inside.

In which case…

Someone was coming in.

Shizue felt something beyond the hallway. She held up Kunugi as he tried to move, and looked around the corner.

It was Yudani and the Frenchman Arvil.

The thin man with the firearm and the large Frenchman were running down the hall in the other direction.

There was an elevator on the other side.

Neither of them passed by the microbe room and probably didn't notice anything.

The large ornamented door was open.

"Let's go, Kunugi. Ishida should be alone now."

"I want to say okay, but what do you plan on doing?"

"That insane, sorry excuse for a police lieutenant has to help us save the children."

Shizue ran out into the hall.

There was no sign of the violent guards.

The large door was still open.

No.

It was closing.

Shizue threw off her shoes and ran down the hall with all her might.

"Wait!"

Beyond the door, Ishida winced.

She would make it. She would throw her leg in.

Ishida's face showed incredulity, and he was unable to close the door for some reason. He simply withdrew into the room. His eyebrows furrowed with fear.

"Miss Fuwa…"

"What happened? Is it terrorists?"

"Well, it really looks like it might be."

"What did you say?"

Kunugi finally reached them. Shizue stepped into Ishida's room. She closed the ornamented door after Kunugi.

She heard the electric lock close.

"You're not surprised? You're letting us in."

"I don't mind. The room will get slightly dirty, but there's no way you're getting out." Ishida, looking ever disgusted, walked over to the desk.

"Wait. You think you're going to call those goons?"

"Relax. There's no need for them." Ishida sat down at his desk and looked at the wall behind him. "Right now, no one's looking for you. Just sit."

"What's the rush?"

Kunugi dragged his feet and sat down in the chair he'd started in.

"Hey, you."

"No need for formalities or anything," Ishida said.

One wrinkle formed on his brow.

Kunugi narrowed his bloodshot right eye and let out a *hmph*.

Ishida pulled up the monitor screen.

"Takasugi. Hey, Takasugi. Hmm? What's going on?"

"Did something happen to your Takasugi?" Kunugi asked.

"That's none of your business," Ishida said.

"Mr. Ishida. Is everything all right?"

"Yes. It's under control," sounded his voice. His face was on the screen. "The results of the experiment were quite satisfactory. I think you'll like what you see."

"Understood. But tell me, what's the situation with the earlier accident?"

"It hasn't reached here," Ishida said.

"Just the main entrance, then. Anything happen after that?"

"We're not sure ourselves," he replied.

There were what appeared to be area patrols in the background of the screen.

The image kept blurring.

The voices were also jarred.

It was noisy.

"What's going on? I can't hear you very well. Perhaps you can send it to me in writing."

The power lines was the last thing they heard clearly.

"Have you confirmed the identity of the intruder? Is there indeed an intruder?"

"Unconfirmed," the zig-zagging image said in a broken voice.

"Understood," Ishida said. He tried paging Takasugi again but closed the call when Takasugi didn't answer.

Then Ishida looked over his shoulder again.

"Why are you so anxious? Is there something important in the wall behind you?"

"W-what did you say? You're not…It's nothing."

For the first time Ishida appeared worried.

"What? It's all right. Tell us about it," Kunugi said. "I'm getting a life sentence, remember? I'm never going to find work in society again. This little lady, Miss Fuwa—I'm going to kill her, right? So you can tell us what you're doing. Why you're killing so many people every year. Oh wait, that's right. You're not killing anybody. I don't know what I'm talking about. But I'd like to know why you're *not* doing any of this. How about it, Ishida?

"You're farming organs from children, aren't you? Say it. What are you doing?"

Ishida glared hard at Kunugi, then spoke.

"I did it all for my great-grandfather."

"Great-grandfather? Yutaro Suzuki you mean? Don't tell me you're offering sacrifices to his statue. I know his believers have practically formed a religion, but—"

"I'm not a believer, but I won't forgive any mockery of my great-grandfather."

"Worshipping the dead isn't a religion? Have times changed? When I was young…well, I was pretty oblivious to religion growing up. Still, isn't ancestor-worship a religious thing?" Kunugi asked.

"Honoring one's ancestors is not technically religious," Shizue answered. "Obviously it's a tenet of many religions, and depending on the region there will be many indigenous informal spiritual tendencies, but that's a little different from so-called religions that own a complete dogma."

"Is that right?" Kunugi feigned ignorance.

Ishida hysterically slammed his fist on his desk.

"You're talking like idiots and we're in a state of emergency. Shut up now!"

"I can't. I don't know about you but this is in no way a state of emergency for me. I mean, unless you count the fact that little girls are being killed for some dead old fuck that was born over a hundred years ago. Then yeah, emergency."

"What did you just say?" Ishida became excited. "Dead? Who's dead?"

"Who's...are you completely off your meds?"

"I'd like to ask you the same."

Ishida stood up.

"My great-grandfather, Yutaro Suzuki, *still lives*."

"What?"

"You didn't know? Tomorrow is his 115th birthday."

"You mean birthday anniversary. I don't care how crazy you are, you shouldn't say stupid things like that. Yutaro Suzuki died over twenty years ago."

"He lives!" Ishida yelled. "Don't you know why this building was built?"

"You said it had something to do with changing the name of the corporation and honoring your dead old grandpa. Am I wrong?"

"Listen. This building was erected only for my great-grandfather. To collect and exhibit all of his achievements, his goals, his ideology, his collections, his history, all of it. Of course, at the very top floor is Yutaro Suzuki himself. We need him to continue on, here, with us."

"Continue on..."

"Yutaro Suzuki shall never die."

"Y-you crazy idiot." Kunugi's swollen eyes widened. "You're saying some crazy things. You've gone completely out of your mind."

"But I haven't," Ishida said as he got up from the desk. "This country needs my great-grandfather. He's a necessary man. Do you understand or don't you?" Ishida asked over and over, stepping toward Kunugi. "Listen, Kunugi. It won't matter if a little piece of shit like you lives or dies, but if he dies, the world as you know it will simply turn inside out. His influence is greater than you could possibly fathom. If this volatile world can maintain happiness and order it's because he's alive."

Ishida placed his hands on the back of Kunugi's chair and looked into his eyes.

"Now do you understand?"

"Of course I don't."

"That man is order. He is order itself. And he's morality. Keeping him alive is the only way to protect the balance of this country, which has lost its way—no, which has completely gone to rot. Yutaro Suzuki is the last stronghold of preservation of this world. That's why it's of utmost importance to keep him alive. At all costs."

He must have gone insane.

This was not a *perversion*. That kind of language was derogatory. However, he'd clearly lost his way. This man, Ishida, was no longer a resident of this reality.

Shizue started shivering.

"So, so, so..." Ishida said.

"So we built this place specifically for the purpose of keeping him alive. We spent fortunes upon fortunes building a state-of-the-art technological facility with the best minds and medical labs. I will do anything and everything to protect the life of my great-grandfather. So..."

"You need the organs of dead girls. That doesn't sound very 'state-of-the-art' to me," Kunugi said. "Wasn't cloning technology the cornerstone of your company's bioengineering reputation? Why do you need to harvest the organs of murdered innocents? Are you transplanting them? Or are you saying there are healing properties in the human body? You could search the entire world and never find anyone who would believe your old make-believe story."

Ishida suddenly went expressionless and moved away from Kunugi.

"You really are stupid."

"What did you call me?"

"Transplants? Healing properties? There's no such thing as a cure. And if there were, there wouldn't be a need to get it from humans."

"Then why?" Kunugi looked up.

"Why it's their taste, of course. *Their taste*," Ishida said.

CHAPTER 027

"WHAT THE HELL!" Rey Mao kicked the door. "Why'd she do that?"

It sounded like she was crying.

Hazuki just stood there wringing her hands.

Tears streamed down her face.

Her emotions ran amok and couldn't be controlled.

Yet she couldn't utter a sound nor move an inch.

And it wasn't as if anything had happened yet.

No.

It wasn't like anything had physically changed in Hazuki.

Whatever Ayumi had done in the past, whatever she might do in the future, whatever the outcome, Hazuki didn't have to have anything to do with it. It wasn't as though Hazuki were in pain, suffering, dying.

Still.

What was this trembling?

This disturbance she could do nothing about, the feeling she knew she wasn't going to be able to control. When it wasn't her life.

"That bitch," Rey Mao said and kicked the door again. And it was at that moment.

Boom. A low reverberation shook the whole room.

"W-what was that?"

Rey Mao lost her balance for a moment and braced herself against a wall.

"What was that? You think that was Ayumi?"

What did Ayumi do? No, it was backwards.

Rey Mao apparently thought the same thing. She narrowed her eyes and furrowed her brow and said, "She must have been caught."

That face went dark for a second. She thought maybe it was the tears, but it was different. The lights started to blink out.

Rey Mao looked up. Hazuki wiped her tears.

It was probably the window outside, facing the ventilation system. The lights in the entrance hall were blinking too.

The lights went out.

"Power outage?"

"Huh?"

A power outage.

The card reader on the door emitted a thin red light. The point of light slowly drifted downward.

"Open."

"What?"

"The door will open now," Hazuki said. She ran toward the door.

It opened without any difficulty.

Hazuki jolted Rey Mao to action.

This.

"The door's probably going to close in thirty seconds, so hurry."

"What's going on?" Rey Mao said as she left the room.

The door closed.

They heard it lock.

This was Mio's magic. Mio. She was alive.

Just as she started to utter the thought, Hazuki stepped into something soft.

She slipped on whatever it was and fell straight on her back. She put her hands on the ground to push herself up.

"What is this?"

She looked at her hands. They were coated in something red and viscous. It was warm.

That smell.

She looked down.

"Aahhh! Aaahhhhhhh!"

With her bottom still on the floor Hazuki lifted her knees and let her legs extend in the darkness. Her feet slipped again and kicked the soft thing over and over.

The soft thing.

Its eyes were open and looking straight at Hazuki.

No, his face was all wrong. *It* was not looking at anything.

Hazuki was splayed on the floor covered in blood.

At the end of her feet was Takasugi, on his side, eyes wide open.

"Aghhhhhh aghhhh!"

"Hazuki! Hazuki!" Rey Mao called at her. "Get it together, Hazuki. Come on!"

Rey Mao pulled Hazuki away from the corpse and stood her up. She managed to stand, but her legs were shaking, on top of which her breath was stopped, and she couldn't move. Her line of sight kept landing on

Takasugi, whose pupils couldn't have been looking at her anymore.

Hazuki kept screaming like a toddler.

Rey Mao firmly grasped Hazuki's shoulders.

"It's all right. It's just a corpse."

"J-just?"

"Is this your first time seeing a dead body?" Rey Mao asked. Hazuki thought she was nodding, but she was shaking so violently she didn't know if she was communicating. Rey Mao hugged Hazuki as hard as she could.

"Hey! That should not scare you. It's not a bad thing. That's what dead people look like. It's just a *thing* now. So calm down."

Calm down.

Rey Mao's straight hair fell across Hazuki's shoulders.

These murders...this is real.

This was what it looked like. This wasn't a fabrication. When you killed someone, they died.

"A-Ayumi..."

"She really did this. What are we going to do, Hazuki?" Rey Mao asked. She let go of Hazuki and placed her hands on Hazuki's shoulders. "She told me to protect you, and I'm going to. Now. What are we going to do?" Rey Mao asked again.

"Do we find somewhere to hide? Do we try to escape? Or..."

Hazuki was still staring at the corpse.

"Stop looking at it," Rey Mao said. "It's nothing to hide, but it's nothing to stare at either. More importantly..." Rey Mao looked down the hall. "How do we get out of here? The door happened to open just now, but the rest of them are closed."

"It wasn't a coincidence."

"What do you mean?"

"That was Mio," Hazuki said.

And at that moment.

Boom. Another great sound.

Through white smoke, the steel door at the end of the hallway burst open. A streak of what looked like lightning arced down the hall. The door fell over onto the floor and bounced once. There was an echo, then silence.

Through the smoke and dust appeared the figure of a human.

"M..."

"Mio!"

Within the cloud of dust stood Mio Tsuzuki, her face scrunched up. She was wearing orange goggles and a metal chest protector from which hung several cables and machines crisscrossing her body. On her hip was probably the battery. And attached to her right arm from shoulder to hand was something that looked like an enormous thermometer, like an old antiaircraft weapon Hazuki had seen in pictures. No, a bazooka.

"Sorry to keep you waiting," Mio said.

"Mio, what are you doing here? What is this getup? You look like some fictional deformée character. Like something from a history book."

"Look who's talking, Cat! And to think I came all the way out here to rescue you. Oh, Makino, you're still alive! Were you crying again? You're such a child. Stop crying. Let's go."

"Let's go where? Seriously, what are you wearing? It looks really clumsy."

"It's Turtle, Mark III. It's running on plasma. But don't think it just spews plasma. It has many more functions than that. The destructive power of plasma is frequently misunderstood. But here I've made it portable. I'm carrying a tremendous load here. I just blew open the main entrance with this thing. What a commotion! Almost all the patrol officers went running. So I came through where no one was left manning their stations."

"Just because you're a legitimate citizen doesn't mean you can do whatever you want."

"Shut up," Mio said, then noticed *the thing* behind Hazuki.

Hazuki turned around.

Mio...

"Did Ayumi do that?" she asked.

"Mio. You knew?"

"I didn't. But after thinking about it I did. She killed Kawabata and Nakamura."

"How did you know?"

"I'm a genius, remember?" Mio said. "Now...I've inputted information about this entire building here. The design of the building, floorplans, building materials, even its valuation. Between what Makino told me and the police stranding me, I was able to do a lot of preparation. First..." Mio pulled out a monitor. The data reflected on the surface of her goggles.

"This building was designed as a hospital. The lower part of the building is all recreational—nothing vital. But there is one room in here that looks extremely peculiar, no matter how you look at it."

The data kept streaming across her goggles.

"Here it is. On the fourteenth floor there's a restaurant. Is it a kitchen?"

"How should I know?" Rey Mao said.

"Only you can see this, idiot. Never mind. Anyway, the whole floor is a restaurant, and so obviously there's a kitchen. However, connected to the kitchen is what looks like a medical operating room. The equipment and goods are all medical."

"Well, this is a hospital, like you said."

"But this is an eating facility. A place for people to eat. There's a room filled with state-of-the-art medical equipment right in the middle of that floor. It's all medical equipment. So why is it all connected to a kitchen and not another hospital floor?"

"Who knows?"

"That's why we need to go there," Mio said as she slid over a compartment on her plasma vest, and added, "Fourteenth floor."

"That's why we need to what? What are you saying?"

"Are you slow or something? It's the only room in the building with a purpose we don't understand. Based on the size, I'm positive that's where they've kept the children. If they're not there it's over. On top of which, it's not just Kisugi anymore. They captured Sakura too."

"You mean that girl, Hinako?"

"Yeah, Funeral Girl," Mio said.

"What do you plan on doing?"

"It's going to take too long to figure out all the ins and outs of this place, so I'm busting down every door."

Rey Mao placed her hand on top of what looked like the nose of Mio's gun. "Stop it."

"Don't touch that! You could get hurt."

"Don't make so much noise. You'll attract attention."

"There's practically no one here."

Mio lowered her plasma gun.

"How do you know?" Rey Mao asked.

"Hey, Cat. Are you forgetting what I am?"

"No, you're an idiot."

"A genius. And geniuses are always thoroughly prepared. I got all the security system data. You see, in this great big compound there aren't more than a few people whose presence I can confirm. The police force outside numbers around two hundred, and they might be sending reinforcements because of the noise I made, but none of them can come inside."

"Can't come inside? Why? What if something happens inside?"

"Something *did* happen," Mio said, and smiled. "It's just the agreement that was made. Contractually speaking it's a win-win. The area patrols are paid contractors after all. On top of which, the security guards are not moving. And if you're wondering why, well in addition to the few people who are inside, there are several people imprisoned here along with us. Normally if you fudged the data on entrants we could fool them, but when the compound is closed to business like today, there's no point in deceiving anyone. There's no big difference between three thousand and three thousand five hundred people, but there's a world of difference between ten and fifteen people. The proportions are small today."

"He said it was a maintenance day or something...that dead man over there. Are there not any cleaning people or anything?" Hazuki asked.

"None. Maintenance ended yesterday. Taking out the trash here doesn't take more than two days. Building maintenance is handled by a D&S affiliate company. They're done with product inspection of the equipment they leased to do maintenance on things like air-conditioning, and have even settled their invoices. Today's supposed to have been a prep day for tomorrow, but it's probably not really."

"You're saying it's something else?"

"Of course. There are only two police affiliates here able to confirm entries into the building. And then two more area patrols on top of that. And for some reason, three technicians for the kitchen. Seven of them altogether. No building chiefs or staff. Isn't that odd? Are those seven people even able to make this building run?"

"What do you mean *run*?" Mao asked.

"Look. You guys are assholes, so maybe you don't have strong feelings about this, but it takes a lot of money to operate a living space for civilized human beings. This building especially."

"You're saying this is a lot of money moving for too few people."

"Even to run a face-recognition system takes time and increases costs tremendously. Running the electricity in this building for one day could feed an undocumented resident like you for a whole year. I mean that's just simple math. Only the outside patrols are on super alert."

Mio made a noise with her plasma gun and swung it over her shoulder.

"So I decided to run with it. If I could take down the seven people in here, I could rescue the captives. I could even avenge the dead. It's not like I have no chance of success."

"Take down…" Hazuki muttered.

It's wrong to kill people.

"Wait, Mio. When you say 'take down the people'…you can't kill them."

"We're the ones getting killed here."

"That doesn't mean we should kill them. It's…"

Hazuki thought about what Ayumi had said.

No, this unbearable thought was all Hazuki's.

"I know all this. C'mon," Mio said.

"What you're worried about is dealing with the simulation. In old fictions, people would go on and on about love and beliefs, to be at peace about killing everyone. Even I know that those things don't mean anything anymore."

"Then…"

"Listen. Maybe you'll understand this, Hazuki. Whatever else happens, we need to save the captives and escape from here. It's no use ending up dead. If you keep objecting, we'll both get killed. Everyone will die. The enemy is not hesitating. They've already killed dozens of people."

But…

"There was even a time when they would have been acquitted. I'm not saying I'm going to bludgeon everyone. If everyone survives that's great. Think positive! But in the meantime, I want to survive this. Eat or be eaten.

"Now move," Mio said. She brandished her weapon again.

A haze of warm vapor rose up around Mio.

The gauge lamp on the weapon turned on. Small blue bolts of lightning crackled around the gun.

The very next moment.

The wall fell down. Mio fell back. Hazuki held her face with both hands.

"Ow! Shit, now I feel funny. Did my electric shield go down or something? But look. Structurally, this is the weakest point of the hall walls. What do you think? Not bad, right? Architecture is so funny."

Mio climbed through the hole in the wall.

"You're insane," Rey Mao said as she went over to Hazuki, who was still crouched with her face in her hands. Mao placed a hand on Hazuki's shoulder. "Hazuki. She's stupid and crazy, but for now I think she's right. If we sit here and do nothing we'll get killed. I don't want to kill anyone either, but I also don't want to get killed."

Beyond the collapsed wall was yet another hall.

"Earlier there were gates on either side to keep the room sealed. You can't get in here directly from either the main way or the back gate. But you take down one flimsy wall and look. An emergency stairwell not normally used."

Mio started climbing the stairs, complaining about how heavy her gun was as she went.

"Will you be okay?" Rey Mao asked. She patted Hazuki's back. Hazuki nodded.

Rey Mao ran up the stairs.

Hazuki followed.

On the elevator this would have taken mere seconds.

Everything shared the same inorganic look.

The sixth, seventh, eighth floor, all looked identical. All it did was elevate. Only the motion let them know how high they were. Only the physical exertion let them know how much time had passed.

"Finally!" Mio yelped. The word reverberated across the stairwell. "This is it. My footing is bad, so I can't fire this gun."

Mio withdrew a universal pass-card from the weapon and slid it through the reader.

The gate labeled 14 opened.

"See how much easier that was! What were you thinking?" Hazuki asked.

"You can call me Crasher Mio. Let's go."

Mio stepped onto the floor.

No one was in the hall.

"The restaurant is over there."

"And that room?"

Mio lowered her body and scoped out the area.

No, she was reading data from the monitor built in to her weapon.

"There are people here."

Hurry. Mio ran to the right.

Rey Mao soundlessly followed Mio and looked around the corner.

She truly looked like an animal.

She signaled for them to come. Mio advanced.

Hazuki followed.

"That's the kitchen. It's huge."

"That big?"

"I thought they cooked in a factory. Boy, was I wrong."

"What do you mean? You've seen me cooking. When you were little I was even still cooking real animals," Rey Mao said.

"I thought that was some religious activity performed by undocumenteds. I was oblivious about religion back then too."

Mio opened the gate to the kitchen with her card.

"This is an antibacterial gate. It *is* a factory. Like we have time to get sterilized," Mio said, and punched some numbers on her keyboard.

Two gates opened simultaneously.

"What do you think? I put it in emergency mode. I've just saved millions of bacterial lives."

The space inside was wide.

There were sinks and preparation tables all along the room. There were heat-treating devices and equipment, and large restaurant-style double doors.

"Look, a freezer," Mio said and suddenly her face went serious. "What if there are humans in there?" She let out a short laugh and went back to being serious.

This wasn't a joke.

"Where's that room?" Rey Mao said, all the while looking out the entrance.

"And, does this door not close now?"

"Not when it's set on emergency mode. If there were a fire or something everyone would get trapped inside and die. It's a trade-off with the bacteria for a second, so just bear with me. Let's see…"

Mio looked up. She was reading data.

Hazuki looked around the kitchen.

"Uh-oh."

The double doors. No unauthorized personnel allowed.

"Holy cow, Hazuki," Mio said.

Just then.

"Ayumi," Rey Mao called out.

Rey Mao fled to the hall before Hazuki could turn her head.

"Ayumi?"

She's here?

They heard a man, howling.

Hazuki sped to the gate.

"Don't come in here!"

It was Ayumi.

Rey Mao's back, holding steady. Beyond it…

The man with the peacock tattoo on his head.

The man who had attacked Hazuki.

He was holding a knife.

Beyond him.

Ayumi standing with her legs apart.

Ayumi stared down the man.

They were frozen.

Can't move.

Can't move.

Can't move.

Only Ayumi.

Only Ayumi's mouth moved.

"Cat. Do as I asked."

The man brandished his knife.

The man...

He barked like an animal and leapt at Ayumi. Ayumi ran with great agility. She was fast.

Rey Mao, confused for a second, turned around.

"Go back inside."

"But, Ayumi..."

"Leave her!" Rey Mao said. She pushed Hazuki past the gate. "I promised. Our kind don't break promises we make with friends. We're just getting in their way."

Inside, Mio was making annoyed sounds.

"What's this 'no unauthorized personnel' bullshit. I don't have time for passwords. Let's try this."

A low rumbling sound.

Sparks flew all around her, and snakelike lightning tendrils ran the course of the stainless steel. All the lights on her electric pack were turned on. The vapors rose.

The gauge sputtered out, and they heard the sound of glass breaking.

The double doors disappeared.

"I'm practically a terrorist. This is a serious crime. No lawyer's going to represent me."

Mio went inside.

Hazuki kept looking backward.

Rey Mao shook her head slightly. Her hair swayed.

Inside...

"Is that an operating table? This is—"

"No..."

"It's a countertop," Rey Mao said.

"Countertop? Look at this thing. It's..."

"Who's there?" Rey Mao yelled out.

A man in a white lab coat was crouched behind the oscilloscope. He was wearing a mask. "W-what the…Hey, who are you? Are you terrorists?"

"We're just little girls," Mio said as she gave the man the once-over. "We're immature little girls. Mister, are you a criminal?"

"C-criminal?"

"You killed them. Our friends."

"Friends? What are you talking about?"

"The people your generation thought weren't worth keeping around because they were tacky."

"*What?*"

"The ones who are tacky because the generation before you thought it was okay to do whatever they wanted."

Mio had her weapon aimed.

"Stop it, Mio!"

"I know. I'm just intimidating him. I have to be intimidating to intimidate. So if you're scared, old man, bring out the other little girls you kidnapped."

The man crept back to the wall. Then.

The other door.

"They're terrorists! Protect the food!" the man yelled. He hit the screen of the touch panel and grabbed for the emergency receiver.

Another door locked. Rey Mao kicked the receiver right out of the man's hand.

The emergency receiver flew across the room.

"No use calling anyone."

Rey Mao grabbed the man in white by his collar and threw him onto the operating table, no, the countertop.

The medical equipment fell over and crashed to the floor, sparking and smoking. Rey Mao pinned the man to the countertop.

"Hey. Did you just say 'food'?" she asked.

The man's eyes widened as he looked at Rey Mao.

Rey Mao looked right back at him.

"What does that mean?"

His mask fell off.

"You girls…"

He couldn't mean…

He couldn't possibly mean…

"Don't tell me you are preparing *humans* for consumption here. Are you?" Rey Mao struck the man again.

"Answer me. Answer me answer me answer me. Hurry up and answer me!"

"Y-yes. Well, n-no."

"Which is it?"

"W-we use the organs."

"What the hell!" Mio yelled.

"Don't be stupid. This is too stupid. In this age, when you're not even supposed to kill or eat animals, you're…humans? What is this?" She smacked him across the face. "Hey, you! Doesn't your company make near flawless imitations of meat? You are making enormous amounts of money exporting that food across the entire world. You changed laws to gain this monopoly. So why humans?"

"The taste."

"The taste?"

"We weren't able to re-create the flavor. The flavor he wanted. We developed great synthetic ingredients and hybrid products, but it seems there was no comparison to the real thing. W-we had very few samples, I mean none of us had ever…we'd never tried it, so we d-didn't know what it t-tastes…"

"Of course not!" Rey Mao yelled and hit the man again. "Why would you go and eat another human being? You're crazy," Rey Mao said. She yanked him off the countertop and held him up by the arms, leaving his feet to dangle.

They heard the door unlock.

"Watch out, Cat!" Hazuki yelped.

Two men flew through the doors.

Spray guns.

The room went white. Hazuki's eyes hurt. She couldn't stop tearing up.

"You think blinding me will get you anywhere?" Rey Mao's voice.

A silhouette appeared in the white smoke. Some men holding metal batons approached them.

The heavy object echoed across the emptiness. The sound of jostling. A short scream.

Something fell on top of something else. The sharp sound of a firing weapon, and then the sound of something breaking.

The smoke gradually drifted to the floor, leaving a rug of white clouds coating it.

Rey Mao stood there with a pained expression.

With her left hand she held one man by his collar. Her right hand dug into his throat.

His neck broke. Rey Mao let go. With his head nearly completely turned around, the man slipped onto the floor, sinking into the smoke.

The other man...

The other man's head was crammed into the readout screen of an electric gauge. After shaking a few moments, his body stopped moving.

The man on the operating table was on his side, quivering. There was a large operating knife in his chest. One of the other men had been wielding it. He must have been caught in the crossfire. The red stain on his white coat kept spreading. It streamed over the side of the countertop, a thread of red liquid pouring into the white smoke. The man turned his eyes toward his own blood and, with his eyes still wide open, stopped moving.

He'd been killed with an operating knife on the very operating table where he'd vivisected so many humans before.

"I killed him," Rey Mao said. "I knew from experience."

"Rey Mao..."

"It's just like she said," Rey Mao said and looked at her hands. "I knew that if I dug in at that angle, with that pressure, I could break his neck. I knew that my hands were lethal weapons. But at that moment, I could think of nothing else."

Nothing except killing a human being.

"So this is what it's like," Rey Mao said. "He had a life. He probably had feelings and dreams too. And it was so easy to—"

"Easy to *get* killed too, Cat," Mio said. "If you hadn't done it, we would have ended up like them. The real crime is throwing a bunch of girls into a 'kill or be killed' scenario. We didn't walk into this situation on purpose. Listen, Rey Mao, this isn't just your responsibility. We're culpable too. We're also all responsible for the guy who was here alone at first doing who knows what. We'll redeem ourselves after it's all over. If we survive, that is."

"You're not bothered," Rey Mao said with a dark expression on her face.

Hazuki closed her eyes, but it wasn't as though she didn't want to face the reality.

She understood Ayumi's feelings, Rey Mao's feelings, Mio's words.

She was angry too. She didn't know why, but she felt like fighting back.

Hazuki thought it would be exhilarating to take all the bad people in the world and obliterate them.

But...

She also thought it sounded horrible. She thought it was mean.

Animals eat other animals.

She thought that was sad.

But.

She wondered what life was.

And that was why she closed her eyes.

"This is no time for pondering," Mio said. "If we dilly-dally we won't be able to think about either crimes or punishments."

So she went into the room from which the men had appeared.

"Come," Mio said.

Inside was a girl wearing an operating gown, sleeping.

She was held down by sturdy-looking restraints. There was something attached to her mouth.

Mio drew up some data with her goggles.

"Umm. This is Ritsuko Kisugi herself. Are you okay? You didn't get eaten yet, did you?"

Mio looked under the bed and found the release to the restraints.

"No, you haven't been eaten yet. I'm Tsuzuki. This is Makino. That's Rey Mao. Hey, are you all right?"

Ritsuko Kisugi sat up and pulled out the object in her mouth. "What's going on? What is it this time?"

"Nothing. We came to save you. We committed a major crime and came as quickly as we could. You were about to be eaten. Aren't you scared at all?"

"I-I know. I *am* scared. I thought it was all over for me. There's another one here. In there."

There was a heavy-looking metal door with a large handle.

Rey Mao rushed over.

Inside that room was Hinako Sakura, seated.

"All right!" Mio said.

CHAPTER 028

SOMETHING PAINFUL CAME up from the back of her throat.

It didn't matter how thoroughly one cleaned one's body, it was filled with germs. It was filthy.

Shizue brought her hand up to her mouth.

She started heaving, her stomach convulsing.

Kunugi was taken aback as well. He didn't have the words. It felt like a practical joke. A joke that had gone too far. But it wasn't a joke.

Little girls were being kidnapped and killed for their organs to be eaten.

On top of which the people behind it were in the police force.

It was absurd. Even the worst broadcast channels would never broadcast this kind of story. Not even a hundred years ago would such a ridiculous story ever be written.

There was no way this could be real.

But...

The man in charge, Ishida, apprised them, candidly.

His stomach turned. The fluids in his stomach coursed the wrong way. He couldn't breathe.

He didn't want to share the air this man breathed.

"My great-grandfather, Yutaro Suzuki...not even I know the full extent of his influence on the world today."

Kunugi didn't want to know any of this. He didn't want to hear Ishida's voice.

"He started with nothing and built himself up. I'm sure there are two sides to his story. But as a result, the core systems of this country have been hugely influenced by him. My great-grandfather's power went beyond just nation-building."

"That's why he's allowed to *eat* human beings?" Kunugi's parched voice finally put an end to Ishida's talking. "Important people get to eat humans?"

"As I said before, we have to do everything in our power to keep him alive and happy."

"I can't see why. You're deluded. I don't even believe he's really alive."

"But of course he is. Though he's withdrawn himself from politics and the like."

"What do you mean, politics?"

"Oh, various things. But staying registered was not good for keeping him alive."

"You idiot!" Kunugi was stammering. He had nothing to add. Not even Shizue could think of an appropriate response to the unreal things coming out of Ishida's mouth. There was no vocabulary for it.

"He's in great health," Ishida said. "He loves watching old historical films. His mind works perfectly and he still remembers everything. His vision hasn't deteriorated, and he hasn't lost the power of speech. Unfortunately his muscles have atrophied, so he is bedridden."

"Of course he is," Kunugi said. "Life expectancy has gone up, and so has the population of seniors, but it's only one small percentage of them that are actually healthy. Ninety percent of them have learned to live again after overcoming some kind of disease. A 115-year-old man walking around would have to be some kind of monster. I take that back, he *is* a monster."

"Take that back," Ishida said. "Did you hear this, Miss Fuwa? He just used discriminatory terminology. Right? There's nothing to indicate he is infirm, but just because he's old, he's discriminating against my great-grandfather. Isn't it a person's right to be whatever age he can, to eat what he wants? Those things shouldn't affect our judgment of an individual's character. To call him a monster is outrageous."

"The kind of person who kills humans in order to eat them doesn't deserve that right," Kunugi yelled.

"That's a problematic statement."

"Damn right it is. It's derogatory, yes. I don't care. It's my own private opinion. Are you going to sue me or something? Oh but wait, none of your surveillance equipment is working. I can say whatever I want and there won't be any proof of it."

Ishida shot him a cold look.

Kunugi rubbed his bad arm.

"There's no record of you attacking me either. There's no data, so it's like none of this happened."

"Didn't I already mention I create the data?"

"Gah!" Kunugi yelled. "Didn't I tell you I'm stupid? I've been trying to understand this unusual situation for a while now, and I still don't get it."

Ishida turned just his face toward Kunugi.

"I mean because your great-grandfather's firm produces synthetic meat, right? It's just like the real thing. But is that just no match for the real thing either? Are you putting one over on everyone because our tastes have deteriorated?"

"SVC's food products have been widely acclaimed the world over. Humanity's past food culture couldn't sustain itself. No company could keep providing the raw ingredients of cuisine forever. Various industries agreed on this point and made a joint statement. Even you should know that."

"It's because I know it that I'm asking, why this?"

"Why what?"

"Don't kill animals. Protect the earth. There's not enough food for everyone. I understand all that. It's all true. If we can concoct meat or fish with vitamins and chemicals, then do it. I get it. But—"

"Yes…it's all true. I understand what you are saying, Kunugi. In fact Yutaro Suzuki was quite instrumental in the movement for preservation of all life, right? In fact he was an honorary trustee of the International Endangered Animal Protection Foundation, and he founded the Marine Life Ecology Restoration Project."

"In his lifetime," Shizue said. She swallowed hard.

She didn't know Yutaro Suzuki so much as the spearhead of the bio-engineering revolution, but rather for those acts—the preservation of life. An antiquated sense of love for animals; a champion of the cause who had a profound influence on the movement.

"He was also a big part of the ban on commercial fishing and helped found the national nature preservation department."

"Those are all my great-grandfather's accomplishments, Miss Fuwa," Ishida said.

"Why does a person like that eat humans?"

"That's why he went into the business of making synthetic meats in the first place," Ishida said.

"I don't understand."

"My great-grandfather fought in that ridiculous war and met a truly horrible fate. He died there. But what brought him back to life was human meat," Ishida said.

"H-human meat?!"

"His troops had been decimated, and my great-grandfather, mortally wounded and about to die, was saved by a commissioned officer. The food that this officer gave my great-grandfather, to revive him, was human flesh."

Shizue felt nauseated again.

"He came back from the dead. However, the whole time he was recuperating he had no idea what he had eaten that day. Then one day, he learned the truth. And then astonished and disappointed, he lost all hope."

"Of course he did. I would have gone insane. But who knows, maybe I'd be okay with it," said the injured policeman, his voice drifting.

"He became religious. He sought mercy from various belief systems. No one would absolve him."

Ishida let his chair fall over and walked over to the wall.

"The fact that he ate it was out of his control. He tried to pretend it didn't happen. He hadn't set out to do that. But he couldn't escape it. He felt worse and worse about it."

"Obviously," Shizue said after taking several short breaths. "It wouldn't be normal if he didn't feel some guilt. Cannibalism is truly an aberration."

"You can't say that." Ishida turned his chair around.

"Why not?"

"You're a counselor. You can't make such a generalized accusation. Listen, my great-grandfather felt guilty about eating human flesh. Continues to feel guilt about it. He thinks about it every chance he gets and *can't forget the taste*," Ishida said.

"Then…oh God…"

Ishida nodded.

"The guilt over not being able to forget the taste of human meat is different from the guilt experienced from the mere fact of eating it. The difference being that he now *wants* to eat it."

He wants to eat it.

"My great-grandfather fears the self that wants to eat it. He feared he'd end up eating it. He knew that even if he really wanted to consume human flesh, it was still the one thing he could not eat. He had no choice but to kill and eat another human being. To quell his desire he had to commit this ultimate crime against humanity. That is the nature of a forbidden penchant."

"You're supposed to resist that kind of temptation," Kunugi said.

"We've earned our careers arresting people who can't, you know," said Ishida.

"My great-grandfather *did* resist. He's a law-abiding citizen. He resisted for a long time. Then he realized something. He could create something like it out of different ingredients. In order to satisfy his desire legally, there was only that."

"That's why he developed synthetic food products?"

The food Shizue had been eating for so long was born from this motive.

"When the war ended, there was something called 'substitute foods,' what with countries defeated in war typically descending into poverty. My great-grandfather made that the basis of his initiative. He wanted to process the game meat he could obtain and make synthetic human meat according to how he remembered it tasting. The idea to create food without killing live animals was all born in this moment. All other food materials were a by-product.

"That's how he's managed to live so long," Ishida said, circling the table with his fingertip. "Eventually, Yutaro Suzuki acquired the wonderful technology and tremendous wealth that would have a huge impact on society. He left many a legacy. SVC technology has raised nutritional standards the world over. Yet despite all this, he was still unable to capture the flavor of human meat."

"You're saying it's beyond technology."

"We weren't able to communicate this to technicians properly. The expressive power of language surrounding taste and fragrance is tremendously attenuated," Ishida said, tapping his desk. "There were millions upon billions of different configurations for compound structure and homogenization of every flavor. We were slowly but surely advancing, but we categorically failed at the nuances of seasoning. It was the same with beef and pork. SVC's synthetic meats were a lot closer to the taste of the real thing than cultivated clones. In fact it wasn't just close, it *was* the real thing. SVC doesn't make replicas. It rediscovered originals. Cultivated meat and living meat are so different. The reason other companies have failed to do what we have done isn't just that they can't master the manufacturing process or because the elements of their ingredients are different. It's because the designs are too complicated and detailed. But the one thing we've failed at is human meat."

"Even if it's near identical?"

"Yes, even if it's near identical. Obviously, cloned human meat was no good. We didn't have any course of action. And the only person who knew the taste was my great-grandfather."

Taste.

What a disgusting word.

"On his 110th birthday." Ishida grinned. "I wanted to give my great-grandfather the most extravagant gift possible. And I thought of the perfect thing. For him. The real thing."

"Don't tell me that it was the flesh of those children in Area 32." Shizue glared at Ishida so hard her eyes hurt.

"Very perceptive. As a matter of fact it was. The medical center was operated by SVC, after all."

My mother.

The boy that strangled my mother.

He's a victim of this man.

Ishida laughed expressionlessly.

"My great-grandfather being so old and everything, not just any meat was going to suffice. I couldn't offer it to him unless I had done a thorough examination of it. Even with successful preparatory examinations, cases like Yuko Yabe, who had that undetected disease, would arise. Even cold medication can leave a taste in the flesh. I had to throw that meat away in the end. So we conducted very thorough examinations before all our abductions."

"Why, y-you…That's why you wanted all the data on the children."

That was why he looked into all the children's records.

Their thoughts. Their backgrounds. Their pasts.

"And I just handed it over to you."

"You're finally getting it. Yes. Medical exams now are so thorough. It was just personal information we lacked. In order to assess the health of a child we really needed that information."

"How could you? That means…"

That meant she had abetted Ishida's crimes.

"Why, you! You you you…" Shizue rushed over to Ishida.

She wanted more than ever to strike at him. She made a fist.

She couldn't speak. She was furious. She was so furious.

Ishida looked up at her.

"We were still struggling. First, what *part* of the human had he eaten? It took us two years to figure that out. We figured out that it was an internal organ, possibly the liver, but beyond that was difficult. Over the course of a long period of time, there weren't actually very many serial killings. When they did occasionally occur they were so intermittent. Some years there were none at all. And even if something did occur, we had to intuit the intentions of the perpetrator first and foremost. Basic police work. And we couldn't pick just anyone from among the victims. So," Ishida looked deeper into Shizue's eyes.

"We had no way of discerning the quality of the product. Last year one of the employees at an affiliate company happened to be a murder victim, so we had all the details and were able to perform the medical exam immediately. However, adult meat was really no good. Comparatively, this year…

"This year was *excellent*."

Shizue threw her fist down at Ishida's face. However, Ishida blocked and responded instantly with a punch of his own to her face.

"Hmph. I didn't figure you for a violent person. It's really disillusioning," Ishida spat out.

Shizue pounded the glossed floor over and over.

You're worse than me.

I've always hated him. We're similar but opposites. I'm still better than…
Better than him.

Still groveling on the floor, Shizue pulled the hair away from her face and glared at Ishida.

The screen on the desk was still scrambled.

"Are you still not reading me? Takasugi. Hey, Takasugi!"

The screen went blank and then back on again.

"Hey. Yudani. Are you there?"

Nothing.

"Lao? Lao?"

The screen kept warping, shifting shapes and blinking on and off. Finally it just glowed, and nothing more appeared. Ishida cursed under his breath and input something on the screen in the middle of the desk. A plasma screen lowered from the ceiling behind him.

"Yudani. It's me. What's going on?"

Suddenly, a large figure of a turtle appeared on the screen.

The turtle breathed fire and spoke in one very strange voice.

CHAPTER 029

MIO THREW OFF her goggles and raised a curious eyebrow.

"Ha ha ha." She wasn't laughing. She was just making the sounds. "Everything is just monsters now. This is what you call data recovery."

Mio let out one strangely contented and angry scream.

Perhaps because of the popularization of voice-recording systems, lately there were more and more children who were not able to use keyboards. But they'd give up on voice-operated systems because they were too fast.

"What the hell are you doing?" Rey Mao yelled. "Stop with the mischief. Think about the situation."

"It's not mischief. Look, I just hacked into the main operational server of D&S through the main system of this building. I'm destroying all the data in this building. Then we'll make everyone else in here give everything up."

"What is this flash movie?"

"That's my favorite turtle monster movie flash. If anyone upstairs tries to access the system now they're going to see this. He's strong, my turtle. I mean I think it's better than there not being anything on the screen at all."

"That's what I mean by mischief," Rey Mao said angrily. She checked the kitchen doors. Then she looked over at Ritsuko Kisugi and asked, "Are you okay?"

She had drawn the medical tubes from around her waist and wrapped herself in a white garment she took from one of the lockers. She wasn't too fearful a girl, apparently.

"I said already I'm okay. I was just restrained, put to sleep, and examined. If I tell you I'm not okay, it'll mean I'm not. I was abducted after all. I was going to be violated or murdered."

"You were going to be eaten," Mio said. "All right. In one hour, the area patrol is going to receive an evacuation order. People who work for the state are like blind sheep, so I'm sure they'll quickly follow orders. I'm not sure if they're conscientious or lazy, but they always follow orders. I'm also sending bullshit reports to the police."

"And…go," Mio let out energetically at the same time she pressed the enter key.

"That's amazing," Ritsuko said, surprised. "I mean, who are you? What are you doing here?"

"We're the bad guys," Mio said. She withdrew the drive from her monitor. "Now all we have to do is escape. As if! Right, Makino?"

That was right. There was Ayumi.

They couldn't leave her.

At least Hazuki couldn't.

"She's just showing off," Mio said as she turned off her monitor. "You think she's fighting the guys that attacked you, Hazuki? They have pistols. She's in trouble."

"Ayumi's not fighting them. She's probably running away."

"Running away? She knows her strengths," Rey Mao said. "She wouldn't try to attack guys like that directly. She's also not going to repent for her sins by getting herself killed, or make a martyr of herself or anything."

"I see. That's how she thinks, huh?" Mio said, acting surprised. "The old movies I see are always like that. They fight for someone, they die, and everyone gets to miss them. It's stupid. And they praise the dumbest fighting moves. The worse it is, the better it is. Fighting an entire battalion all alone, for example. Plain stupid. No way they'll win. Really stupid. No way they'll win. But then they do. They kill all the bad guys and no one blames them. It's unbelievably insensitive. Man's adventurous spirit, freedom of the rugged individual, etcetera etcetera."

"But we're neither men nor adults," Ritsuko said with a strange accent.

"That's right," Rey Mao said.

"We aren't solitary either."

Mio lowered her goggles and pulled up some more data, started searching.

"Children are more cunning and more realistic. That includes her."

"I don't know about that," said Mio. "There are a lot of rooms here. The whole place is ridiculously big. If we just flee now we'll get lost. I mean we'd get caught and then killed. Hmm, this 3-D map is really annoying. You think it's been about an hour and a half since we came around here?"

"A little longer than that, I think. If she's hiding somewhere that's one thing, but if she's escaping, it might be too late." Rey Mao pulled her hair up.

"I just unlocked all the doors earlier, but you think that was a bad idea? I mean Kono has an ID card, right? She could go into the rooms with them. If she's hiding—"

"They all have cards. It's the same."

Up.

"She's up there," said a soft voice.

It was the voice of Hinako Sakura.

"Up? What do you mean?"

"She's headed up. There's a demon up there. *A demon.*" Hinako's blue-white face didn't move, and her gray lips only opened slightly as she spoke.

After she finished her sentence she looked at Hazuki and the others with black-lined, green-tinted eyes.

"Huh?" Mio said. "Is this a divination?"

Hinako looked down without answering.

"What do we do?" Rey Mao asked Mio.

"What do you think?" Mio asked Hazuki.

"I think Ayumi is upstairs," Hazuki answered.

"If she were going to escape alone she'd be heading down. But if she's letting us escape, she'd go up. And of course upstairs...there's one last person."

"Right," Mio said.

"Sheesh. Writing messages in blood on scraps of cloth, ghost-hunting...You guys are truly from a different era. It's like you've traveled through time from the past. I mean it's cool and all, but..." Mio said, looking at Rey Mao.

Then she looked at Ritsuko and Hazuki.

"Hey, there are hardly any more enemies in the building, so why don't you guys go find somewhere to hide?"

"Hide? That's not my style," Ritsuko said. She looked around the kitchen, then grabbed a large stick. "My grandpa always said only I could protect myself."

"Grandpa? Whatever. Anyway you're safe now, so it would be stupid if you went and died," Mio said, then hoisted her enormous weapon onto her shoulder and passed the gate.

Rey Mao led the way down the hall.

They went to the emergency stairs.

"What's above us?" Hazuki asked Mio.

"It's the whole medical center compound. They've got an incredible amount of medical equipment. It's all worth more than the building itself. They've got every kind imaginable, and according to this, the eighteenth floor is something of a research center."

Mio had unlocked all the doors in the building, so all of them opened easily.

They climbed to the fifteenth floor.

The electric lock to the door was already open.

"This is so different from the underground clinics we go to," Rey Mao said, referring to undocumented residents. She stared at the glass walls of the exam room while holding the door open.

"It's a horrible examination. When I woke up from it I thought I was going to die. It hurt worse than when they attacked me," Ritsuko said.

On the fifteenth floor were several comparatively spacious open rooms, making it easier to search them.

But it wasn't as though they could call out Ayumi's name.

They had no idea where the enemy could have been hiding.

They went up to the sixteenth floor. There was a small booth there. It looked like a counseling room.

It was quiet. All they could hear were their own footsteps.

The floor and the walls were all made of sound-absorbing materials.

It was all shiny but not slippery. It was all perfectly maintained and cleaned. Not one speck of dirt.

Every step Hazuki took left a muddy footprint; she started to feel apologetic. She felt bad for the cleaning people who worked so hard to maintain this level of cleanliness. They hadn't done anything to deserve this. But then Hazuki realized how strange it was to be thinking of such a thing at all. There was a part of her still unable to digest this entire situation.

Wait.

"Mio," Hazuki said in a small voice. Mio turned around.

"Footprints."

"It's all right for us to make a mess. I've put *holes* through parts of this building."

"That's not what I mean. Ayumi had to have come at least up to here on the same path we did. So…"

Mio pondered for a moment, then said, "Nice, Hazuki."

She stopped everyone from advancing farther, pulled out a portable scanner from her chest protector, and took a snapshot of one of Hazuki's footprints.

"There's hardly any change in color."

"What are you doing?"

They were going to find her footprints and follow them.

"Watch."

She connected her scanner to the weapon and downloaded the image.

It seemed Mio was right about her plasma device having more than one use. It was a multi-functional machine with many capabilities.

Mio lowered her goggles.

She looked up something on the panel on her weapon.

"There it is. She was here."

It was invisible, but there was the faintest trace of dust on the floor.

"I'm determining the difference in hue and augmenting the contrast. There's an AI up ahead. Okay, it looks like she went upstairs. Let's take the stairs."

"You're like a dog," Rey Mao said, but Hazuki had no idea why she said that.

"The illumination of the footprints is slightly different, so it's not clear. But…they're there. Up."

They followed Mio up to the eighteenth floor.

Rey Mao carefully scoped out the area.

The eighteenth floor was almost totally cleared of any partitions. It was one large, no, one *giant* floor.

There were several large beams holding up the ceiling. There were desks and all kinds of measuring instruments lined up neatly.

A window.

An unbelievably wide window.

Outside the window it was night.

In the sky, a full moon.

A large, round moon hung glowing in the middle of the window.

Like it could swallow them whole.

Hazuki was mesmerized by the heavenly body.

Soon.

She took a step forward.

There was no indication of anything.

No sound.

No smell.

Hazuki couldn't feel Ayumi's presence.

Mio aimed her weapon.

She signaled to the others with her eyes.

Rey Mao soundlessly advanced.

She waved a hand behind her back.

Don't move. Ritsuko and Hinako stopped.

Hazuki turned torward Mio. She could hear her own heart beating.

Her heart was beating.

It was the first time in her life hearing this sound. A sound that had certainly never stopped in her lifetime. A sound she could have heard at any moment.

Boom. Boom. Boom.

Boom.

Mio advanced one leg ever so slightly, and it was at that moment.

The desk closest to them sprang up into the air and a large black shape leapt forward. The shadow jumped at them with tremendous force. Just as they captured what they saw, and probably too late, the desk made a tremendous sound, crashing to the floor.

It was him.

But they realized it too slowly. The large man with the head tattoo threw Rey Mao across the room and wrapped a hand around Mio's neck. Flung her away. No one moved. No one could make a sound. Mio swung her legs and fought back. It did nothing. Rey Mao jumped on him.

She was no match for him. He was simply too large. Rey Mao was tall, but still only half the man's size. And yet his arms reached down to Rey Mao's waist.

Then, finally and much too late again, Hazuki was seized by her fear.

"Stop! Stop it!" Hazuki screamed.

Slam.

On top of the desk, with the full moon casting light from behind was Ayumi's silhouette.

The man looked back for a moment. Ayumi whisked down.

Then...

It looked like she had just disappeared.

With the speed of a wolf.

The delicate shadow moved without a sound to the man hoisting up Mio and, in one gesture, went for his throat.

And slashed it.

It was a matter of one second.

Ayumi's shadow moved away from the man. The otherwise normal-looking face, touched by moonlight, eventually let out an abnormal noise.

He let go of Mio's neck. Mio fell to the floor. The man turned his back to her. He brought both his hands up toward Ayumi.

Blood from his wound spewed violently in Ayumi's face.

It made the sound of a winter's wind.

The large man held his throat with his hands. The sound stopped.

But the black-red blood kept pumping through his fingers. As if in rhythm with his heart. *B-boom b-boom b-boom.*

B-boom.

Then the man fell forward, as if trying to make one last lunge at Ayumi.

He fell like a rag doll, unceremoniously.

The pool of blood spread across the floor.

Bleached by the moonlight, Ayumi looked at the man.

"Ayumi…"

She lifted her face.

Her eyes were clear, brave.

Very short hair.

A refined face. Delicate arms.

Covered in blood. The moonlight illuminated the bright red blood.

Ayumi's shoulders heaved with her breath. She had probably been fighting him this whole time.

"Ayumi," Rey Mao said as she stood up.

"I was waiting for both his hands to be occupied," Ayumi said. "Are you okay, Tsuzuki?"

Mio rubbed her throat with her left hand and said, "Of course I am *not*! Why'd you wait so long? I had two, maybe three seconds left."

"Is everyone okay?"

"Yes," Rey Mao said.

"Then get out of here. There's one more person here."

Suddenly, they heard a bang. Hazuki thought maybe only she'd heard it.

"Get down!" Rey Mao yelled.

A bright red burst of light.

"Shit! Get out of here!" Mio said. "Hide!"

Ritsuko ran from the doorway.

They heard the sound again.

Was this the sound of a gunshot?

Someone let out a short cry.

"Kisugi!" Mio yelled. Blood poured from her left arm. Hinako disappeared, rushing over to help her. Mio left.

"Hazuki!" Rey Mao called out, and not a moment after hearing it Hazuki fled to the entrance. A red line. A red laser pointer.

No.

She was just a pace faster than the sound of the gun. She made it past the entrance.

Ayumi had pushed her away. She tumbled across the ground and passed the entrance.

Another gunshot.

The sign that read 18 flew from the wall.

Rey Mao simultaneously flew past the entrance.

"Where's that girl? The injured one."

"She was only grazed. I had her run upstairs with Sakura."

"Up?"

Ayumi looked puzzled.

"Cat, go up too," Mio said.

"Funeral Girl and Ritsuko are in danger even if no one is there," Mio said and lowered her goggles. "You too, Hazuki."

"Ayumi…"

Mio looked at Ayumi through her goggles.

"You know why I made them go upstairs?"

Ayumi looked at Mio, confused.

"Because this idiot with the gun is going to go downstairs. And you know why he's going downstairs?"

"What? Tsuzuki—"

"So that you'll go upstairs. Now go."

Mio pushed Ayumi toward the stairs and then stood up in the middle of the entrance.

"If we're taking turns, it's mine now. C'mon, you gun-toting asshole!"

Mio held up her plasma gun.

The red light steadied on her forehead.

"Crap, he's going to get me. Hurry up, Ayumi! I'm gonna get killed here if you stay!" Mio withdrew as she said that.

A gunshot.

"Shit! That was too close!"

"Mio!"

"Don't worry, I won't do anything stupid. I'm a genius, remember?"

"You're an idiot," Ayumi said and ran up the stairs.

"Makino! You too!"

Mio pointed just the barrel of her gun around the entrance.

She was using the viewfinder to look inside the room. She was no doubt scoping the room with her goggles.

"Here he comes! Stupid Makino, stop stalling! Get out of here!"

"Aghhh!"

"Aghh nothing! Seriously, you have to leave. Get away from here!" Mio screamed, and ran down the stairs.

Hazuki followed.

Seventeenth floor.

"This way, Makino."

Mio ran to the seventeenth floor and across the main hall.

There were several semi-private cubicles lined up with short partitions.

There were glass dividers, lockers, and bizarre scientific instruments everywhere. It was like a maze.

"He's coming." They heard running footsteps coming down the stairs.

Mio hid behind a pillar.

"Makino. Stay put right here."

Mio hefted her gun.

The red laser beam traveled across the dark floor.

Mio suddenly jumped out.

A light shone on her.

She flew to Hazuki's side.

A monitor exploded on a desk at the same time the gun sounded. The man ran. Mio, now on her knees, started to move.

She stood up. Another gunshot.

First a hole in the glass partition, then the whole partition shattered and collapsed into a rain of shards. Mio quickly ran around it.

But every time she stood up he would shoot at her. She couldn't run or charge him, and she obviously couldn't attack. Was she going to wait till he was out of bullets? Or was she going to keep hiding?

Still, her movements were explosive.

Suddenly, Mio turned her back to the man and sank to the floor. At almost the same time a hole opened in the wall.

"Shit! He thinks he's hot shit just because he has a gun. Bang bang bang bang, stop it! Man, I can't believe Rey Mao actually attacked this guy. This is unforgivable. Nicking Ritsuko and everything. It's just not civilized to be shooting a gun at fourteen-year-old girls in a developed country. But you know what?"

Her plasma gun made a beeping sound.

"It's also not normal for us to want to go upstairs. You think I'm going to let you get me, you pervert? You were prancing around so much I have your whole movement pattern down. Plus, I have all the blueprints for this building. Now. I'm here…That means you're…"

The numbers reflecting on Mio's goggles scrolled rapidly down.

All the lights on her body suit lit up.

Whoosh. A shadow stood up.

"Charge."

And as Mio spoke, she stood up, pointed the gun slightly left of where the man stood, and yelled, "Don't fuck with little girls."

The man moved. Electric tendrils scattered all around Mio and a beam of light hit the ground.

All the lights on the floor went out at once, and the monitors glowed with the reflection of the plasma burst.

The sound of static crackling. A short burst of lightning.

The last sound they heard was *shoo*.

The floor was completely still.

The man stood there, still holding up his gun.

But he couldn't fire it. Even the laser pointer disappeared. Then.

Bam. The destructive sound reverberated through the entire floor.

The gun—and the entire arm holding it—exploded to pieces.

From the man's ears and nose wafted a white smoke.

He was dead.

"Mio!"

Mio pointed her plasma gun at the ceiling. Her hair was standing on end, and she just stood there with her eyes wide open.

"Mio! Mio!" Hazuki slowly approached her, and Mio slumped to the floor.

"Dude, that was scary."

"Scary?"

"Yeah, because it was different than how I'd imagined it. I didn't know what would happen. But this thing was like an electromagnetic oven. That guy is burnt to a crisp inside."

Hazuki placed her hand on Mio's shoulder. It was trembling.

"This makes me a k…" Mio stopped talking, looked at Hazuki, and hugged her.

"I was about to piss myself," she finished.

CHAPTER 030

ISHIDA STARTED SCREAMING when the walls shook. It was the most human look Shizue had ever seen on him.

Her calm and collected mother was also suddenly deranged, right before she died.

Kill me, just strangle me.

There was no situation in which it would ever make sense to ask a patient you are treating to kill you.

Anyone who thinks for even a second about what would happen afterward would never do that.

The boy ended up killing himself.

If he hadn't, he would have been a convicted murderer anyway.

Even if he weren't apprehended for his crime, the memory of having murdered another human would stay with him.

That was why Shizue had decided her mother was no longer human. She couldn't forgive her.

She hated her as much as she hated herself.

Sometimes people just couldn't think that far ahead.

Looking at Ishida in his deranged state now made her realize all this for some reason.

However.

"Gra-ndfather. Gra-ndfather...Gra-ndfather," Ishida muttered over and over.

Then with his hands on the floor, he suddenly realized Shizue had been watching him.

He cocked his head to one side like a veritable slapstick comedian.

Then, as if playing around, he made his face rigid and, half facing her, glared at Shizue. "What's your problem? What? What? What? What?" he kept repeating, now approaching her.

"Hey!" Ishida kicked Shizue. Unable to understand his demonstration she just said, "That hurt."

"What the hell are you...Why are you looking at me like that? Hey! Hey hey hey hey!" Ishida kept kicking Shizue.

"Stop that!" Kunugi said, and with his good arm pulled Ishida by the shoulder. "What's wrong with you, Lieutenant?"

Ishida grabbed Kunugi's hurt arm and twisted it hard.

Kunugi let out a ferocious scream and fell to the floor, but Ishida wouldn't let go. "What? Why are you bothering me? What? Hey, say something. Speak!"

Kunugi was gritting his teeth.

Shizue took Ishida by the hand and said simply,

"Stop it."

Ishida guffawed, let go of Kunugi, and drifted over to the ornamented door.

He said, "What did I do wrong? Why? Everything was going so well. What happened to Takasugi? Why did everyone disappear? Has it all fallen apart? I'm okay. This is all trivial." Ishida suddenly spun around. "I'm sure this is just an electrical malfunction. The electromagnetic waves are unusually strong. Maybe the medical equipment downstairs just malfunctioned. I can't get ahold of anyone because the wires are all mixed up, that's all. There's nothing wrong."

"You think the secret door's just going to open now?" Kunugi said, still lying on the floor. His voice was hoarse.

Suddenly, the wall behind Ishida's desk parted to the left and right, and indeed opened wide. Beyond it was another gate, and that opened too. Beyond that gate was an old wooden door.

"What? It's just a couple open doors," Ishida laughed. "Right now, the tresspassers, Hazuki Makino and Ayumi Kono, are being captured. And that filthy undocumented brat Rey Mao too. They're most certainly restrained by now. Ritsuko Kisugi is being sliced open, and her delicious liver is being extracted. Anyway, this time, we'll have plenty of ingredients. We can keep eating and eating and eating…" Ishida said proudly, spreading his arms as he uttered the words.

"My great-grandfather will be so happy. When you're 115 years old, eating good food is one's only joy. And you two, yes…you will have to die. You'll have to commit double suicide."

"You're going to kill me too, after all?" Kunugi said.

"Having an idiot like you in the police force is a waste of taxpayer money. If you live, my great-grandfather won't be able to eat human flesh anymore. My great-grandfather is going to keep eating lots and lots of humans and keep living living *living*!"

The ornamental door crept open.

Ishida jutted his head out and peered around the door half-wittedly.

Right next to his neck he heard a *swoosh* sound.

Standing by him was a little girl.

Ishida stared at the little girl's profile, perplexed.

Blood.

She was covered in blood.

"K-Kono…"

The blood-soaked girl stood there unblinking.

Ishida.

Ishida, whose face still bore a perplexed expression, slowly collapsed to the floor.

Blood was dripping from Ayumi's aquiline jaw.

In her delicate right hand was a unique-looking weapon.

Kunugi raised himself. Shizue still couldn't swallow what had just happened.

"M-Miss. You…"

"I'm a murderer. He was a criminal," she said confidently, without so much as wiping the blood from her face.

Shizue raised herself up too.

"As you just witnessed, I killed this man. I also killed the police officer named Takasugi, and the man with the peacock tattoo on his head. I killed Ryu Kawabata and Yuji Nakamura. I confess to all of those killings."

"Kawabata and Nakamura?"

"Miss Kono…" Shizue stood up. She thought herself so weak. If what she just saw was real, and if what this girl just said was true. Despite it all, this little girl was standing firm. Despite being drenched from head to toe in blood.

Behind Ayumi was Hinako Sakura and probably the girl known as Ritsuko Kisugi. And behind her…

Cat.

She had the face of an adult. Ayumi walked into the room without so much as a glance at Ishida's dead body.

The others followed.

Ayumi faced Shizue and politely thanked her.

"Are you injured at all?"

"I'm fine." The counselor couldn't tell them she was in pain.

Mio Tsuzuki appeared in the doorway.

And Hazuki Makino, covered in mud.

They were all all right.

They were all alive.

No…

These children had attacked the building.

This impenetrable fortress, overrun by little girls.

Ayumi kept her gaze straight ahead and walked through the room, past Ishida's desk, through the hidden door, and past the gate beyond it.

"Miss Kono," Shizue called out.

Ayumi turned around slightly. And then she opened the wooden door in the very back.

Mio and Hazuki walked past Shizue and followed after Ayumi. Rey Mao, Hinako, and Ritsuko followed suit. Shizue lent Kunugi her hand to help him stand, and they followed after them.

They passed the doors, the gate, the wooden door.

The girls were lined up, two-by-two.

The room was so white it was glowing.

A huge window.

The giant heavenly body.

For some reason the moon shone brighter and closer than ever.

It was encircled by a large inorganic machine, inside which was a small white bed.

On it.

On it was a tiny old man, shriveled and covered in wrinkles. He raised his head and looked their way. There were tubes sprouting from all over his body, and on his hairless head were several electrodes, cables leading from them.

There was a small tabletop attached to his bed, and on it was a white plate.

On the plate was one morsel of meat left over from his meal.

Ayumi, dark red, stood at the side of the bed.

Stood there silently.

The old man looked at that crisp face with utter dread.

"Are you a demon?"

"I'm a wolf. I butcher everyone in my path. I'm a werewolf. Loup-garou," Ayumi said.

The old man let out a short laugh.

"Are you here to ease my pain?"

"No, I'm here to kill you," Ayumi said, and grabbing all of the wires connected to the old man, cut them with her knife.

Beep.

The small lights all flickered and one by one were extinguished.

The sound of the machines stopped.

The fan stopped.

The monitor went black.

Even the lamp turned off.

The machine stopped.

The old man looked around him several times, looked at his wrinkled hands once, frowned his wrinkled face, and then quietly, so quietly, ceased to exist.

The old man was not alive. He had been *kept* alive.

Ayumi slowly turned on a heel.

"Police officer. I have killed another man."

Kunugi lowered his eyes.

"Miss Fuwa," Ayumi said to Shizue. "Killing people is wrong, right?"

"Yes."

Shizue tried to answer as calmly as she could.

Not for her own sake but for the child's.

"Please arrest me. And then take me to prison."

Kunugi, however, turned his head.

"I'm sorry, but, miss…I can't do that," Kunugi said. "I can't arrest or convict any of you girls. I didn't kill anyone, but I might have committed an even greater crime. In fact I'd understand if you wanted me arrested along with you."

"If no one is convicted of murder this tale won't have a conclusion. This leaves me—"

"There is no conclusion," Shizue said, and she really believed it. "A conclusion is something the records will conveniently provide. In reality there is never any clean resolution. You can say it however many times you want with words, and you can even convince yourself of it, but humans aren't that simple. Or, on another level, humans are much closer to pure than that. Confessing to a failed middle-aged cop isn't going to start anything," Shizue said.

"I'm…"

"It's okay."

Shizue hugged Ayumi. Just the way her mother had held her once.

"I understand. I'm entrusting this to the police, the law. That's what you want."

"The police will be here soon," Mio said. "I timed their arrival perfectly. Though they don't know what happened here."

In that case.

We could get out of here before daybreak. We could leave this impenetrable fortress.

Shizue looked at the girls' faces.

This was an impenetrable fortress, but it was also man-made, not the work of gods. We can take it down.

Despite the misery, despite the pathos, despite the horror. Despite the sadness.

Even though so many people were dead now. Even though so much blood was spilled.

Despite all this, Shizue was glad to see the girls were alive.

Even if it turned out they had committed serious crimes.

She was a horrible woman.

In reality, people had died, and people had killed those dead.

To be happy despite all that made her a horrible person.

In the window illuminated by the full moon, Shizue could see her tired face reflected back at her.

Shizue looked at the pathetic face and couldn't stop crying.

The moon was slow.

And cold.

"And then the wolf ate Little Red Riding Hood."
                                        –Charles Perrault

CHAPTER 031

IN THE END.

There was no conclusion to the tale of Hazuki and the other girls.

Actually, there is no need for fairy-tale conclusions in the real world.

Everything just went along as usual without any more understanding, and at the end of the day, nothing changed.

Yuko Yabe, Asumi Aikawa, Ryu Kawabata, and Yuji Nakamura, plus all the others who lost their lives, were almost thought of as people who'd *always* been dead when you read about them on monitors.

They were branded victims.

The myth-making of the lives of the victims was extremely compact and easy to understand. For example the Yuko in the monitor was completely different from the Yuko that had once been alive and breathing.

It didn't matter how many times Hazuki watched her surveillance video of Yuko, she could no longer recall the soft sensation or scent of her that day they carried her to Ayumi's house.

The Area 119 SVC Memorial Building was one day attacked by terrorists from some -ism, and since it took place on a non-workday, fortunately the casualties were limited.

With all that blood, and all those explosions and that many deaths,

How dare they call it limited, Hazuki thought.

Hazuki was received warmly by her father.

He did not ask any questions but said, "I was worried. I don't ever want to worry like that again."

He scolded her lightly.

Hazuki never found out what happened to Ayumi. Had no way of finding out.

They were each interviewed by different people and afterward escorted home. She didn't know what happened with Mio or Rey Mao either.

In her interview Hazuki described everything she saw and heard, and didn't think to lie or make up anything about Ayumi or Mio. Hinako and Ritsuko had no reason to hide anything either.

They should have been punished accordingly.

However.

After the three-month summer break, Mio and Ayumi were present at the communication sessions. Hinako and Ritsuko too. No one said anything. Like nothing had changed from before. So there was nothing to ask.

Because it was all the same.

Hazuki had never talked to Mio before, and hadn't even known who Hinako and Ritsuko were. Ayumi...

She eventually also went forward and didn't stand out.

Ayumi was always looking outside during the sessions.

Afterward, Hazuki went to their spot alone.

She folded her knees and sat down.

The vaporous ambitionless cityscape.

Buildings that looked like flash drives.

Hills that went on forever.

I was there, she thought.

I went over those hills.

But it was probably from a different angle. She knew that.

"Miss Makino," a voice called.

Hazuki turned her face up and saw Shizue Fuwa standing by the handrail of the stairs.

"Miss...Fuwa."

"Hello," said Shizue and sat next to Hazuki.

Hazuki remembered that Miss Fuwa was not at the day's session. A substitute counselor had come and said nothing important. Hazuki hadn't listened to any of it, so she didn't know what the substitute had said.

"Miss Fuwa..."

"I'm on break," she answered before Hazuki could finish her question.

"I'm taking a short vacation. Sorry."

"Um..."

"No one was punished. It was like nothing had happened."

"Nothing?"

"It just makes you want to give up on humanity, doesn't it?" Shizue said with a laugh.

Was this the kind of person she was?

Miss Fuwa?

Hazuki looked at her.

"According to the records, that man on the top floor was already dead. He was kept alive with those machines. The master of that body was the machine. Biologically speaking too, he was dead. So he couldn't be killed. Even if he were, he wasn't."

"How about the others?"

"Terrorism."

"And the serial killings?"

"It's a huge maze. Some of those people...I mean the Kawabata and Nakamura cases were even broadcast on the public channel. But the person who killed those two and Yabe aren't to be found anywhere."

"But Ayumi confessed to it."

"It's a tremendous nuisance for the truth to be revealed. The man on the top floor of that building was a very important figure. The criminal had said that when he died, the whole world would turn upside down."

"Criminal?"

"His name was Ishida," Fuwa said. "But you know, it was just his delusion. That man was certainly important. He had the money and the power to run this country. But he died, and it's not like the world fell apart. Nothing changed. You know that, right?"

"Yeah. Nothing changed."

"Of course it didn't. Humans aren't that extraordinary. We're small. The more humans tell themselves they are giant, the more I feel like I'm losing sight of myself. Humans are only as big as a human can be."

"Ayumi said something similar."

"Miss Kono..." Shizue said, looking far away.

"What's going to happen to Ayumi?"

"Probably nothing."

"But."

"It was a lie. The police determined that she must be a pathological liar. That's what they said in their data. I guess that really makes her a wolf girl," said Shizue.

Hazuki didn't know what that meant.

"It's not very satisfying, is it, Miss Makino?"

"Not...not necessarily," Hazuki said.

"Yes it is," Shizue said. "Good, bad, weak, strong, holy, evil. The stories created around polar opposites are easiest to understand. But nothing's that simple. I don't think. I mean I don't know," Shizue said. She leaned on her side.

"Then there are those people who can murder people and then take a nap," she said.

"Huh?"

A hand came out of the grass and waved.

"That was legitimate self-defense. He had a gun."

"Who was the one with the gigantic gun, Tsuzuki?" Shizue said.

"M-Mio?"

Mio popped her dried-grass-covered head up from the lawn.

Ayumi was not there.

There was no scent of a beast.

"I wonder where she's going to go," Shizue said, looking high up into the sky.

"It must be hard. She can't even repent for her crimes."

Hazuki didn't know.

She looked up at the sky.

The moon was not visible in the daytime.

But it wasn't like it was gone.

Hazuki was here.

Mio was here.

Ayumi was nowhere.

It was in the past now.

There once was a beast called the *wolf*.

But.

The wolf went extinct.

That's what they said.

ABOUT THE AUTHOR

NATSUHIKO KYOGOKU: Born in Otaru, Hokkaido. Studied at Kuwasawa Design School. After working at advertising agencies, he established his own design studio. He still works as art director, designer, and bookbinder for various projects. He is also an expert in *yokai* (Japanese folklore of monsters and ghosts). His novel, *The Summer of the Ubume*, was published in English in 2009.

1996 | Mystery Writers of Japan Award for *Moryo no Hako*
    (Grave of Goblins)

1997 | Izumi Kyoka Award for *Warau Iuemon*
    (Laughing Iuemon)

2003 | Yamamoto Shugoro Prize for *Nozoki Koheiji*
    (Inquisitive Koheiji)

2004 | Naoki Prize for *Nochi no kosetsu Hyakumonogatari*
    (Going Around a Hundred Stories, the sequel)

HAIKASORU
The Future is Japanese

SLUM ONLINE by Hiroshi Sakurazaka

Etsuro Sakagami is a college freshman who feels uncomfortable in reality, but when he logs onto the combat MMO *Versus Town*, he becomes "Tetsuo," a karate champ on his way to becoming the most powerful martial artist around. While his relationship with new classmate Fumiko goes nowhere, Etsuro spends his days and nights online in search of the invincible fighter Ganker Jack. Drifting between the virtual and the real, will Etsuro ever be ready to face his most formidable opponent?

THE STORIES OF IBIS by Hiroshi Yamamoto

In a world where humans are a minority and androids have created their own civilization, a wandering storyteller meets the beautiful android Ibis. She tells him seven stories of human/android interaction in order to reveal the secret behind humanity's fall. The tales Ibis tells describe the events surrounding the development of artificial intelligence (AI) in the twentieth and twenty-first centuries. At a glance, these stories do not appear to have any sort of connection, but what is the true meaning behind them? What are Ibis's real intentions?

LOUPS-GAROUS by Natsuhiko Kyogoku

In the near future, humans will communicate almost exclusively through online networks—face-to-face meetings are rare and the surveillance state nearly all-powerful. So when a serial killer starts slaughtering junior high students, the crackdown is harsh. The killer's latest victim turns out to have been in contact with three young girls: Mio Tsuzuki, a certified prodigy; Hazuki Makino, a quiet but opinionated classmate; and Ayumi Kono, her best friend. And as the girls get caught up in trying to find the killer—who might just be a werewolf— Hazuki learns that there is much more to their monitored communications than meets the eye.

THE NEXT CONTINENT by Issui Ogawa

The year is 2025 and Gotoba Engineering & Construction—a firm that has built structures to survive the Antarctic and the Sahara—has received its most daunting challenge yet. Sennosuke Toenji, the chairman of one of the world's largest leisure conglomerates, wants a moon base fit for civilian use, and he wants his granddaughter Tae to be his eyes and ears on the harsh lunar surface. Tae and Gotoba engineer Sohya Aomine head to the moon where adventure, trouble, and perhaps romance await.